✦



Leto's eyes glimm[illegible]
ing as the accents on h[illegible]rmor. They narrowed. Dark brows drew together. Only a person who was really looking for those clues would find them. "If we win, we'll be congratulating each other. You remember what I said about how Cage warriors are rewarded," he said. "Don't you?"

"Sex."

"Yes."

"Winner's choice."

"Yes," he said again, his intensity as strong as any touch.

Nynn stepped to within inches of his armored masculine beauty. She cupped his skull and smoothed her thumbs over his temples, where his exotic serpent tattoo burned beneath her skin. "And what happens if we both win? Will you choose me, Leto?"

"No. You'll choose me."

✦ ✦ ✦

LINDSEY PIPER

# CAGED WARRIOR

The Dragon Kings
Book One

POCKET BOOKS
New York London Toronto Sydney New Delhi

Pocket Books
A Division of Simon & Schuster, Inc.
1230 Avenue of the Americas
New York, NY 10020



First Pocket Books paperback edition July 2013



Manufactured in the United States of America

10 9 8 7 6 5 4 3 2 1

ISBN 978-1-4516-9591-5
ISBN 978-1-4516-9594-6 (ebook)

To MB and KL.
Thanks for Billie.

# Acknowledgments

I am grateful for my family, my friends, and my agent, and to Lauren and Kate. I held the keys to a wonderland. You encouraged me to open the door.

*Malnefoley:*

*No time for formality, cousin. Forgive me.*

*My darling Caleb is dead. Jack and I have been imprisoned. Dr. Aster is obsessed with learning how Jack was born naturally. Endless experiments and torture. He removed one of my ovaries. My knuckles have yet to heal. He'll cut off my hands if I fight back again, but I'm tempted every time my little boy screams.*

*Those who've been ruined are sent to the Cages. Some never return. Reed, of our own Clan Tigony, will try to escape before that fate. I hold little hope. He's been driven insane. One leg taken. No tongue.*

*Please help us! You lead the Council. I know we've had our differences, but to keep punishing me will destroy the Dragon Kings. Aster guards the secret to our survival, but at <u>this</u> price?*

*Hurry, Mal.*

*In love and faith of the Dragon,*

*Nynn*

# CHAPTER ONE

She wasn't in the lab. That's all she knew. The smells were different. Fewer sterilizing cleansers and less recycled air. More body odor. Piss and sweat. Dirt. Wet rocks.

Audrey opened her eyes and blinked. She pushed up onto her hands and knees. Pain banged at her temples—the ache of still-healing blows to the skull and her own frantic pulse. Lifting her head was an effort like swimming through wet cement.

Her fuzzy vision sharpened as she got used to the dim lighting. Just a pair of bare incandescent bulbs. A humid mist hung heavy in the cavelike room. Even when her eyes worked together, focusing, that mist ebbed away at details. She couldn't tell where the algae-covered walls began and ended.

The bars of her four-by-four cage were a prison. Solid iron. She lifted swollen hands and grasped the cold metal. Frustration ate at her insides. Rattling the cage bars, she shrieked.

"Where is my son?"

At least in the lab, she and Jack had shared a cell. No bars. Only walls painted black. Just as disorienting. But that confinement had almost felt safe. She'd held her boy, thankful the darkness concealed the worst of their wounds.

Now she had iron bars, algae, and a black pit where her heart had been.

"Where is he? Aster! You son of a bitch!"

Footsteps.

The hair lifted on the backs of her forearms. As her heartbeat jacked, she noticed her dirty body. Her vulnerability. She wore a paper hospital gown—no underwear, no shoes. Had she been dragged straight from the lab? The last thing she remembered was being strapped to an operating table after having slipped the note to Reed. A mask had pumped anesthetic into her mouth and nose but she'd been hopeful for the first time in months.

Maybe that explained her grogginess. From surgery to a Dragon-damned cave.

Now she wore a damping collar. *But why?* Her powers had never manifested. Giving birth to the first natural-born Dragon King in a generation was the only remarkable thing she'd ever done.

She forced the distracting details away. *Look for a way out. A way to survive.* The iron bars were a lost cause, but the floor was pitted concrete.

With a crack in the corner.

Audrey picked where moisture had worn away a small crevice. Her fingertips bled. Aching knuckles stretched shadow puppets along the wall. She wiped sweat from her forehead. Her toes gripped for balance as she scraped harder, faster.

The steps echoed more loudly. Heavy. Determined.

Certainly male. His footfalls hit too heavily for a lean man. A bruiser. One of the Aster cartel's bodyguards. She didn't stand a chance, but she kept clawing. Her breath became hot steam in her lungs.

A piece of concrete about the size of her fist gave way. One pointed end had promise. If she could strike just the right spot on the man's temple . . .

She edged away from the bars until her spine pinched against the rock wall. After twisting her long hair, she shoved it down the back of the hospital gown. She balanced on the balls of her feet, ready to spring.

As a member of the Honorable Giva's immediate family, she'd been instructed in martial training from an early age. She'd never wielded the powers of her kind, and she was seriously out of practice, but she was not helpless. The chunk of concrete rested in her palm. It was the difference between dying—and dying while fighting.

A flashlight's beam penetrated the recess of the cave. Audrey narrowed her eyes. She watched through her lashes. The man had so many advantages. That realization should've cowed her. Should've turned her backbone to mud and left her weeping. But after having been a victim for more than a year—drugged, bound, helpless—she felt mighty. No manacles. No hallucinogens. Just a rock in her hand and a blaze of pure rage.

The man stepped into clear view.

Easily more than six foot, he was built for breaking bones and ripping off limbs. Brawn. Solid muscle. Powerful biceps. Plate metal covered his heart and vital organs, leaving his arms free. Calf-high boots were made of toughened leather. Bare, muscular thighs flexed with the slightest movement. But he didn't seem the kind of man to make slight movements. Everything about him was overwhelming.

His jaw was fixed in an expression she'd learned to recognize: *You will find no mercy here.*

Audrey gave her flight instinct a hard shove. She pushed far into the shadows. Futile, really, when he aimed the beam directly at her face. She squinted and kept her right hand out of sight as the cage was unlocked.

"Disgusting," he muttered.

"And you're a traitor," she spat in the language of the Dragon Kings. A language she hadn't used for nearly a decade.

Since meeting Caleb, she hadn't given much thought to the old ways. Her happiness as a human wife had been too easy. Too good to last. But long ago, the ways of the Dragon Kings had been her entire life—the ritual and the covert power.

No matter her ostracism from her clan.

Years of rage came rushing back. The coiled ferocity in her legs exploded. She leapt. The cage door swung open on hinges that squealed a rusted protest.

Not even the momentum of her leap shifted the man from his kneeling stance. He only grunted. Audrey's quick instincts brought that chunk of concrete up, up, in a violent arc. Her aim was true. The jagged edge struck the side of his face. Another grunt.

Then Audrey was thrown across the room.

Her shoulder hit the ground, followed by her head. A cry ripped from her throat. She slid three feet. Agony stabbed down to her marrow, as if pain had always been a part of her body.

He'd simply . . . hurled her.

The big man needed only two strides to cross to where Audrey was sprawled. He stripped the chuck of concrete from her hand and tossed it down the tunnel.

"Can you hear me, lab filth?"

The old language rattled in her brain. Words passed down from the blessed Dragon. Nothing quite worked. Her lungs wouldn't take in air. Something ground painfully in her hip socket. She nodded out of pure reflex.

"If you ever attempt to strike me again, I will snap your spine in two. Think you could recover from that? Our kind can endure a great deal—much more than humans. But we're not immortal."

"Where is my son?" Only a rasp now.

"He's better off dead. Now get up."

He yanked her up under both arms and thrust her against a wall. Shots of fire spiked her joints. She gasped as panic set in. She wanted to fight. *Wanted to.* Yet just as when Dr. Aster had drugged her, or when her brain short-circuited because of his torture, she could not.

That didn't stop her from snarling and spitting.

Because he spoke the language of the Dragon Kings, he belonged to one of the sacred Five Clans. But to actually work for that madman? *He* was the filth. Bile surged into her mouth.

"You've still got some spirit." His muscles were tense, holding her immobile, while his breathing remained calm. "I can see why Old Man Aster has plans for you. We're going to have quite the time."

The flashlight had rolled across the ground until it illuminated her captor's face. Blood streamed down from where she'd gouged a ragged hole in his cheek. He was smooth-shaven, and his black hair was shorn close to his head. Eyes the color of teak were fathomless, unreadable. Dark lashes cast shadows along his sharp cheekbones. A scar on his upper lip told stories of past battles. A damping collar encircled his thick, muscular throat.

A tattoo of a serpent wrapped around the back of his head. The tongue hissed toward one temple and the tail flicked toward the other. The Aster family symbol.

Realization settled ice in her belly. He was far deadlier than a brute from the laboratory.

Part boogeyman, part myth—he was a Cage warrior.

"The Aster cartel owns you now, lab filth. But they're done with experiments." His scarred lip curled into a snarling smile. "You're here to fight in the Cages."

Leto had not expected so much resistance from the woman. The prospect heated his blood. For too long he'd only found satisfaction in preparing for the annual Grievance—the ultimate prize for the most dedicated warriors.

Warriors like Leto.

Performing in monthly Cage matches was essential to keep his skills sharp. Training Dragon Kings—called neophytes until they won their first fight—for those monthly matches was a drudgery. Most were volunteers who had debts to repay. They rarely possessed the true courage that deserved combat. Some were as weak and sniveling as humans.

Yet others went on to greatness. Leto had trained such victors.

His cheek was bleeding profusely. This nasty castoff from Dr. Aster's lab had surprising spark.

"You're insane," she snarled. "I'm not going in there."

"Have you ever seen a Cage fight?"

She shuddered. "Of course not! They're for barbarians."

With a swift movement that had nothing to do with his Dragon-given gift, Leto spun her. "Now is the time you listen. You believe me a barbarian, then believe my threats aren't idle. Your suffering won't weigh on my conscience."

"Because you have none." With her cheek pressed against the damp cave wall, her words were muffled.

Leto loosened his grip. If he pulled any harder he would dislocate her shoulder. The goal was not to impair his charges but to ready them. Instead, he added another incentive for her to obey. With his free hand he grasped between her legs.

"No conscience," he repeated coldly. "I will have my way."

She stiffened. She stilled. But Leto realized his heart was beating far too fast. Need had gathered in him for three weeks. Cage warriors were permitted female flesh only after a victory—unless they chose to violate their charges, as he threatened now. Some mentors indulged too often. Their neophytes became submissive, not resilient and strong. Leto had never needed to use such crude methods. He had other means, including stores of patience.

And he never lost a match. The regular reward of satisfying his sexual needs was not something every Cage warrior could claim.

She bucked against his hold. "If you think worse wasn't done to me in the Asters' lab, then you have no idea what goes on there."

"Doesn't matter to me." He gave her pussy a last, hard squeeze. At least this time she flinched and tried to pull away. Any reaction could be twisted to his advantage. "Maybe you'll enjoy it. Pleasure can be another incentive."

She slammed her head backward. Her skull smacked the bridge of his nose. Pain rocketed through his brain. The woman scrambled from his arms and ran. Leto shook his head. Part of him was dazed that she'd got the jump on him. Mostly he was amused. Where did she think she could go?

From down the short corridor that led to her cell's gate came a feminine shriek. Pure frustration. She was certainly loud enough to use the sonic assaults that accompanied the berserker rages of Clan Pendray. They annoyed the fuck out of him. Shaking off a weeklong migraine was the price of victory over those Dragon-damned Reapers.

He took a strip of linen from beneath his chest armor and wiped his face. The gouge in his cheek was nearly a puncture. The woman continued her tirade. High-pitched bellows echoed up the corridor.

"She-devil bitch," he muttered to himself.

Still, he was surprisingly eager to get started.

Leto set his shoulders and lifted his chin. The Aster family ran the most powerful human crime cartel in the world. His victories over their cartel rivals—the Townsends of England and the Kawashimas of Hong Kong—had earned him many privileges. First among them was the right for his sister Yeta and her husband, Dalnis, to conceive a little girl. Soon, with the Dragon's blessing, his efforts would earn protection and care for his comatose younger sister, Pell. Up in the human world where they'd made their home, Yeta and Dalnis had taken on the burden of Pell's care for nearly a decade.

He would win the Grievance, year after year. To keep his family safe. To ensure Clan Garnis would live on.

Confidence gave him extra swagger as he strode down the sloping corridor to retrieve his screaming neophyte. She stood with her back against the gate made of floor-to-ceiling wrought iron. Leto had no key. He was let in and out by the Asters' human guards. Cattle prods, Tasers, and napalm bullets kept even the most powerful Dragon King in check. The collars made it so.

Leto had never fought back. Why would he? This subterranean complex had always been his place of glory and purpose, where his father had fought. Where, in service to his loved ones, his father had died.

Decapitated by a Dragon blade.

"Stay away from me!"

"I won't." His words were as assured as he felt.

She darted sideways. Though slender, she was wily and surprisingly strong. But she would never be his match. He caught her around the middle. Momentum threw her onto his forearm. Again he hurled her to the ground. He pinned her with his boot heel on her collar, right over her larynx.

"You'll only hurt yourself. Save this fire. You'll need it for the Cages."

She cradled her elbow and glared up with pale, pale eyes—maybe blue.

"I'm to train you for your first bout in three weeks,"

he continued. “Normally we’d have more time, but Old Man Aster wants you ready by then. He’ll be hosting many important people.”

He removed his boot and grabbed a fistful of hair—a honey blond shade that trailed down her back. He’d need to fix that. His actions were proof of how dangerous long hair could be in battle.

“Let go of me!”

“No.” He dragged her back to the main body of the training room. He shoved her into a crevice that had been carved by a steady trickle of water. “Wash yourself. I won’t work with garbage.”

She hissed as cold water drenched her face, sluiced down her back. The thin paper hospital gown clung to her body. Soon it would be as useless as wet tissue. He had proper armor for her to change into. Eventually. First, she needed to learn her place.

“Soap?”

Leto crossed his arms. “What was that?”

She pinched her lips into a tight white line. That honey-colored hair darkened beneath the water’s trickle. Her arms and legs trembled. She closed into a protective ball.

If the woman didn’t ask, Leto would have a despicable chore ahead of him. On a certain level he would enjoy breaking her. Yet he craved a real opponent. She had that potential, if she proved smart enough to know when to back down.

“May I have some soap?” The effort of asking contorted her features with fury.

“Perhaps.”

Slowly, he knelt before her. He’d trained enough for

the Cages to know when the appearance of gentleness held greater power than aggression. She backed deeper into the crevice, but her fear was nowhere to be seen. Those pale, almost silver eyes were visible through the water dribbling down her face. Already she was cleaner. He could see more of her features. *Stubborn.* Every feature stubborn.

"I will not give much advice beyond techniques for fighting. But listen to me now: Save your hostility. I am not your enemy."

"Bullshit."

She whipped wet hair back from her heart-shaped face. Her pointed chin was haughty, but her lips were delicate. Thin. Tremulous. As with every Dragon King, her skin was naturally tan. Hers was overlaid with a shimmering luster, like gold beneath a blazing light. Wide cheekbones were streaked with freckles, not the dirt he'd assumed. The water darkened her lashes and framed those nearly translucent eyes. Her gaze was canny. She assessed every detail, even through her fury.

Intelligence in a trainee was a double-edged sword.

"Become a half-dead cripple for all I care," Leto said with a shrug. "You know it takes a great deal to kill a Dragon King. But the crowd loves when combatants bleed and scream. No one mourns."

"My son would mourn me," she whispered.

"He already does. Dr. Aster will have told him you're dead."

"I was promised my son. One year more."

*One year.*

He almost pitied the woman's naïveté. She'd be lucky to stand or talk or chew after her first match. Yes, she would heal, as all Dragon Kings did, but the process was imperfect. Amputated limbs never grew back. Minds cracked into mad pieces. Scars remained. His split lip and lashed back were a testament to that.

He masked his pessimism and long-ago pains. This was his responsibility. He had yet to fail the Old Man. He wouldn't let this woman destroy the respect Leto had spent years acquiring.

"Learn to fight," he said. "Or you'll suffer as others have."

She shuddered. The hospital gown clung to her. She tucked her legs beneath her and crossed shaky arms over her breasts. The water let her keep few secrets. "And you're here to teach me?"

"You would've saved yourself a lot of abuse had you asked that question twenty minutes ago."

*"Bathatéi."* The worst curse word in the language of the Dragon Kings.

Leto only laughed. "Your name. Now."

She lashed out with a tight fist. He caught it easily, then the next one. The only weapon she had left—one she might not have realized—was the surprise of her breasts. The soaked paper gown outlined their lithe, luscious shape. Leto forced his gaze back to her face.

"Your name," he said with growing menace. "Unless you enjoy being called lab filth."

"My name in exchange for soap."

He grinned. This was going to be fun.

"Agreed."

A swallow disappeared beneath the edge of her collar. She lifted her chin. "My name is Audrey MacLaren."

# CHAPTER TWO

"Your real name."

Dragon be, his calmness was irritating. He let go of her fists.

Audrey had lost feeling in her fingers and toes. The hospital gown disintegrated into little balls of paper along her shoulder.

"It is. I'm Audrey MacLaren."

"Maybe out there with the humans. I won't speak that dirt down here."

"Sure, because this place is so pristine."

"My rules."

"You sound like my son. Petulant. Expecting to get your way."

He stared down at her with abject condescension. "And I suppose he got his way in Aster's lab?"

"You piece of shit!"

"Call me what you like. That won't change your situation."

Everything about his raw brawn and arrogant posture said fighting back would be a useless waste of energy. She was too weak with hunger and too shattered by pain to resist with more than words.

But she *did* have words.

"I was born Nynn of Clan Tigony."

The man flinched. She'd dented his arrogant exterior. "A Tigony? In the Cages?"

"You heard me. Malnefoley, the Honorable Giva, is my cousin."

Malnefoley was the leader of the ten-person Council that protected the Dragon Kings' ancient traditions.

"Your origins don't matter down here." The man recovered as quickly from mental surprise as he did from physical attacks. "Here, we only fight for the Asters."

She couldn't read his eyes—eyes the rich brown of an antique book's leather binding—but she compensated with other clues. His shoulders were not quite as relaxed. Tension had replaced the grace of his assured movements. Lines around his mouth tightened.

Just what power did he possess? If she could learn his clan, she would know. Each had particular abilities, passed down through dwindling generations. The Tigony had not inspired myths of Zeus's lightning bolt by accident. They harnessed and concentrated kinetic energy—which wound up looking very much like an electrical storm.

But her tormentor could be crossbred.

Though Audrey had been raised among the Tigony, few had let her forget her origins. Her unknown father was Pendray, one of the vicious berserkers that had inspired Norse and Celtic myths. Only Mal had forgiven her mother. Audrey's place among the Tigony had been granted at his discretion alone.

Crossbred children could possess extraordinary—and dangerous—gifts in unique combinations. Or they could possess nothing at all. Like Audrey. She'd never been immune to the rumors and scorn.

So she'd adopted the name Audrey after hearing it in an American movie. She and Malnefoley had agreed it best that she leave their Tigony stronghold in the high, craggy mountains of Greece. She had received her education at a boarding school in the States. Money and influence meant she'd eventually become an American.

She'd met Caleb at an innocuous college bookstore, amid used texts and supplies. Imperial Russian history—turned out they'd shared the class, rolling their eyes at their slightly insane Scottish professor. They wed before graduation, and she'd loved him with all her heart.

But she'd kept secrets. She was a Dragon King. Life before boarding school was a lie. He'd married an alias.

Despite her guilt, she'd protected her new life—and had buried the pain of her exile. Now she would never return to either of her homes. Jack was not only her son; he was all she had.

Standing, Leto glared down at her. "If you move from this spot, I'll leave you for the night. Cold. Wet. No soap, clothes, or food."

Clothes and food. "Any other threats?"

"You'll be confined to your cage instead of being allowed free rein of the training room."

"This is a training room?"

"For one such as you."

His voice was almost powerful enough to force obedience. It was low and throaty, as if wounds could speak. The collar might as well have fused with his larynx. She shivered for reasons that had nothing to do with the chilly water.

He strode down the corridor. His swagger was as maddening as it was fascinating. Ridged, well-built thighs powered his body with surprising grace. His bare back was a lacework of scars. Leather straps crisscrossed below his shoulder blades to hold the chest plate in place.

Sinew. Brawn.

Another shiver.

Audrey scrubbed the paper hospital gown from her skin. Naked, she turned away from the cavelike room. Dragon be, the brute was right. She was filthy. Dirt and dead skin sloughed off beneath her palms and fingernails. Although she was frozen through to her bones, she relished the feeling of starting over.

She would stay strong and learn what she could. No one would keep her from Jack. She only prayed to the Dragon that something of her little boy would remain.

The man returned. A chunk of soap landed by her hip. She snatched it up. A scant lather was enough to finish washing her body. She glanced behind her when she was about to wash between her legs. He squatted on the balls of his feet, with his back against the opposite wall. A folded pile of fresh clothes waited by his boots.

Goose bumps shivered up her wet back. He had grabbed her between the legs. The *lonayíp* bastard.

The human laboratory guards had used her that way, when she'd been drugged and bound. Deep instinct told her this man would want her to fight back.

Turning away, she lathered her grimy hair. A year ago, she'd lived with Caleb and Jack in a sunny Manhattan condo overlooking a small park. Her bathroom had been filled with sexy indulgences. Loofahs. Bath salts. Moisturizers of all scents and purposes. It seemed so ridiculous now.

The woman she'd become appreciated a scant chunk of soap. At least it wasn't an astringent, hazmat-level disinfectant. Her skin had toughened, like the rest of her. This soap was something almost . . . pleasant. A small change in the scheme of things, but a change she desperately needed.

"Come get your clothes."

Of course. What man would miss the opportunity to ogle a naked woman? She'd only waited for him to command her in that rasping, broken timbre.

Clothes. Then food. Each step stretched before her like Dorothy on her way to the Emerald City. She nearly smiled. Jack had been four the first time they'd watched *The Wizard of Oz*. The flying monkeys terrified him so badly that Caleb had traded out the DVD for *Cars*. Audrey had made popcorn. They'd let Jack stay up late to finish his favorite movie, but he'd fallen asleep on the couch, sprawled across Caleb's lap. Her husband, so blond, had stroked their little boy's wheat-pale hair.

Whatever this barbarian planned to do to her had nothing on that memory. Or the ones that followed: Caleb shot through the heart. She'd watched him die in an instant. Then came Jack's screams. She'd caught sight of a Dragon King in a trench coat, just before a hood blacked her vision—but none of the horror.

Good and bad memories burned until she couldn't breathe. Bodily pain could be disconnected, like flipping a switch. But messages from her heart attacked at unexpected moments.

Even when she stood wet and naked in front of a stranger.

Still shivering, she walked toward where he knelt. Never had she been so conscious of the surgical marks left by Dr. Aster's experiments. Some scars never healed, not even for a Dragon King.

"Are you going to give me my clothes?"

"You have no possessions."

She gritted her molars. "May I borrow them?"

The amusement in his eyes made her want to pluck them out. He flicked his wrist. A tank top and plain women's briefs landed on her wet toes. A strange leather outfit followed.

"Get dressed."

"Here?"

He nodded.

Let him look. Dignity had been replaced by one instinct: survival.

"My little boy is named Jack," she said softly, just to herself.

She focused on her words rather than the vulnerability that punched her heart against her ribs.

The pants were tough, tanned leather lined with denim and what felt like . . . silk? The shirt was made of the same odd combination. Both fit snugly but with enough room to move. Had they taken her measurements while she was unconscious? Dragon be, there existed so many ways to violate a human being.

But she wasn't human. Never had been, no matter how many Pixar films and bags of popcorn and bottles of lotion. That didn't mean she could restrain the grief filling her chest like hot sand. She needed to speak it aloud. Audrey MacLaren had been a high school art teacher, married to a marketing exec. So content, she'd taken it for granted.

Now, that contentment was nothing but pain.

"Jack Robert MacLaren." Stronger echoes touched the back wall of the training room. "He's almost six. My husband's name was Caleb Andrew MacLaren. He was thirty-four when he was murdered trying to defend our son. I would've liked the closure of attending his funeral. Instead, I was strapped to a laboratory table. Dr. Aster had taunted me that no one would investigate the crimes. 'Our family has a great deal of influence, Mrs. MacLaren.' He always used my married name. Salt in every wound."

"I didn't say you could speak."

"So stop me."

The beastly man stood. So damn tall. Audrey was a respectable five foot eight, but he dwarfed her. "Is that a dare?"

"I'm doing what I was told. Why do you care what I talk about? I needed a distraction while you slavered over me." The clothes were armor, like wearing a fortress. Assurance lined her bones with steel. "Did that turn you on? For a defenseless woman to shiver and beg? If I grabbed between *your* legs, you servile, brainwashed dog, would you be hard? I hope not. I hope you fondle your limp little prick tonight and cuss a blue streak because you can't get it up."

Massive fists bunched along his thighs. His scarred lip twitched. Eyes narrowed to slits that glittered like deep brown topaz. A heavy pulse ticked at his temples, where his serpent tattoo stopped short. Branded by the Asters.

*Disgusting.*

"I didn't say you could speak." It was no idle repetition. It was a prelude to violence.

Audrey smoothed back wet hair and met his gaze. "If the Old Man wants me here, he won't appreciate seeing me harmed. I bet you can't risk that, *warrior.*" She sneered the word. A warrior fights to be free, not to grovel in the dark. "So hit me, throw me back in that cage, or get me some Dragon-damned food."

During combat, Leto would've laid waste to the insulting bitch. He'd have crushed her ribs before she uttered another infuriating syllable. With the collars temporarily disengaged, his speed and reflexes—the hallmark of Clan Garnis—would've made that possible.

He couldn't remember the last time a neophyte figured out how their relationship worked. Symbiosis. If this woman failed to entertain, Leto would share the blame. To lose face left him seething.

He checked his thoughts. There was always something to be done when a neophyte got lippy—no matter how clever. No matter how fucking sexy.

Leto shut down that thought even faster. Just as he tried to forget the healed surgical incisions on her lustrous golden skin. A violation.

"Get in your cage."

"Go to hell."

"You can stay out here, but I won't feed you."

Defiance dazzled from her bright eyes.

This time Leto was able to hide his renewed surprise that she knew how to pick her battles. The Tigony made no secret of their disgust for the Cages. They were the

Tricksters of the Five Clans, more eager to wheedle than fight. They could storm fire from the heavens, yet few tapped into that potential. They simply talked too much.

"Get in your cage, Nynn of Clan Tigony. Or I'll throw you in."

"What happened to letting me have free rein of this . . . cave?"

"That was before you insulted me."

She shot a disdainful glance toward his crotch. "Hit a little too close to home?"

He pulled until her ear nestled against his mouth. She smelled delicious now. Fresh. Scrubbed clean of the sweet, unnatural scent of decay that the lab refugees always carried. He never let his mind journey to Dr. Aster's lab. Imagination was best left to techniques in fighting. But he couldn't deny what his senses told him.

Whatever happened there was simply *wrong*.

Leto used his grip to shove her into the four-foot-square iron cage. He hated being unprepared against *any* opponent. No one of her rank wound up in the Cages. The Tigony were practically royalty, ever since their days as patron gods to the Greeks and Romans. Combat was saved for the poorest, most desperate Dragon Kings. Or for those like Leto who'd fought since early manhood to perpetuate their bloodlines. But to train the Honorable Giva's cousin?

He threw the lock and knelt. "Your identity won't make a difference when we train. What will make a difference is your gift from the Dragon. And I sure as hell know what that is."

"My gift never manifested!"

"Save your breath."

He said it flatly, because he'd seen proof of her destructive powers: Dr. Aster's lab, with its roof obliterated. Her lie was obvious.

Unless . . . unless she had been subjected to the same procedure as his sister Pell. Leto had survived the disorientation and fear of his first manifestation, but his sister had not. Vigorous powers required the intervention of a telepath. Sometimes the process of installing unconscious restraints went badly. Very badly.

Leto shook off his foreboding. Time to get food. She would respond to food.

He walked away without explanation, unsurprised when her shouts followed.

He'd been confident in what to expect when first entering her training cell. Now, he knew what she looked like naked.

He exited at the guards' discretion and walked between them toward the mess hall. He knew the turns and sloping underground tunnels well enough to walk with his eyes shut. He may as well have. Images of Nynn overlaid his vision. Waist and hips designed for a man's hands. Supple legs to curl around a man's lower back. Tight nipples waiting for a man's eager mouth.

She'd got it all wrong. He had tamped down his arousal out of sheer mental discipline. He would not be limp when he bedded down that evening. In his private quarters, he would indulge those erotic images and release the grinding tension she'd ratcheted into his joints.

The mess hall was no more elaborate than Nynn's training room, only bigger, having been carved out of granite deep within the earth. Dozens of human workers, all male, had gathered for the evening meal. Long wooden tables were flanked on each side by plain benches. Durable pewter plates held beans, rice, chunks of beef, kernels of corn, and buttered bread.

The guards accepted their meals from a stumpy man named Kilgore. "Here for your portion, Leto?"

"Yes, and for my neophyte."

"The girl? Caught a glimpse when they brought her from the lab. Is she a looker? Couldn't tell."

"Food first."

"You can be such a bore."

Leto stood over him. "Earning the roar of a satisfied crowd is never a bore. Can you say the same for ladling beans?"

"Don't rub it in." Kilgore's puckered face didn't need much incentive to curl in on itself. "Not all of us can be stars in the Asters' empire."

The man served up dinner and assembled a second plate.

While Leto sat in the mess hall, he ate with silent relish. Quality fare. He'd heard rumors of Dragon Kings who fought for the Townsends and Kawashimas. Some were fed no better than scraps. Their holding cells were riddled with vermin and disease. They fought for meager prizes. Only Dr. Aster had perfected the process of reproduction among Dragon Kings. No one knew how he'd managed to solve the problem—or why conception was a problem in the first place.

The two other cartels had achieved limited successes. Their warriors bore as many insane, malformed children as ones delivered healthy and vital. It was a chance more were willing to take by the day.

Leto, however, was a god to the Asters. Praised above all who shared this warrior's life. That Yeta had given birth to a healthy child meant he was more than a warrior. He had helped pass down their bloodline. His niece, Shoshan, and the few others who remained represented the future of Clan Garnis.

He returned his empty plate and faced Kilgore. "You ready for it?"

The small man stopped in the midst of lifting a scoop of corn. He ignored the thin, sallow-faced worker who waited for his food. Nearly every human in the compound looked that way—pale, sunken, wasted. Life underground turned them into two-legged moles.

Leto hid his disgust. For millennia, the Dragon Kings had ruled over these people, and for good reason. Mere herd animals.

He only wore the Asters' collar because he benefited.

"Go on, then." Kilgore's dark, beady eyes were eager. "Her tits. Tell me."

"Small but shapely."

"And?"

"Tight buds. Dusky. Best I've seen in years."

A shudder of pleasure jerked the loose skin along Kilgore's jowls. "You really are without peer, my friend."

Leto hid a scowl. He counted no humans among his friends—as if such a word existed for him. Sharing physical details about his neophytes spoke to Kilgore in the language of small minds. His lust for news about new arrivals was insatiable. Kilgore would embellish those curt descriptions, earn clout among the workers, and spread proof of Leto's superiority. Such men eagerly bet on their favorite champion.

Distasteful. But necessary.

Leto took up the second plate of food. "Now if you'll excuse me, I have a neophyte to break."

# ✦ CHAPTER ✦ THREE

The *lonayíp* bastard.

He left the tray of food out of reach beside her cage, and resumed his place against the wall.

Audrey's stomach was a raging beast gnawing through her skin. It wanted the freedom to scramble between those iron bars and gorge. Dizzy on the scent of fresh meat and vegetables, she closed her eyes. There was nothing to do but beg.

She had begged for mercy in the labs. Needles, scalpels, saws—torture brought out the animal in a girl. When survival hinged on a sadist's caprice, the words had babbled from her lips. Before Aster's men stole Jack from her arms each morning, she'd held his frail, injured body for as long as possible. And she'd pleaded. Every day. She'd turned into some servile little creature.

But here . . .

She had a chance.

Audrey went through her list of assets. She was clean and clothed. She had endured years of ostracism among her namesake clan, bearing the brunt of her mother's supposed indiscretions—years that made her stronger. She was free of Dr. Aster's lab.

Risking an entire year before seeing Jack again was unbearable. Cage fighting was a temporary measure. She needed to escape and save her son.

That meant learning this complex inside out—from its physical layout to every single person inside it. Roles. Timetables. Coveted bribes. She would need to try getting another message to Mal. Pinning her hopes on one hastily penned letter wasn't enough. At the lab she'd managed to conceal three Post-it notes before her hands were cuffed. The pen had taken longer to find. Months of vigilance. Amazing that she'd lived in hope of finding what other people took for granted. Opportunity had come in the form of a careless assistant and his gaping lab coat. Writing had required as much of her blood as it had dried-up ink.

Reed of Tigony had been so broken. She had no way of knowing his fate, or the fate of her letter. She had no faith in the Council senators, either, who'd pressured Mal into sending her into exile after her marriage to Caleb. They'd been waiting for any excuse to exert power over the Usurper—the derogatory name used against Malnefoley. Common sense said the Council wouldn't sit back while Dragon Kings were yanked out of their homes, tortured, and forced to fight as slaves for human crime bosses. But common sense rarely applied in politics.

Buying time meant she would need to survive in the Cages.

That meant getting stronger. Eating. Training. And, yes, that meant begging.

"May I have the food? Please?"

He shoved the plate forward with the toe of his boot.

Audrey pounced. Beans and rice. She ate with her

fingers, relishing each bite. The buttered bread was as sweet as chocolate cake. Such an indulgence. With her mouthed crammed, she looked up at her captor. Was this why he made no protest against being enslaved? If the Asters kept her too much longer, she'd lose herself. She'd become like him.

*Never.*

"Enough." He knelt, tossed her plate away, and grabbed her hair through the bars. "This has to go."

"My hair?"

"See how easy it is for me to immobilize you? No weakness allowed."

He unlocked the cage and dragged her out.

No weakness? *Yeah, right.* Her knees were liquid. Sleeplessness and the cramped cage had left her weak. Adrenaline had propelled her initial fight. That fuel was long sapped.

"Turn around," he said, his voice a gravelly rasp. "Hands on the bars. If you so much as move, it won't be your hair I cut."

Audrey took a deep breath. *Do this for Jack.*

Other words began to coalesce in her mind. New words.

*Vengeance. Judgment. Reckoning.*

She liked those words—would live for them. For the first time, she had a goal beyond rescuing her son. She'd burn the whole place down for what had been done to her family.

She gripped the cold iron bars, blinking back surprising moisture. Caleb had loved her hair. Corn silk, he'd called it. He'd loved when she trailed it down his stomach on the way to sucking him into her mouth.

A lifetime ago.

She tightened her grip and heard the slide of metal being unsheathed. Was her captor so trusted that the Asters permitted him a weapon?

"Hold still."

An inexplicable shiver danced up her spine. His voice was hypnotic. Just enough steel, just enough calm. That she could analyze it at all seemed a minor miracle.

The first cut was the toughest. She watched long, caramel-colored strands float to the grungy cave floor. He didn't hack, but he didn't take care either. Just another duty he performed without thought. More hair scattered on the ground.

He sheathed the knife and stepped away. "That will do."

Audrey turned her back to the bars. She ran shaking fingers over where he'd cut close at the base of her skull. Choppy, uneven strands ran along her crown and temples.

Her mysterious guide down this dark rabbit hole stood watching her. Sizing her up. She would sketch his body using blocky shapes. Unapologetic rectangles for his limbs. Strong squares for his trunk and head. Yet a true representation would demand flowing arcs, too. Swoops. Supple curves. His muscles were that graceful, that prominent.

*Charcoal and paper,* she thought. *With golden brown oil pastels for accents.*

Her artistic training was making him into something impressive. He was not.

"We'll train here in close-quarter combat," he said. "But for now I want to see what you can do."

"You already got a taste of that. I was brought up learning the martial styles of the Five Clans."

"No. With your powers."

Audrey's heart beat with thunderous pain, which always happened when she thought about her lack of a Dragon-born gift. *But why?*

"Maybe you didn't hear me the first time. I have none. Never have."

"Lie all you want. You'll still need to adapt. The more entertainment we provide, the better we fare."

"I don't care about that shit," she said. "You know what I want."

"Your son."

"That's right."

The man rubbed a calloused hand along his hard, square jaw. "Regaining your son is your reward. You were promised."

"I don't believe it. Dr. Aster won't give him up until he's cut down to Jack's marrow, dissecting him alive."

"A Cage warrior named Honrovish won ten straight matches. As reward, the Old Man overruled Dr. Aster's protests and released Honrovish's brother."

"Where's Honrovish now?"

"Dead." No inflection. No hint of emotion.

"What a waste."

"No. His brother and sister-in-law lived. They bore a son. Their bloodline continues because of Honrovish's sacrifice. Now, come this way."

Always that long, confident stride. He simply expected her to follow.

"What's your name?" The question jumped out of her mouth.

He stopped. Looked over his shoulder. His cropped black hair shone in the dim lighting. The serpent tattoo across the back of his skull looked alive—a representation of a warrior's potency. And a slave's captivity.

"I am Leto of Clan Garnis. But you'll call me *sir*."

She stayed rooted to the hard cave floor. *Clan Garnis?* Many believed them extinct for centuries, although Audrey knew they yet maintained a place at the Council table. Mal believed them scattered so far across Russia, China, and the Americas that they'd assimilated into the human population. They maintained no known government and no stronghold. The myths they had imparted to their human worshipers were scattered to the winds.

Clan Garnis were the Lost.

That explained so much. This man Leto's admiration for his dead comrade was plain. Perhaps he intended to forge a similar path in order to perpetuate his scattered clan's bloodline. Brainwashed or not, he had as much reason to step into the Cages as she did. The futures of their families depended on it.

The last thing she needed was a feeling of kinship with this brute.

"Come," he said more harshly.

With her teeth gritted but her belly full, Audrey obeyed.

The guards slapped manacles on Nynn's wrists. Leto refused to think of her by whatever human name she'd taken.

She stared at her metal-wrapped wrists. "What the hell?"

"They don't trust you."

The guards escorted him and his charge down a bright, open corridor. This one led away from the human quarters and mess hall, toward where the Cage warriors slept in personal dorms, and where they trained. He enjoyed the familiar sights and sounds and smells of being among his colleagues. His domain.

"You'll never be without escort," he said. "Unless you prove yourself beyond doubt, you'll never be without manacles."

"What about our collars?"

"They're never removed. Why would it matter? Topside, I'm a holdover from long-ago gods that no one believes in anymore. I'd have to hide like a coward, as you did."

"*You* talk of hiding and cowardice?" She laughed—a hard, grating sound. "Marrying Caleb was the bravest thing I've ever done. You let human criminals lead you around by your throat."

To so thoroughly deny her heritage by uniting with a human . . . What Dragon King could do that? "You don't deserve the honor of fighting here."

The guards led them to a wide double door made of reinforced steel and the same restrictive properties contained within a collar's matrix. They couldn't escape the main training arena's room by using their powers. In fact, the matrix of the door was amplified to paralyze anyone who breached it.

He told Nynn as much. "Some have tried, the fools. They became drooling cripples."

The guards removed Nynn's manacles and departed, locking the door.

She scanned the large square facility. Leto looked as well, though he knew their perspectives would vary radically. He saw the basics: the high domed ceiling lined with sound-muffling materials, weapons along the left wall, the X-shaped whipping post in a shadowy corner. His back itched at that harsh reminder of past indiscretions. For the most part, however, he remembered moments earned, taken, beaten into submission. Those memories were more powerful than the cool air, the lingering scent of sweat, and the matrix's buzzing ozone.

"Once locked inside the Cage, the collars can be deactivated." He pointed to the mesh steel that comprised its ceiling and octagonal sides. "The training room's doors keep us inside, but the reversed matrix of the Cage allows us free use of our powers. This floor is padded. Real Cages are twice as large, with brushed concrete floors with a five-inch layer of clay."

"How does that affect fighting?"

Leto raised his eyebrow, surprised but gratified. "The clay is slippery. Makes for a tricky start. But it wears away. The concrete offers more grip. It also means the end to the fight is near. Combatants get tired. One wrong hit and bones are broken. Skulls cracked."

Understanding shone behind her silvery-blue eyes. Leto didn't like her sharp tongue or her obstinacy, but his initial enthusiasm returned.

He'd already assessed her body, but this was the first time her features had a more powerful hold on his attention. Wide, wide eyes caught his attention first. Equally wide cheekbones, exotic and high, came next. She had a full lower lip that dragged down at the corners in a stubborn pout. Even her nape was worth notice—

slender, with strong tendons that accentuated her upright posture. Across her cheeks and the bridge of her nose was a smattering of freckles. When he found himself tracing patterns with his gaze, he looked away.

"We have three weeks before the first combat match," he said. "And a lot of ground to cover."

"What does a match entail?"

"Dragon Kings from here in the Asters' compound compete in nonlethal contests. We perform in a genuine Cage, with seating in the round for the Asters' guests. Betting is rampant. Winners are rewarded, and take one step closer to the annual Grievance."

"A Grievance? That's ancient—from when the Five Clans needed to clear bad blood."

"Now it's where the best warriors of the cartels fight for the ultimate prize."

"Conception."

Leto nodded. "And with the ultimate risk. At a Grievance we can be beheaded by a Dragon-forged blade, as punishment for losing."

She blew breath out through her nose. "They've co-opted our traditions and made them into something disgusting. What's the point of earning conception if it comes at the cost of slain Dragon Kings?"

Leto led his charge toward the Cage and opened the gate. "The perpetuation of our own lines. Protecting the futures of our families."

She shrugged from under his touch. "That's a selfish way of looking at our people's march toward extinction."

"Not my problem."

He ignored her obvious disgust and locked them in together. The hum of the mesh steel's reversal surged to life. His gift returned to him, following by white noise. It was a signal deep in his brain to prepare. The collar felt lighter. He stretched his neck from one side to the other. Muscles and joints loose. Ready for battle.

"So what can you do?" she asked, arms crossed.

"I'm Clan Garnis. What do you think?"

"Speed. Reflexes."

In a blink, he shot behind Nynn. His crooked elbow held her in a chokehold. She gagged when he pressed just above her collar. "A great deal of speed, and *excellent* reflexes."

His reflexes were so astonishing that, on occasion, he felt as if he could see his opponents' moves before their minds twitched with the thought. To his knowledge, there were no other Cage warriors of Clan Garnis. He had no one to ask. Besides, why would he reveal something so advantageous to anyone he might one day face?

He shoved her away. Nynn landed on hands and knees on the padded floor. A coughing fit arched her back.

"Fight me," he said. "Or I get nasty."

She held up her middle finger.

Another blink of speed. Another surge of power. He kicked her in the gut.

She clutched her stomach and clasped one hand over her mouth, as if she was ready to be sick. The heavy supper would fuel her body. Eventually. Right now it was a hindrance. He'd be impressed if she managed to keep it down.

"This will only get worse if you resist."

With blond hair in disarray around her heart-shaped

face, Nynn glared at him. Fiercely. Her unearthly blue eyes took on the intensity of a predator. Leto was surprised by the snap of primal awareness. Manhandling her, watching her wash, hearing her beg—nothing had jolted him so strongly. Instead, it was her outright defiance.

A killer instinct, with titanium behind it. A true warrior.

He had hoped for competence. Maybe even skill. The wrath in her expression was a bonus that affected him physically. He would teach her, watch her win, and then he would have her for his prize.

Shaking his head, he reminded himself that her training was his true goal.

Again, a blink. He moved with speed that could barely be seen, or so he was told. He landed a punch against her right kidney.

"You freak! Give me a chance, for the Dragon's sake."

"You speak of the Dragon but you lived as a human," he said, not even winded. "It's blasphemy."

"I can't help how I was raised."

"Bullshit, as you say." Leto leaned against the mesh steel. "You were cast out, I assume. I can't imagine he was worth it."

She stood. Slowly at first. Knees unsteady. She lifted her chin. That killer instinct had returned. Leto breathed in and relished the sight.

"He was worth everything I've endured, everything I ever will. And you've never felt its like."

Anger lifted in Leto's chest. Almost pain. Almost shame. Because she was right.

Blink. Kick to the lower back. Scream.

This time she didn't fall. She whirled on the balls of her feet. The blaze of her silvery eyes caught with his. An uncanny glow stopped him cold.

Fireworks.

He tried to shake away the illusion, but it remained. Intensified. Thousands of fireworks bubbled inside a concentrated circle between Nynn's hands. Sparks. Pinging blasts of flame were trapped in a sphere of energy that built and built—a balloon ready to burst. Her face contorted. Sweat trailed down her cheeks. She shrieked with the fury of a Pendray in the throes of a full berserker rage.

The bubble burst. Leto scrambled out of its path, but even he wasn't fast enough.

Pure concussive force threw him against the mesh steel. He hit face-first and grunted. He couldn't hear. Had he landed on the brushed concrete of the genuine Cage, he would've busted both kneecaps. With any more force, she would've broken every bone in his back.

He used the mesh steel to climb to his feet, ready to defend himself. But Nynn was on her hands and knees, shaking.

He hadn't expected her to leave her first Cage match with all four limbs intact. Part of him hadn't believed the pictures of Dr. Aster's damaged lab. A hoax? An incentive to challenge him? Yet Nynn possessed the most remarkable gift he'd ever witnessed. She was a volcano bursting open and flinging burning, breakneck debris.

Nynn rasped, "What was that?" Then she sagged onto the Cage floor.

He staggered forward. His extraordinary senses returned.

From a corner of the arena room came slow, deliberate clapping. A shuffle and the thump of a cane followed. Leto's gaze sliced through the darkness. Entirely bald and pushing eighty years, Old Man Aster emerged from the shadows. His maniacal grin carved wrinkles into the pantomime of a clown's smile. He was only missing the face paint. His sallow complexion—after having spent most of the last five decades belowground—was eerie enough.

No matter his value to the Asters, Leto was always disturbed by that warped, skeletal appearance.

"I told you." His voice was cultured, but scratched by his advanced age. "She's amazing. She'll rival you one day, my champion."

Leto straightened to his full height. Upon the raised floor of the Cage, he had the higher vantage. That didn't matter when staring into his master's eyes. His pride twitched. "Is that what you want, sir? For her to best me?"

"No, Leto. You are going to do what you do best: make our family very wealthy and make me very proud." He nodded toward Nynn's fallen body. "To do so, you will fight with Malnefoley's cousin . . . as your partner."

# CHAPTER FOUR

Partner. With her."

"Yes, Leto." The Old Man stroked a mustache as wan as his skin and as thin as his hair. Had he not possessed piercing green eyes, he would've appeared an albino. "The crowd grows weary of your successes. Betting has been poor—all in your favor. It's become a losing prospect for the bookies. Some have refused to take wagers on you. The other cartels refuse to pit their best against you in a future Grievance, which would exclude you from the games." He grinned again with that warped joker's smile. "Apparently there exists the possibility of too much of a good thing."

Indignation burned in Leto's throat. To have his victories so insulted was something he'd never imagined. Couldn't comprehend. After the blow he'd suffered at Nynn's hands, the insult to his pride was too much.

A faint glow radiated from her body, even through her armor. The training arena took on an eerie light. Her power shocked him. Stayed with him. A headache had burst across his temples—the constant beat of unreleased tension.

He swallowed in an attempt to regain his patience.

He couldn't argue with the head of the Aster cartel. Perhaps the facts could be plainly stated.

"Sir, I've never fought with a partner. She's an untested threat to herself and to me."

"My point exactly. She adds an element of uncertainty that you no longer possess. The crowd will hold its breath and the exchange of coin will skyrocket." The Old Man thumped forward, near enough to touch the bars of the Cage. "You will do this, Leto. I don't care how you manage it. If Nynn of Tigony survives three matches, I will provide your sister Pell with whatever medical care she requires."

"For life?"

"What remains of it."

Leto's focus returned, as did a sudden lifting of his heart. He didn't like the situation, and rebellious thoughts doubted he could make it happen. But his purpose remained as clear as the sunlight his mother had described to him as a boy.

"Pell has been under the care of my older sister and brother-in-law for many years," Leto said with a tight roughness in his throat. "My family would be very grateful for the assistance. I will do this, sir."

"Good."

The Old Man thumped away—three sounds with each step. Step. Cane. Shuffle. Leto would've recognized that pattern anywhere. His master's cadence was nearly as familiar as his own heartbeat.

Over his shoulder, the Old Man called, "I'll return in the days before the match. Arrangements will need to be made if you're not ready."

*I'll be ready.*

To turn this woman—practically a human, but for her remarkable powers—into a fighter would be nothing short of astonishing. What better opportunity to demonstrate his prowess as a warrior? Three matches. Keep her alive. Then his comatose younger sister would be protected forever.

Leto returned to where Nynn had fallen. Cropped, golden blond hair glimmered beneath the floodlights that lined the Cage's octagonal posts. She appeared asleep. Again he was fascinated with her freckles. He'd never seen their like—light brown, not tinged with red as with pale human women. He recognized that her stubbornness resided almost entirely in her pert chin. That stubbornness disappeared while she rested. Flaring brows gave her an exotic look, even among the Dragon Kings. Their women were perfection, hewn of centuries of power and flawless genetics.

Perhaps that was why they could not reproduce. What if such perfection came at great cost?

Leto was not the man to speculate.

"Wake." He gave her a hard shove. "Lab filth. Get up."

"I thought you'd decided on Nynn. Sir."

He indulged in a tight smile because her eyes remained closed. "I did."

Feathery gold lashes fluttered open. She assessed him in a way that belied her depleted sprawl. "What happened? I'm . . . Shit, I hurt."

"You don't remember?"

"Light. An explosion. I thought you said you had speed and reflexes. You decide to blow my head off instead?"

She truly didn't know? Dragon damn, this was getting messy.

"Get up, or I'll haul you out of here," he said. "Your prickly pride wouldn't like that. Or I can introduce you to Hellix and his allies. They'll be here to train soon."

"Hellix?"

"A Pendray. He wasn't trained for the Cages from youth, as I was. He was a criminal—a rapist and molester of the innocent, including the daughter of one of the Old Man's backers. Hellix was sentenced to die in a Grievance."

"But he survived?"

"He was *allowed* to survive after two straight hours of fighting. The Old Man thought his salacious history made for a good story. He lost that backer but gained a novelty."

"More about entertaining the crowds," she said, dragging to all fours. "They sound charming."

"Hellix's sycophants believe him a god for having dragged up from that low beginning."

Her mouth drew into a crooked smile. "And here you made me think all Cage warriors held hands and sang Boy Scout songs."

Leto scowled and arose. He didn't consider Hellix a warrior. When he thought of the men and women he respected, he never included that monster.

"Stay, then. I regret that you won't fare well."

She held out her hand. "Please, sir."

*Surely a trick.*

They were still inside the Cage, with their collars deactivated. He did not relish taking two huge blows in such a short span. From a neophyte, no less.

As was common practice among their people, he assessed her body's unspoken language. Shaking legs. Unsteady fingers. Sweat-slicked short strands of hair against her nape. Their gazes met, where her icy pale blue eyes revealed her fatigue.

She was in earnest.

He pulled her to her feet. "Walk or be carried."

Steps ragged, she followed him out of the Cage. She scratched at her forearms as if energy bristled inside her body. A glimmer of that electric explosion still raced through his veins, too. She was a wild creature hewn of untapped potential. He'd witnessed her unflinching determination. The memory of it stirred him in disturbing ways.

He reached the training facility's exit, having cleared his unwelcome thoughts, when Hellix barged through. Three arrogant shits followed like puppies after scraps, although they matched their idol in size and training.

Hellix's hair was bright red, which contrasted with his darker skin and piercing blue eyes. He bore scars on his face—from combat, of course, but also a brand in the shape of a dagger on his forehead. Only the brand marred the otherwise handsome features of a Dragon King.

"Leto. You look worse for wear, brother."

Standing chest to chest, Leto dared not assess his own appearance. He hadn't considered the effect of Nynn's powers on his armor and would reveal no such weakness now.

"You are no brother to me," he said.

The monster's keen appraisal of Nynn raised Leto's hackles. "And who is this? Your new project? I should fight harder in my matches. Whores and wealth are satisfying. Still, I'd like to train a neophyte of my own. Imagine the possibilities."

Leto needed to get Nynn out of there before things got ugly. She was barely able to stand, let alone fight. Free of the rules of the Cage, Hellix never played fair.

Yet Leto couldn't resist a pointed look at the puckered scar on Hellix's forehead. "Too bad. Forever banned, knife-branded scum. No neophytes for you." He looked down at the man he despised. "Now get the fuck out of my way."

Audrey watched the men square off. A primal shiver dusted her limbs with goose bumps. Fear? Curiosity? Or worse, anticipation? She'd never seen such a contest in the making. That she could respond on such an instinctual level was a surprise.

But then, everything inside her felt changed. She couldn't remember what had happened in the Cage, only that she still ached. Her body was jittery. Her lower jaw trembled. The ends of her fingers tingled as if she'd stuck them in a light socket.

*Why do I feel like there's a tiger in my skin? And what the hell happened to his armor?*

But how to demand answers from a man who had more in common with a brick wall than a sentient creature?

Any interrogation would need to wait. This contest was more immediate. Audrey's senses were supercharged and buzzing. She took in every nuance.

"Seems you're in *my* way, champion," Hellix said, sneering the last word. "I suggest you step back."

"I don't think so."

"So rude. What of your legendary honor?"

Hellix really was repulsive. His body and his features

were as appealing as any of their people, but his lips twisted in a way that set off her defensive reflexes. He exuded a cocky, malevolently violent nature.

And that brand. What did it mean? Audrey couldn't look at it without cringing.

Leto's expression was a hundred times more condescending than he'd shown her. Maybe it was a small mercy to know he held some people in even lower regard.

"My honor doesn't apply to men who have none," he said.

"Yet you work without question for our master." Hellix flashed an arrogant smile. "You're none too smart, my friend."

Leto unleashed a low growl. His fists bunched like hunks of steel at the ends of his corded forearms. Audrey's view of his back was impressive. The leather straps holding his damaged armor did little to conceal a patchwork of old scars across rippling, tense muscles. Those muscles made her stomach watery. Taut tendons at his nape were all the more impressive because of his closely cut black hair. She could practically see him twitching with eagerness for the standoff to explode.

The effect of witnessing a commanding man on the verge of savagery was undeniable. Her breath was strong and fast, just like her heartbeat. Her own fists were at the ready. She would back Leto if matters came to blows—bizarre, considering their inauspicious start. The odds weren't in his favor, and she was smart enough to recognize any ally. She squeezed her fingers even tighter, hardly daring to exhale. Her only desire was to leave with her body and brains intact.

That meant leaving with Leto.

However, a very deep, surprising part of her wanted to see him pound the shit out of Hellix.

The allure of oncoming violence stuck a blade of betrayal between her ribs. Audrey was a thinking, civilized woman. She had valued logic, books, long conversations with Caleb about history and politics. He'd teased her for making her way through Shakespeare's plays in chronological order.

*This* was fascinating on an elemental level.

Only then did she notice that Leto had angled his body between her and Hellix. Intentionally? She didn't dare believe it. Her tormentor-cum-ally had kicked her in the guts. Repeatedly. He'd dragged her by the hair and watched her dress. Only shards of his conversation with the Old Man helped make sense of his protective stance.

She was valuable to him.

Their postures coiled with menace. "I await our next contest," Leto said, his voice impossibly low. "Just as I await a repeat of the last outcome."

Hellix's mask slipped for only a second. Beneath the posturing was shame. Audrey wondered if she'd have noticed it before what had taken place in the Cage. The acuity of her senses was amplified. Although Hellix hid it quickly, she was certain Leto had also caught that moment of doubt. No wonder he could stand in the face of Hellix's hulking body and fierce scowl. Shame could be as debilitating as pride or fear.

Leto seemed a master at exploiting weaknesses.

Hellix laughed, as if none of it mattered. "One day I'll throw you down. I'll sever your head from your body and you'll leave this world."

"If you even came close to earning a place in the Grievance, I might take that threat seriously."

"You arrogant—"

"I've earned my arrogance." Rather than push the physical tension, Leto stepped back. The gesture from any other man would've seemed like retreat. His condescending expression, accented by the silver scar on his upper lip, said otherwise. He owned the moment. "You boys need the practice. We'll leave you to it."

He took Nynn's clasped hands in one of his and tugged her through the cluster of savagery. "Oh," he added, meeting the eyes of each of Hellix's cronies. "The Old Man is here today. Not a bad time to try impressing him—unless impressing Hellix holds more meaning."

Hellix's men were surprisingly susceptible to Leto's ploy. They broke into overtly masculine trash-talking and slapped one another like football players before a big game. Their interest in Leto and Nynn dissipated in a breath. Hellix remained a fuming, intimidating barrier, but even he didn't stop them from exiting.

Instead, he took control of what resources he had left: the men who'd abandoned him. "Come on, you shit stains. Get in that Dragon-damned Cage."

Audrey didn't look behind her as Leto's grip was replaced by the guard's manacles. Her exhale was pure relief. The incident added new layers to her situation. Being trained by a fool or a sadist would only get her killed. Now, she trusted Leto more than she would've thought possible upon waking that morning.

Morning. What a joke. She had no idea whether the sun shone, or the moon instead.

"How did you know he would back down?"

Leto walked ahead of her with long strides. He cast an assessing glance over his shoulder. He seemed to do that most frequently when she used logic rather than mindless hysterics. Not the best first impression she'd ever made, but screw it. Anyone who'd suffered in Aster's labs would've behaved the same way.

"I've lived in close quarters with Hellix for six years," he said. "I've never seen him strike first."

"And the others? No concern?"

His impressive back gleamed bronze beneath the corridor's fluorescent lights. "My skills are not limited to the Cages."

"I've seen that much." She ran a hand over her raggedly shorn hair. She wanted a mirror, if only to even out the damage he'd done. Or maybe to see herself as he saw her. "Brawn seems to be your lifeblood. I'd like to survive, thank you very much. That means learning from you."

He chuckled so softly that his lips barely moved. The sound was as throaty and scarred as his voice. "I'm not going to need to break you."

"You sound disappointed."

"Maybe."

Something close to amusement hovered in his glittering black eyes. Even with the fluorescent glare and the strange brightness of her senses, she couldn't be sure. She'd forgotten how many subtle human emotions were cloaked among the Dragon Kings. Facial expressions were generally placid and restrained—the better to keep the Five Clans from slaughtering each other millennia ago.

Living among human beings, she had learned to

smile and laugh and cry with abandon. She had learned to express what she felt. Here, that was a dangerous weakness she would have to unlearn. Otherwise, every ploy and intention would scream across her features.

*More thefts. Now I can't even laugh or cry.*

"I don't doubt you'll find new ways to keep me in my place," she said quietly.

"An invitation if ever I heard one."

His scant smile was Audrey's first glimpse of the man behind the armor. She hid a smile of her own. Women possessed advantages that balanced obvious vulnerabilities. From the dawn of time, they'd latched onto the biggest and strongest males. Safety among alphas. Out among humans who'd layered civility over old instincts, she would've been appalled at such a thought.

Leto was the alpha she needed in order to survive. To get her son back. To make the Asters pay.

The guards returned them to Audrey's cell and locked them both inside.

Leto leaned against a damp wall and crossed arms that bulged with sculpted muscles. Everything he did led back to the Cages. Be the best. Save his family. But he was incurably brainwashed by the Asters. He was part of the system she was going to burn to the ground. Only when it came to surviving the matches did their goals align.

"Are you going to tell me what happened in there?"

He lifted his brows a fraction. "With Hellix? You were there."

"No, in the Cage."

Hard masculine features shifted into an expression of . . . confusion? Disbelief? "You really don't remember?"

"I damn sure remember you kicking the crap out of me."

Audrey dared to approach him, which she wouldn't have hours before. The energy buzzing in her blood was like a venomous toxin, but she didn't feel sick. Only different. More radiant, although that word didn't make sense. People weren't *radiant*. That was the stuff of cosmetics commercials and descriptions of brides in wedding white.

Still. She couldn't deny that she'd come away changed. Whether that was good or bad would have to wait.

Within arm's length, she touched his blasted armor—a burnt edge of leather and flame-curled iron. His chest remained concealed, but the pitted metal and singed padding were exposed. The champion had been bested.

She preferred him whole and shielded. Powerful. Useful.

*More potent.*

"But I don't remember this," she said. "What did this much damage?"

"*You* did."

"No way. I told you, my gift never manifested."

"Don't make me repeat myself, neophyte. You blew a hole in Dr. Aster's lab. That's how the Old Man found out about you, and that's why you're here."

Flickers of memory pushed through. Fire. Lightning. Pain and rage fused into energy she couldn't control. She wanted to protest, but she was too uncertain to contradict Leto's outrageous claim.

*That's how Reed escaped.*

How had she forgotten? She'd unleashed chaos enough for him crawl to freedom. In her previous memories, he'd simply . . . gone.

The truth remained stark. Her hopes were no stronger now than when rage had given over to a burst of power she couldn't remember unleashing.

Instead, she was left with a new truth. She had a gift from the Dragon.

She'd become reconciled to her lack. Dragon be, she hadn't lived among her own kind for years. Now she recalled kinship, deep roots, and matched instincts. It should have been a joyful realization. Only, Audrey was ready to vomit. Sick, shadowy fear clenched inside her chest. She sank to the damp floor and leaned against one of the algae-covered walls. Eyes unseeing, she fought to remember just as hard as she fought to forget.

"We start again tomorrow," Leto said. "Sleep now."

The sound of the clanging gate echoed through the dank space. Audrey barely noticed. She pushed her fingers against her temples. Something was there, lurking in her mind—something dark and terrifying and ready to erupt.

# CHAPTER FIVE

"The letter is the most important development we've had about the cartels in a decade," said Malnefoley, the Honorable Giva. "You refuse to acknowledge it."

Sath Wisdom sat forward in her chair. "Watch your tone."

He whirled his gaze toward the seemingly ageless woman. "What did you say?"

She pressed her hands flat against the meeting table hewn of wood older than memory. It, like everything else in the Fortress of the Chasm, was storied and inviolate—a functional memorial to the creature that had given life to them all. Even their robes were hundreds of years old, sewn from heavy black cloth and accented with each clan's color. Copies of copies of copies of those worn by the first Council of the Five Clans, when Sath, Tigony, Pendray, Garnis, and Indranan bridged their divisions to secure an armistice that had kept the Dragon Kings strong for millennia.

Only the Sath knew their people's entire history. They kept secrets they weren't meant to hide, just as they took powers that weren't their own.

"You heard me, Malnefoley," Sath Wisdom said with

narrowed eyes. "You won't get anywhere by bullying us into submission."

For the sake of harmony and, more important, as a means of keeping his temper, Mal didn't call her on the obvious slight. His family still called him by his given name. To everyone else, he was the Honorable Giva—the only one of the Council to wear robes of endless black. No clan color. Senators relinquished their identities when they assumed their positions, the better to secure non-partisan consensus. Two came from each clan. The old women were referred to as Wisdom for their sagacity and maternal patience, while the impetuous men were dubbed Youth for their spirit and eagerness to go to war.

Checks and balances, with the Giva as their fulcrum.

Of all the senators, Sath Wisdom was his most formidable opponent. She was a Thief.

*No.*

She was Sath. That she challenged him at the start of their twice-annual assembly was not a good sign. It was not a Giva's place to resort to name-calling, and with what he had planned, the meeting was only going to become more contentious.

Outside their mountaintop Tibetan shelter, a snowstorm raged as if it would wake the Dragon from its forever sleep. Snow swirled against the wall of glass tempered in the deep fires of the Chasm. Unbreakable. Shimmering and golden. Only its unknowable properties kept them safe from the force of a Himalayan blizzard.

He hated the cold and couldn't wait to return to Greece. Yet he couldn't govern at a distance. Nynn's letter changed everything.

With his fists clenched beneath the table, he breathed calmly, using time-honored techniques. The other clans thought the Tigony preferred politics to violence. Far from true. They possessed gifts so overwhelming that control was essential. Mal fought the electrical current gathering in every cell. To outsiders, particularly the Council, his control could appear as weakness. He didn't feel weak; he was a man whose honor and will held a thunderstorm at bay.

"We are here to disagree," he said, his voice practiced and even. "That much is necessary before we can agree to take action. We are *not* here to hurl insults."

"What if 'usurper' is not an insult, but fact?" This from Pendray Youth, whose expression always revealed his powers. He forever stood on the precipice of untold frenzied violence.

*Usurper*. That word had followed Mal for twenty years.

The Council reminded him whenever they convened—not always with outright snipes, but with their refusal to cooperate. The previous Giva had guided the Five Clans for just over eighty years. He had been an authentic choice. Two children from each clan had looked into the churning, fiery maw of the Chasm where the Dragon had been birthed and where the Dragon had died. There, ten mouths had simultaneously screamed the name of the chosen Giva.

But Mal . . .

He'd been chosen by six whispers. Clans Pendray and Garnis were so few in number that they'd refused to condemn even two children to a mountaintop life of semimadness. For millennia, it had been considered an honor to choose the Giva. Never again wholly sane, the children grew into fierce warriors whose only duty was to protect the Fortress of the Chasm. Now it was regarded as a waste of what few children remained. Those who'd chosen the previous Giva were growing old, leaving the fortress vulnerable. Their skills were dwindling, as was the population of Dragon Kings.

Mal was an obvious symbol.

Only six whispers, when tradition required ten screams.

Four crucial votes had been missing since his first day as Giva, always raising suspicion about his authority. Giva meant fulcrum. Plain and simple. Mal fought to tip the scales in an attempt to save their race, but he did so without unanimous authority.

That didn't mean he was without power. Or the element of surprise.

"Pendray Youth, if you have a better solution to my standing as the head of this Council, I'd like to hear it. Are you ready to assume my position? You as much as any senator know what we face, as clans and collectively. You have the privilege of speaking, arguing, making trouble, being useful—but ultimately, you'll remain one of ten. Any consensus will be my responsibility to defend, for good or for ill. Are you ready to bear that scrutiny?"

"Fine." Pendray Youth was the most contentious. Even Sath Wisdom knew when to back down. "Just know that 'woe is me' sounds pretty pathetic, *Giva*."

"There is nothing woeful about stating a matter in plain speaking. Petulance, however—"

The young man banged his fist on the table.

"Enough," said Sath Wisdom, her white brows narrowed. "We speak out of turn and with a lack of respect."

From long experience, Mal knew she was quietly mocking his leadership. At the moment, he didn't care. Her intervention gave him a moment to cool his temper as Pendray Youth's posture lost its aggression.

"Now," Mal continued, as if the outburst hadn't occurred. As long as he kept calm, he could play any political game. Twenty years of contentious rule—and before that, years as the head of his clan—had made him a master. "The letter from my cousin is our most decisive proof that the human cartels have overstepped. We're no longer talking about volunteers, desperate to pay off debts or to gamble on the possibility of a child. Human criminals are taking Dragon Kings from their homes! I'm struck dumb by how easily you're letting this happen."

"Because even if it can be proven, the information *is* from your cousin." Sath Youth lifted his chin in an obvious sign of disdain. "She was banished for good reason."

"She was banished because she married a human, and if we're all honest, as retribution for circumstances surrounding her mother. But not because she was someone to spin tales. That Nynn bore a natural son is something we should be praising. Something to be thankful for. You'd rather dredge up what happened years ago."

"Her son is only six," said Indranan Youth, with his dark, steady eyes. He always spoke for himself and Indranan Wisdom, who sat stooped and shrouded to his left. Their telepathy made whispered discussion unnecessary. "No one yet knows whether he possesses a gift from the Dragon."

How the Indranan chose their representatives was a mystery to the other clans. Northern and Southern factions had been engaged in a bloody civil war for three thousand years. Mal would never know if these two hailed from the Indian subcontinent or from the wilds of the Australian outback. But he resented them because they represented all that stood in the way of the Dragon Kings' survival. Ridiculous rivalries. Long-held grudges. Jealousy and hatred and all the emotions they'd long disdained of human beings.

The humans thrived. The Dragon Kings held off extinction as if by chance.

The Indranan senators never failed to disagree with Malnefoley. He didn't attribute it to their unnerving telepathy. They simply didn't want to acknowledge what he had to say, for reasons he could never comprehend. Personal? Political? A means of manipulating the emotions he kept in check?

Then there were the senators from Clan Garnis. Useless. They were almost always quiet—even their Youth. Compared to the organized, even powerful governments of the other four clans, Garnis had nothing. The Lost. In twenty years, Mal had yet to discern whether their lack of involvement in Council discussions was because of their clan's ways or because they had little power to reinforce any point of view. Surely they believed *something*.

He wanted to pace—or rain lightning down on those who opposed him. Too much temper for a Giva. He'd known it from the beginning. A slow-boil fury made him vibrate with things unsaid, actions not taken. He pushed his anger into the pit of his stomach. No one would humble him. For all the doubts others harbored about his legitimacy, Mal knew the truth. He had the insight and resolve to see his people through this crisis.

"We all know her husband was killed. No one has seen her or her son since. This letter is the first communication anyone has received from her. It's half-scrawled in blood, for Dragon's sake."

Arguments burst across the table as the senators took his words, warped them, turned them into weapons to brandish at one another.

*Aster guards the secret to our survival, but at* *this* *price?*

Nynn's words haunted him day and night. Even the fierce mountain winds sounded like his long-lost cousin. Her voice was strong enough to compete with the ticking clock in his mind that said they were running out of time.

His aunt, Leoki, had been dead since the accident no one mentioned. She had given birth to Nynn by a Pendray man. Perhaps one day she would've been accepted back into Clan Tigony, especially with Mal as Giva. Instead, Nynn had killed her.

Grief still pounded in his joints. Leoki had been his aunt, but they'd been separated by only five years—more like siblings. He'd lost so much that day. Leoki dead. Nynn subjected to the process that had boxed away her dangerous powers. She'd emerged practically human, so that his decision to have her educated in the States was an easy one to edge into her consciousness. After only a few weeks, she'd taken up the idea as her own.

And marrying a human man . . . That had been the end of Nynn's life as a Dragon King.

He'd fought the Council. He'd even fought Nynn, hoping she would relent and come home. But layered over that wretched era had been one moment of goodness. She had appeared happy for the first time in years. Even when the Council delivered its verdict, she was a woman relieved of deep burdens.

Only, she didn't know what burdens remained in her mind.

"That's what I'd expect to hear from a Thieving liar like you!" came a shout from Pendray Youth.

"Quiet!" Mal's voice thundered around the wide circular room. "You're spoiled children, not senators. I *will* act without this Council's consent if name-calling is the extent of your involvement."

"Act without our consent?" Sath Youth looked ready to turn his chair into a weapon—whether to strike Mal or Pendray Youth didn't seem to matter.

Tigony Wisdom cleared her throat. She was the only person who could stem the tide of so much anger with the arch of one brow. The Pendray and Sath Youths glared, but one cast his eyes toward the table and the other fussed with draped robe sleeves.

Named Hobik, Tigony Wisdom was Mal's adoptive grandmother and the only senator whose name he still used in his mind. Despite no blood relation, they looked a great deal alike: thick, straight bronze hair and eyes so deeply blue as to appear black in the low light of the Council room. Elegant, the Tigony had always been called. Cultured. Gracious.

Another reason they weren't taken seriously in times of war.

Mal could've laughed. His people had taught the

Greeks and Romans how to fight. How to build cities and raze them. At that moment, a crackle of static was taking the form of sparks in his blood, inside him, all around him. If he let his concentration slip, those sparks would amplify into violent kinetic energy. He would become a living turbine.

Not now. Maybe not ever.

He gave his grandmother the barest nod.

Hobik turned her attention to the rest of the Council. "Whether or not Nynn's child has been blessed by the Dragon, the other two human cartels remain our clearest stream of information. They are openly jealous of Dr. Aster's acquisition. Because of the timing of her kidnapping, we can assume some truth to the Asters' involvement. Why would he hold them captive if they weren't important?"

That logic was apparently the key to coalescing the Council's attention. Mal had been too agitated to think of it.

He breathed deeply of the mountain's thin, chilly air, thankful that Hobik's logic had quieted the senators. For now.

Nynn was a piece missing from his life since her departure for the States, and then gone from him forever after marriage. She had never treated him as a man apart, but as a friend. Worse, she had since become an obsession. She represented the first and only significant time he'd given in to the Council's demands. As a result, he'd never met her husband or her son. Her resentment had been too strong.

Now he had her letter. What might be her last. Her disappearance finally warranted the Council's involvement. He'd been waiting for such an opportunity.

Mal cleared his throat. Time to bring this meeting to a head. "What's more, new information suggests the existence of an underground network of Dragon Kings. They work in secret and are unaccounted for among their clans. More than that, they have reached across clan boundaries. No politics. No allegiances other than to our people as a whole."

Gasps of surprise and disbelief met his words. Every senator believed that he or she held sway over their territorial, increasingly bureaucratic governments. They likely thought it impossible for clansmen to escape entrenched lore and self-importance. Managing Council meetings even twice a year was becoming more and more difficult. No one was willing to compromise for the greater good.

Not even this small group.

Yet out there, he believed others might see the world—and their pending extinction—with more pragmatism. That gave him as much hope as Nynn's letter.

"They don't have a name," he said, with all of his calm and focus. "No codes. No way of getting in touch."

"Then who delivered the letter? Carrier pigeons?" Wearing a sneer, Pendray Youth made as if he were ready to retire for the evening.

Mal paused, looking the rebellious senator in the eye. "It was Tallis of Pendray."

No one spoke. Mal could see them processing this new information, testing it for truth. Finding it lacking.

"The Heretic," Tigony Youth whispered. "He's been dead for years."

"He hasn't been dead, because he's been a Pendray myth all along." Sath Wisdom shook her head. "Some legendary assassin? I don't believe any of this."

Mal smiled coldly. "Careful. Calling me Trickster is one thing. That sounded very close to calling me a liar. I refuse to discount any possibility."

The pair of Indranan senators shared a glance before their Youth spoke. "We're with Sath Wisdom on this. He doesn't exist. Never has."

"Pendray Youth?" Mal stood, placed both hands on the table, and let it take his weight. The senator's natural golden color had drained to a sickly pallor, as if he'd seen ghost. "He's of your clan, so tell me. Is Tallis of Pendray a myth? Is he dead?"

"The Heretic is not a myth," he said, his voice hushed and monotone. "And as far as the Pendray government is aware, he is not dead. We would've seen the celebratory fires from here in these mountains. Our people have hunted him for decades." Although he appeared to have aged in a matter of moments, he snapped out of his daze. "And he just *delivered* this letter? Like some Good Samaritan?"

"Don't think me so generous," came a shadow-dark voice.

Mal stood to his full height, pleased with Tallis's timing.

Guards materialized out of nowhere. The Council's Youths jumped to their feet. Only the crackle of electricity from Mal's fingertips silenced the chaos. "Stand down, senators. Now. And I suggest you introduce yourself. Quickly."

"The Council spoke of the devil, so I appeared. I *am*

Tallis of Pendray. I assumed you'd want to have a little chat."

Everything about him, from his posture to his words, was laced with sarcasm. He radiated an impression of complete disregard. He was a man who didn't care about a thing, not even dying. As with any Dragon King intent on blending into the world at large, he wore inconspicuous clothing—a pair of black jeans, a long-sleeved T-shirt layered with a black sweater. The casual, almost sloppy disregard for fashion was meant to detract from, not accentuate, the classically handsome features of their people. His hands were in his pockets, as if interrupting the Council's twice-yearly meeting was as common as going to a cinema.

Shock and curiosity layered in the Council meeting room like smoke twining with clouds. Despite having brought the man to the fortress, Mal held no respect for the Heretic. The man's list of crimes was nauseating. "Tell us, then. How did you come by Nynn's letter?"

"You're near to the general idea of it," Tallis said. "Which is impressive for a Council. Well done."

Mal gritted his teeth. In the midst of fighting ten recalcitrant senators and the slow-wash tide of extinction, this bastard was testing the last of his patience.

"Yes, there exists a collection of rebels who refuse clan associations. They found the letter. Reed of Tigony wasn't a kilometer from the Asters' complex when he froze to death. They'd known its general vicinity." He chuckled softly. "Only when your cousin blew the roof off the lab did they know for sure. Reed escaped in the aftermath."

"You dare laugh about this?"

"Save it, Giva. You need them to hear what I have to say. I was willing to deliver that letter when none of the rebels could. Anonymity is their great asset. My asset is to become anonymous when I will it."

"There are other rumors." Mal stepped forward. He lifted his chin and prepared to kill a fellow Dragon King upon Tallis's next answer—not there in the Fortress of the Chasm, but wherever the deed needed to be done. "There are rumors you killed Nynn's husband, then handed her and her son to the Asters."

Tallis stared at Mal, emphasizing their impasse. Under the flippancy was a flicker of something deeper. Flash and gone. "Funny things, rumors."

"But you *are* a killer."

Tallis nodded.

"Tell me why we shouldn't keep you here and force you to stand trial? Or, more fittingly, return you to the Pendray who despise you?"

Pendray Youth practically growled his agreement with that idea.

"They do hold grudges, my beloved clan." He shrugged. "But you, Giva, would rather believe me in hopes of saving Nynn."

Mal felt as if he held the weight of his people in his hands. The entirety of his race depended on his next decisions. Luckily, his great weakness was an overabundance of tenacity, not a lack of resolve.

"Nynn and her son are in pain," he said. "For now, for me, that is enough. With all due respect, senators, I'm adjourning this meeting. None of us are leaving until we reach a consensus. Take action against the cartels? Ignore them and hope Nynn's fate is a single event?

Follow this man's lead? We owe our respective clans the answers they'll surely demand."

The crackling energy in his blood could stay. It was the purest part of him, giving him strength from inside out, providing a reminder to remain stronger than his gift.

"Take the night," he said, his words spoken with deep confidence. "Take days if need be. Find it in yourselves to put away this petty bickering and lead our people. It's your Dragon-damned duty and I expect nothing less than your full cooperation."

He turned to the Heretic. With a flick of his wrist, Mal signaled the guards to take him into custody. "As for you," Mal said, "I will listen to what you have to say. I may even accompany you to a stronghold—the Asters' or otherwise. But first you will answer every question I have about my cousin."

# ✦ CHAPTER ✦ SIX

Audrey was exhausted—body, mind, soul. But she couldn't sleep.

She lay on the rugged ground and stared at irregular shadows distorting the depth of her cell. Training room, he'd called it. Sleeping quarters. She knew better. Bars and keys meant imprisonment. A breath of free air had not been hers in more than a year. Each one she drew was tainted with acidic pain. Helplessness should've become part of her after such demoralizing captivity.

It *had* been.

She'd nearly given up in the labs. Another few months, maybe weeks, and she would've done anything to end her life. And Jack's.

Every morning, she'd wondered if murder-suicide would be better than another day of torture. She was scarred, inside and out, but she could place blame where it belonged. A child, though . . . Jack wasn't even six. He would never outgrow this cruelty.

In the end, Audrey's survival instinct had been too strong. Over and over, she'd decided to give them one more day. One more chance. She hadn't been able to abandon hope. She'd cursed it almost as often as she clung to it—almost as strongly as she'd clung to her little boy.

She was swathed in darkness once again, yet she wasn't holding Jack. No slight warmth. No soft breathing when he finally drifted toward dream. Not that his dreams were without trauma. Even there he was not free. His nightmares broke her heart.

She'd rather have a broken heart than empty arms.

Her back ached. Regret and uncertainty were parasites digging into her mind. She was to become a Cage warrior. The decision whether to release Jack from that misery was no longer hers. Instead, she would free him and rebuild their lives. She had the power to make it so.

*You blew the roof off Dr. Aster's lab.*

She no longer needed to wonder why she'd been plucked from one hell and deposited into another. New questions sprouted.

*How?*

*Since when?*

*And why this dread in the pit of my stomach?*

Every part of her body hurt. Her scalp burned where Leto had dragged her across the floor. Her arm creaked where he'd yanked it behind her back. Her gut cramped where he'd kicked her. The energy beneath her skin stung with pain close to pleasure. At least this pain had purpose.

Audrey curled into herself like an infant in a bassinet. Only by remembering long-ago Tigony techniques for calming her restless mind did she finally feel the warm blanket of sleep.

For a moment.

A key rattling at the end of the sloping corridor

roused her with a start. Noise meant danger. She was on her feet in an instant. Cold made her clumsy. She wobbled, focusing beyond shadow after charcoal shadow. Yet her muscles responded with surprising grace. The aches had eased. She buzzed with the need to move.

"Awake so early?"

She flinched away from the sudden spark of the two bare lightbulbs. But even that disoriented sense returned more quickly. Had releasing her powers done something? Maybe it was nothing more than shedding the sluggish hopelessness of Dr. Aster's lab, but she doubted it. She wished she could remember or understand. Then she might feel more satisfaction, and banish the queasy, lingering dread. She didn't have time for unknowns.

Leto stood half a dozen feet away. He wore similar armor, but this set was free of damage. His right shoulder was covered by alternating layers of metal and leathers of different thickness and texture. The other shoulder was bare. Striated muscles flexed and shifted with every small movement. Biceps, forearms—even his hands. He was the most impressive man she'd ever seen. Something out of an impossible fantasy. Darkness and intensity. Vigor and power. A pulse of purpose surged in constant waves from his magnificent body, potent enough to feel against her skin.

A man in control.

A man who needed her.

That she could be of any importance to such an intimidating mountain of skilled, deadly brawn almost made her laugh. *No way.* For Dragon's sake, she'd clipped coupons and taken Jack to Mommy and Me swimming lessons. She was no warrior.

Her amped-up body and sharpened senses said otherwise.

She had no chance at survival, let alone rescuing Jack, if she didn't transform into something like Leto of Clan Garnis.

She nodded toward the small crisscross of surgical tape, where she'd pierced his cheek. "The bandage doesn't suit you."

"Then don't strike me again."

"I'm going to land as many blows as possible."

The heavy bag he dropped at his feet sounded overly loud in the cell. Two shields followed with twin clangs of steel against rock. "You're in a mouthy mood. No breakfast."

As if spurred by the mere mention of food, Audrey's stomach chose that moment to rumble. The guards at the end of the tunnel could've heard it. Leto's smirk twitched.

He walked through her small cell like a god. There was no other way to describe his stride, his straight back, his proud shoulders. He moved with refinement despite the weight of each step. After kneeling before the large leather bag, he pried it open. Metal. Gleaming metal of all shapes and sizes. Each piece shone with deadly purpose.

Dragon-dark eyes lifted to meet hers. "First, we learn materials."

One by one, he introduced her to the weapons available to them in the Cages. A machete and a mace. A wicked dagger and a sickle. Even something that resembled a metal skull.

"I don't understand," she said once he finished. "You

haven't mentioned anything more about what may be a mystery Dragon-born gift. And now you're teaching a course on Medieval Weaponry 101."

"Your gift needs to be developed. But even a warrior in complete control cannot rely on it. During a match, an arbiter controls the Cages. With the flip of a switch, our collars activate again. Survival becomes a matter of blood combat. That means working with steel and martial arts—even if your pyrotechnic display was impressive."

"And completely gone from my memory."

"Another problem, yes." He leaned closer. Breath against skin. Lips near enough to brush her ear. They never did. "My job is to make sure you can survive those random minutes when our powers won't mean a Dragon-damned thing."

Audrey shivered. Her body was already edgy with an energy she couldn't control. To feel Leto's warm skin so nearby added another layer of sensation. *Want.* She tried to push it away. She called it a betrayal against the husband she still missed with every heartbeat. Yet the craving for physical contact was undeniable—contact that didn't mean pain and fear. She took a deep breath, filling her lungs with the heady power of his scent.

Feeling out-of-body, she reached to pick up the metal skull.

Leto snatched her wrist and glared. "Do you take me for a fool?"

"How am I supposed to learn to use them if I can't touch them? Tell me, at least."

"It's a *nighnor*. Are you really so ignorant of our ways?"

"I'm sure circumstances have taught us very different things. Can you read?"

"Yes." His mouth pinched tightly. "My mother taught me. She taught me many things."

"And when was the last time you were aboveground? The last time you saw the sun?"

His subtle glare intensified, but his tension was more evident in his shoulders. "How is that important?"

"I'm just curious what you barbarians learn down here, other than ripping out spines. And besides, a *nighnor* is the ceremonial weapon of the Sath." She felt pleased at having taken him by surprise. Again. "You forget. I was raised among the Tigony. That meant years of learning our lore and rituals. I don't know how to use it, but I know what it is."

He hefted the *nighnor*. "Your turn to tell me. Prove it."

"Each one is ancient, from the time when the Sath ruled as Pharaohs. They're said to be the heads of men who denied the superiority of the first Dragon Kings. The fearful made the Sath into gods rather than suffer the same fate." Her stomach knotted for reasons other than hunger. "Coated in iron. Lacquered and polished over the years to add luster. But beneath the metal is bone. Some ancient peasant's skull."

Leto shrugged. "So they say."

"Let me touch it. Sir."

"That's not a question."

"Forget the mind games, remember? You need me to learn." Their gazes met. "More than that, I think you want me to."

The set of his jaw became as ruthless as the skull he

held. Metal over bone. "Do not assume anything about me, neophyte."

"How can I not? We know the stakes. Give me the damn thing and teach me how to use it."

"No lunch either."

Audrey huffed a breath. "You *are* dense. Even Dr. Aster fed me. 'Keep up your strength, Mrs. MacLaren,' he always said. 'More work to do tomorrow.'" She stood and glared down at the strongest man she'd ever seen. "You can't harm me, *sir*. Not like he did. So get on with what we know needs to be done."

His slow rise from a kneeling stance seemed to go on forever. Deliberate. Controlled. Just taller and taller until he was a ruthless warrior once again. "Oh, but I can do you harm. And win. I'll do that at any cost, even if it means knocking you unconscious during our match."

"What purpose would that serve?"

"I could fight on. Unencumbered."

Audrey's blood slowed. "You're giving me quite the education."

"And don't forget about Hellix," he said, that rumbling voice bathed in menace.

"What about him?"

"Your days are mine to direct. Your nights are not my responsibility."

"But the guards—?"

"Are lonely and easily bribed. Don't expect quarter from them either."

The pinch of her lips was almost painful. She forced herself to calm, valuing information more than the urge to answer his taunts. "Will you tell me something? Sir?"

"What?"

"The brand on Hellix's head. What is it?"

Leto's expression hardened. She wouldn't have thought it possible after the harsh way he'd spoken to her. Apparently his distaste for Hellix trumped almost anything else.

"Sometimes, humans with huge debts volunteer to fight in the Cages, too."

"That would mean death, surely."

"The other choice is for the cartels to harm their families."

Audrey shook her head in vehement denial. "That's no choice."

"Do you want to know about Hellix or argue the way of the world?" He held her gaze as she breathed deeply and remained silent. "The humans in the Cages are killed with ordinary knives. Dragon Kings set for execution are done so as a prelude to the annual Grievance."

"Hellix survived."

"But he still needed to be punished."

"I don't get it."

"How do you kill a Dragon King?"

Bile rose in Audrey's mouth, along with the age-old fears of her people. They could live far longer than humans. Some for centuries. That didn't mean they were immortal. Old age eventually caught up with even the strongest of the Dragon's children. And then there was . . .

"Decapitation," she said, as if by rote. "But only by iron forged in the fiery Chasm where the Dragon was born and died."

"*That* is an honorable death for a Cage warrior. Hellix was branded by an ordinary human knife—a shameful reminder that he should've died. The lowest of the low. I think he'd peel off his face just to get rid of the thing." He cracked a knuckle. "He takes out his anger on the women he earns. Do you get my meaning?"

She shivered. Just because she'd survived degradation in the labs didn't mean she wanted more. Somehow she knew that surviving against Hellix would be at least as difficult a Cage match. At least in a Cage, she would have Leto as her ally.

With a tight swallow, she firmed her spine. "I understand, sir."

"Let's get to work."

Leto had made a number of threats in order to secure Nynn's active cooperation—threats he had no means of carrying out. Using Hellix as a living, frothing boogeyman had worked. But she was a perceptive creature. Soon she might realize that to be subjected to Hellix's notorious sexual ferocity would destroy her. Leto would have no warrior left to partner with; he would have a broken shell of a woman.

The idea of beating her into unconsciousness during a match and taking on their opponent alone also had its appeal. Yet that would be a failure of another sort. He was tasked with keeping her alive through three matches, but the crowd wouldn't appreciate an unconscious fighter.

He would need a fallback plan when threats no longer worked. In Nynn's case, he believed the key was how much she secretly craved an outlet for her anger. Given the right tools, she wouldn't need to be coerced or intimidated anymore.

One such tool sat in his palm. The *nighnor* was an

old, brutal, effective weapon. A single crushing blow. To the spine, the nape, the forehead. It meant instant death for a human, while a serious blow to a Dragon King permitted enough time to sever the head with a Chasm-forged sword.

That method was the finale he'd enacted at the last Grievance.

"Here," he said.

"You don't fear my wild reprisal?"

"I would, if I thought you could wield it with one hand."

Nynn cupped the heavy iron skull. Her shoulders slumped to keep it from dropping to the damp, slippery floor. Training cells were kept damp for just that purpose, to make finding purchase even harder. Once this woman fought on rougher ground, she would be even more sure-footed and skillful.

The chilly dampness would test her endurance, too, as would the cell's complete austerity. Neophytes were denied every creature comfort. No pallet. No toilet. Just a slit trench that was washed clean where the crevice water flowed out a drainage pipe. The four-by-four-foot iron cage remained a lingering threat.

She would only have what he gave her. Until she won. The thrill of victory combined with basic rewards made reluctant fighters into eager ones.

The close-fitting training armor he'd provided was not a reward but a necessity. She needed to learn how to expose her limbs to harm. Protecting one's body was instinct. Only patience and practice would override her urge to shrink from an attack, rather than surging forward and putting her trust in leather and metal.

One of her arms, bare of armor in order to permit more maneuverability with a shield, flexed with a gratifying degree of muscle tone. She was lithe, beautiful, and fit for combat. Now all she needed were techniques—not to mention her gift, which she couldn't even remember after the fact.

He had three weeks.

Pell needed him. Never had he been promised a reward for so little work. Usually a favor so extraordinary required winning a Grievance. Although, in truth, watching Nynn struggle with the hefty *nighnor* promised work enough.

"Come at me." His voice echoed off the domed ten-foot ceiling. "This is your chance to let loose the hatred I see."

He didn't think she would. Too much sense. Too much pride, when she already knew the futility. Yet the vigor of her sudden attack was impressive. Rather than charge, attempting to strike him, she spun and hurled the weighty weapon. Leto arched backward using the reflexes he'd honed for two decades—no matter his collar. The *nighnor* hit the wall just over his left shoulder. Shards of raw cave rock splintered out from a crater.

She breathed hard, hands propped on her knees. Without food, pushing that hard would continue to test her endurance. Her eyes shot sparks that were nearly literal. He didn't like how he was drawn to her blue fire.

He braced his stance. "Learn anything, neophyte?"

"That *nighnor*s are heavy?"

"They are."

"That I can take you by surprise?"

Hiding his reaction took effort, because she certainly

had. As Leto had seen in the Cage, she was a fighter. He would see her blossom into a vicious creature who wouldn't recognize her own face. *That* would break her. And that would make her a worthy partner.

"No, you should've learned that I do everything with purpose. There are other weapons better suited to your frame. Now you've lost dinner, too. A day's rations gone, with nothing gained." He knelt to retrieve the dagger. "Take this instead."

She studied the blade for several moments, as if she could read its purpose. He'd never seen a warrior—let alone an untested woman—assess a weapon with such immediate understanding. And where were the aftereffects of her hazing the day previous? She believed she possessed no gift, but Leto knew otherwise. She was a changed woman.

Now to keep changing her.

Nynn extended her hand and took the dagger. With a slight movement, she twisted the handle until it fit snugly in her palm, the balance just right. Leto felt the rightness like the stir of a distant dream.

"Now the shield." Without warning, he threw a small round shield straight toward her face.

She deflected it using the dagger. A quick spin found her crouched on the ground. She'd moved so that the shield's leather strap already hugged her left forearm. Ready to defend.

Slowly, Leto knelt to retrieve his shield and weapon of choice—the mace. His pulse was up, surging as it always did when anticipating a fight. More troubling was how his cock stirred beneath the hard plating of his armor. Sex and violence twined together. Had for generations. There was a practical reason why victors were awarded the prize of flesh. Potent aggression didn't fade. It built and built, seeking release. Allied warriors were tempted down from that high by means even more satisfying than wringing each other's necks—by slaking the primeval shock of life-and-death combat. It was glorious when done so between slick thighs.

He'd never reacted that way *before* a fight. Release came afterward.

Leto kicked the rest of the weapons down the corridor that led to the gate of her cell. Beneath the wan light of the bare lightbulbs, he and Nynn circled one another.

"I will be your first opponent in combat," he rasped.

As if claiming her. Making her his, even in this violent way.

"Seems we've been evenly matched so far. You wear a bandage and new armor." She grinned. Slinky. Sly. "Give me what you can, *sir.*"

With that, she attacked.

# ✦ CHAPTER ✦ SEVEN

Audrey had only wanted to knock that smug expression off his scarred face. He was mortal. Fallible. The scar angling on his lip and the whip marks crisscrossing his back proved as much. He could be injured, bested, maybe even defeated.

Not that day. Not by her.

Her dagger glanced off his armor. He didn't need to use his mace, only swung his shield as easily as a kid with a Frisbee. The edge of blunt metal hit her in the gut. Her thick leather training armor protected her from the worst of the damage. Yet the hit still rattled her bones. She bit her tongue as she landed on hands and knees.

Instinct commanded her to lift her shield. The head of the mace cracked down where her head would've been. She rolled out of the way and again crouched in a defensive stance.

"You asshole! Are you trying to kill me?"

"I'm finding your limits," he said with a tight grin. "Apparently that wasn't one of them."

Audrey gasped for breath. The dagger's hilt fit as if it had been molded to her palm. The shield was the perfect weight. Why was this remotely possible? She had trained from childhood to defend herself, and worst case, to defend Malnefoley. Never with weapons like these. She shouldn't have the foggiest idea how to hold these implements.

But she did. It felt like coming home to a home she'd never known.

Sweat gathered under her arms. "What's the silk for? In the armor."

"Clan Garnis taught the samurai how to use it, centuries ago. Silk prevented arrows from embedding in the skin. Tug the fabric. Out they come."

"It's hot as hell."

"At least I won't withhold your water rations."

"Small mercies."

He kicked the toe of his boot beneath the edge of her shield. Her forearm wrenched upward. For a split second she was undefended. Only when the mace descended again did she act. A quick roll. A slice of her dagger. She missed setting metal to skin, but so did the mace. The round, spiked club swung past her armored shoulder. The breath of its movement was close enough to tousle her short hair. Leto caught its momentum by collecting the slack of the chain with one swift adjustment of his grip.

"Nearly."

"Nearly," he echoed.

"And the armor on only one shoulder. Why?"

"Do you always talk so much when fighting?"

"I'm *learning*, remember?" They breathed in tandem. Audrey licked her lips. "My martial instructor never let his students say anything other than *yes* or *no*. Maybe you're a step up."

Muscles bunched on both sides of his jaw. She could see his pulse where it throbbed at his temple, where shorn hair revealed the tips of his snake tattoo. The vigor of his blood gave life to the ink.

"Hold still and I'll answer your question about the armor." He dropped the mace and his shield. "I mean it. Hold perfectly still or this session will be very messy."

The intensity of his hypnotic voice—a weapon in itself—meant she could only nod.

Faster than imaginable, he stole her dagger. A single slice cut through her shield's leather cinch. It dropped, useless, to the ground. She was stripped within a heartbeat. Every cell in her body wanted to fight back. Run. Scream.

She held still.

Leto stabbed the dagger in a sharp, angled arc toward her armored shoulder. His right hand. Her right shoulder. The blade glanced along the metal and leather, as if shooting down a slide. He switched the dagger to his left hand and cut upward. Again the blade had no effect. It caught in the layers.

"Twist away!"

She responded instantly, spun and dropped low. The dagger stayed embedded in the leather, yanked out of Leto's grasp.

He was far less winded than she, but his breath still echoed through the dark cell.

Leto nodded tersely. "The armor hugs the arm you use to hold your weapon. The exposed arm. An attack would need to be incredibly forceful to pierce so many layers."

Audrey glanced toward her bare left shoulder. "And

this one is free to maneuver with the shield. I guess that lesson was 'don't lose your Dragon-damned shield.'"

Admiration flickered across his features. The thrill of their sortie had momentarily obscured her true goals. She hadn't even wanted to best him.

She'd only wanted his approval.

What the hell did that matter? She needed this condescending brute for what he could teach her.

"But you," she said. "You can fight equally well with both hands."

"Honing my gift—my reflexes—helped guide me. Now my muscles react before I do."

"A Cage warrior acting with brawn instead of thought? I wouldn't have guessed."

"You would do well to keep from taunting a man who stripped your shield."

She grabbed the hilt of her knife. Pulled it free of the leather layers. Settled it into the palm of her right hand. "I'm not defenseless."

He stalked toward her. She stared at the movement of thighs forged of pure muscle. Looking up his body sent an ancient shiver of awareness to her fingers and toes. His features were perfectly symmetrical, with a decisive brow that probably revealed more than he realized. Straight nose. Surprisingly wide eyes rimmed with thick lashes as dark as his hair. There was no telling his age. Few lines creased his smooth, flawlessly tan skin.

And his mouth. Lower lip just this side of full. Upper lip slashed by that old, silvery scar. It was the only hint of imperfection on an otherwise captivating face.

Her awareness shot inward, deeper than fear or hunger or vengeance. A shiver settled low in her belly. To admit she was aroused seemed tantamount to betraying Caleb's memory and Jack's innocent struggle to survive.

Yet he was sexy in the basest, most primitive sense. Weapons and armor and strength. Unequaled skills. He possessed confidence she doubted could ever be matched. Rather than wanting to divest him of that confidence, she wanted to get closer, soak it up, know what it was like to look at the world with such unabashed certainty.

She truly couldn't remember what certainty felt like.

He crossed his arms. Default stance. Proving a point, marking his territory, and ready for attack—all at once. Power coiled there, barely leashed. Dark eyes glittered. The lights bathed him in garish bronze that shadowed his features and accentuated his blunt, prominent muscles.

"Do not get cocky, Nynn. This is still training. The first *hours* of your training. Admit what you must and I will give you one ration."

Inhaling deeply, she looked down at the ground. She realized she was bowing. It didn't matter. She needed food. Whatever he wanted her to admit would be worth what he offered. Energy for another round. Maybe he could break her after all, beyond the physical. The journey between pride and submission had shortened.

Again, she wanted his confidence.

*One day. Soon.*

"Admit what, sir?"

"Stand. Lift your head."

She did as she was told. Limbs that should've been weak from exertion had recovered in record time. The feeling of inhabiting a body that wasn't her own added to her disorientation. Dragon damn, she wanted to remember what had happened in that Cage.

Leto stripped the knife from her hand and tossed it behind him. Metal slid across concrete. He took hold of her wrists. Vises and manacles had nothing on his incredible grip. He could snap her hands clean off. Her shudder must've traveled between them because his lips parted. That was new.

She liked it.

"I wear new armor and a bandage because I was not at liberty to kill you," he said quietly. "Your skills are already impressive. I cannot say I've trained your like before. I'm twenty years a Cage warrior, but this is only the beginning for you. To survive, you must admit that I could've bested you at any moment. You would be dead now had I not refrained."

The truth of his words hit her like a blast of cold water. His grip slid from her wrists to her hands. Squeeze. His hypnotism wasn't limited to his voice. She could barely detect what subtle devices he used to manipulate her body and mind.

But he was right.

"Yes, sir. I would be dead now had you not refrained."

He nodded tightly. "Retrieve your dagger. We have hours to fill."

Two weeks later, Leto stood outside the locked gate that led to Nynn's training cell. To his left, one guard's chin drifted tellingly toward his chest. His eyes were closed. The other flipped through an old issue of *Playboy*. And why not? It was nearly midnight, and they knew Leto's purpose was to check in on his new charge, as he'd done several times a day. That he brought an extra ration as reward for a good day's work didn't matter to them.

Soon, after her first match, Nynn would be ready to meet the rest of the Dragon Kings in the compound. She had already faced a half dozen during practices in the training Cage, but that wasn't the same. He wanted her to bond with them. To see this place as an unexpected haven that could provide security and purpose. Yet custom had it that neophytes didn't associate with proven warriors until after a first victory.

Knowing her, as he was beginning to, she would use any such interactions as a means of resisting him. He could imagine her crafty enough to foment rebellion and form new alliances. Leto wanted his domain just as it was. *His.* He'd spent years aligning patterns and relationships to his advantage.

Only when Nynn knew victory would it be time to fit her into the hierarchy. In the meantime, he was the center of her world.

Even with the collar in force, his senses were remarkable. He'd perpetually developed the blessing. Once experiencing the rush of what he *could* be, he refused to let it go. He worked at it. Fought to keep what the collars stole. Trained until muscle memory followed him out of the Cages. Because of those senses, he knew she was still awake.

He also knew the habits she'd developed. When she managed to sleep. When she cleaned her body. When she trained.

Which was almost always.

Since those first contentious days after her arrival, she ate regularly and followed the regimen he dictated. Stretches. Weight training. Cardiovascular. She'd even found a way to do vertical sit-ups by hooking her legs over the top of the door of the cage. She'd progressed from a weak creature into a woman on the verge of untold boldness.

He peered through the gate bars and down the corridor that led to her dank, dark quarters. He shut off the bulbs at night—though, on occasion, he kept them on. Her training included being able to adapt to any situation. Only with his keen sense of sight could he discern her movements. He narrowed his eyes and concentrated. Scant glimpses of her body at work were erotic, dancing shadows. Every panting breath wove into his chest. She grunted. Gasped. Cursed.

Too faint for humans to hear, those sounds were for Leto alone.

Without the details of light, he recalled how she looked naked. Audible proof of her determined physical labor laced into his nearly perfect memory.

He could make her sound like that.

They could *fuck*. Hard. Aggression and combat layered over a fierce coupling. Afterward, they would lie together in a tangle of naked, sweaty limbs, as after twelve hours of training. Tenderness was for softer people in softer places.

He craved the release not even combat could provide.

Another of her determined grunts stirred his cock. He remembered bare flesh. Sensuous hips and pert breasts. A flat stomach. Long, graceful legs.

And scars. Scars she had not earned in combat.

The intensity of that memory spiked down to the base of his skull. What had been done to her was disgraceful and disgusting.

He blew out a sharp breath. *Dragon-damned fool.*

Past torments meant nothing when preparing for the Cages. Enduring the unknowns of Dr. Aster's laboratory had likely made her stronger. He would use her past to forge her into a warrior, not wonder at the abuse she must've suffered.

She was a survivor, which made the mystery of her gift even more frustrating. How could she be so dedicated to martial training, yet refuse the most powerful asset at her disposal? She might as well be a human in a boxing ring. The Asters' guests didn't venture underground for anything so mundane. Their disappointment would be Leto's failure to bear.

Clenching his fists into tight balls, he put the night's goal ahead of every other consideration. He would push and push and push until something broke. Or until they forged into a single unit.

"Checking up on me?"

Nynn had walked down the sloping corridor to meet him on the other side of the gate. That she'd done so without his sensing her approach caught him off guard. Was she that good, or had he been lost in thought? Sweat glistened on her supple, golden skin. She'd stripped down to her underwear and tank top. Simple white cotton. Damp. Clinging. Her breasts and stomach and lush hips were his to admire, overlaid with new mysteries.

"Because you've given me cause to think you need

to be observed," he said. A brush of cool air against his forehead revealed he was sweating, too. Leto nudged the guard who stared at a flexible blond centerfold. "We're going to the practice Cage."

It wasn't a request.

The guard only shrugged, although his bulkier, full-body armor nearly concealed the movement. They dressed as part SWAT team goons and part medieval warriors. The two might as well be the same thing. Things Leto hadn't seen in person were difficult to comprehend. Refusing to be left alone, his mother had followed her young husband into the cartel's complex in the hope of starting and raising a family. Leto's father hadn't believed in educating his son in the ways of the outside world. After all, Leto would become a Cage warrior. His future was set, while Yeta and Pell were prepared to emerge from the dark and find husbands from among the Five Clans. Yeta had succeeded; Pell had never been afforded that chance.

Yet their mother had been adamant in teaching each of her children life aboveground, including Leto. She had insisted that he understand all that existed beyond the cartel's dark walls. A deep, edgy corner of his mind still doubted any of it. They were words, not concrete facts accumulated by his senses and his experiences.

Guards from the Townsends and Kawashimas wore their own distinctive uniforms, although Leto rarely noticed the details. He only thought about the other cartels' Cage warriors when the Grievance pairings were announced. That was when he called in favors from the likes of Kilgore. Leto learned all he could about the opponent he would take down.

Nynn dragged her hand along the back of her neck, slick with sweat. "*Now* we train? I was just about to sleep."

"I can leave you here. But I thought you might appreciate an extra ration." He held up a wrapped tray.

After banking her obvious surprise, Nynn stood a little straighter. "What's on the agenda tonight?"

She no longer called him *sir.* A trivial thing when she was obeying. He wasn't sure what to make of her mood that evening. Or his. In all other respects, she should have been the perfect neophyte: a quick study, skilled, and with a powerful motivation to success.

*Should have been.*

Just like he should have been able to keep his gaze off her breasts as a guard wrapped her wrists in metal. She lifted her chin—that distinctive gesture she must've learned among the humans. It accentuated the elegance of her neck, the pout of her lower lip, and the width of her soft, round cheekbones. She glared at him with pale, narrowed eyes, as if she were ten feet tall. That lithe elegance didn't stop with her neck, but trailed down a body that was tempting. So tempting. She was strength and curves. Power and femininity. Nynn of Tigony would be as much a challenge to bed as she was to battle in the Cages. Leto wanted his hands around her bare waist, down her sinuous back, between her thighs. He would find her wet. He would taste her. And she would taste him, making use of her stubborn mouth.

The guard dragged her into the open and roughly guided her toward the arena. Leto found it more disconcerting than arousing to see her bound and hauled like an animal. He liked her best when she blazed with confidence, because the last thing he wanted was to pity her. Or to sympathize with her pain.

His own pains burned hot enough.

The guards left them alone in the Cage facility and locked the doors. One of them handed Leto the keys to Nynn's manacles.

They were alone.

"Now what?" she asked.

With calm and patience, his sensual thoughts banished, Leto set the plate on a bench against the wall. He walked closer. He unbound her wrists. And he grabbed the pale gold hair at the top of her head, where the strands were longest. "Tonight, Nynn of Tigony, we see how you react to complete unknowns."

# ✦ CHAPTER ✦ EIGHT

Leto probably should've kept her bound.

She pulled against his hold, wincing in the process. "What is this, some version of underground barbarians' seduction?"

"Seduction?"

"You drag me out of my room in the middle of the night. *Alone.*" She clawed at his hands when he wouldn't release his hold on her hair. "Might as well be a Neanderthal dragging me to his cave."

Her words rocketed through his body, just when he'd thought his desires were under control. "I intend nothing like seduction, neophyte. Or anything else you imagine."

Shutting down his acute senses was as much a skill as using them. Rather than indulge in her scent, her gasping breaths, and the way her body still hummed with the energy of her exertions, he pushed a hard clench of desire down to where he locked every selfish impulse. He would bust through the bricks she'd stacked around herself. She could keep her physical armor, but he meant for nothing to remain between her mind and victory.

Leto released her hair, gave her one more look up and down. She held her body stiffly. Straight back. Tense limbs. He couldn't tell if she was truly confident and waiting for his next move, or poised on the edge of terror. He wanted her snarling, not anticipating the worst. Maybe that was the drawback of working with a woman so fresh from the labs. Yes, she was resilient. She also flinched too much for his taste. Only in the Cage had he seen her shed all doubt and use her past as a weapon.

A radical idea took shape in his mind, unlike any he'd ever considered. Then again, he'd never been permitted three short weeks to bend, break, or understand a neophyte. And he'd never trained a woman like this. All he'd managed from Nynn was a semblance of obedience and augmented physical conditioning.

She expected him to treat her like a piece of meat in a lab.

She expected more pain. More degradation.

She did *not* expect choice.

Although she still glared, Nynn had stopped struggling. Fatigue showed in every feature. The slackness of her brow. The deep purple crescents beneath her ice blue eyes. The tight pinch of her upper lip. She pushed herself hard, and her ability to recover from injury and physical stress had increased since the first outburst of her power, but that seemed to be waning. Just his luck that she'd be as vulnerable as a human by the day of the match.

The goal was to train her, even if that meant dredging up some gentleness. Maybe it wasn't a matter of busting through brick defenses so much as slinking through their cracks.

He walked toward the bench where he'd left the food. And sat. "I promised a ration. Will you come eat?"

Wariness altered her features. She was beautiful. More than that, she drew the eye. Even if Leto hadn't been charged with her care and training, she would claim his attention. That wariness, however, made her look younger—more like how she must've appeared among the humans. He didn't like reminders that she'd once had a life beyond the walls of the complex. In part because that life was obviously holding her back. In part because he didn't want to sympathize with what she'd lost. In part because he never dealt well with things he couldn't understand.

Fighting. Feeling the burn of muscles well used and injuries on the mend. Soaking in the balm of applause. Bedding a woman who took his victories into the primal vessel of her body.

Leto knew those things.

And he knew that even the wariest creature eventually responded to food and a soft voice.

Nynn rubbed her face, then the back of her neck again. She assessed the arena, her eyes blue on silver on suspicion. Then she shrugged.

"What was that for?"

She walked toward him with defiance in her steps. Moments of doubt . . . gone. "You could hold out your hand and offer me food, then take it away. In the scheme of risk and reward, this has more potential for reward."

"Too many words for a caveman like me. Does that mean you'll eat?"

"Only if you tell me if that was almost a joke."

"Almost."

And she almost smiled. A different sort of awareness eased over Leto's skin, then deeper, into his bones.

Still graceful despite her fatigue, Nynn sat beside him on the bench. "Sandwiches, eh?"

"Plan on being picky, woman? Just shut up and eat."

That was definitely a smile. Her mouth was small when compared to her other features, but she used it well. Small, straight white teeth and curving lips. Nothing too overt, but the effect was devastating. Her eyes lit with amusement. The freckles across her nose and the apples of her cheeks held his attention as they did every time.

She opened the wrapper and began to eat, as he'd commanded. An apple, a sandwich made from rough wheat bread and cold ham, and a large portion of almonds. Protein for fighting. They sat in the arena, which felt cavernous when used as a simple dining facility. They took up so little space in a place where Dragon Kings trained to be larger than life.

He wasn't used to feeling small.

After glancing toward Nynn, he stopped hesitating and flat-out stared at her profile. The haircut he'd forced on her was uneven, but the short, spiky style suited her. It was aggressive and showed off the strong line of her jaw. She had small ears, which came to a subtle point at the top.

"Is this the price for my food? You staring at me?"

"Not at you. Just your ears. Like a pixie."

"You don't seem the sort to wax poetic."

"I wasn't. Legends of fairies and pixies originated with Clan Pendray, their Celtic mysticism and Highland secrets. Just wouldn't expect a feature like that on a Tigony."

She shrugged again, but the movement was tighter. Definitely defensive. Possibly lying. Leto's senses flared to full alert. Mentally, he pushed past the barrier of the collar. Extending. Reaching out.

"So you've met every Tigony?" she asked.

"No. Just never met one I wanted to study so closely."

Nynn whirled her face toward his, then backed away. "Really? Don't start."

"You'd rather I be like the other men here? Those workers in the mess hall, who sneak around corners to catch a glimpse of you? Because I won't do it." He stroked a finger along her jaw. She flinched. When he did it again, and again, she closed her eyes. "If I'm going to stare at you, you'll know it. And I won't apologize for it."

Tension pulled her mouth into a grimace. His senses expanded yet again. He could detect pheromones, tiny tremors, the prickling of her hairs beneath his touch. Finally, he detected the change in her breathing. She relaxed. Minutely. Not like sleep, but that place of calm just before drifting off.

"You're making me proud," he said roughly.

Dragon be, where had that come from? He'd been more frustrated with her than pleased, right from the start. And even if his words were true, he wasn't in the habit of praising neophytes.

"I don't want to make you proud." Her voice was whisper soft. Her eyes remained closed.

"I know what you want. And you'll have it. You resist me at every turn, but we work toward similar goals. Tell me that you understand that much."

A shuddering exhale bowed her shoulders. She didn't pull away. "You want to stay here. I want to escape so badly that I'd chew your leg off for the possibility. How is that similar?"

Leto cupped her shoulder and stroked damp, bare skin. The strength contained within her lithe limbs was heady. He'd thought about the obvious. They would fuck. Body on body. Rough hands and even rougher satisfaction. He'd never thought about touch.

Maybe because touching like this—soft, urging—was something he'd never thought to use when indulging in a woman.

"Think nearer to today." He dipped his head. Gave her time to back away. Made her aware that, yes, he meant to kiss the shoulder he held. "What do we both want in one week's time?"

His lips met her salty flesh as she whispered what he'd needed to hear. "To win. We want to win."

"*That* didn't make me proud," he said against her skin. "That was pure pleasure."

The kiss didn't end so much as shift. Farther up her shoulder. Past the metal collar that kept him from tasting her throat. He settled his mouth against the hollow just beneath her jaw. Sipped her. Inhaled the perfume of her body. Goose bumps raised in the wake of his lips. Too tempting. He flicked his tongue to smooth them away.

Nynn lifted her face to the ceiling. She gripped the bench with both hands. Wearing nothing more substantial than her underclothes, she breathed quickly. Her chest lifted and lowered. This flimsy cloth, already so near to mimicking the contours of her breasts and her flat stomach, was a weapon only a woman could wield.

Memories overlaid his present state. Only in his small room did he think back on how she'd appeared on day one. Elegant and bold, frightened and clumsy from the cold. Through the centuries, tales of goddesses in possession of untold beauty had been inspired by Dragon King women.

Nynn was Venus made real.

She silently taunted him until, alone in his quarters, he took cock in hand and stroked as hard as he would thrust between her thighs. Or she would follow him into dream where she smiled, opened for him, and took his full, hard length into her mouth. In those dreams-like-nightmares, he didn't put as much force behind each deep drive of his hips. The pleasure was in seeing how much she could take. How deep. How fast. And how long he could hold out before losing his mind.

Lust stiffened his cock and snapped his limbs taut. Anticipation, desire, *want*. He tilted her stubborn chin and brought their lips close. A whisper of air between them. If she touched him, she'd ignite him as surely as she'd blown holes in his armor. But she didn't, with her knuckles still bone white as she clutched the bench. This was submission—to a point. It certainly wasn't participation.

He'd been working toward her participation for weeks. Only now, he had two goals. They were interwoven in his mind as surely as their limbs would twist and wind together when sharing his bed. They would win their match, and Nynn would be the woman he chose as his reward.

Her heavy-lidded eyes fluttered, trying to open. "Stop touching me."

He did. Hands off.

Just before he kissed her.

She gasped into his mouth—the only place where their bodies met. Lips slid over lips. She stiffened. Leto wouldn't have expected otherwise. But she didn't pull away. Again he thought of a wary creature coming to him by shy steps and little gestures. Victory was a long way off when taken at such a slow pace.

Yet what a victory.

She moaned softly. She opened to him. She nipped his lower lip between her teeth.

It was Leto's turn to moan. If she meant for the delicate blend of sweet and raw to drive him mad, she succeeded. Without thought, he had slowed to her pace. His tongue pushed inside. He angled his mouth over hers, taking her kiss and taking everything he wanted—all at half speed. Quarter speed. The agonizing slowness still sped his blood, fast, faster, just as his gift could power his body around a Cage. He dragged her taste into his mouth, pulled her scent into his lungs.

That deliberate, aching kiss tested all he was.

How much control could he give up?

How much pleasure could he find in holding back?

He'd never asked either question. But then, he'd never kissed a woman when he was so certain she'd hurtle out of his grasp at any moment, even if that grasp was simply the magnetism of their exploration. Not his strength. Not his skill. He held her by no concrete means.

With the same aching slowness, he withdrew. That whisper of air settled between their mouths again, cooling his lips. He had kept her awake when she needed sleep. He had fed her an unaccustomed ration. And he had spoken soft words.

He petted one finger along her jaw, lifting her chin so that their eyes met, and realized how well he'd played the moment. Her blue eyes shimmered with an iridescent glaze, where desire mixed with relaxation. She probably hadn't known its like for more than a year.

She was, in effect, what he'd intuitively needed her to be: Receptive. Pliable. Open.

"Nynn," he said against her cheek, "do you want to use your powers?"

"I don't have . . ."

"You do. Now tell me the truth. Do you want to use what resources you have? To win?"

She shuddered. "Yes."

"Why do you resist?"

A blink changed the color of her eyes, from iridescent to ice. She appeared even more vulnerable than during their kiss. He expected her to rear away from their intimacy at any moment. She would realize exactly where she was, who she was with, what she was doing. And she'd take her softness away.

*Stay.*

He shoved the disconcerting plea away. Far away.

"Dragon damn you, Nynn." Only, his curse was a whisper. "Make this possible for both of us."

"I can't remember some things. Parts of my youth. Just like I can't remember when I used them, in there." She glanced past him, toward the practice Cage, as if it was the enemy. "How is that possible? It's all blank."

*Telepathic block.*

In an instant, Leto knew it was true. He and his siblings had all required blocks of varying strength. Coming into one's gifts could be difficult—or even impossible, as in Pell's case. Telepathic blocks from powerful Indranan, those Heartless monsters, were sometimes the only means of survival.

No one could come into a gift like Nynn's without trauma.

"Memories can be restored," he said. "You know the methods."

Nynn flinched as if slapped. Her eyes clouded. She shoved against his shoulder, away—just away. Any distance seemed good enough.

"I won't do it."

He'd never heard a statement spoken with so little conviction.

Leto was exhausted from the challenge of moving so slowly. He needed to shake out of this trap. Standing from the bench, he grabbed Nynn's forearm and hauled her to her feet.

She tripped once as he dragged her to the Cage, but soon she strode beside him. Up they climbed. In they went. With the door locked behind them.

The deactivation of her collar made Nynn cry out. She slumped to all fours. That same rush surged over Leto as if swept over by a wave of pure energy. The lingering taste of Nynn's kiss turned violent as he savored every little detail.

That was his gift. Every time the collar held him in check, he missed his gift as he would an absent limb.

Nynn's gift was a ghost hiding somewhere in her mind.

"If you had no powers, you wouldn't drop to your knees," he said. "You wouldn't have cried out if you didn't feel it. Humans can walk into a Cage and feel nothing." He stared down at her as she crawled to her feet, with eyes like the blue center of a flame. "I hope you enjoyed your seduction, neophyte. Break's over."

# ✦ CHAPTER ✦ NINE

The release of the collar's damping hold shot power to the deepest recesses of Nynn's body and mind. Energy coursed through every cell—energy she needed. That vitality was even more potent now, after the adrenaline rush of Leto's persuasion. He was right. A human wouldn't have noticed that empowering shift. The woman named Nynn was exhilarated and freed.

*No.* She caught herself. *I'm Audrey. I've been Audrey since high school.*

Did it matter?

He had kissed her, she had let him, and something chilling was pressing in from the back of her mind.

She was losing herself.

Even in the labs, she had rarely felt as helpless as when Leto had traced his lips across hers. The intensity of his attention had been . . . enticing. Unsettling. Full of potential.

*Wrong.*

The gold-flecked mask of his eyes and the exploring touch of his tongue had been terrible enough. Terrible, because she'd responded. Not by running or shouting. She'd been too shocked for that. She'd responded by relishing each honey-slow caress. Just his mouth and her mouth and what sick spell they'd brought to life. Her body was keyed up and aching in ways she'd never known. The call and response of ancient needs.

Needs she'd thought dead and buried with Caleb.

The depth of her betrayal was staggering. Her heart stuttered, and the taste of ash settled at the back of her mouth. For that alone she needed to stay clear of Leto.

As if that were an option.

She couldn't shake free of those moments when his exhales had tangled with her inhales. She'd shivered through the entire encounter—not from fear, but from an elemental exchange. His curiosity about her. Her unconscious response to that curiosity. She'd practically stopped her own heart. Wondering. Searching. What did he see when he looked at her?

Now she was nauseated to realize how easily she'd responded.

Her limbs buzzed all the way to the tips of her fingers and toes. Not fear. Not hatred. Dragon be, not even simple lust. For those moments when he'd stroked her jaw and her cheek, she'd wanted comfort. From a beast. She'd only found real comfort when in the company of her cousin, Mal, and in the arms of her late husband. Any reaction—*anything*—to Leto's enticements was like personally shooting Caleb in the heart.

That was where the torture had started. She had wanted to fight back. She was a Dragon King. She should've been able to do *something*. Her gift had failed her, as it always had.

Another darkness slunk forward. Distant fear. Grief

she couldn't identify. A terrible thing sat at the edge of her vision, like being stalked by a wraith.

Muscles coiling, blood surging, she faced her tormentor—the brainwashed brute who'd just kissed her.

"Use logic, Nynn. You know I'm right. You have greater potential than you've yet tapped."

"What would an animal like you know about logic?"

With a casualness that mocked the situation, he glanced around the Cage wires. "Animal? Seems we're both locked up."

"But you're so subservient that you stay locked up by choice." She couldn't stop moving now. Spinning. Her head was a tornado. She couldn't keep still. *Didn't want to* keep still. "How can you sit down here in the dark? You're a circus freak, not a man. I knew a good man and I loved him and he's dead—murdered—by the cartel family you serve without thought. I look at you and I want to throw up."

He didn't react. He didn't even taunt her with the kiss she'd just accepted. "Who did you lose?"

"My husband!"

"No. Farther back. There's a hole where something happened. Where someone should be."

"No one!"

"Think about it. I didn't hit you. I didn't threaten you. I only asked who you'd lost. Now look at you. Look around you."

As if of its own accord, a ball of light appeared before her. It grew and grew until it was half her height and twice her width. Explosions sparked at its heart. She was mesmerized by what she had wrought.

Beautiful. Fascinating. Destructive.

"Let it go," Leto called. "Release, Nynn."

Her impulse to hold on to the magic was strong. She only wanted to look at it a while longer. Otherwise she wouldn't believe it. She couldn't even trust that she'd remember it. The bursts of color and hot violence were like vicious fairies in pitched battle. She could watch it forever. Let it grow. See if she could crack a crater in the earth with one blow.

In the back of her mind, where the woman once known as Audrey MacLaren still thought and assessed, she saw the truth in an instant. Such a release would kill her.

She closed her eyes. Arched her back. Spread her arms.

The ball that shivered out from deep within—it was part of her. She had to let it go.

It *burst*.

A wave of heat and electricity shot around the Cage in whirling circles. That power hit her back in the face. The ricochet effect knocked the air from her lungs and threw her back in a lopsided stagger. She landed hard on her ass. The back of her head connected with one of the Cage's metal posts.

"Aw, fuck," she muttered. Blood seeped from the base of her skull. Leto strode toward her and knelt. She touched a strip of that leather woven through his armor—leather singed black. "How?"

"Less damage? I was ready this time. Flat on my back, or it would've been shredded to pieces." He grabbed her upper arms and gave her a hard shake. "Tell me you remember that. Nynn, you stubborn little shit. Tell me."

"I'm not stubborn. I did what you wanted." She wiped the blood on her pants. No number of blinks cleared the image of what she'd just done.

*Dragon be. I have a gift.*

She had expected Leto to remain as still as statuary, yet his features spoke of surprise—and something close to approval. "You did. We can move forward now."

She shook her head, which added dizziness to her pain. Or maybe that was another aftereffect of her gift. He was right. Audrey MacLaren was not a Dragon King. Yet *Nynn* was. This demonstration, the unnatural way she took so quickly to Leto's training, maybe even how she'd responded to his physical allure—all proof.

But to let go of Audrey? That would mean turning her back on the life she'd shared with Caleb. She would not be the same mother Jack loved. Perhaps that might be for the best. For his safety, he needed her to become a warrior like Leto. Only later could she offer comfort and the pure affection she longed to give. Warrior and mother were interlinked.

A year in the Cages.

She didn't want to become such a monster.

"The next step is for you to control it," he said plainly.

"That I managed to do it at all is as good as it gets." She pushed to her feet. Her balance was unnaturally steady. "How are we going to fight with that bomb ready to mow us both down?"

"Energy can be controlled. If you want to learn how."

"You act like I'm doing this on purpose!"

"I thought that. Not anymore."

This talk was more than just talk. He was prodding a place as tender as a wound that had never healed.

"Dragon damn," she whispered. "I *hate* you."

If he shrugged in reply, she was going to smack him until her hands bled and he wrung her neck. Instead, he stood and walked toward the center of the Cage. Big man. Big, confident steps. Eyes the color of his singed leather armor were sharp, but his arrogance had dimmed. Why? Perhaps less need to posture? Or the inherent faith in what it was to be a true, unencumbered Dragon King?

Maybe she didn't hate him. The word didn't take into account how he made her terrified of her own impulses. She wore the same skin, but beneath it were new urges. She was struck by how the energy of their gifts reminded her of sexual potency. He looked stronger, bigger, and more intimidating, and her body responded—no matter that he still bought into a system so corrupt that no decent person could possibly defend it.

They squared off. Audrey was furious at him and the Asters and herself. Leto was as calm as she'd ever seen him.

"Let me tell you five words." His voice was low. Hypnotic again. "See if it jars your memory."

"Do it."

He paused for three heartbeats. "A box in a corner."

Cold covered her skin. Flashes. Old memories. From inside out, her body convulsed.

"Follow it, Nynn. Talk."

"Can't."

"I can't read your mind like some Indranan witch. *Talk.*"

"Some gifts are too dangerous." Her voice sounded different. "No. Those weren't my words."

"It's what they told my parents about my sister Pell. Now she'll be in a coma for the rest of her life. What there is of it." He crossed his arms, appearing defensive. "Did they beat you? When they forced their way into your mind?"

"I don't remember." Audrey shook her head. "Did they beat you?"

"Yes."

No wonder he looked so wary. She couldn't imagine anyone or anything strong enough to cow Leto of Garnis.

Bitter acid had collected at the back of her tongue. Flickers returned. Whispers and secrets and fear as painful as needles piercing her eyelids. Entire years were missing.

Leto reached out to touch her clenched hand. A zap tingled between his skin and hers. Their gazes caught. "They took it from you, Nynn. There are steps to reverse the process. You know that."

"And let some Heartless witch in my head? If that's what's happened, I'm sure as hell not letting it happen again. There has to be a better way. More training."

"We're almost out of time." His anger, and all of his emotions, were becoming easier to read. Was that Nynn's doing, or was she affecting his personality as much as he was altering hers?

"Then I want to make the most of that time. That means sleep. Will you let me, or will this argument go on all night?"

He caught her chin and looked at the back of her skull. "You're still bleeding."

"And that'll be healed by morning. Don't tell me you haven't realized I'm changing."

"For the better."

Audrey pulled free of his taut fingers. "Are we done?"

"Fine. Limit met. Loud and clear." From beneath his armor he pulled a fist-sized packet wrapped in white butcher paper. "Here. One of the guards wanted you to have this."

The scent of mint hit her with an old memory. Jack with a candy cane stuck in his hair. His third Christmas, when anything Tonka yellow made her little boy squeal with a child's enthusiasm.

"Why?"

He lifted his brows. "To buy your attention with trinkets. Would you take one of them as your lover to secure gifts and privileges? Or would you fight to earn them honorably, as I have? I pass them on to you as a reminder. Trust anyone here but me and you're a fool. I've always been clear about my motives. These humans would trade Dragon knows what for trinkets and pornography. You're above them."

She took the package from him. *You need to make a choice.* That meant knowing what, exactly, she was choosing.

"Were you given the chance to hold your niece?"

He flinched. "Sometimes you make no sense."

"Answer me, please. Sir."

A long exhale. Was he merely frustrated with her? Tired? Or did he feel the same buzzing aftereffects of their kiss? The fizzing snap in her blood—part Leto, part aftershocks of her explosive gift—was tantamount to infidelity. Caleb was dead, while she'd been turned on in the midst of a sick power game. Leto's mouth. His hard restrained strength. His beautifully masculine body and oddly innocent reserve.

"Did you?" she asked more sharply.

He studied her for a long time. She didn't waver, just waited for his answer.

"Yes, I held her. A little girl they named Shoshan. She has my sister's dark hair. Fairer skin." He looked away. Shook his head. "It was an honor to see her. To know I'd earned such a gift for them and for our clan."

"Then it *is* possible. The Asters . . . ?"

"I told you. Winning is important. Keeping their family profitable is vital. Without them, the system collapses."

"Maybe for the best."

"My father died in a Grievance after fathering three children. He didn't believe it a useless system, and neither do I. There's too much to be earned for those we cherish."

*Cherish.* Such a tender word from a brick wall of a man.

"We will never agree on this," she said, almost to herself.

"Just do your job. That means controlling your powers. Indranan live here. They could unlock what we haven't been able to."

She stepped away. Once. Again. "My mind is not theirs and it's not yours."

No matter Leto's faith and his skills, no matter the birth of his niece, she didn't trust that her son would be returned out of the goodness in Old Man Aster's heart. He and his warped son had no hearts. They didn't give away anything that didn't earn them something in return. Letting Leto hold little Shoshan only kept him focused on earning their respect and adding to his family's glory. The incentive had successfully bought the rest of Leto's life, and had taken the life of his father.

She sure as hell wasn't letting anyone into her mind on that scant possibility. Already her thoughts were blended, distorted, and still aching with an old, forgotten tremor of bloodshed she didn't want to see.

"What else do you get out of this system?" She was trying to shed her uncertainty. For nearly three weeks, that had meant baiting Leto. "Maybe extra beans at dinner time? A pillow for when you sleep on the floor? Or do you just like to feel important once a month? I'm assuming it's not only for procreation, otherwise your sister would have half a dozen children."

"I've won eight Grievances. Shoshan has been the only child to survive." He blinked once. "You're not the only one here who's suffered."

His emotions shut down. Closed off. He was as opaque now as when he'd first strode into her training cell—further evidence of how many of his subtle clues she'd unconsciously learned to interpret. He exited the Cage. A brief shudder marked the moment when the collar revoked his gift.

Leto was skilled in all methods of combat, but the amazing power that set him apart from human beings could be withdrawn on a whim. Even among the Dragon Kings he was special. Clan Garnis. The Lost. He had the heart and soul of a warrior. The taunt of having his greatest asset offered, then stolen again . . . Surely he must regret losing that precious blessing.

Nynn had only just discovered her potential, and

even she felt its loss. As soon as she followed him out of the Cage, her new potential flipped off like a light switch. The tease was nearly as cruel as the promised rewards. Deep beneath his misplaced loyalty, Leto must hate it, too.

Shadow claimed most of his body. Only a glimmer of golden skin shone where his breastplate left room for muscles to maneuver freely. Bare. Smooth. Flexing with each movement. She remembered her vision of him as a work of art. Charcoal and warm, fluid pastels. She wondered briefly how she would draw him while he fought. Blurs of color. Smudges of steel gray and swirls of his mace.

Shutting her eyes blocked those visual distractions, but the details of his body followed her into the dark. She was free to imagine Leto posing for an artists' class on the male anatomy. An exemplary specimen, with every muscle and ligament ripe for study.

Nude and *glorious*.

With a frustrated noise, she ground her knuckles against her eyes. She was behaving like some desperate victim succumbing to Stockholm syndrome. Sympathizing with his cause. Changing her beliefs to suit his. Accepting his praise like a cracked desert floor drank the rain. Her fears were coming true, that she would wind up just as brainwashed.

Jack was her lifeline, as was her vow that the Asters would burn for their crimes.

Ten minutes later, Leto and a pair of guards walked her back to her training cell. He left without a word or a backward glance.

Alone, Audrey opened the butcher block paper. Inside were peppermints—the round kind that only old people ate, or what children left for last after Halloween. Didn't matter. She grabbed one of the candies. The mentholated sweetness was a shock. Work and work and more terrifying work. Now she rolled candy across her tongue.

The contrast was nearly as shocking as how tenderly Leto had kissed her.

She glanced down the corridor toward the gate. There stood the sleepy, ridiculously overdressed guards. What was the purpose of their SWAT-style armor if they traded for peppermints and *Playboy*? What sort of men were they to imprison and torture and snivel like moles in the ground?

Only the locks held her prisoner. Not those fools. They were as useless as the rest of the humans in that complex.

Audrey froze. She spit the peppermint onto the ground.

She'd been trained since birth to believe the old, pompous prejudice that Dragon Kings were better than humans. Millennia of examples proved it. Only, Audrey had fallen in love with Caleb—with his caprice and warmth and lack of centuries-old ego. Here, she was sinking into the morass of ancient bigotry against the resourceful, thoughtful, amusing people she'd spent years among.

No matter how much she disliked that thought, Audrey recognized the pragmatic truth. Her heritage was impossible to deny. She was a Dragon King, and she would need to embrace that old, powerful arrogance to save her son.

# ✦ CHAPTER ✦ TEN

The next afternoon, Leto and Nynn squared off against two other warriors within the octagonal framework of the practice Cage. A dozen others had gathered to watch, taunt, cheer.

Leto had expected Nynn to see sense, break down, and beg for an Indranan to help unlock the gift she couldn't control. He'd been a fool to expect her to be that rational.

In two more days, they'd fight in a real match.

Too much of her old self remained. Why did she let resentment and a stubborn, impossible grasp on her human life keep her from embracing her fate? Now it was worse. She knew of her gift's existence and chose to ignore it. She was a fighter who refused to use the weapons at her disposal, choosing a rock instead of a broadsword.

"Get up!"

"Fuck off!" she spat from all fours.

She could conjure a nasty temper. Nothing wrong with that if she aimed it at the right opponent. Instead, she was going to ruin his chances at keeping Pell safe. He would be humiliated in front of the Old Man and his guests.

"Don't make me fight you, too." His shout echoed off the domed ceiling above the practice Cage. "Get back in this! Now!"

She jumped to her feet and readjusted a practiced grip on her dagger. Had her glare been a gift from the Dragon, she could've leveled continents.

Leto knew their opponents well. The first was a bulky middle-aged Southern Indranan named Fam. If the man had ever been muscular, his brawn had since turned to fat. Fam had sold himself into service after gunning down three people in a failed robbery. The Asters could protect such criminals from the human justice system. Lately, Leto was surrounded with more thugs and delinquents than true warriors.

Fam was sorely lacking in martial skills. His clan's unique telepathy, however, made him formidable when the collars were randomly deactivated. Always birthed in sets of two, the Indranan were born with what amounted to half of the Dragon's gift. Some decided that wasn't enough. Fam, for example, had killed his twin. Decapitated her. In doing so he stole her abilities to make his gift whole.

The Indranan were known as the Heartless for that reason.

The other opponent was a female Sath known only as Silence. Five years hadn't been enough time for Leto to determine her real name or her reasons for fighting for the Asters. Only her lover, another Sath named Hark, might know those secrets. He'd descended to the Cages six months earlier, when Silence had returned from a mission to Hong Kong on behalf of the Old Man.

She was called Silence because she never spoke. Fit and slender, her ghostly blond hair and fathomless eyes added to an unnerving aura. The Sath had the ability to mimic the powers of another Dragon King within a certain range, which varied widely. A Sath's real skill was in picking which foe to mimic.

The collars deactivated.

Dragon-given powers surged back to life. Leto breathed. He gathered the rush of being the warrior he was meant to be.

For but a moment.

He was bombarded by the combined attack of Fam's mind-scrambling telepathy and the lightning-quick reflexes Silence stole from Leto. She swept around, sliced her shield behind his knees, and used his shoulders as a launching point to jump away.

The small assembly of spectators cheered their approval.

"Thief bitch," he growled.

Those born to Clan Sath were known as the Thieves. Leto had been raised to believe them parasites, but he couldn't deny that Silence's long years of surviving physically stronger opponents had served her well. She never used a traditional weapon, instead using a shield as confidently as Leto wielded his mace.

Although he needed but a moment to recover from Silence's attack Leto couldn't see past the white-hot glare Fam painted across his vision. If Nynn's gasped outrage was any indication, Fam had her in his grips, too. The Sath were limited to one theft at a time, but the limits of an Indranan's mental meddling were untold and unpredictable. Some were weaklings in mind as well as body. Some were as powerful as devils, digging into the psyche, exploiting unacknowledged weaknesses.

Some were the witches who had locked Nynn's gift in a mental box.

He didn't need to see. Although Silence could mimic Leto's reflexes and speed, she hadn't refined those gifts for a lifetime as he had. He located both opponents by minuscule clues—the vibrations of footsteps, the warmth of skin heated by exertion, the scent of sweat, leather, and metal. Fam had never been able to obscure all of Leto's senses at once.

Nynn gasped. "Get the hell out of my head!"

Silence's hesitation was almost nonexistent, but it was the moment of weakness Leto needed.

He sped around the Cage in blurring fast circles. Every time Silence tried to swipe the serrated edge of her shield, he stopped, changed direction, struck out. He identified Fam by the unique cadence of the man's breathing; his respiration slowed when he concentrated. To locate calmer respiration within the adrenaline-filled Cage was simple. Leto used his agility to snake the chain of his mace around Fam's calves. He yanked hard. The man toppled to the padded floor and cheers erupted from the onlookers. Fam only cursed.

Dragon Kings could only be killed one way, but that didn't mean they were immune to pain.

Leto shook his head to clear the last of Fam's telepathic interference, just in time to see Silence swing her shield in a glancing swipe across Nynn's mouth. Blood welled from his neophyte's split lip.

Although Nynn didn't stop moving—which was at least proof of her resilience—she only used hand-to-hand techniques. Silence, however, was thriving. Her reflexes and speed, sapped from Leto, outmatched Nynn at every turn.

"Dragon damn you, Nynn," Leto bellowed. "Use your gift!"

She spewed curses of her own. The warriors surrounding the Cage laughed and hooted. He'd seen her practically explode with concussive force—the promise of undeniable victory.

Then it was too late. The collars reactivated.

Leto growled his frustration. He always felt bereft when his gift was curtailed. His energy, potency, even confidence took a dip. He shrugged off that split second of weakness, knowing the others felt it, too—the cruel switch from gods to the pitiful equivalent of humans.

He hauled the mace's grip back and away from his body. The chain snapped taut. A quick yank spun Fam onto his back. The ball of the weapon swung in an arc that Leto controlled with long practice. He twirled in a sharp circle. The spiked spherical head slammed dead center of Silence's shield. She staggered back.

At the corner of his vision, Leto saw Nynn grapple with Fam. The latter was bleeding from his shins and calves. He'd dropped his sickle after Leto's attack, while Nynn still held her dagger. She didn't need it now that the collars put her on equal footing. She was quick. Observant. Graceful. The softer, older Indranan man didn't stand a chance.

The match continued until the stench of sweat was almost too much for Leto's senses.

Collars off. Collars on. Again and again. Always random. Taunting. Returning and hampering his gifts.

With his powers back in force, he chose another strategy. Not Silence. Not Fam. He attacked Nynn. Their eyes locked just as he swung his mace. A moment in time caught between them. So clearly, he could still see every detail. Her narrowed ice blue eyes and distinctive freckles. Damp honey blond hair streaked across her forehead. He even caught the tiny lines creasing her top lip as she pinched her mouth.

She raised her shield just in time to save her skull from the arcing smash of his mace.

Leto didn't stop. He kept at her, again, again, trying to provoke her. Only when the mace caught her inner thigh did he relent. She sprawled on the Cage floor among shouts and groans from those gathered to watch.

"Enough!" He signaled that match's Cage operator to shut it down. The spotlights on each octagonal post dimmed to half intensity. Leto's collar resumed its damping properties. "Well done," he said to Fam and Silence. "We're finished for today."

Some good-natured heckling accompanied the Indranan as they left the Cage. Fam had a slight limp. He would be in pain for the next few hours, but with a Dragon King's physiology, he'd be back in fighting form in mere days.

Disgusted, Leto knelt where Nynn lay in a sweaty heap. She clutched her thigh. A massive contusion turned her thigh ugly colors. Welts and spots of blood showed where the mace had bit her skin.

"Idiot." Her lips curled back in a hateful grimace. "No armor for thighs. Why not?"

"It limits mobility and encourages speed. If you'd

done your job and fought back, you'd be standing as victor. Not lying here defeated."

"You wanted this. To teach me another *bathatéi* lesson."

"That was last week. And the week before. Now, I'm pissed. I'm two days on from a Cage match with a piece of lab filth who won't use her greatest asset."

"I *can't*."

"You did. And you sure as hell remember it."

"But control it? *Make* it happen? No way." She waved an unsteady hand at her bruised thigh. "This should be proof."

Leto grabbed her chin with wrenching force. She gasped, struggled. He held fast. Her ragged breathing heated his skin. He could make out every blond lash and each delicate freckle.

"Do you want to lose?"

"I wouldn't be working this hard if I did."

"Do you want *me* to lose?"

"What the hell does that matter?"

"If you do, if you want to show me up, if you seek revenge for these weeks, then I will kill you after the third match." Her jaw clenched beneath his gouging fingertips. "Do you understand me?"

"What, no 'lab filth' on the end of your threat?"

He pried her hands away to get a better look at her wound. Rather than apologize or even assess the need for medical treatment, he raked taut fingers over the damaged skin. Nynn screamed. She whirled her good leg in a well-aimed arc. Leto caught her ankle, threw it away from his body, and felt only disgust. She lay gasping on the Cage floor.

"Nynn of Tigony, I can't think of an insult strong enough to justify your failure."

Audrey crawled onto all fours. The welt on her thigh throbbed as if on fire. The sharp points of Leto's mace had cut a stippled pattern in her skin. Just as disturbing was the way she could still feel his blunt fingernails dragging across her marred, trembling muscles.

Fucking sadist. No wonder he was heralded.

Body, mind, soul—stabbing pains became the full measure of her world. Only that wasn't true. Somewhere beyond these cavernous burrows, her son was in pain. And in a place she had never seen, her husband lay dead in the ground. Who had arranged his funeral? Probably his parents. She'd always told them she was an orphan. Because she was. She'd just never told them that she was an orphan born in shame, high in a fortress in the northern mountains of Greece.

Dragon Kings adapted. That had been the key to their survival for so many thousands of years. She wondered how many, if any, had envisioned such a fate for their race. Hiding among the humans. Retreating to spend isolated lives in clan strongholds. Grasping at any chance to bear a child.

The woman she'd fought still stood in the Cage, in a pose that reminded Audrey of Leto. Arms crossed. Leaning against one of the eight support beams. She had black-on-black eyes and spiky, luminous silver hair. Tall and thin, her limbs were like those of a track-and-field athlete. Maybe a high jumper.

Here, she was every inch a warrior.

Silence, she was called.

Even her expression was silent, if the word could be applied to a set of features. She revealed nothing as she stared at Audrey. No disdain. No pity. No empathy. Just . . . staring. The only thing Audrey might discern was curiosity. Why else would a person stare so long?

The Indranan man, Fam, fell into limping step with Leto outside of the Cage. He looked like a puppy trailing after the alpha of the pack. Perhaps he had been fighting for some time, but Fam carried himself with no grace and little authority, especially considering the wounds on his shins and calves. Had Leto trained him? Instinctively, Audrey knew that wasn't the case. He possessed few of the traits and skills Leto had been droning on about since her arrival.

Yet Fam was popular. Fellow warriors greeted him with ribald comments and slaps on his bulky back. His only strength came from the gift the Dragon had inexplicably bestowed on the Indranan. Telepathy. She shuddered at the remembered feel of Fam's mind plundering hers. That eerie feeling stayed with her long after the contact. A slithering familiarity.

No wonder she resisted contact with the Heartless. She . . . Dragon damn, she'd lost something. What if getting it back was even worse?

When Fam embraced Hellix in that masculine football player way, her respect sank even further. He was sloppy and cocky. He was soft. Yet she was the one still breathless and quivering on all fours. Pride pushed her to her knees, then to unsteady feet. A stumble. A hearty laugh from those who still watched.

"Useless Tigony bitch," Hellix said. "Tricksters aren't worth anything more than a bad fuck."

Fam dropped his sickle. "I'd take her. Trickster or not."

"You'd take a hole in the wall if it got you off," said another of Hellix's followers.

Audrey noticed Leto's reaction, even if he refused to look in her direction. He had taken up a towel. Face, bare shoulder, upper back—he scrubbed the sweat from his incredible body. Upon hearing the comments from Hellix and his friend, he dropped the towel and picked up his mace and shield. Not aggression. Just a reaffirmation of his place within their society. Champion. Default leader.

While she'd made him look like a fool.

She would have no dependable ally in Leto of Garnis. As for the world at large, she needed to find it. Soon. Before pleasing that man and winning ridiculous sparring matches became as important to her as it was to him.

Silence finally pushed away from the post. She walked forward and held out an arm. Warily, Audrey considered refusing, but in a place of such isolation and mistrust, she chose to accept the gesture at face value. With Silence's help, she tested her leg's ability to hold her weight and found it resilient enough to walk. Silence looked her up and down with that unnerving black stare, and nodded. Dragon damn, even her body language was unreadable. Audrey couldn't have interpreted that little nod had her next breath depended on it.

The woman returned to the Cage wires and retrieved her shield, with its serrated edge.

"Thank you," Audrey called.

The slight lift of Silence's brows was practically a spoken question.

"You could've taken off half my face." She touched her bleeding lip and nodded toward the shield. "I appreciate that you didn't."

"Hey, quit flirting with the new kid," came a man's voice, although this one had none of Hellix's aggression. "That was me once, all shiny and useless. I might get jealous. But food first. You know how hungry I get sitting around and watching other people fight. Just *famished*."

Silence nodded her slight good-bye to Audrey, then joined a man at the base of the Cage's steps. He was Silence's lover, Hark. He didn't look like the rest of the muscle-bound warriors. He didn't need to. His lean, street fighter's build was a deceptive trick. He could carry the Sath's traditional *nighnor* as if it weighed nothing. With cheekbones high and elegant, and his eyes the clearest, brightest blue—his combination of strength and grace was surprising, but in that, he was perfectly paired with Silence.

Audrey watched as the pair stealthily, unhurriedly moved past Hellix and his sycophants. The bullies didn't heckle or jeer. Only watched them pass.

Strange.

But useful information.

Audrey staggered toward the Cage's exit. Surprisingly, Leto met her there. He looped the mace over his shoulder, offered his hand.

"What, some pity gesture?" she asked.

"You should know by now that pity is of no use down here."

"If you think I'm touching you after what you did to me, you're insane."

The nearly placid set of his features didn't change. "Let Hellix or Kilgore touch you instead. Makes no difference which way you want to torture yourself." He dropped his hand and nodded toward the whipping post in the corner of the training arena. "*That* will be your next lesson if you fail to learn from this one."

A shudder ripped up the length of her spine. The agonizing pain in her leg was only a taste of the pain a whipping post could entail.

Leto stalked away. Much as had been the case with Silence, the others made no sound as he passed. Only Hellix stabbed a hard glare his back.

Audrey berated herself as she slowly, unevenly made her way out of the Cage. Between the menace of Leto's threat and the admiration she couldn't yet admit, she realized exactly how much danger she faced. Stick. Carrot. And losing herself.

She couldn't stay in this underground prison any longer. But did she dare risk her life and Jack's to make an escape?

# CHAPTER ELEVEN

Audrey actually had no idea *how* she'd escape until the opportunity presented itself.

Kilgore. The galley cook who never looked at her as if she wore clothing—always straight through her garments, searching for skin.

She hid a shudder when the guards summoned her to the bars of her training cell. Kilgore waited for her. He appeared as spit-shined as a man could manage in that underground prison. Hair washed and combed. Threadbare uniform clean. In a warped way, he looked like a man picking up his date.

For Audrey's plans, the strange little man with the round, too-large head would do nicely.

Leto would never let her out of his sight, and the guards were like machines. She'd gone over every crevice and crack in the training room. She'd even gotten completely soaked probing the trickling waterfall, as well as where it transformed from clean-flowing water to a one-woman latrine. Not the best evening.

"Leto keeps you locked up in here," Kilgore said, pityingly. "Would you like to go for a walk?"

She glanced at the guards, who watched with some

interest. Each of her words would be important, chosen with the same precision as a well-timed roundhouse.

"Of course. I'm yours to command."

Kilgore's eyes widened. They were tinged with yellow. Jaundice? Audrey hid a shudder.

He handed the guards one package each. They accepted them without fanfare, only secreting them into their armor. What was inside each . . . she didn't want to know. One man unlocked the iron bars. He literally looked away.

Audrey had learned that the entire complex traded black-market goods through Kilgore, even though it was obvious he hadn't been outdoors in a very long time. He was revolting. Jaundiced eyes. Sallow skin. Sunken eyes. His hair barely covered his scalp. Proof that human beings shouldn't spend forever in the dark.

"Come on, then, Nynn of Tigony."

Even the way he said her clan name was enough to make her skin itch with disgust. He thought he was going to fuck a Dragon King. Better than that—a Tigony woman from the Giva's inner circle.

*Not going to happen.*

"I'll be right back," she whispered.

She hurried back up the corridor to her room. Leto had started the habit of leaving a training knife with her overnight. With no way out of her personal prison, why not spend free hours practicing? Although made of wood, the knife might be enough to disable one unsuspecting opponent. Then she would need to find a real weapon.

And find her way out of the complex.

Carefully, somewhat impatiently, she'd interpreted

slivers of sentences and carelessly exhaled facts. The human quarters were her best bet. When the workers' contracts expired, they needed a means in and out. The Dragon Kings never left except for matches, and so far, that procedure was swathed in questions. How were they transported? To where?

She would be gone before that was her issue.

The most important piece of information had been a guard's casual grouse that he needed to help transport another lab patient into the complex. *I hate the walk to that place. It's creepy as fuck.*

Walk.

Walk to that place.

It made sense, considering Audrey had been dropped into this underground hell while still wearing a hospital gown. She must have been transported without the possibility of outsiders seeing her curious state of undress.

She would get free. Save Jack. Contact Mal.

Malnefoley would not fail her on this. They would put their differences aside. He would not bow before the Council's wishes again.

Wearing her silk-lined leather clothing, Audrey tucked the practice knife into the strap of one of her boots. She wanted the armor Leto had begun training her to wear. Kilgore's expectations, however, were clear as glass behind his sickly yellowed eyes. She needed to be a neophyte, dictated by his whims.

The butcher paper from the peppermints, mud, and the tip of her practice knife had come in handy for her second letter. She'd composed its words using using the Tigony's ancient language. Then she'd re-coded so that only those among Mal's inner circle could read it. The Sath knew too much about all of the houses. No language was considered safe without private ciphers. She'd spent an evening scraping mud into the paper's waxy sheen.

She would get Kilgore to deliver it—and learn enough about Jack's whereabouts to hazard an escape. All while manipulating an avaricious man who apparently hadn't touched a woman in forever and a half.

*Dragon help me.*

After a deep breath, she returned down the corridor.

She automatically presented her wrists. Manacles. An advantage in this case. By Leto's example with the mace, she knew how effective chains could be in downing an opponent. She'd rather chew nails than admit what his instruction had provided her by way of skills and resolve.

But it was true.

Kilgore hadn't lost his half–puppy dog, half-salacious expression. He was too desperate for it to be called leering. She almost pitied him. *Almost.* She knew too much about what he expected of her.

"Shall we?" He even offered his arm.

Again, that date analogy. While she wore manacles.

Audrey would've laughed. Her thundering heart, however, reminded her to keep quiet and focused. She was right to be afraid, just as she was right to be amped up on a double shot of adrenaline.

She cupped her hand around his forearm. "We have business to attend to, yes?"

He literally licked his lips. The further she delved into this situation, the less Audrey liked it. And it had started out unpalatable.

With her free hand, she touched the fabric of her tunic, over the spot where a scar was a constant reminder of what Dr. Aster had done to her. Although he had cut her in a hundred different places, her emotional losses centered there, where he had removed an ovary.

Kilgore led her toward the mess hall. Then past it. She hadn't been allowed any farther, so she gathered as many details as possible. Cinder block walls, just like the rest of the complex. Painted white. Cheap fluorescent lights stretched along the ceiling in a single-file line. They made the paint seem to glow with a ghostly blue aura. Goose bumps prickled the skin beneath her sleeves. She only noticed she was reflexively gripping Kilgore's arm more tightly when he lifted a pleased smile.

Good. Whatever made him believe she was there to meet his needs.

Using old mnemonic training, Audrey memorized the twists and turns. He steered her left, then right, right again, and down another endless corridor of blue-white fluorescent and cinder block. The long hallway was dotted with doors at intervals of roughly five feet.

"The workers' quarters?"

Kilgore nodded. "Mine is better."

"Oh?" She returned his smile. Hers felt meaner. "That's where we're going, yes? On our little walk?"

"You're coming with me willingly." Kilgore's mouth puckered as if having scraped his teeth along the inside of a banana peel. "What do you expect of me, neophyte?"

"The fairest trade we can both agree to."

"Good. You're no more naïve than I am. Don't think

the guards would side with you if they happened on our negotiations." His eyes were beady, but they glittered with a menace she fully believed. "They get their dirty magazines, extra rations, and even their mail through me. They'd just as soon hack off their own balls rather than lose my services."

No allies. No real weapons. One mercenary piece of slime.

This was going to be tricky.

"Thank you for the compliment," she said. "Because you're right. Neither of us is naïve. I have a letter I'd liked mailed. You have physical favors you want fulfilled."

"That I do."

Another left, then a climb up shallow steps that curved to the right. By the time Kilgore pulled out a set of keys, they stood before another unmarked door. This one, however, was at the end of its own hallway. Practically private. Just the sort of place where skin-crawling sounds would never be heard.

Her optimism remained. Kilgore had more than one key on his ring. She watched which he used to enter, which narrowed the possibilities to four others.

One particular door during their journey had been colder than the rest. The light beneath it had been different, too. Darker. More like pale gray than eerie blue. She'd identified two other possibilities as well. Exits. Chances. All she had were chances. And Kilgore's self-importance could be to her advantage. He liked to boast. She just needed him to brag about the right details.

His touch turned suddenly rough. With a fist closed over her manacle chain, he threw her into his room. She landed hard on the bare floor. Her forehead slammed against the iron encircling her left wrist. Blood. Instantly. Its coppery warmth dripped down toward her cheek.

That was nothing compared to how her heart lurched, then froze, when Kilgore slammed the door. *Slammed* it. She'd been right. No one would hear them.

"We haven't reached our agreement," she said calmly, despite her injuries and fight-or-flight fear.

"You'll need to give me a great deal if you expect me to smuggle a neophyte's letter out of the complex."

"Tell me what."

"Oh, no. That's part of the fun. I want to see the look on your face with each new surprise."

She didn't apologize or contradict his threat. Kilgore was a haggler by trade. He wanted a good negotiation before either of them gave in.

And, apparently, a good fight.

He moved faster than she would've imagined. Maybe that was because her forehead still throbbed. He retrieved a pair of handcuffs and locked her manacle chains to the foot of his bed. Not even *on* the bed. Just sprawled on the floor.

It was almost worse to know she possessed a gift from the Dragon—no matter how erratic—when her collar kept her powerless. She felt no better off now than she'd been when a Dragon King in a black trench coat had watched the Asters take her and Jack hostage.

She indulged in that one flicker of panic. Self-pity, really. Because she had a hell of a lot more resources now. She didn't need her gift to best one lust-blinded human.

Flipping onto her back, she thrust up with her legs and caught Kilgore around the waist. He tried to push her off, but she squeezed with the strength of her thighs and calves. A hard grunt indicated when she'd found his kidneys with her heels. With one hard slam, she planted the soles of her boots dead center of his chest. He staggered, coughing and clutching. His back connected with the bedroom door.

Bedroom. Hell. It was just another cage, this one with a bed, a dimly lit lamp, and only one way out.

Although Kilgore still coughed and reeled, he dredged a warped smile. Subservient weasel? No way. He was calculating. His yellowed eyes shone with a cruel glint she hadn't seen since her internment in the labs.

"Do you know why I've been down here for so long?" he asked, spitting the words at her.

"Don't care."

"You do. You're smart, and that means you've wondered." He pushed off the door and limped toward a waist-high chest of metal drawers, like a filing cabinet. "Why is Kilgore still here, when all the other human workers leave after three months?"

From the top drawer he removed what looked like a child's pencil case. All black. Plastic. Unassuming—like he was.

"I was one of Dr. Aster's assistants. A PhD in genetic engineering. Now I slop beans for human moles and put up with the scorn of your friend Leto. We're both slaves. Only he thinks his servitude is a good thing." He opened the case and removed a hypodermic needle. "I don't think that at all. But it does have certain advantages."

"What the fuck is that?"

"The way I'm going to make you cooperative. I'm not delivering any letter for you, Mrs. MacLaren. I like my guts intact. And I'm not so stupid as to let you escape either." He raised one brow. "That was your other plan, yes? Tell me the truth or I'll start with your asshole before the sedative sets in."

*Oh fuck.*

She flipped a short lock of hair back from her temple. "Tell me one reason why I'd want to stay in this piece of shit basement? Of course I want to escape. I thought you'd be smart enough to take the right side in this little . . . negotiation."

"And what do you have to offer?" He eyed her breasts, then the apex of her thighs. His grin was demonic. "I wondered if I'd be able to get the jump on you. For all your vaunted training . . . you're a piece of meat now. I particularly enjoyed that privilege in the labs. So many oblivious bodies to choose from. But you, Mrs. MacLaren, will feel everything. Sedated doesn't mean unconscious."

Audrey swallowed to keep from vomiting. The idea that he'd taken advantage of Aster's patients was too reprehensible to dwell on. *Was I one of them?*

She hid what she could of her reaction. "You know damn well who my cousin is. Get me out of here and he'll—"

"Be lenient? I doubt that. My list of crimes is too long. And besides, life is too short. You've seen that. What was his name? Caleb? That was it. See, the good Dr. Aster trusted me with even that detail. I'd rather take my chances with the feast lying before me. The Giva can suck his own dick. He has no influence down here."

Audrey sneered, although her stomach was a boiling knot of nerves. "But *you* do? Answer your own question. If we're so special, why are you here now?"

"Make one little attempt on the mad doctor's life, after one insult too many . . ." He grinned, appearing half-mad himself. "I knew too much, but I was too useful to kill. You should see how he reacts to catch-22s. My current occupation is to keep the guards happy, keep ambitious bitches enslaved like good little girls, and keep you from learning where Dr. Aster is busy cutting your boy into bits."

"You sick fuck."

"No, that's for later." Advancing, still clutching his injured chest, he stood with the needle ready. "How else will we have any fun?"

Leto knew Nynn wasn't in her cell the moment he came to retrieve her. No scent of her skin, either freshly cleaned or tinged with sweat after a hard workout.

And he knew who'd set her free—not that she would be free in Kilgore's quarters.

*Bathatéi.*

She couldn't just let things be. Dragon Kings used their powers. Cage warriors used every means at their disposal. She'd been given a task and promised a reward.

*She never had a choice.*

His anger pushed that objection aside. She didn't have much time.

"How long has she been gone?" His gaze was needle-sharp as he skewed each young guard. The one to his left was the first to drop his eyes. Toward a breast pocket.

Leto pounced. He felled the man in a single lunge. The guard grunted, then squeaked a token protest when Leto dragged out a tin of dipping tobacco. The other guard made a halfhearted attempt to help his comrade. Leto glared over his shoulder and rasped, "You'll be next."

The man resumed his post on the far side of the training cell bars, as if a scuffle weren't taking place four feet away.

"This is mine now." Leto shoved the tin into a fold in his leather armor. "And I'll report you to the Old Man for possessing contraband if you don't tell me. *How long* has she been gone?"

"About twenty minutes," the guard said, a warble in his voice.

Really, he was big for a human. Maybe six foot. Brawny, with a decent amount of muscle. In his own world, he might have fought in boxing matches—human cages, with as scant honor and significance as humans themselves. Leto only felt disgust.

"When I find her, I'm bringing her through here. Past you both. And you won't say a fucking word."

The downed guard nodded, his brow soaked in sweat that smelled like fear. The second man's face has gone a sick, milky white. "Yes, sir."

*Sir.*

That's what Leto called the Old Man. For the first time, he wondered what purpose the guards really served. They could be bribed, overpowered, even harmed. If Leto killed one of them, what punishment would the Old Man inflict? Not physical pain. That was easy enough for Leto to slough off now. Maybe harm against his family.

The guards were tradition. Ceremony. Show ponies. The real prison was on a much deeper level—hostages, and the two-sided coin of promise and threat. No number of victories would change that.

Leto kicked the felled guard to hide his shudder, then barreled past the mess hall and humans' quarters. He shoved his sudden, unwelcome realizations into the pit of his stomach.

He was risking more than he ever had. He was risking his place in the Old Man's favor, his place as the Asters' champion, and his own family.

For a neophyte.

*For Nynn.*

Who'd thought she could outsmart a devil.

# CHAPTER TWELVE

Leto didn't knock. He didn't listen outside the door to confirm his suspicion. He just burst inside. Hinges gave way to the release of his coiled strength.

During his run through the human complex, he'd pictured what he would find. He hadn't thought to find them so far progressed in Nynn's subjugation.

She was bleeding from her forehead and chained to a metal-framed bed, which was topped by a flattened mattress. Hunched into himself, moaning, Kilgore held a needle between his teeth. The blood Nynn had shed was nothing compared to the stream oozing out from where her wooden practice knife pierced the man's forearm.

Kilgore turned. His eyes were huge yellow discs. Even if the man was a grasping snake, he knew when to be afraid. Perhaps that made sense. The lower the animal, the stronger the instinct to recognize imminent danger.

He spit the needle onto the floor where it rolled to a stop by Leto's boot.

"Leto." He was quick to recover. Always had been. "We were in the midst of completing our transaction when she attacked me."

"And you decided to subdue her?"

"Exactly."

"Chains work." He smashed the hypodermic beneath his heel. "Drugs are best saved for the lab you came from."

"You don't blame me for this. The fault is hers. Surely you'll punish her."

"I would've been more likely to take your side had you *asked*. Instead, you tell me how to discipline my own neophyte? That isn't your decision."

Leto loomed tall over the man. His anger was well out of proportion with the situation. Although he should be furious at Nynn for doing something so stupid, he was ready to rip Kilgore into pieces and leave his useless carcass. Maybe someone would miss him come mealtime.

Again . . . That realization of his limits. Dragon damned, he didn't need another unwelcome thought. No matter Leto's status, dismembering even one as humble as their human chef was prohibited, when a man like Kilgore should be below a Dragon King's notice.

But Nynn was bleeding. Which meant Kilgore was *not* beneath his notice.

He yanked the wooden knife out of Kilgore's arm and tossed it toward the door listing on its hinges. The man's yelp of pain was satisfying.

"Strip your shirt," he said.

At Kilgore's compliance, all hissing agony, Leto ripped the flimsy hemp material into strips. Two minutes later, he'd wrapped an expert field dressing around the three-inch gash in the man's forearm. Despite his boiling turbulence, Leto tamped down a tight smile. Nynn had cut deeply and with careful aim. Kilgore wouldn't be able to use that muscle for weeks. Even chained, she'd taken the man's right arm out of the contest.

He could comment on her technique later. Once she was safe again.

*Safe?*

Dragon be, he was losing perspective.

"Now come here," Leto said, voice rasping.

Kilgore raised his brows. The surprise and even the fear of Leto bursting through his door was gone. His rat-sly expression followed every movement. Trying to gain advantage. That wasn't going to happen. No matter the intricacies of power Leto was only just untangling, he was still a Dragon King. And still a foot and a half taller.

He grasped Kilgore by his scruff and stood him on solid footing. "Stay there. Don't move. Nynn had a good try, although I'm fairly sure you can serve food with one arm." Close to Kilgore's ear he said, "The Old Man would be upset if I killed you, but I wouldn't be. I'd finish what she started, and I'd make it agonizing."

Kilgore swallowed. His forehead looked squashed in proportion to the rest of his face. It was slick with sweat. Although he didn't acknowledge Leto's threat, he didn't move either.

Leto turned his attention to Nynn, who lay watching the exchange with an expression of rage. A mirror of his own anger. What the fuck was he going to do with her?

She should've broken by now.

That she hadn't made him proud and furious. He

wasn't a man used to processing contradictions, yet the night had been full of them. Leto knelt before her. Although loath to use Kilgore's ripped shirt for the task, he wiped the blood off her forehead. Softly. Almost soothingly. As if lulling a child. She'd behaved like a child—one with a woman's body. But she was a warrior, not a seductress. Otherwise Leto would've found them in some state of undress, in a sexual position he didn't want to imagine. Instead, they'd been bleeding and spitting at each other like cats in a bag.

Kilgore must've sensed her potential for violence. He usually liked his girls complacent but conscious. Leto would admit to admiring her technique with the knife later, but he'd also grill her about letting a little man get the jump on her.

Then he'd spend hours making sure it wouldn't happen again.

Her punishment, however . . . that was his priority. What came to mind made him ill, but maybe it was just what had to happen. He needed to bust into that stubborn skull of hers. Kilgore would help, only under Leto's watchful eye.

She winced.

"That hurts?"

"Yes," she said.

"Imagine what pain you'd be in now if he'd got hold of you."

"No telling." Her eyes darted to the metal drawers in the corner of the room. "Tranquilizers or something like them. From Aster's lab. What I felt would depend on the drug."

He took her chin in his palm. Met her eyes. Pale,

silvery blue was turbulent and fraught with emotions Leto wasn't sure he'd ever felt, let alone all at once. "You'd have felt every cut and bruise and violation once you awoke. If you did."

That focused her. *Good.* If she couldn't see the consequences of a mistake, she would be useless to him. And she'd get herself killed.

"As it was, I think you were trying to accomplish something underhanded. Kilgore specializes in that. He asks a great deal in return for some favors." Leto held out his hand. "The letter, Nynn."

Her steady stare meant she was getting better at hiding her emotions, but he felt her thigh jump where it pressed against his.

"I could strip it off you," he said. "Just like I stripped contraband off your cell guards. I thought I'd let you keep a little dignity. For the moment." He flexed his fingers. "Hand it over."

"How did you know?"

"Because you're a clever woman."

Her manacles rattled as she dug into her tunic. He was familiar with that sound—the sound of life in the complex. But the tinny, hollow sound of handcuffs against the metal bed frame sent a shiver of unease up his back. Had he been only a few minutes later . . .

She retrieved the letter and handed it over, her eyes churning with hatred.

It smelled of the peppermints from the butcher paper she'd used. Unceremoniously, Leto ripped it into pieces. "And that's that."

"Bastard."

He gripped her chin with much more force. Now

that she was no longer in danger, he had the luxury of letting his anger return. Full. Powerful. "We have two days left before our first match. And another pair of matches in the months to follow. You *will* fight with me. Or would you rather forfeit your son's life? Here you are, risking his safety, believing the lies this creature spins. Or maybe you intended to chance an escape. Where would you go, idiot girl? Maybe since you've been free of your child for a few weeks, he's no longer a concern."

Nynn lashed out—within inches of wrapping her manacle chain around his neck. He caught both wrists. So much proof of her redoubling skills would be something to celebrate later.

"Nearly there, neophyte. What would you have done after you caught me?"

"Enjoyed watching your eyes bulge."

"Would've been fun while it lasted?"

"Very."

"Too bad, then." He slipped two fingers between her collar and her neck, then jerked her close.

He kissed her.

And just as he'd expected—Dragon be, just as he'd secretly wanted—she fought back. Kicked. Twisted. Tried to wrest free of his hands.

The slow softness of their first kiss was some distant dream, something that had taken place between two different people.

This . . . *this* was who they really were.

Of course he enjoyed it. Her spark and fire had been his to observe and nourish for weeks. But his enjoyment wasn't the goal. For a moment more, he indulged in the feel of her. Strong but lithe and feminine. Hot. She tasted of blood, although he knew that couldn't be right. Maybe it was because she made him that crazy. Blood-lust. Needing an outlet.

He pushed her down against the floor. Arms, legs, torso—she was a thin, chained woman, which meant she was easy to pin, no matter her fight. Leto levered above her, stomach to stomach, and held her writhing body in place. His own body was hard. Rock hard. Strung tight and wanting and *demanding*. Against the dictates of his mind, he found himself thrusting his hips, seeking the tender flesh that would slake the tension he'd battled for weeks.

He forced his tongue into her mouth. Grinned when she bit him. One swift move and he cupped her bottom jaw with his palm. The throat was such a vulnerable part of the body. Her gasp of surprise—she had no air now—was a sick invitation for Leto to take more.

He wouldn't.

He reined in his screaming, aching needs. Breathing hard, he was needy in ways he hadn't felt in years and years. Maybe ever. He was stretched to the point of breaking and couldn't afford that luxury.

His turmoil was nothing compared to the fury on Nynn's face. The streak of blood on her forehead and the streak of his blood on her mouth. Her hair a spiked tangle. Her tunic ruched over one hip, which bared a sliver of golden skin. She looked as disheveled as if she'd just been fucked by a group of men.

He would do murder before he let that disgusting scenario come to pass.

In truth, she'd only been kissed by one Dragon King. By him.

Leto growled low in his throat. He had to get this done before his imagination and his lust got the better of his plan. Because he did have a plan. Successful Cage warriors took bars of steel and bent them into the weapons needed for victory. Nynn was just such a weapon. He still needed to bend her to fit his needs, for *both* of them to thrive.

Through it all, Kilgore had stood transfixed. The greed in the man's wild eyes was as obvious as the bulge between his legs.

"Take down your pants," Leto told him.

Kilgore blinked.

Nynn shrieked, fought harder, and managed to land a solid punch against Leto's temple. He ground out a curse and hauled her up to her knees. After trapping her manacled wrists at the base of her spine, he caught the back of her collar with his free hand. She was as trapped as when he'd pinned her against the floor. Only now, her mouth was level with Kilgore's pathetic erection.

Pants down, the man was stroking himself.

"What the *fuck* is this?"

"This is your punishment, neophyte," Leto said against her cheek. "He would've taken you. You'd have been awake, or tranquilized, or even asleep, but you never would have left this room before some part of him was in some part of you."

"You ripped up my letter." Again, her voice was flavored with emotions Leto couldn't parse. Fear, yes. Disgust. Pleading? She even backed up, as if being closer to him would protect her—even though he was the one holding her immobile. "What else do you want from me?"

"I want you to continue your negotiations with this human slime."

She squeaked when he gave her collar a shake.

"Tell me, Nynn," he said. "You planned more than asking him to deliver a letter. You planned to escape. And you were going to give this man favors in return."

Her hiss held the sinister potential of a gas pipe and an open flame. "Are you not hearing me? Every single day? I have to save my son!"

"Two steps closer, Kilgore."

"Hurt her," came the man's lust-roughened voice. "Fight her again."

"Shut up, unless you think I couldn't hack through *any* part of you with her practice knife."

Kilgore only moaned as he worked himself. "Yes, sir."

Nynn's eyes were watering. The back of her head was pressed against Leto's breastplate. Her gaze never left Kilgore's throbbing little cock. The man's expression was one of absolute, entranced pleasure.

"And you haven't been hearing me," Leto said softly. He was restraining her in the most violent, most vulnerable hold he'd yet used, but he'd never spoken to her with more compassion. "Nynn, you are *here* now. You will become a Cage warrior because you have reason to. Because they've taken every other choice away from you. Because they will never let you succeed any other way."

She twitched her shoulders, then pounded her head against his armor. A sound of pure frustration reverberated around the walls of that tiny room.

He beckoned Kilgore even closer. "The alternative is to let men like this use you. To become a victim. You were a victim when they killed your husband and took you and your son."

A sob ripped out of her chest, but he didn't think it was because of the situation. "I tried," she said, almost soundless. "Caleb was dead before I knew what was happening. Blood sprayed across the refrigerator. Jack's mouth was covered in masking tape. They used a Taser on me, covered my head with a hood, and zip-tied it into place. Late on a Thursday evening. We'd ordered a pizza. But in thirty seconds, they destroyed my whole life."

"Here, today, you put yourself in the position to be a victim again." He nudged her temple with his chin. "Look at him. The man is disgusting. You're a Dragon King of the Tigony, on her knees. How will this save your son?"

"You could let me go. You could *help* me find him!"

"That would mean the deaths of my sisters and my niece. I can't let that happen. We do this together. We fight as one. Or you open your mouth right now and take your chances with this man."

Kilgore was out of breath now. His eyes were glassy.

"Go ahead, Nynn. Give him what you were willing to give. Taste him. Let him thrust into you."

"You are *sick*."

"It's what you were ready to do. Forget fighting in the Cages. Forget showing the Asters exactly what you can do. No, instead, you'd let this toad fuck your pretty face on the chance that he'd hand-deliver a letter to the Giva, or open a magic door that set you and your boy free. Give it a try. Now's the time."

"What would you do if I did?"

Leto was swinging between the arousal of holding her trembling, infuriated body and the revulsion of forcing her into such a position. All he knew was that even then, as helpless as a woman could be, she was still fighting. She *was* a fighter. Forget her clan. Forget that she'd married a human. For Nynn of Tigony to do anything less than destroy her enemies was an insult to her potential and their kind.

"I would be disappointed," he whispered. "And you'd make Kilgore very, very happy." She gagged when he tightened his grip on her jaw. "So open up. Show both of us what sort of woman you really are."

She snaked a leg out and around. Not the most effective angle, but it was enough to catch her boot behind Kilgore's ankle. One quick tug landed the man on his back. She slammed her elbow toward Leto's ear, and he let her have that small victory.

Quicker than any human, but slower than any member of Clan Garnis who remained free of the collars, he jerked her to her feet. She gasped.

"Now," he said, his breath rough against her cheek. "A trade."

Kilgore writhed on the floor. She watched him as if keeping an eye on a venomous insect. Dangerous, but vulnerable. She nodded slightly.

"You'll walk out of here with me. Very calmly. No more fighting. Otherwise the guards will wonder what the hell happened. Bribes and intimidation will only work for so long." He grinned. "And in exchange, you get to let loose one more kick."

Sputtering, still dazed, Kilgore began a pleading sort of moan. He cupped his withering erection and doubled over himself. "Leto. No. Think of what I do for you! Your matches! You'd never know who's coming up next."

"And won't that make it more interesting." He nestled a cold smile against Nynn's temple. Her pulse was manic, but she'd stopped struggling. "Do we have an agreement?"

"I don't get a say?" Kilgore bellowed.

Nynn relaxed, then nodded to Leto. "Agreed. If you hold him down on the bed."

Leto exhaled slowly. Trusted. And let her go. She didn't run and she didn't try to strike him. The measure of faith they'd given one another in that moment was priceless.

Yanking Kilgore into place was no great task. Leto was happy to do it.

Rather than kicking the man, or stomping on his face, or whatever manner of violence Leto could imagine, Nynn calmly walked to the chest of metal drawers. She retrieved another syringe. Her expression was fierce. Only her silvery blue eyes gave her away. Leto was surprised he could read her vulnerability so plainly.

"Time to go to sleep, Kilgore," she said sweetly. The needle slipped so easily into the vein on the back of his hand. "And when you wake up, you can wonder what *I* wondered for a whole year. Just what was done to me while I was drugged? I bet your cock is the first thing you check."

Kilgore thrashed and cursed . . . then slid into unconsciousness.

Leto raised an eyebrow. Not the choice he'd expected.

She met his gaze. "You gave me enough room to kick my leg free."

"Yes."

"And you let me get the drop on you—when I hit your temple."

"Yes."

"You're still a sick fucking bastard."

She wiped the blood from her lip. If anything, her posture was straighter, prouder than Leto had ever seen.

Had she learned a damn thing?

She was impetuous and thought too far ahead of him. Her imagination was more developed than his would ever be—except in matters of combat, when he thought three steps ahead of every opponent. She had no sense. She showed no due deference to the tasks laid out before her like a path. Why would she? Glaring, her wide-set eyes dared him to try again, to make her a victim resigned to her fate.

*Resigned.*

He would never associate that word with her—his lethal neophyte.

Then why did the word weigh so easily, so heavily, in his own mind?

# ✦ CHAPTER ✦
# THIRTEEN

Leto needed to be away from the woman. Instead, he led her through the corridors, as if dragging a dog that needed to be put down. He gripped the chains of her manacles as he led her toward the guards standing watch at her training cell. Both men raised eyebrows. Nynn looked like she'd just endured two rounds in a Cage. May as well have. The laceration on her forehead was raised on a bruise.

She stopped at the gate and turned. Blue fire sparked in her eyes—a quiet imitation of the gift she couldn't use. "I hate so much of my life and so many people, but you're the only one here to hate in person. Thank you for making it easier to do."

"I'm tired of you."

"You should've made the most of your chance," she ground out. "Turning a blind eye is easy. Let me show you."

She presented him with her back and the guards with her wrists. One fumbled to find the right key.

There, so close to where he would sleep that night, where the other warriors took their meals and, in their own uneasy ways, socialized—Leto could almost imagine her becoming part of his world. But she never would. Her escape attempts would continue. Her barbs and insults. Hatred, no matter how justified, was blinding her to the value of playing along.

The Old Man wanted them paired in matches, and Leto had never fought with a partner. What a farce. It was hard enough to win without keeping a muzzle and chains on Nynn, knowing she would knife him in the back at first chance.

"Well, now," came a voice Leto couldn't place.

Not at first.

Nynn whirled. Her eyes bulged. She tried to dart. Only Leto's quick reflexes kept her from bolting back down the corridor. He held on with all his strength, because she'd gained the ferocity of a lioness. Vicious. Manic. A perfectly placed kick to the back of his thigh gave her the opening she needed to break free.

Only, her features were contorted by abject fear.

"No," she gasped. *"No!"*

She moved too fast for her own limbs. Spun away from Leto. Slipped. Fell backward onto her ass, scrambling away. The manacle chains draped in a noisy clank around her abdomen.

"Lovely to see you again, Mrs. MacLaren."

Dr. Heath Aster.

Leto's gaze was quick. He couldn't keep both Nynn and the doctor in sight at the same time, but he came very close. One placid smile. One expression of surprised fear morphing into the most powerful anger he'd never seen.

Nynn surged to her feet. She grabbed the practice knife from Leto's waist belt, spun, and snatched the guards' set of keys. He'd never seen her move so swiftly, with precision and grace despite the fury warping her pixie features. Stance wide, she edged away from the wall in a tight, controlled circled. Her attention on the doctor. Knife in one fist. One key thrust between the knuckles of the other.

"Where the fuck is my son?"

"Where you should be, my dear," the doctor said. "No matter what my father insists. Leto, restrain her."

Leto might have hesitated. He *might* have. A pause waited in the space between one breath coming in and another going out. Nynn forced his hand by lunging at the doctor.

Leto lashed out and wrapped an arm around her stomach. Her makeshift weapons hit the floor in quick succession. He caught her manacles and wrapped his inner elbow around her neck. She shrieked as if he'd captured a Pendray animal rather than a woman raised among Tigony royalty and lowly humans.

Sweat formed along Leto's brow as he held her thrashing body for the second time that night. Both times fighting. But this was a moment outside of his control. His neophyte was his to command only as long as he was alone to make the decisions. Those decisions were no longer his.

That knowledge grated up his spine.

"And silence her."

Leto dropped from champion to slave in the span of three words.

He adjusted his grip to keep her immobilized and silent. Sharp teeth grazed the inside of his palm—her tongue, her lips, her vicious snarls. When Nynn tried to kick, he looped one thigh around both of hers. She still tried. He'd known that about her from the first moment she'd stabbed his cheek with a piece of concrete. She would still try. That didn't mean she would win. Not against him and not against the Asters.

Why did that make his stomach lurch?

The doctor stepped closer, his chin lifted, inspecting.

Likely mid-fifties, Dr. Aster was glossy as a photograph. His suit was immaculate. Light brown hair was carefully combed back from a face that greatly resembled that of his father. Hawkish. Predatory. With the same jester's smile. Only, the doctor seemed able to keep his smile just shy of unsettling. More contained. Nothing about him said sadist. Madness. Brilliance. Just a well-ordered sense of competence.

His eyes, however, gave Leto pause. Dull gray. Slow to move. He took his time to linger over every surface, especially Nynn's face. Collecting details? Leto didn't know how to do that without racing at high speed, when he could suck up information as quickly as slurping water from a glass. To move so slowly worked against every instinct he had ever honed. It actually bothered him to watch the doctor's careful, slothful movements.

He'd met the man only once or twice. With nothing between them other than a connection to the Old Man, they'd had little to say. In fact, in his twenty years as a Cage warrior, he couldn't remember having spoken with the doctor. Now Leto's skin was itching as if bugs were crawling beneath.

"Cutting your hair hadn't occurred to me," he said. "Do you miss it, Mrs. MacLaren? I suppose your husband must have enjoyed its beauty a great deal."

Aster was tempting fate by taunting her. Leto caught

her renewed blitz of venom as if holding back lightning. At first he couldn't identify the wetness along the outside of his hand, but it was her tears. Two blinks of salt water trailed down her cheeks and settled in the crevice between his skin and hers.

That lazy gray gaze returned to Nynn. "Greatly changed." Aster wiped one of her tears, then touched his finger to his tongue. "But still broken. I like to see even our champion hasn't been able to change that. Although you have tried, haven't you, Leto?"

"Yes, sir. She's a good fighter."

Dr. Aster stared directly into Nynn's eyes. Leto could almost feel the earthquake her hatred was going to rip open beneath their feet. Had she been free of the collar, she would have done just that. "True. But alas, her son . . ."

She shrieked. Leto's arms were beginning to burn. They'd both have bruises from how roughly he needed to keep her contained. And all the while, his anger lifted to new heights. Nynn was *his* neophyte. This mental and emotional torture would set their training back by weeks. Possibly longer. He'd only just determined that her anger stood in the way of greatness. Now the personification of that anger was playing marionette with nightmare thoughts of her son.

"Maybe that isn't such a welcome topic," the doctor said. "I'll leave talk of young Jack for another time."

More salt water against Leto's hand. This was a torture he'd never experienced.

What was right? Dragon be, he couldn't tell.

Dr. Aster smiled. "And you remember my companion, I assume?"

He turned to beckon a young woman forward. She

walked with slinking grace, moving with a cat's animal ease. Only when she reached Aster's side and he snapped his fingers did she squat by his side. Her twisting elegance was unnatural, if only because she retained an air of dignity even when kneeling. She curled against the doctor's upper leg, as if a part of his anatomy, not a separate being.

Leto shivered.

The Pet.

Leto's interactions with Dr. Aster had been limited, but his contact with the Pet was entirely new. He only ever saw her from a distance. She was the doctor's constant companion. No one knew who she was or how she'd come to be more animal than woman.

A *beautiful* woman.

"Up, Pet."

Dr. Aster's voice was as deliberate as his slothful gaze.

She stood. An agile unfurling. Leto thought of petals opening—something his mother had described. A blossom went from tight and closed to radiant and ready to receive. In this case, to receive instruction from her master. She eyed Leto, then Nynn, but everything about her posture said that her true attention was riveted to the doctor.

Beautiful, yes. But eerie.

Leto had never seen a Dragon King so pale. He'd never known it possible. She was white. White like marble struck by floodlights. Her hair was just the opposite. Stark, incomprehensibly black. Her eyes blazed green and gold. She wore clothes made of what looked like latex, as black as her hair and as shining as her unsettling skin. Elfin features. Narrow shoulders. Tiny, tiny mouth.

Beyond strange.

Rumors abounded about her.

Lobotomized. A failed experiment in the doctor's lab. No one knew if she had a clan, if she had a gift, or if she was even a true Dragon King.

Of all the rumors, Leto couldn't believe in the possibility of a lobotomy. In contrast to her master, her eyes were shimmering, keen, cagey. An unsettling aura pulsed from her in chilling waves. She stared at Nynn. Stared outright. She even frowned—the touch of a crease between her dramatic black brows.

"She hates you," the Pet said to her master.

Toneless.

Leto half expected the doctor to smack her for such a blunt assessment. He only stroked her nape. "Of course she does. And we're not even through with the evening. Leto, bring her with us."

After taking a deep breath, he grabbed the chain that dangled between her arms and pulled. Nynn was shrieking like a Pendray priestess. Long-forged habit demanded that he exert his dominance, especially in front of Dr. Aster. Leto was their champion. He did as he was ordered—but not with the violence he would've used on anyone else. She stumbled as she fought his hold. He pulled her up and into his embrace, then tightened his arms.

Holding her.

Curses forged with fury and hurt were the most vicious Leto had ever heard—and he'd heard the worst dying men could spew before taking their last breaths.

"Save your strength," he whispered against her temple. He couldn't save her, but he could do as he'd always done: teach her how to survive. "Nynn, hear me. You're going to need it."

It galled him to realize that was all he could do: offer her words. He couldn't do a Dragon damn thing but carry his neophyte toward the training arena. Two guards fell into step with the doctor. The taller of the two pulled a Taser from his belt.

"Let go of her," he said to Leto.

Reluctantly, enraged by the frustration that he could do nothing more, Leto dropped the manacles and let Nynn slip to to her feet. The guard shoved her down and kicked her in the stomach. She jackknifed. He wedged the sole of his boot between her shoulder blades, then pushed the Taser against her left ribs. The Tigony could wield electrical impulses, and even generate their own electrical currents by hauling energy out of the air and amplifying it.

That didn't mean they were immune to its effects.

Nynn screamed, vibrated, slumped. The guards hauled her off the floor, working together until all six of them were locked inside the training arena. Leto was the last to enter. Everything he'd known about life in the complex—his home—had changed in the span of a few hours.

There, on the far side of the arena, waited the whipping post. As did Hellix and Fam.

"Dr. Aster, what is this about? She's my neophyte. She makes her debut in two days and needs her focus."

The doctor looked over his shoulder, but he didn't stop his deliberate walk toward the whipping post. "She also tried to escape tonight, did she not?"

"She did." Leto decided on complete honesty. No telling how Dr. Aster had learned what he did. Lying would only hurt them both. "I dealt her punishment. That's my right as her trainer."

"Oh, I saw your punishment," the doctor said with a smirk. "Very entertaining. You're still reeling from that one. I know it. So close to taking what you wanted. Yet so good and loyal, trying to teach her what's right." He looked down at Nynn, where she slumped between the two guards. Nothing about the woman Leto had trained remained in her eyes. "She's very, very stubborn when it comes to learning lessons. Now it's my turn."

Dr. Aster reached the whipping post. The Pet curled up at his feet, holding his calf with one hand and the base of the post with the other, so feline and watchful. Unlike the doctor, she didn't smirk or smile, only assessed the scene. Leto found no hint of judgment in her expression, or pleasure. Whoever—*whatever*—she was, the Pet was not a sadist made in the doctor's image.

She looked up the length of the whipping post and exhaled. Leto barely heard her say, "Inevitable."

Crystal clear memories still twitched across his back. He bore scars from combat—honorable scars. He also bore shameful ones. Whip marks. Welts had lifted from strike after strike of chains hurled at full force. Sometimes Leto's trainer had administered punishments for youthful disrespect. Sometimes it had been Leto's own father, under orders from the Old Man. Another lifetime, yet he was as helpless now as he had been at fifteen, still learning what it would take to become a respected, respectful warrior.

The guards pulled Nynn forward. Hellix reached far

overhead and inserted a hook through a link from her manacle chain. Her toes barely reached the floor, with her arms stretched taut overhead. Her collar pressed upward on her throat. Sweat dampened her brows. The doctor grabbed a hunk of hair at her crown. He lifted until her eyes were level. Leto had come to expect fight and fire.

She was *blank*.

Dr. Aster pushed the Pet from his leg and faced a selection of whips and chains hanging from a pegged board. Perhaps the concealment of shadows had prompted the Old Man to have the whipping post erected in that particular place—half hidden but visible enough to send a shiver down the backs of any warrior who'd been chained to its unforgiving wood.

In the center of the training arena, the Cage lights cast gruesome slices of black and white over the doctor's smile, one of pure anticipatory glee. Had Leto any reason to suspect that tales of the laboratories were false . . . those reasons were gone now.

The doctor selected a thick whip. Three inches in diameter at the base. No more than four feet long. Although it tapered to a point, the thickness would deliver as much punch as sting. Aster tested the heft, but lifted his eyes as if to turn over the responsibility. Why not? The Old Man had never delivered any of Leto's whippings. He'd liked to watch.

Leto was sweating. He had to make one more attempt. "Sir, I cannot whip her. She's to be my partner. This . . . She'll never forgive me for something so extreme. Fighting at her side will be impossible."

For a moment, the movement of Dr. Aster's sluggish,

measured gray eyes made him seem almost kind. Almost sympathetic. "That's very logical, Leto. And accurate. You won't be the one to deliver this woman's sentence."

He handed the whip to Hellix.

Leto sprang. No calculations. No thought toward how his actions would affect his future or his family. He simply couldn't let Hellix whip Nynn.

He'd never made such a rash choice. He'd never seen a choice come to so little fruition. One guard cocked a napalm pistol. The other hefted the recharged Taser.

They needed ten minutes and both weapons to take him down.

# CHAPTER FOURTEEN

Audrey woke up screaming.

She'd screamed for hours, even in her dreams.

Bricks of pain slammed down on her head. Fire like the lick of the Dragon's breath scorched her back, ass, and upper thighs. What must've been burns from the Tasers nettled and itched—between her shoulder blades, down her ribs. One at the base of her skull.

She moaned. Her head was too heavy to keep upright. When she stopped fighting gravity, she hit pitted wood with her forehead. Must still be the post—the whipping post where agony threaded through every inhale, every shrieked exhale. Was the training arena in near darkness, or were her eyes failing? Hard to tell past her mangled senses.

Moving, ever again . . . wasn't possible. She hurt too much. That pain would never stop.

A noise—the scuff of leather soles—pulsed panic across raw nerves. She moaned once more, then fought, *fought* to move. Manacles still circled her wrists. The chain would still be looped through the ring at the top of the post. Drawing from reserves she didn't know she had, she dug her knees into the post. Flexed screeching abdominal muscles. Tried to find a position that wasn't just hanging by a chain. If she could climb high enough, she might be able to release the chain from its loop.

She needed a weapon. Manacles would do.

Leto had been right. By accompanying Kilgore and trying to play his game, she'd volunteered to be used. Maybe so many months in the labs had left that possibility open. Nothing had been out of pride's reach when begging for her son. She'd done unthinkable things on the chance of some small reprieve. What was the difference, giving in to one more sick bastard?

That wasn't her anymore. She wasn't scared Audrey MacLaren anymore. She wasn't even some halfway-committed neophyte. Dr. Aster had handed a whip to Hellix, and the sick sadist changed her life once again. Weeks of Leto's training and his strange, twisted faith in her coalesced around her pain and hatred. Making her new.

She was Nynn of Tigony. Fully. And she'd strangle the fucker who tried to touch her again.

Hoping for something other than hazy shadows, she blinked and kept blinking. She couldn't trust that the lights had been dimmed. But she'd fight near-blind if she needed to.

Up. Up again—two more pushes, with all the strength she had left. Another inch. Struggling. No part of her body was free of agony, so it didn't matter when the insides of her knees became ripped and bloodied, pierced with splinters. Her palms, too, as well as the inside grooves of her knuckles.

She reached the hook, the loop, the chance to hurt someone. It wasn't going to be her.

Manacles and collar remained, but she was free of the post. She dropped to the ground. Although her legs gave way, she held a low, crouching defensive stance. Both shredded hands clutched the chain.

"Nynn."

The shock of Leto's low, hushed whisper was not as startling as the relief that followed.

"Where are you?" she gasped.

A light flickered on, far across the arena. The Cage waited between them. Slowly, her eyes adjusted to that slight illumination. At least she wasn't blind as well as half-crippled. Small comfort, but she didn't have any other kind. Any last softness in her life had been crushed.

Slowly, Leto appeared. He walked with the same deliberation that shouted ego and attitude and victory. But something was different. She stayed crouched low, watching. His pace was the same. His balance was not. He favored his left leg—nothing so obvious as a limp, yet she spotted the change. His shoulders, too. Tighter and set higher, hunched almost defensively toward the lower band of his collar.

She waited. Stunned, really. She remembered . . .

He'd lunged at Hellix, or perhaps he'd even aimed his strength at the doctor. She hadn't known his target, and despite all of his courage and strategy for battle, she doubted he'd known either. Just pure *fury*. The memory of his fight materialized in full, grotesque detail. In the Cages, he was unbeatable. That confidence allowed him to attack every opponent, knowing its outcome in advance.

He had acted on quick, violent instinct. *For her.* That

had been his failing. Rage had given him the power to hold off the guards, but he'd been an animal. No strategy, and none of the advantages a Dragon King had over humans—*armed* humans.

What had happened afterward, when her consciousness had slipped away like a raven taking flight? Had he kept fighting? Did that explain his strange gait and taut shoulders?

She didn't know what to make of that. So new and unexpected.

He'd been the one to debase her in front of Kilgore. He'd carried her into the arena. He'd handed her to them, where she'd been beaten on the floor. Did any of that overwhelm how he'd warned her to save her strength, or his attempt to set her free?

Which warrior was walking toward her now?

Nynn hefted the chain. Enough slack.

After a sharp inhale, she was beset with a dizzying wash of black.

She fell face-first against the concrete floor. Her chin split. A sound of rage burst from her lungs. Maybe she would've lain there forever. Deflated. Defeated. Angry as fuck, but unable to do a damn thing more.

Only, Leto knelt. He touched her shoulders. She winced, tried to shrivel away.

"You're not going anywhere," he said softly.

"I want to hurt you."

One of those nearly indecipherable emotions crossed his rugged features. Disappointment? She didn't want to disappoint him. Not after what he'd done. He'd dented his reputation, suffered pain, kept brawling.

Again those two words: *For her*.

"I got that impression," he said, with a grim downturn to his full lower lip. That frown made his scar more prominent. "But your skills deserve better weapons than these chains."

She made noise more than any concerted effort to move. Brain. Bones. Muscles. She was an orchestra without a conductor. Dissonant pain blared over every command. So when he wanted her sitting up, she sat up—all under his power.

That's how she wound up huddled against his chest. He sat cross-legged and pulled her close. She winced, hissed, but even she realized when her protests stopped: when he kissed the top of her head and tucked her close beneath his chin. Strong arms circled her. Stronger legs braced her lower body. Every shaking and twitching muscle no longer needed to struggle. She slumped.

And wept.

She was too depleted to cry as forcefully as the pain demanded. Leto's tenderness, however . . . just when she'd thought all softness crushed . . .

"I'm here, brave girl."

Indignation forced her to suck in a hard, fast gulp of air. "You're here? Now?" A push. A twist. She tried to get free of how dangerous he was. Four words—and she'd wanted to melt into him forever. "Where were you when Dr. Aster planned to beat me? You *carried* me here and handed me over. Hellix tried to break my back, one strip of flesh at a time. You fought, but by then it was too late."

Keeping her close must've been as difficult for him as restraining a mad kitten. He closed his big hands over her upper arms, held her, wouldn't let her go. Protests or not. Insults or not. He wasn't letting go.

The light was scant, but it was enough for Nynn to catch sight of his right wrist. That perfect golden skin was circled with angry red welts—the bracelet only a sadist would bestow. She was strong enough to find his left wrist, where his large hand cradled almost the entire length of her forearm. Another repulsive welt.

Fascinated, sickened, she traced the red weal with her fingers. Every movement was spasmodic, like a junkie three days into detox. Didn't matter. The tender, raised flesh banding both wrists was proof that what she'd witnessed hadn't been the last of his torture.

It was safer to cast him as yet another villain, but to think of Leto as a villain was an outright lie.

"I'm here now," he said, low voice impossibly rough. "They wouldn't let me before."

"What else did they do to you?"

"Nynn, there's no changing it now."

She coughed out something manic and twisted—something like a chuckle. "We still gonna argue? Just let me know. I'll save my energy for words. Forget keeping body systems from shutting down."

"They . . . restrained me."

After pulling back to study his profile, she waited for more detail. Dragon damn, she would've gotten more forthright answers from talking to the Cage. But she didn't have the energy to be angry with him. He kept touching her hair. Softly, as if by instinct, he avoided the places where she hurt the most. In that bizarre, terrible place, Leto of Clan Garnis was becoming more than a mere ally.

She *wanted* that. Wanted someone to confide in, and who might confide in her.

Defying her body's juddering protests, she climbed his body until she pressed her lips against his strong jaw. Stubble abraded her lips with gentle sensation. He'd always been immaculately clean shaven in her company. Just how long had they been awake and, for the most part, suffering?

"Please," she whispered against his skin. "I don't want to be alone anymore."

His big body was fiercely powerful, but at her hushed words, he shuddered. His head listed toward hers, until their cheeks met. The jaw muscle by his ear bunched, as hard as teeth and metal and Hellix's strokes across her back.

"*I'm* not alone," he said.

She frowned, gripped his unblemished forearm. "I never said you were. That's proof, though. You feel it, too. Being isolated here. I've seen how the others avoid you. They move aside when you pass. Respect. Not companionship."

"I have what I want."

"But you needed to be restrained. What did you want that you couldn't have?" The defined ridges of his forearm tightened until he made a fist—open, then closed, as if trying to reawaken a deadened limb. Nynn put her hand over his restlessness. This time they shuddered into one another and connected in a way that resonated behind her breastbone like the bass notes of a cello. Fear and hope—hope, that evil thing. "Leto, I'm being torn to shreds. My life, my thoughts, now my body again. You want me to be your partner in the Cages. That means trusting me. And I need to trust you. Please."

His swallow was audible. "I didn't want them to hurt you."

She might've taken comfort in his words had he said them with any more passion. She would know the truth, even if she needed to pull it out of his mouth with both hands. "You've hurt me. And you've punished me. What's the difference?"

"Because you're mine."

She reared back to look into his eyes. He'd already looked away. Blank again.

"My neophyte," he added quietly. "Mine to train as I see fit."

"So, a beating is worse than what you threatened with Kilgore."

"You said it yourself. I gave you an out. You took it." He'd stopped stroking her hair, instead cupping the backs of her thighs. He pulled her closer, and she accepted that comfort. "I've worked to make you stronger. You'd be able to stare anyone down, with red in your eyes. Even those first few days, I never doubted we could make that happen."

Maybe it was pain or fatigue—no telling—but Nynn blinked a surprising sheen of tears. "And now?"

"Now they've undone everything. Made you a victim again."

She found her same ragged chuckle. She sounded insane. "I climbed that post to get free. Had you been anyone else, I would've died defending myself." She sat up a little straighter, as much as her trembling, aching limbs would permit. With his jaw in her hands, she forced him to see her eyes. "I wouldn't have been able to do that without your training. Sick as some of it's been."

"Necessary."

"Fine. Necessary." She touched his injured wrist again. "Tell me what happened. The real reason."

"I didn't want Hellix to hurt you. Or the doctor . . ." He turned to kiss her forehead. "Kilgore looked like a man should look. Turned on. Eager for release. It was disgusting but predictable. Whereas the doctor never changed that sinister expression."

"Scrutiny . . . It's all for posterity. How much can a person take?"

"That. Yes." Another kiss. This time he didn't pull away to talk. Just spoke against her skin, pushing his rasping words right into her mind. "I fought back. Tasers, napalm bullets—the whole arsenal."

"I saw," she forced out. "For a few moments, anyway. After?"

"I was chained over there, in that corner."

Nynn looked toward where he indicated with his chin. "I never noticed them. Locks on the wall?"

"To force me to watch."

She lifted his injured wrist and kissed the bruised skin on the tender inside. Then the other. "It was my fault. My impulse to try to play Kilgore's game."

"Maybe to start," he said, shifting their positions. "But how can anyone predict what a man like Aster will do? No rules. No honor."

"Do you see why I hate him so much?"

Leto nodded, then slowly, very slowly, got to his feet and helped her stand. She wavered. Clutched at him. She bowed her neck and pressed her dizzy, pain-spiked head against the chest plate of his armor. His muscles would be just as hard as that protective metal, only warm and pulsing with life. She shivered, then shivered again when he gingerly gripped her upper arms.

"I'd carry you," he said, "but I think I'd do more damage than if you walked."

"Walk where?"

"To the Cage. Turn off our collars for a while. It'll speed the healing process."

She dumbly followed him toward the wired gate entrance. He flipped a switch on the outside control panel. Step up. Walk inside. *Breathe*.

She gasped, but it sounded less like surprise or pain. More like freedom, no matter the bars and locks. She stumbled, then knitted her fingers into the wire mesh. Leto entered, too. She saw the exact moment when the collar released him from bondage. Pleasure washed across his expression, too potent to be concealed. Eyes shut, neck tilted toward the ceiling—he looked like a man who'd just come. Pure satisfaction.

He stood behind her and laced his hands over hers. His warmth layered across her back. Maybe that was the rush of sensation that came with being free again.

And to think she believed she'd never possessed a gift from the Dragon. Now she felt its power coursing through her body as strong and sure as her own thunderous heartbeat.

Leto was so careful. He didn't touch her anywhere other than where their hands fused with the charged metal that gave them back what made them special. But his voice had always been a force, an enticement, a touch of its own.

"I can see why you hate him," he said, as if their discussion about Dr. Aster had never ceased. "And how much danger Jack is in."

A sob coughed out of her lungs, which burned as if she'd run for miles in the searing winter cold. "That's the first . . ." She coughed again, leaned her head back to rest against his solid strength. "That's the first time you've called him by his name."

"Maybe it was time." He let go of her hand and smoothed his fingers along both of her cheeks, back across her hair. He turned her, held her, would not let her look away. "You need to decide now, Nynn. Are you ready to do what you must?"

"Will you be here, too? I mean, an Indranan witch . . ."

"Yes. I'll be here."

A chill unlike any she'd ever known stole over her skin. Not even Leto's nearness kept it away. But she had no other choice. She needed to control her powers, no matter the cost.

"Then, yes. Let me meet her."

# CHAPTER FIFTEEN

Within minutes, Leto had secured the gates to the training arena, locking Nynn inside. He couldn't trust the guards, so he behaved as he always would. Champion of the Asters. With any luck, they wouldn't notice his slight limp. Most of the napalm bullets had missed the mark, but one had pierced his thigh. The bullets didn't go through flesh; they nestled just inside the skin and burned and burned.

Even with time spent in the Cage, they'd both be long to heal. They were in no shape to fight at top form. Not physically. Not mentally. Despite the embrace they'd shared, and the awkward kisses, they weren't partners either. For the first time, he envied Silence and Hark. They were both Sath. Same clan. Same history and abilities. When they stepped into a Cage together, they moved and breathed as one. Unified and deadly.

He didn't want that—not permanently. But to feel it just once?

*I don't want to be alone anymore.*

Shunting those thoughts aside, he focused on a more pressing matter. He felt as if eyes followed him everywhere. Aster had seen Nynn and Kilgore together, and what Leto had done to punish them both. Who was to say they were alone, completely alone, in the training arena?

Why hadn't he ever considered that possibility before?

Because since his youth, he'd never done anything to make being observed a concern.

The guards were especially wary of him. Since he'd been attacked from behind—and because, frankly, he'd taken to believing all the human rabble looked alike—he didn't know whether these two men had done him harm. He wanted retribution. He fisted his hands and kept walking toward the Dragon Kings' quarters. They flanked him closely. He couldn't remember the last time a human had thought to encroach on his space.

In trying to save Nynn from the inevitable, he'd lost much of his standing in the complex. Only a fresh victory—still doubtful—would help restore his importance and trustworthiness.

At least Nynn was on his side for the first time. She wanted to control her powers.

He knocked on a dorm room door. A haggard-looking old Indranan woman name Ulia answered. What must've once been the golden, flawless skin of a Dragon King woman was creased with wrinkles and so wan as to be unnerving. She might be two hundred years old, for all Leto knew. Stooped. Gray-haired. Eyes clouded to the point of blindness. She didn't need sight. Her telepathy meant she used other people's eyes to compensate for her own.

One of many, many reasons why Leto avoided her.

She had once fought in early Cage matches. Her telepathy was legendary among those who'd served the

Asters—and likely among those who'd feared facing her in a Grievance. Only when she'd lost her leg to a Pendray berserker did the Old Man offer her freedom. She'd refused. After decades in the complex, the outside world held no appeal. She had purpose among the other warriors.

*The outside world is frightening.*

At his own errant thought, Leto bit his back teeth together. He wasn't afraid of anything. Only the thought of disappointing the Old Man and risking the safety of his family held any sting. Surely Dr. Aster would tell his father of Leto's transgressions. He had a lot of ground to make up with his mentor. *That* was important. The outside world held no appeal because it couldn't honor a skilled warrior. Where else would he be hailed as a living god? Nowhere but in the Cages.

"Young Garnis," she said, her smile cagey. "No courtesy for your elders? No greeting? This is no time for conversation."

The night was in its ninth hour. Not quite time to rouse. Dragon Kings renewed on a twenty-six-hour cycle. Ten sleeping. Sixteen waking. The actual hours of an Earth day had no impact belowground. That he hadn't slept in longer than he could remember was probably doing his judgment no favors.

He wondered how Nynn and the Dragon Kings coped while living among the humans. Perhaps they adjusted as Yeta had, learning to accept the constant touch of sluggishness that came with being awakened too soon from a solid rest. Perhaps that had affected Nynn's ability to channel her gift. She'd never been in touch with the rhythm of body.

"My neophyte. You've heard talk of her, I'm sure."

"The Giva's cousin. How could anyone close their ears to such a temptation? And she's to partner with you."

"As the Old Man bids."

Her grin widened. It was unnatural to see a Dragon King use such a breadth of facial expressions. Ulia was animated, as was Hark—that disturbing, chattering jester. Leto had only just gotten used to the variety Nynn could produce. Perhaps other rumors—that Ulia was just as mad as she was powerful—could be true as well. No one outside of their clan knew how the Indranan's gifts worked. For all Leto knew, she had three personalities in that small, almost shrunken old head, grappling for control. Perhaps they only came together when it was time to crawl into someone else's mind.

He stiffened his back to hide a shudder. The Pendray were easy to understand. Simple brawn and mindless rage. The Sath were secretive but manageable thieves. When the Tigony weren't playing Tricksters and sidling up to their human subjects, their gift of concentrated electricity could be evaded. Fellow Garnis—well, that was just a matter of knowing one's own weaknesses and turning the tables. So few of the Lost remained that Leto had never faced one in competition. Frankly, he didn't know if he could kill one of his own.

But the Indranan. They were so devious, with a gift so potentially devastating, that a millennia-old feud had broken the clan in two. Northern versus Southern, separated by the Indian Ocean. They would kill a fellow member of their clan as surely as they would kill a sibling.

Revolting people.

"She was blocked at the onset of her gift," he said. "She's needs it reversed."

"As the Old Man bids."

"How do you mean?"

"He instructed me to provide any services you requested for your neophyte. What is her name?"

The surprise of Ulia's statement came first. Was Nynn so valuable that the Old Man hadn't trusted Leto with her training? The truth—that Leto *had* been unable to see her properly prepared—lanced shame between his ribs.

Then came another concern. The Indranan witch didn't know Nynn's name? Perhaps she was playing games. Testing his patience. Or pretending to be a doddering crone. She might not know Nynn's name. Maybe she hadn't cared to learn, or had forgotten.

And she was going to have the whole of Nynn's consciousness to mold.

Leto had learned as a young man that few would discuss having blocked the gifts of a loved one. Fewer still wanted to talk about the particulars. He only had two experiences to draw from: his own and Pell's. One had succeeded in bringing order to frenzy. One had failed, leaving a husk of a young woman.

The ceremonies were private for a reason. This was a time when minds touched. Vulnerabilities could be exploited when both individuals slipped into the world on top of the world. Of course Leto's had been private as well. Much to his agony. That time alone had given his telepath free rein to exert physical as well as mental dominance. Leto still bore a trio of parallel scars on the backs of both calves. Not only that, he carried a crystallized, infallible memory of the moment those wounds were inflicted.

The guards walked them back to the arena, but their vigilance was waning. Like all the humans, they worked on a different sleep cycle. After twelve days, the day guards became night guards. Always a species out of step.

Locked once again in the training arena, Leto led Ulia toward the entrance to the Cage. He presented the stooped-back woman to Nynn, who still looked like a shredded piece of cloth. Blood had caked in slashes across her back. Blond hair was streaked pink at her nape. She moved with noticeable pain when she pushed away from the wire framework. Her icy gaze moved instantly to Ulia's prosthetic.

"Don't worry about staring, young one," Ulia said. "Lost it in a match. No shame. I still won."

"That's . . . good."

Nynn's posture had changed. Stiff. Wary. But she straightened her graceful shoulders, even if the adjustment pinched her lush lower lip. He'd tasted that mouth and he knew that stance. She'd made up her mind to be stubborn. At least it wasn't aimed at him for once. He'd come to depend on her resilience. Unlike Dr. Aster, his goal had never been to see her cowed. He'd only wanted her to be an asset, strong and working with him side by side.

A partner. This was how she would become his.

Even if he only thought of it in practical terms, he needed her. Other emotions—darker, needier, unfamiliar—had no place in a warrior's mind.

"Our champion says you've been blocked." Ulia tsked. "Not right. Dragon Kings deserve the full use of their gifts."

Nynn remained wary. "But wouldn't it have been an Indranan who blocked me in the first place?"

Ulia scowled. Leto still cringed at the old woman's free use of such telling expressions. She was too vivacious to be trusted.

"Could've been a Northerner. Who knows what those maniacs believe? Maybe they believe we Dragon Kings don't deserve to be set apart. But we do. Without our powers, we're no better than humans."

The tightness of Nynn's jaw spoke loud and clear. She was offended.

The old woman climbed the steps and settled awkwardly onto the padded floor of the practice Cage. She wrapped a shawl more tightly around her shoulders and spread the fringe along her thin, wiry thighs. "We'll find a way to undo this damage. Join me."

Leto was surprised at how quickly Nynn obeyed, even though she walked with a shuffling limp. Her mouth was pursed. Her hands danced restlessly along her hips. A hard frown creased the skin between her pale, angular brows. But she seemed to have renewed the sense of purpose.

He didn't want to think well of the beating she'd suffered. That he shouldn't have protested. He shouldn't have fought. Perhaps the doctor had been right in going to such an extreme. Aster had pushed her to the edge of desperation. She would be a different woman after this.

Leto was surprised at his slight shudder. If he shouldn't have protested and if he shouldn't have fought back, then why had watching her suffer hurt worse than the metal that bit into his wrists and the napalm still sizzling under his skin?

It made no sense.

What made sense was that Nynn sat cross-legged in front of Ulia. His neophyte was behaving with more clarity than he was. Time for that to end.

He entered the Cage and backed against its wires. At least Ulia would be more gentle with her charge than how Leto had been treated. He told himself his only concern was making sure Nynn came through the process with as many resources at her disposal as possible.

But then he met Nynn's eyes.

She was as brave at that moment as he'd ever seen her. A pulse of light shone between them, but he could see through it. See *her*. What wasn't possible was possible. At that moment, he didn't want to distinguish between the two.

Ulia chuckled softly. "So much distance, champion. The light between your gazes says you need to be with this woman."

Shared light? It was a rumor. An old, old tale. That certain Dragon Kings had the ability to generate shared powers—separate from their individual gifts. It was as unknown to him as life outside of the complex. He could believe on faith or trust his senses. This required some of both. Not his greatest skill.

He inhaled very, very slowly as he looked away. In doing so, the golden glow dissipated. The training arena looked drab and hazy in its absence.

The old woman motioned for him to join them on the floor. "Come. You're a part of this."

"The ceremonies are private."

"But she is to be your partner, in more ways than you see. Trust begins now."

Again, the word *partner* rang behind his sternum with more force than it warranted. Yes, Nynn would be his partner in the Cages. He was resigned to that. Ulia, however, suggested a deeper meaning. Her eyes, clouded to the color of dull copper, seemed to hold no malevolence. A by-product of her blindness? Or honest truth?

He forced his unease to abate.

Nynn remained still, even determined, but she was not calm. Tendons stood out from her nape. That shimmering blond silk drew him. The softness. The way it framed her golden features. The memory of its luxurious length—long gone. Her hair was one of the only things he'd ever admired that held no purpose.

Lost now.

He straightened. Walked. Looked down at the pair. "What do I do?"

"Sit with her."

Rarely did he let another Dragon King direct his actions, but this was quickly becoming very important. A heaviness of purpose, even destiny, hung above their heads. It lowered inch by inch with each passing second. Soon it would touch his shoulders and claw inside until it was reality. He'd resigned himself to such changes before. Easier than thinking about them. Simpler than resisting them.

"No, no." Ulia waved her hands, dislodging her shawl. "Together. Behind her. Hold her."

Nynn flinched. "Wait, what?"

"Believe me, child. You will need a link. He is your link to this world, is he not?"

For a long moment, Nynn stared at the Cage floor. The muscles above her collarbones tensed. She nodded once, but her voice was tissue thin when she asked, "Can we just get this over with?"

Kneeling behind Nynn, Leto splayed his legs on either side of hers, in a pose that mimicked how he'd held her after her climb down from the whipping post. She smelled of sweat and blood. There in the Cage, his senses were free to search for more elemental shades of her perfume. The primal bitterness of fear. Salt from her tears. Damp mold from the age-old whipping post. And even him—he smelled his own scent layered over her skin.

Then more and more. Details upon details. He could hear when her heart slowed and sped. See individual hairs prickle to life on her bare left shoulder. Feel the heat of her body with each cell of his. His senses bathed in her.

With his chest gently shielding her injured back, he crossed his arms around her stomach. She tensed, then forced an exhale. Their hands twined. He rested his forehead against her nape, just below where a slight trickle of her blood had crusted.

"Good," Ulia said. "We'll begin. Leto, keep this woman safe."

He did not look at the crone. He was too busy absorbing the cadence of Nynn's breaths. Until they . . . aligned. He'd never felt anything like it, while four words echoed endlessly in his mind.

*Keep this woman safe.*

# ✦ CHAPTER ✦ SIXTEEN

Nynn could not remain stiff. The woman Ulia's voice intoned sounds like bell chimes, urging Nynn to sink deeper into a recessive state. With her last conscious thoughts, she clutched tighter to Leto's hands. So intimate once again. Wrapped together. Arms over arms. Legs twined with legs. They sat like lovers offering respite after an arduous task—in their case, surviving Dr. Aster.

They weren't lovers, but that comforting pose was not entirely unwelcome.

Part of her still rebelled at the idea of including Leto in this ceremony. What if some part of her slipped free? What if Ulia opened his mind, too, and let him see all her secrets? He'd see how much she'd come to rely on him, even desire him. She shivered. He gripped her fingers more tightly.

His presence couldn't be helped. There was danger in this operation. Ulia could lose her grip on Nynn's consciousness and leave her somewhere dark and adrift forever. Perhaps a physical anchor—Leto's body-to-body strength—could help lead her home.

They both faced Ulia. Their skin touched. He burned

and she burned. His heavy muscle pinned hers. Pinned, but embraced. Large, strong hands seemed to be everywhere. Or was that her mind slipping? She only sighed when he found more skin to hold. Fingertips, throat, cheek.

The room was dark. Ulia became a bronzed glow between Nynn's temples. The woman's lined face, stooped back, and prosthetic leg never materialized. Only the color that matched her faded copper eyes. Nynn blinked against the disorientation.

Leto was there, too. She couldn't see him. No other senses found him either—smell, touch, sound. Even taste. She wanted more of his taste.

That shock made her struggle past the anesthetizing hold Ulia had over her mind. But again, Leto held her stable. Some *element* of him, beyond senses. Outside of the darkness, he held their bodies together on the floor of the practice Cage. Held her. Held . . .

*What sadness do you bear?*

Nynn flinched. The bronze glow was sharper now. The living entity of Ulia without taking her shape or form. "My husband was murdered. A Dragon King stood by while the Asters' men ripped us from our home. Caleb was already dead in the kitchen. My son is being tortured. I'm here alone. *My family is gone.*"

Even in her mind, she cried. The grief was more raw there. No inhibitions. No physical limit to how loud she could scream or how deeply sobs could rock her body. No one to hear her, look at her, punish her for what could not be contained. Dr. Aster had used a scalpel. And he'd handed Hellix a whip.

*What do you fear?*

Nynn flung hideous images toward the glow that centered just behind her forehead. Worst-case scenarios. All of the nightmares she'd had time to conjure for more than a year. Jack . . . oh, Dragon be. Jack in *pieces*. How he'd cry for her. He'd think she had abandoned him. He would die alone and so would she.

*What else do you fear? There is more. Deeper.*

An ancient memory surfaced. Nynn gasped. Struggled. Had she been outside her mind, she would have vomited. Only, in that place, she was the silently screaming witness to an old, old crime. A crime she'd committed.

She'd used her powers. Only thirteen years old. A house demolished. A woman dead.

Some things are too dangerous to set free.

Among the Tigony, she had been suspect because of her mother's indiscretion with Nynn's Pendray father. Barely trusted. That explosion had marked the end of even that scant trust. Where had her mother gone then? Gone . . . gone . . .

No . . . *dead*.

Nynn thrashed against the pain stabbing through her mind, lashing, like that whip across her back. They'd stripped her gift and made her fear it. Made her think it had never even existed. Most had cast her out in all but deed.

*Then let go.*

"Let go? I have nothing left! Why am I here, if not for my son?"

*You are here because you have no choice.*

Certainty began to seep deeper and deeper. It slid like molten rock through her veins, arteries, and every pinched little capillary.

"No choice?"

*No choice. Let go.*

"My son!"

*Will be returned to you in one year. Remember?*

"One year." She was slipping. Even Leto's ethereal presence had faded, as distant now as a man waving across a vast chasm. "I must fight."

*With your powers, Dragon King. Harness it. No distractions. Join Leto in victory. You are Nynn of the Asters.*

That name didn't sound right. She was spinning and falling without moving. Only the most important thought refused to be submerged. "I *will* have my son back."

*The promise will be kept.*

"And I will burn down this hellhole."

*Of course not. This is your home now.*

Was it? Nynn was sure she'd hated this place. The gentle lulling of her thoughts, however, set aside images of such violence.

The dull bronze light faded. In its place, a rush of stinging energy burst to life. She shrieked. It surged through her limbs, shot out her fingers and toes. Even the ends of her hair lit and lifted. She ran through her thoughts, hearing bittersweet memories that gouged her heart into crimson strips.

Memories. Deep memories.

The first time . . . she'd *exploded*. And her mother had been put to death.

Nynn's gift from the Dragon was a curse. An abomination.

She grabbed at flashes of remembered light. Caught every strand. Formed electric pulses into potent, controlled beams. From her eyes or from her hands, she was in control. A sense of power unlike any she'd known filled her chest and made her laugh. When was the last time she'd had *control*? All she knew was that it felt good. Right.

Devastating.

She closed her hands, her eyes, and breathed out. Her raw gift was tamed. She coiled it back within her breast. Even among that vacant, formless place, she remembered Leto's snake tattoo. Now she had a serpent, too. Waiting to strike.

*But a trade, Nynn. Put* them *away.*

Ulia's voice was whip-sharp now. An undeniable command.

At first, the only sound in that infinite space was Nynn's heartbeat. Others soon joined. Overlaid. And cracked open her heart. She heard her clan's laughter when a pair of acrobats had performed at a Tigony feast in honor of Mal's ascension as Honorable Giva. Then fire. Crashing wood. Terrified shrieks.

She felt her mother's touch across her cheek. "So beautiful, my child. You will not be ignored." Then . . . that touch was gone forever.

Caleb next. Oh, Caleb. His quiet voice never entirely left her thoughts.

At the bookstore where they'd met. "Would you like to get a cup of coffee?"

At the topmost pod of the London Eye, on their first vacation together. "Will you be my wife?"

At an outdoor altar in Central Park on a sunny spring afternoon. "I do."

Their first kiss as husband and wife. Gasps of passion. Groans. Awed whispers in the night. So many plans.

And the best. The most perfect. The hardest to hear again. "It's a boy, Audrey. Our son."

After Jack took his first breath on a gusty cry, their nighttime whispers had been for him, about him, centered on keeping their little family happy and whole.

Her mind was crying again.

"Hush, now," she'd whispered while trapped in a cell in Aster's lab. Jack's baby-fine hair had smelled of antiseptic and iodine. "Everything will be all right."

She'd lied to her boy. Nothing was all right.

*Everything will be all right. The voices . . . That pain is gone now.*

Yes. Gone now. Thankfully gone. The painful weight Nynn had carried for more than a year lifted and lifted. The agony was a bird escaping, flying, disappearing into a blue too bright to follow. It carried away the sharp brambles of her mind.

The space was empty now, quiet now. What had been there? She'd lost something.

*Just the pain, child. You've only lost the pain.*

"What do I do?" she called into the black. "Ulia, help me!"

*You will fight for the glory of the Asters. Keep your promise.*

Relief washed her like a cleansing rain. Her skin was new. Her mind was clear. Her gift was ready to surge. She would wield it as easily now as Leto swung his mace and circled the Cage with unimaginable speed.

Leto. Holding her.

"Yes," she whispered. "Yes, I promise."

Although she could no longer remember what promise she'd made.

Leto stroked back the sweat from Nynn's brow and temple. Her body raged with a sudden, fierce fever. Unnatural. Overwhelming. She shook uncontrollably no matter how firmly he pulled her against his body. Lithe feminine limbs twitched without warning. Strong. Punches and kicks to the air. More than a few struck him.

The strangest Cage match of his life.

The consequences extended beyond winning and losing. He wasn't accustomed to long games.

All he could do was tend to the woman he held. He focused on Nynn. The hair he'd cut short was not entirely blond, as he'd assumed in her cell. It was tinged with streaks of copper. A half dozen strands here and there. Thin as filaments. Ethereal as ghosts. Her freckles covered more than her cheeks. Nape, shoulder blades, and forearms—all touched by a faint dusting of beige color. He traced a line of them up her neck. He didn't know what caused her to shiver at that moment, but he tightened his arms.

He wanted the cause to have been his touch.

"Promise, promise, promise . . ."

Her chant grew stronger as her body began to still. More voice. Less frantic fighting. Leto exhaled against her damp skin. He forced his muscles to release. Slowly. The adrenaline rush of combat, no matter how strange, began to ebb. First his legs, where hers no longer kicked. Their limbs were sticky with sweat. Locked together. Then his arms—softer now, as she eased back.

His chest became her wall, although he remained hyperconscious of the damage done to her back.

A quick-fire fury reignited at the thought of what he'd seen done to her. Hellix. That thick, powerful whip. Nasty smiles and debauched taunts.

Nynn's breath shuddered with every ragged inhale and sloppy, off-tempo exhale. Even that pattern wasn't normal. Warriors breathed hard and fast after a tough contest, yet always with the rhythm of lungs and heart working together. Her body had no grace. No balance.

He pressed his mouth against her damp, salty temple. "What do you promise?"

"Save my son."

"One year, Nynn. You will."

"Burn it all down . . ."

Leto frowned on a sharp intake of hot, electric air. He banked his surprise as Ulia was the first to emerge from her trance. The old woman looked toward him with those eerie, dull bronze eyes.

"Was it a success?"

That was not worry in his voice. He was only evaluating whether a tool at his disposal would be ready for its time in the Cage.

Ulia smiled in a way that gave him no assurances. "Of course. Nynn will have full control of her powers now. She may even outshine you, champion." She cackled softly, as if her pun about Nynn's powers was intentional.

Shaking off his frustration, he stretched his aching legs. "What happened in there?"

"We freed what needed to be freed, and tucked away what needed to be tucked away."

More foreboding. Leto hated this. He couldn't remember a time when his skills and reputation hadn't been enough to solve a problem. The whole night had been a study in just that. Frustration built under his skin. With the collars deactivated there in the Cage, his gift became a flood of water ready to burst through a dam. He could destroy concrete and wrought iron and steel.

Nynn coughed. Gasped. Jerked nearly to her knees. Only Leto's arms kept her from toppling. Watching her wobble because of muscle fatigue after a hard day's training was one thing. Satisfying. Goals achieved. To see her disoriented and graceless for so many hours was disconcerting. This creature hadn't returned from a hellish place. Not yet. That it existed in her own mind was not something he could shake away. He'd suffered it as well. Looking too closely would mean admitting the same dark places lurked inside of him—darker than he already knew.

"Nynn," he said. "Sit still. Breathe with me."

Slowly, with exaggerated care, he showed her the rhythm she needed for respiration. He stroked her bare arm with the same tempo. She nodded in time as well. They were more attuned than Leto had ever been with another being. Rather than push that realization away, he hid it. Kept it for later. A Cage warrior could not afford softness.

Yet he was a champion. Surely that meant one small concession.

"Leto," Nynn whispered. She turned in his arms. She touched the head and the tail of his tattoo. Soft fingertips shook where she traced lines of ink and his throbbing veins. She lowered her head until her mouth nestled behind his ear. "I have a serpent, too."

"Where is yours?"

The touch of her hot, wet tongue against his skin was as unexpected as it was provoking. "Behind my breast. It waits to bring down our opponents."

"Good." Better than good. He smiled against her roughly cut hair. "It will be a treat to share victory with another. Something new."

He swallowed. Exhaled. She had barely emerged from a psychic trance. The desire he felt had no place in that moment, but the need remained. Changed. Stronger. More dangerous.

He meant what he'd said. The prospect of standing beside this unflinching woman while the crowd cheered their shared triumph was incredible. He wouldn't be alone. His heartbeat sped and his body swiftly roused. Concern plunged straight back down to primal need. He'd never had a partner in the Cages. They shared the same goal: win. Win again and again.

They could share that triumph as lovers. Fierce. Together.

Yet her groggy words would not leave his mind.

*Burn it all down . . .*

He wanted to ask Ulia what it meant. Something stilled his tongue. For now, the ritual had been a success. He had a partner who might be more than a burden, more than a tool. That was all he needed to know.

Ulia levered onto her feet with great difficulty. Leto would've aided the old woman, but Nynn needed just as much help in standing.

Her smile quirked. "You can let go now."

Leto nearly matched her grin. Nynn seemed lighter. More at ease. The change was hard to pinpoint. A certain cockiness in the set of her shoulders? A brow smoothed of so many worry lines? Even his ability to read a fellow Dragon King fell short.

Forcing himself to release her arms, he stepped back. Nynn took a deep breath that seemed significant. Exhaled. Tossed her head in a way that once would've flung long, pale hair back over her shoulder. "I'm eating today, Leto. I'm sleeping. And I'm not training for a single minute."

A laugh escaped him. He couldn't help it. She was no longer a neophyte, despite her lack of experience in an actual Cage match. The confidence and competence shimmered off her. Stronger now. Undeniably powerful. Almost savage.

Dragon be, he wanted her.

"Yes, you're eating today. Tomorrow we'll learn to coordinate our strengths and weaknesses."

She tilted her head, still wearing a teasing smile. "You have weaknesses?"

"Few. Very few."

"That *will* be interesting."

Drawn by a newfound camaraderie, he stepped closer and touched her chin. Perhaps it was his relief that made him relent. She wanted a piece of her old life. Who was he to deny whatever would propel her through the tough months to come?

"Audrey, you will get your son back."

She flinched. Drew back. Frowned—just when he'd gotten used to her fine, smooth brow and another pattern of freckles. "My name is Nynn."

He shrugged. "If you'd rather."

"And you must have me mistaken with some other neophyte. I had no idea you trained so many."

"What do you mean?"

"Leto, I have no son."

He went very, very still. His lungs had stopped working. Quickly, he searched for Ulia. She stood outside the Cage. An enigmatic smile turned her face into a mass of overlapping wrinkles. "The Old Man will be pleased, don't you think?"

Leto grabbed Nynn's arms. Gave her a shake. Harder. Her injuries would heal but he needed to get through to her—to her mind—as if his will alone could undo the last few hours. As if that would ease the sudden plummet in his gut.

"If not for your son, then why will you fight? *Tell me.*"

"For the same reason you do," she said calmly. "For the glory of the Asters."

# ✦ CHAPTER ✦ SEVENTEEN

Nynn woke with a massive headache and little memory of what had happened the night before.

Night. As if anyone could tell light from dark when underground. The bare bulbs were out, so that meant night. There was no other way to mark time other than the schedule Leto set for her training. She was grateful for the attention from the Asters' champion. Being given over to a lesser warrior's tutelage would mean her defeat.

The idea of defeat was as powerful as the idea of death.

Leto was fast becoming more than a trainer. She remembered being at odds with him as if watching the memories of another woman. Why had she been so contentious? She should've been paying attention from day one. And why, for so long, had she denied her attraction to him? He was a godlike man—a living example of why Dragon Kings should be revered. All graceful power. His skills made him impressive, and his teachings had made her strong, but he possessed a magnetism she no longer wanted to refuse.

Despite her headache and how her back throbbed,

she lay in the dark and combed through the images of how he'd held her. How he breathed. How he caressed. How he kissed.

She hadn't seen him with the right eyes. Blinded by pride, she was of Tigony blood. From the house of the Giva, no less. Her condescension and a few years of martial training in her youth had made her stubborn—just enough knowledge to be a danger to herself. She'd wasted too much time.

Why she'd put old Tigony biases above her survival was beyond her. Aside from Mal, they'd treated her like dirt. Worse than dirt. Dirt could nurture crops. She was more like the barren rock aisles jutting up from the Aegean. Pretty. Useless.

Not anymore. That wasn't her world anymore, trying to fit in where no one wanted her. This was a new day.

Or it would be soon.

Aside from her pounding skull, she felt good. Refreshed, even. She sat up and ran a hand over all of her aching places. Her recollection of their last training session was fuzzy. Her powers were still so big and strange that she closed her eyes when she set them free. Gaps in her memory made sense. They must've gone a full twelve rounds with how much pain pulsed down her back and thighs. Yet the flesh beneath her fingertips was whole.

A Dragon King's gift was a mysterious, powerful thing.

Nynn of Clan Tigony could harness lightning. Pull it into a sphere so beautiful that she was reluctant to let it go, make it burn, set it free. But she would. Leto would be her partner in her first Cage match. He needed her. Relied on her. And they both had reasons to fight.

He would provide comfort to his sister.

She would . . .

There in the dark of her cell, where the only sound was trickling water from the crevice in the corner, Nynn frowned again.

The lights above her winked on. She blinked away her confusion and stood. Stretched. Shook out the last of her foggy fatigue. That strangeness must be the remnants of an unpleasant dream. She knew who she was and she knew her place: in the Cage.

Excitement merged with a case of nerves. She'd only ever practiced. The idea of stepping into a real Cage, with clay beneath her boots and a crowd roaring its approval, was too much to imagine. Her first time would give detail to her vague, eager visions.

"Armor on," Leto called as he strode up the corridor. "Today's the day."

"Today . . . ?" Even as she tried to sort her memories, she was already obeying his command by gathering her things. "I thought we had more time to prepare."

"You must've lost track of time. You've worked hard these last few days."

He crossed his arms and leaned against the nearest wall, as was his habit. He looked . . . magnificent. Whatever armor he'd worn in the past must've been for the sake of training. This set was immaculate. Polished bronze accented black metal as dark and lustrous as onyx. Protective layers over his right shoulder accentuated the breadth of his upper body, while his bare left shoulder revealed striated, defined muscle. The leather wrapped around his forearms seemed to be a part of him. Stronger. More supple. Not on its own, but because of the toned flesh it protected. More leather tucked around his waist and laced around his thighs, clinging and accentuating his strength.

He was freshly shaved. Defiant jaw. Lean cheeks. Raised chin. Even his hair was shorter. Dark. So dark. She ran a hand over her own cropped hair and felt a rush of camaraderie.

"You're going to need to dress faster than that," he said, "if you want to meet the Old Man before we begin the match."

"Of course."

One eyebrow lifted only a fraction. She read more of his cocky, amused mood from the way he widened his stance. He pushed his shoulder blades flush against the wall. Chest out. Taller now. More intimidating. Only, she wasn't intimidated anymore. She couldn't remember why she had been.

More likely, she'd probably thought him beneath her. Clan Garnis. The Lost. What did they know about tradition and long millennia of controlling their human subjects? The idea of having anything to learn from a man of such wandering stock must've been laughable.

She wasn't laughing now; she was staring.

Rather than rush through her preparations, Nynn crossed the training cell—not toward the pile of her armor, but toward Leto. Wearing only her leather trousers and the tank top she slept in, she was conscious, so conscious, of his dark eyes following her. No animal. No beast. This was a man who knew his place in the world. Reveled in it. She was becoming the woman he wanted her to be, but he was still Leto. Her mentor. She wanted to touch him, to bask in his courage.

"Do you believe that I deserve to stand in a Cage with you?"

"Yes." He said it with such confidence.

She needed to close her eyes. His approval. It meant more to her than she could explain. All she knew was that the rush of sensation upon hearing that one word was liquid and warming.

"May I?" She lifted her gaze to the head of his snake tattoo. His fresh buzz cut left it clearly visible. "I want to see it. All of it."

"That would mean turning my back to you."

"I'm not your enemy, remember?" She grinned. "Besides, you haven't armed me yet. Collar on. No knife in hand. What could you fear from me?"

"Nothing." But then he swallowed.

Nynn hid her surprise, her curiosity, and reached up to touch the snake's hissing tongue. First, just skin beneath her fingers, where that tongue licked toward his smooth temple. She pushed back. Farther. The hair beneath her fingertips was stubbly but not coarse. She traced the body of the serpent until he was left with a choice: let that be the end of her exploration, or turn.

He watched her with unmistakable curiosity. Unmistakable even for him. Normally reading his expressions was like casting rune stones, a trick only the wild Pendray in the Highlands knew how to do. Right then, however, he lifted his coal-dark brows even higher. A muscle twitched along his scarred lip. Nearly a smile? A dare?

No, *accepting* a dare.

He turned slowly. Nynn had free rein to continue the path of that black serpent. It lay only partially concealed behind rich velvet hair. The tattoo ink was so dark. She tipped her finger to another angle. Fingernail now. The clash of swords and the swing of a scythe weren't enough to make this fantastic male specimen flinch, but the scrape of her fingernail did. She shivered in response.

Still he turned. So slowly. She flicked her gaze between the tattoo and the portion of his back left bare by his crisscrossed armor straps. Muscles flexed and pulled, even with that achingly patient pace. The overhead bulbs cast extreme shadows. Every ridge sharper. Every curve more graceful. New patterns of light and dark and flesh were revealed no matter how insignificant his movement.

That sounded poetic, even to Nynn. Had she always thought to describe things with an artist's eye, or was Leto just special? After all, he was man enough to inspire poetry in any mind. Throughout human history, odes had been written and masterpieces had been created to honor Dragon Kings.

Olympus. Thebes. Varanasi. Cahokia. Skara Brae.

No matter the city, no matter the tribe, men such as Leto had walked among human beings and reigned as gods. Awed subjects had looked upon such perfect bodies and found generous muses. Now she was touching him. Scraping his skin with one ragged fingernail.

He turned to face her, so that she finished with the serpent's tail—slim, slimmer, gone—just at his other temple.

Their eyes met. Gold sparked between them. They both blinked and Nynn drew her hand away.

"Why the tattoo?"

"Initiation ceremony. If you do well tonight, you might be offered the same honor."

She smiled, which always seemed to catch him off guard. "I don't intend to do well."

"That's not the attitude of a—"

"Of a champion?" Her smile widened. "I know it's not. Are you listening to your neophyte, Leto of Clan Garnis?"

His brows pinched toward the bridge of his nose. Confusion didn't suit him but she enjoyed taking him by surprise. "Yes, I'm listening."

"I intend to be *astonishing*. Be ready to keep up."

Leto didn't need to watch her dress for the Cage. He'd seen her prepare often enough. Details stayed with him, whether he wanted them or not. Three weeks had emblazoned her across his senses.

Except for touch. He would never get enough of touch.

So he lingered. This was her first Cage fight. He wanted her to help him show up the Old Man. Not that he'd dare say it. Too petty. Even petulant. All he knew was that the head of the Aster cartel had reservations about Leto's successes. With Nynn at his side, he would prove those reservations ridiculous.

He adjusted her armor and cinched the straps across her back. He lingered. Just as she'd traced his tattoo, he also needed to touch. Her back was a mess of cuts and whip marks. Most had healed, even if the skin still appeared puffy and red. He placed two fingers on either side of a long, angry slash and traced it down—from shoulder to where her skin disappeared beneath layers of metal and leather.

Hellix. The bastard. And Dr. Aster as his puppeteer.

Leto needed purpose. He found the fruition of that purpose staring up at him when Nynn turned. An untested warrior. A resilient woman. Her potent femininity collided with his body's repressed needs. They were trainer and neophyte, but the fire in her icy eyes said she wanted more. A rough sort of want, no more gentle than the armor they wore.

Any gentler touch had no place between them.

Yet he'd held her while Ulia probed Nynn's mind. He'd felt every tremble and each unconscious twist of her fingers against his skin. He'd smelled her hair and the sharp stench of dried blood. He just kept holding, as if in penance for the pain he could not save her from on that whipping post.

Or in the labs.

Or when her family was destroyed.

She'd come out of that session a different woman—apparently one who could stare him down. A woman who could touch him. Study him. Make him feel something very new. For a warrior who'd honed his reflexes and his senses for two decades, feeling anything new was both novel and unsettling.

Of course he remembered the continuous burning bite of the tattoo needle after his first victory in a Grievance. He'd been only sixteen—too young to receive an official initiation. But the Old Man had made an exception, because no sixteen-year-old had ever been invited to fight in a Grievance. No one had expected him to live. Possibly not even his father.

Leto had triumphed.

When he'd bowed his head to receive his tattoo, adrenaline yet pumped in his veins. Celebratory cups of *golish* had softened his brain. He'd been lucky that his heightened senses were damped. Back then, he hadn't been able to carry over as much of his gift once the collar was reactivated. Otherwise the prick, prick, prick of the tattoo needle might have been too much to handle.

After a lifetime of practice, he'd learned to control all of it. When to feel. When to cut off feeling. Yet he still felt her nail trailing along the serpent's undulating body. Over and over. A tickle across the back of his skull. And he still felt the skin of her back where he'd traced his fingers.

All he could do was keep her safe now. They would conquer all comers.

"I'll wait for you outside the gate," he said roughly.

He left her cell—which wouldn't be her cell much longer. Victory in that evening's match would see her established in a warrior's dorm. She would have privacy and small luxuries. In other words, she would not be his to control so completely.

Frustrated, edgy, he waited outside the locked gate for Nynn to emerge.

A shiver crept up his back like a spider's eight legs. The neophyte who'd insisted on being called Audrey had defied him at every turn. Only the goal of saving her son had given her strength and purpose. That goal had helped him justify why he pushed her so hard. That their goals were so compatible only eased the process.

This woman . . . This was Nynn of Tigony.

She wore her perfectly fitted armor with confidence as she strode into the light. Blond hair glimmered and cast spiky shadows across her forehead and cheeks.

Those freckles gave her features extra depth. Texture, even. Something untenable and unique to her.

Any woman could move with poise when wrapped in flowing silk. It took a warrior to move with the same grace when outfitted for battle.

Underneath it all, she still bore the red slashes of punishment for having tried to escape. And she didn't seem to recall any of it.

Leto smashed his doubts into pieces. If he tried hard enough, he wouldn't remember them by the time they reached the Cage. The workings of her mind were not his to ponder. He couldn't afford to care, not with Pell's future at stake.

The guards let her out of the cell and secured her hands with manacles. Leto held his hands out as well. She angled him an arch look. "You, too? Why?"

"Because we're leaving the complex. The Old Man never hosts visitors down here. We're escorted to where the guests assemble around the full-size Cage."

"Ah, so you have been outside. You've seen the sun."

He kept from curling his hands into fists. No show of limitation. The simple recitation of fact. "No."

"What do you mean, no?"

"What would you think of such a thing if you lived your whole life belowground?"

Her lower lip rubbed over the upper, which plumped them both. He hated his gifts for cluttering his mind with distracting details.

"I'd see it as an enemy," she said. "A disadvantage."

"And the Old Man knows it. We travel in buses and wear blindfolds between."

"Safer."

"Necessary. Any visiting warrior would be at a serious disadvantage."

"But if we looked?" She shook her head.

"What?"

"If we didn't wear the blindfolds, we could see where we are? Cities. Mountains. Rural Dragon-knows-where. That could be important."

She sounded as if she were speaking through a long, long tube of glass. Distant, even to herself. Whatever Ulia had done, Nynn had come out with her powers—and no apparent memory of fighting to free her son. He didn't want to mention her little boy again, for fear of reversing her real potential. Or splitting her mind in two.

So he maneuvered her. He didn't like it. It felt more like the sort of games the Tigony would play. Tricksters.

"Glory is only found in the Cages. Why would it matter where they are?"

She nodded firmly. The clouds of confusion ebbed from her eyes. "Then let's do this."

# CHAPTER EIGHTEEN

Leto had proven honest about all matters pertaining to combat, and to Nynn's survival in his world. Why wouldn't he? Arming her with information was as much of an advantage as arming her with skills and weapons.

So when human guards blindfolded her, she acquiesced. Every advantage. She would face genuine opponents. None of the contests between Dragon Kings would be to the death. Her pride, however, was on the line. She wanted to prove herself to those she served, and to Leto.

She was led outside. Two guards held her elbows. Guiding. Restraining. They didn't need to bother. She was as eager as she'd ever been. Only when the rush of cold, fresh air, hit her face did she flinch. She hesitated enough for the guards to jerk her forward.

The smell of snow.

*It's been more than a year. Free air.*

The cold tingled in her nostrils and spread goose bumps across her exposed left shoulder. Her nape prickled. She'd had long hair the last time she walked in the cold. Like a soft blanket draping down her back.

*When was that? Where was I?*

A headache gathered between her brows. The guards prodded her lower back. More force. Less patience for whatever fit had taken hold of her mind. Soon she had climbed three steps onto an idling vehicle that stank of diesel. One of the buses Leto had mentioned. Old and new collided in her mind, no matter how she tried to focus on the next few hours. A sort of panic made her heart speed.

The darkness of the blindfold. The pressure of the guards' hands. The biting manacles. Her pulse raced and her headache intensified. Panic. She couldn't breathe. Cold snow. Diesel. Long hair. She struggled, fell, groped for purchase.

A pair of strong hands hauled her up and deposited her on a seat. "I should've included walking lessons, too? Didn't realize."

Leto's voice was a low purr against her neck. Darkness. With him. Excitement of a different kind replaced the Cages and the disorientation. To be alone in the dark with him. But with no boundaries of leather. Skin on skin.

Breathing had been difficult, cluttered with strange thoughts. Now it was impossible. He had seen all of her. She had not seen all of him. Her imagination did its damnedest to fill in the mysteries. Her personal darkness, there behind the blindfold, was shaded with images of tan skin. Flexing muscles. Sweat. Swagger. Deadly purpose and strength. Dark eyes that watched and assessed. A mouth meant for bold kisses. A body honed for combat and sex.

"You can't see either?"

He grunted an affirmative. "I told you as much."

"You sound so calm," she said. "At ease."

"We're on our way to victory. Of course I'm at ease."

What about the disorientation? Or the terror Nynn couldn't articulate? Or the restlessness of spirit that burned her sightless eyes with tears. She couldn't feel at ease. Not like that. Not like him. Some facet of her training, maybe. She was missing something.

"You're ready for this, Nynn. You have no reason to be this skittish."

The bus's engine fired to life and began to move. It sounded familiar, yet altered. All she could do was cling to what she knew. Leto's voice—that hypnotic, magnetic rumble. His words of encouragement. His warmth created a bubble of intimacy between them. She fumbled for his hand.

He flinched again, the same as when she'd touched his temple. Yet he'd been bold as well. Touching her back. She had enjoyed the attention, but she also remembered that they'd kissed. Hard kisses. His body had levered above hers, strong and resolved. The why and where didn't matter, only a ghostly impression of having been entirely at Leto's whim.

He was her compass now.

Nynn tightened her fingers. A simple gesture. Hands together. She needed that reassurance. The contact seemed to unmoor him faster than any attack. Images of bare, damp flesh were replaced by the comfort of having something warm to hold on to in the dark.

She'd needed that before. Holding . . . in the terrible black . . .

"Breathe."

His low command wove into her like hot honey. Just

enough sting. Just enough sweet. Nynn exhaled. Inhaled. He kept hold of her hand and she gave up the unknowns. Too many awaited in the Cage. At least there, she had the skills and confidence to take on whatever stood in her way.

"I'm breathing," she said. Then more firmly. "I'm breathing."

The trip wasn't long, more or less a half hour. Nynn spent that time mentally running through drills and holding Leto's hand. He made no move to encourage her. No move to push her away.

When the bus stopped, he let her make her own way. How very like him. The brief minutes of silent connection—done now. Good. She needed to focus on something other than how reassuring his touch was. The roughness of his palms. The blunt weight of his bones. Again she felt a surge of wonder and awe that she would fight beside such a warrior.

And again, she wondered why she'd resisted his instruction for so long. A waste of time.

Outside. The smell of snow. She didn't like it. Too much disquiet in her soul.

The warmth of a new building couldn't come soon enough. It enveloped her and blocked out the eerie strangeness of being outdoors. She belonged in the complex.

*The smell of snow.*

A guard removed her blindfold. She, Leto, and ten other Aster family warriors stood in a hallway. It was probably larger than it seemed, but so many tall, broad, bristling men stole every square inch of perspective. They may as well have been crammed into a child's dollhouse.

Silence stood nearby, with Hark beside her as close as a shadow—that curious, formidable pair. They watched the world as if it contained as many secrets as their clan harbored. Nynn would never consider them allies, but she didn't tally them among her enemies either.

Hellix, however, seemed born to make enemies of everyone. He looked as if he'd lost more contests than most would ever fight.

"Virgin match." His brand looked even more hideous in the dim light. No telling skin from shadow from lumped tissue. "You'll share the spoils with me."

She disliked the man. That was nothing new. But the desire to run, just *run*, almost overpowered rational thought. Pain lanced through her head. Deeper. Lower. She could feel it flailing at her back and hear strangled, pleading cries.

Just nerves. Eagerness. She swallowed a surprising twist of bile at the base of her tongue. Hellix was not going to intimidate her.

"If you want," Nynn said with a shrug. "Would be fun to take you down first."

His armor was highly polished but plain. Perhaps it was a reminder that he would only ever hold so much status. The reverence Leto had achieved would always be out of reach. "I'd wager it's been a long time since you've been fucked."

An instant reply formed in her mind.

*Leto would kill you first.*

It was ridiculous. Beyond satisfying the Old Man's expectations, Leto needed her for no other purpose. His dislike of Hellix would be more of an incentive to beat the man than anything to do with her. Yet she liked the thought. It warmed her in the same way that holding Leto's hand on the bus had warmed her. Something to clasp in the dark, even if it was just a delusion.

"You try that and we'll see who lives to see the next day," she said quietly. "It might not be me, but you'd lose a limb or two. Maybe even your prick. And then what would you have left to use when throwing around threats?"

"I'll bring the whip. We enjoyed it so much last time."

Nynn frowned in confusion, but an insult was ready on her tongue. "Save it for the ring, knife-branded scum."

He stepped within inches and leaned close to her ear. "I'll break one bone. You'll scream. And before you finish screaming, I'll have broken *all* of them."

"What's your clan, Hellix? I don't remember which one's gift is wishful thinking."

Hark laughed. "Leto, is this how you've spent your time? Teaching her how to talk trash? That's a bold approach. I should consider a refresher course."

"No need, you idiot clown," Hellix snarled.

Leto shouldered through the other combatants and looked down one inch. The exact difference in height between him and Hellix. "Shut up."

Although Silence didn't say anything, a slinky smile tipped the edges of her lips. Hark grinned and rested his chin on her shoulder, as if settling in to watch. He whispered something in his partner's ear. Her tiny smile increased. The pair was as enigmatic as the Sphinx, there in the Nile Valley where the Sath staked their territory.

Another woman named Weil of Clan Pendray looked on with utter detachment—which wouldn't last when she let loose her manic fury. Leaning against one of the beige walls, Fam laughed outright. After so many weeks deciphering Leto's tightly reined expressions, that laugh was grating, like shouting during a wedding ceremony.

The sooner she could fight, the better.

When the doors behind them were secured, the ones ahead of them opened. A long airlock. Leto turned away from Hellix without haste. He pushed a path through the others and led the way. A primal shot of lightning struck pleasure through Nynn's body. The hollow behind her breastbone tingled. Her fingers prickled with the remembered feel of his short hair and the soft, warm skin of his temples. Her lips tingled, wanting another taste of him.

She ignored Silence, Hark, Hellix, and anyone else who wasn't Leto, then followed him toward the other doors. There, guards removed the manacles. She shook her wrists and circled them clockwise, counterclockwise. She popped her knuckles. Rolled her neck. Adrenaline mixed with the scent of Leto's skin and the warmed leather of his armor. They stood that close.

"This way," he said. "The Old Man wants to meet you before the matches begin."

Although the guards technically encircled them, Leto strode through the maze of hallways, sloping corridors, and stairwells as if he'd been born to the task. Very nearly. Every glance she shot toward his profile revealed the same locked-down expression. Stoic, calm, but with a concealed, buzzing energy. Maybe it was the way his eyes never stopped moving, or the way he occasionally slid his jaw from side to side. From Leto, it was practically fidgeting.

She anticipated the moment they would stand together in the Cage and she would see when the collars deactivated. His powers returned to him. Sexual release had never looked so enticing. She wanted to see it, then see it again—a unexpected reward for surviving each match.

"Leto," came a voice.

Beneath wrapped leather, the hair on Nynn's forearms tried to stand on end. Those on her nape did. Before their assembly of large men and formidable women, all deadly warriors, stood warped and stooped Old Man Aster. He supported his weight with a cane, although there wasn't much to support. Skeletons had more bulk and more color. He was a corpse with a jester's wide smile.

"And Nynn," he continued. "Welcome. I anticipate what you have to show us this evening."

"I hope to earn your respect, sir."

He angled a bizarre look toward Leto. "Interesting."

That seemed . . . anticlimactic. He added an extra layer of strange to the moment by turning to greet other combatants. Was he that detached?

She caught up with Leto's long strides. "How many times did you say that the Old Man had picked me out? That he had some big plan for me?"

They were admitted to a weapons room, full to brimming with every manner of metal and steal and wood. "Enough for you to believe it," he said, selecting his favorite. The mace.

"And that was all we get? A sneer and a noncommittal comment? He should've offered some kind of congratulations."

"He didn't sneer." From a wall of swords and daggers, he selected three before turning to face her. "And why congratulate a warrior who has yet to win? There's no value in praise offered before it's earned."

"Is that why you never congratulate me?"

Leto's eyes glimmered, as black and shining as the accents on his armor. They narrowed. Dark brows drew together. Only a person who was really looking for those clues would find them. "If we win, we'll be congratulating each other. You remember what I said about how warriors are rewarded, don't you?"

"Sex."

"Yes."

"Winner's choice."

"Yes," he said again, his intensity as strong as any touch.

Nynn stepped to within inches of his armored masculine beauty. She lifted her hands and cupped his skull, tracing her thumbs along his temples. The head and the tail of the serpent. "And what happens if we both win? Will you choose me, Leto?"

"No. You'll choose me." He pulled away from her hands, turning toward the wall of weapons. "Now. We will select your dagger."

He didn't make a suggestion. He didn't even hold one blade slightly more forward than the others. All he did was present them as equals. Other warriors from the Aster family came and went, took what they needed. Their insults and buoyant boasts were the buzzing of insects. Leto would shut them all out until he needed to see them again—as opponents, or as victorious comrades.

He only waited for Nynn. "Choose."

"You said 'we' will select. That implies you giving me a clue."

"These are the three that will best fit your frame and the size of your hands. They're lightweight, sturdy, and you should be able to hold on to them even when you use your gift."

The trio gleamed in the armory's ambient lighting. One was decorated with gold leaf. One copper, edged in green. One plain steel.

"So is this some sort of test? Pick the plain one. Or pick the ugly one. Dragon forbid I go all girly and choose the pretty one."

"It's a test, but not like that. How well do you know your abilities?"

A tight pressure gathered in his lungs, which were already tight from the prospect of sharing one another after their victory. They had to get there first. No matter his outward confidence—confidence in himself, really—he couldn't deny that Nynn was a wild animal.

As for the long daggers, he knew which one would make her a champion. He wanted *her* to know as well. Proof he'd done well. Proof they had more than a chance at victory.

*I intend to be astonishing.*

He wanted that nearly as much as he wanted victory for himself. And afterward, after the applause . . . they would unleash that potency on each other. Dragon damn, he wanted this woman.

"Let me hold them," she said.

Leto nodded. Yes, that was the first step toward making the right choice.

One by one, she took the blades in hand. Hark and Silence entered the armory. Per their custom, he chose a silver *nighnor* and she picked a shield with a slim profile and razor-sharp edges. Both stopped, watched Nynn for a moment, then moved on. Hark was markedly quieter than usual. Before a match, even their resident chatterbox had enough sense to know when to shut up.

"This one," Nynn said.

Something close to disappointment settled in his lungs, as if he breathed heavier air. She'd chosen the plain steel sword. Fine. A good weapon. But it was not as elegant as her movements. The blade had little give and no flair.

"Good enough," he managed to say.

What had happened to the easy confidence he'd felt during the ride over? The closer they got to the start of the match, the more he doubted.

"You think I made a bad choice?"

"You made a choice. Who knows what way the match will play out." He handed her a particular shield, offering no room for error this time. "We haven't much time."

Nynn gnashed her upper teeth into her lower lip. She shook her head. "You're impossible. I'm trying to learn and you're playing cryptic master of secrets."

"What happened to being astonishing?"

"It'd be nice if I had some help!"

"Shut up, neophyte."

"Save it for Hellix, *sir*." She strapped the scabbard around her waist. "Now, who do we butcher first?"

"Is this still a joke to you? Even still? Dragon damn, woman. I will not step foot in a Cage with you if that's how you think."

"Go take it up with the Old Man."

She hefted her shield into place. The pivot of her heel turned her in a perfect half circle.

She froze, screamed, and drew her sword. Because Dr. Aster stood in the doorway, with the Pet at his feet.

Leto jumped forward and hauled her away. "Put that away, you maniac," he growled.

Nynn blinked and . . . she did as she was told.

Leto's heart became a wild beast, beating and clawing, as she sheathed her weapon. If he'd needed any more proof that Ulia had changed Nynn, perhaps irrevocably, he had it now.

# ✦ CHAPTER ✦ NINETEEN

Dr. Aster smiled, just short of repulsive. "My father informed me that tonight would be a special occasion. Our newest champion?"

Leto nodded, his stomach lurching. "She is untested, but I believe her ready to honor the Asters."

"Good. Then many lessons were learned the other night." He glanced at Nynn, who was puzzled. Or angry. Or sleepwalking. Leto couldn't tell, but Dr. Aster seemed very pleased. "And what do you say, neophyte? What is your name?"

"Nynn of Clan Tigony."

"Hmm. I thought you were called something else. Are you sure?"

"Yes, sir."

Leto slowly let her go. Part of him was convinced this was some elaborate ruse on her part, that she'd attack and murder the reptilian man. Dragon be, part of him *wanted* that to be true. He was on the verge of caring too much. Nynn's pain had been so obvious—nearly as obvious as the scars marring her gorgeous body.

That scream. Instant recognition. Then gone.

"And I'm Dr. Aster. A pleasure to meet you, Nynn."

Her fingers were tight around the hilt of her sword. Tight enough to clear the blood from her knuckles. Bone white. "Thank you, sir."

"I'm impressed, Leto. Few would've thought this one possible to tame."

"She's not tamed, sir. She's *trained.*" If Nynn could manage to be calm, so could he.

"Exactly. I'm glad you haven't taken it personally. You know now what had to be done."

"All I know is what you'll see in the Cage."

"I look forward to it. Come along," he said to the woman at his feet.

The Pet didn't leave right away. She glided toward them as if she floated rather than walked. Again she wore a bodysuit of skintight black leather. A spiked collar circled her neck, but Leto couldn't tell if it had damping properties, or if it was just a jagged bauble to decorate a strange, beautiful creature.

She stopped within inches of Nynn, who remained still. Although the Pet moved with unbelievable grace, her voice was sure and clipped. "The Chasm isn't fixed."

Leto frowned and was glad to see when Nynn did, too. "I don't know what that means," she said.

"Fight well, Nynn of Tigony."

Only when the woman departed did Nynn press two fingertips to each temple. She clenched her eyes shut. Sat heavily.

"No time for that," Leto said roughly. There was no time for patience. "We fight. Now."

She opened her eyes and blinked back what looked like tears. But her gaze was clear, strong, energized. "Good."

He led Nynn—a little dazed, but remarkably steady on her feet—toward a gathering anteroom where the combatants were given their assignments.

Nynn stood at his shoulder, trying to read the paper he held. Her smile was brilliant, with teasing lips that bordered perfect, almost small white teeth. Whatever shock and possible memories from her encounter with the doctor had faded entirely. "So, who do we get to humiliate?"

"You're taking to this rather well."

"Careful, Leto. That almost sounded like a joke."

He stilled. Chills shivered beneath his armor. The hair atop his head itched with a sudden prickle of sensation. She had used his given name before, but now they had the promise of victory between them. All that could entail. He would hear her gasp his name when he entered her.

Another weakness. And another reason to win.

"The Pendray woman, Weil," he said. "And Urman, sent by the Townsends."

"What's his clan? I can't recall."

"Tigony."

"Too bad for him. No trickster gets by another." She walked an appreciative glance down his body, then back up to his face. A deep pulse of awareness radiated out from her smile, into him. "Let's do this."

Nynn followed Leto. She had never been so overwhelmed.

The crowd surrounding a real combat Cage was thick. Loud. Eager. Men in suits and women in evening gowns. Bodyguards and strange shadowy figures. Possibly even other Dragon Kings, if their distinctive bronzed skin and larger-than-life auras were any indication. That they would associate so freely among humans struck her as peculiar. She couldn't make sense of it.

There was a lot she couldn't make sense of lately.

Like why seeing that doctor had propelled hand to hilt. She'd been ready to take off his head. She'd envisioned it. The spray of blood. The strike of metal against flesh, then deeper into bone. And then deeper still, into a place of satisfaction. Even justice.

Those images were the remnants of some dream. Leto had done her a favor by intervening. Her opponents were in the Cages, not among the Asters.

There was no mistaking the grandeur of where she would do battle. Leto had described it perfectly. Larger. Brighter. An ominous pall of significance made it far more than a place to spar and learn. This was a place where futures were determined.

Probably a thousand people circled the Cage—a complete circle of spectators around the familiar octagonal framework. Lights shone with the brightness of day. Only then did she realize that each corridor since the one they'd entered upon arriving was slightly brighter. A slow means of acclimating them to what would shine down like another enemy.

She kept her eyes on Leto's boots. Better to ignore the crowd. Better to focus. She wore armor, carried a weapon and a shield, and climbed up eight webbed wrought iron stairs behind one of the greatest warriors among the Dragon Kings. Their names were announced.

A Cage warrior. The stuff of legend and nightmares. Nynn didn't feel like a nightmare; she felt like a blade. Sharp and ready to cut.

Despite countless distractions, she waited for the moment she'd come to relish: when Leto stepped into the Cage. He tipped his head to the ceiling. His expression became as animated as any she'd ever seen. He was in his element and *reveling* in it. Holding his mace and shield, he lifted his arms as if to encompass the arena, then turned to stake his claim over the entire building. He roared back at the crowd.

Part man. Part animal.

Nynn followed him inside. The same gorgeous rush of freedom stole her breath. Power. Just *power*. This was what it meant to have full possession of her Dragon-given gift. Her cells quivered inside skin two sizes too small. The clay floor was like gritty mud beneath the soles of her boots. Glaring lights atop each of eight support posts bathed them in an unearthly shimmer. The visual echo of the Dragon, perhaps, as it dove into the fiery Chasm and birthed their kind.

Two opponents entered the Cage. Weil was a short woman, as were most Pendray. She had wild red hair that stood out from her head as if zapped with electricity. But the one who truly commanded electricity was the Townsend warrior, Urman. Nynn's allegiance to the Tigony did not exist here. The only person she wanted to please right then was Leto.

Only when an official entered the Cage did she catch a shift in Leto's posture. He stood straighter, chest out. Posturing. But bristling with something close to confusion.

The official carried two manacles connected with a ten-foot length of chain. "Leto. Nynn. Your ankles."

"What in the name of the Dragon is this?" he asked.

With a triumphant sort of smile, the human official nodded toward where the Old Man sat with that doctor and the strange girl in black. "You knew the Asters wanted to make these matches interesting."

"And fighting with a partner isn't interesting enough?"

"When the Old Man meant partners, he meant it. You'll be chained together."

"Fuck that. We fight as we were meant to, not chained like dogs."

The small man—small compared to Leto, as most were—grabbed Nynn's ankle. He affixed the manacle too quickly for her to protest. Frustration like she'd never seen tightened the tendons of Leto's muscular throat. Then it was too late. They were bound together.

"And our opponents?" Nynn asked. "What of them?"

The official sneered. "Do you see another chain here, neophyte?"

Nynn removed her sword from its scabbard and absently twirled it through the air. She fairly hummed with potential. Already she could feel the bubble of electricity—all those beautiful colors, a whole spectrum—building inside her body. "No one calls me neophyte but the man who trained me, and he won't call me that after tonight. Shut your mouth."

She lifted her chin and found Leto's gaze. Their gazes locked. Without the damping properties of their collars, they produced a burst of gold and even green and blue—right there in the five feet between their bodies. The crowd gasped. She almost felt the light on her skin. It was like staring down the length of a kaleidoscope. Colors didn't wait for her at its end. Just Leto's dark eyes. Her awareness narrowed. Centered. Focused.

Only him.

Spellbinding.

"What *is* that?" Her voice was an awed whisper.

"I don't know."

She wanted to know what Old Man Aster thought of their little party trick, but she didn't want to look away from her partner.

"Do this," she said softly. With his senses, she knew he'd be able to hear. "Best fucking show they've seen in years."

The chain rattled between them, dangerous as a snake's hiss. His jaw was a granite vise and his temple throbbed, pulsing that serpent to life.

The roaring beast was gone, but the seething, outraged man remained. He would not bear this humiliation well. Nynn couldn't wait to see what he would unleash. She only hoped that she could keep up. Because no matter how much she would depend on him to emerge triumphant, his only objective was to keep her alive.

He'd do so by whatever means necessary.

Leto swallowed his anger. To be shackled again . . . chained, for the second time in as many days. Treated like an animal rather than a warrior of worth. Every fiber of every muscle protested. What good was a Garnis who was chained to a Tigony? His reflexes and speed would be useless with Nynn as his anchor.

He grabbed her shielded arm and dragged her close. "Now who needs to keep up?"

"Not ideal, is it? Think of something. Quickly." She was deadly serious.

Yes. Dragon be, *yes*.

The cheers were growing in ferocity. Across the Cage, Weil and Urman circled one another, pacing, as if taunting Leto with their unencumbered legs. Weil used her long lance to spin practice circles—strikes that would turn deadly earnest in a matter of seconds. Urman held two sickles, without a shield. If he got the timing right, the Tigony trickster could use those sickles as electrical conductors.

"I'll stand in front of you," Leto said. "We'll leave as much slack as possible, to let me move. Weil is the least predictable when she rages, but we've trained against her. Urman is the one most likely to fry our brains. Watch my back and make sure you fry them first."

"How do I do that without taking you out, too?"

The bell rang to signal the start of the match.

"Figuring that out is your job."

Within seconds, Weil was on them. Pendray warriors had the gift of a rage so intense that it eventually earned its own name: berserker. The Nordic and Celtic peoples worshiped that power. Leto thought it the least graceful method of attack. Not that it mattered when Weil charged in. She spun in what looked like wild circles. In truth, they were perfectly timed and with a precise line of attack. She never faltered or tripped, and her lance didn't dip as she became a living blender.

Leto countered her with his mace and shield. He snatched out a hand. Grabbed the end of her lance. Pain shot up his arm, from wrist to shoulder. That stopped her momentum. He caught her by the neck and tossed her against the far Cage wires.

The crowd's appreciation added to the adrenaline of a match coming into its own.

The collars reactivated, which reduced them back to hand-fighting. Weil had recovered, but her lance was in two pieces. She improvised with the skill of a long-trained warrior.

Urman whirled his sickles and edged toward Nynn. She countered as well as she could with the high angle of her shield. The ferocity of her defense made up for any lack of technique. Even Urman seemed taken aback. He retreated a pace, then renewed his scissoring assault. Sweat made her blond hair spiky and her cheeks damp. A look of wild excitement blazed from the palest eyes he'd ever seen, as if she were lit from inside with a new color of fire.

The collars flipped off and on and off again. And the chain binding him to Nynn didn't give Leto the rhythm he liked to find during a match. But there came moments, gorgeous moments, when he knew victory was in hand.

"Get behind me!" he shouted at Nynn.

She obeyed. Instantly. Leto smiled tightly.

"No more hand-fighting for you. Keep out of the way of the mace. Keep your shield up. And dredge up some Dragon-damned fireworks."

With his gift returned to him, Leto concentrated on keeping the two opponents at bay. Not defeating them. Simply keeping them away from Nynn. The chain was deadweight on the end of his leg. He'd once thought

Nynn would be that sort of hindrance. Now he was relying on her to conjure more power than anyone in that arena had ever seen.

A burst of lightning shot from Urman's sickles. Leto took the bolt with his shield. Electricity shuddered up his left arm.

"Leto?"

"Numb. Can't move it."

Urman attacked again but Leto was able to avoid it. He was born to Clan Garnis. He was a man fast enough to dodge lightning.

Weil shrieked—that wailing sonic attack. Her voice alone was enough to pierce Leto's sensitive hearing. She'd burst his eardrums before the match was over. He braced for the strike of her lance, but the clay floor was giving way. His boots slipped. He took hit after hit, where the violence shook from his shield into his numb, paralyzed arm. Only the ball joint of his shoulder directed the shield now. Graceless. No precision. Still he held the position, ready to stay there all night in order to fend off Weil.

Heat gathered at his back. At first he thought it was another burst of Urman's lightning, come to separate more of his nerves from his brain. But Urman was lying on the clay floor. Nynn's sword was embedded in his thigh. When in the Dragon's name had that happened?

That heat increased. Popping showers of sparks shimmering around. A waterfall of light.

*Nynn.*

"Get down!" she shouted.

Leto's knee hit the Cage floor. He pulled the shield over his neck and head. Pure instinct. The concussive blast propelled his face into the clay. A scream ripped through the noise of the crowd. He groaned in pain at that unearthly sound—the sound of Nynn ripping the roof off the Cage. The crowd shrieked its awed panic. Even among that chaos, Leto was disgusted by their hypocrisy.

*You wanted to see us fight. This is how we fight.*

Lights on the octagonal posts burst. Only the crackling sizzle of Nynn's gift lit the arena.

When Leto lifted his head, he grinned. Flat-out grinned. Urman was still on his back. Smoke trailed up from his thigh, where Nynn's firestorm had touched the man's sword. *May the nastiest Tigony win.* Urman hadn't stood a chance. Weil was shivering against a Cage post. She held stumps that had once been the pieces of her lance. Her eyes were wide disks. Had her chest been still, instead of furiously pumping, Leto would've assumed her a corpse.

Leto turned to congratulate his partner, only to find her equally felled. Nynn lay sprawled on the clay. Her shield was a burnt-out hollow.

The chain still connected their ankles.

He dropped his weapons, knelt, and looped the slack chain around his forearm, which was slowly regaining sensation. He grabbed Nynn beneath her arms. Dragged her upright. Shook her until she gasped. Her eyes had lost their silver shine, yet that strange, colorful glow was still there. Quieter. Maybe even spent. It was still breathtaking.

"Can't." She coughed and nearly fell. "Can't walk."

"Yes, you can," he said, fierce and low. "I'm not carrying you, neophyte. You have to stand on your own to accept this applause."

In truth, it was the loudest applause Leto had ever heard.

# ✦ CHAPTER ✦ TWENTY

Nynn could only hold on.

Leto held her hand aloft. The crowd bellowed its approval, in shades and waves of noise she couldn't process.

She held on to his sweaty, tense shoulders as the official unlocked the manacles binding their ankles.

And barely, just barely, she held on to her sanity.

Her only focus was that she had survived. More than that, she had devastated their opponents. The Pendray named Weil limped out of the Cage, while the Townsend man—some Tigony whose name bounced through her head and slipped free—was carted away by what looked to be medics. Nynn's sword was on the ground where his body had been.

"Stay with me," Leto growled. "You pass out and I'll find some new pieces of your soul to steal. You stand here and behave like a Dragon-damned champion."

He'd hit that particular timbre, even among the crazy cheers—the tone of voice that she recognized as hypnotic but was powerless to resist. She nodded. With his hand at her back, she was able to refashion the numb lumps at the bottoms of her legs into feet. Feet in boots.

Boots on scuffed floor. Leto still scowled down at her. How could a victor appear so dissatisfied and angry? Well, in her case, how could a victor feel ready to vomit and lie down on the clay?

That wasn't Leto, and that wasn't her.

She grasped his hand and lifted her chin. "I told you. Astonishing."

His lips quirked. "So I'm to trust your word now, neophyte?"

She hadn't wanted to let go of his bare shoulder, so she didn't. This was not a gesture of necessity, but one of greed. She wanted the feel of his flexing muscles and pulsing blood where she dug her fingertips into his flesh. His eyes briefly fluttered shut. She raised up on tiptoes and pitched her voice above the echoes in the Cage room. "I am no longer your neophyte."

Leto abruptly let her go and circled the Cage with a shout of victory, even more powerful than the intimidating growl he'd postured to the crowd before the match. Every step was powerful, his thighs taut. His back was arrogantly straight. His outthrust chest was accentuated even more because of that beautifully crafted armor. He swung the mace in quick, deadly arcs.

*Show-off.* But Nynn soaked up every minute, as did Leto's audience.

Only when he turned, met Nynn's eyes, and flung the mace aside did she shiver in what could only be described as anticipation. He strode toward her and positioned his body within inches of hers. "You're not wrong. You're no longer my neophyte. But you will be mine. Tonight."

"What happened to that arrogant crap about how I'd come to you?"

They stared at one another. That tingle of something otherworldly and profound glimmered between their eyes. Nynn wanted to blink if only to clear her senses, but the sensations were too seductive.

"Does it really matter who chooses whom?" Pitched so low, beneath the diminishing applause, Leto's voice was an earthquake ready to rip her open. "We're both victors."

"And if I choose someone else?"

Rather than continue his posturing menace—much better suited to those who wagered on his prowess and adored his blunt ferocity—he licked his lower lip. "Then I'll convince you otherwise. Or I'll convince your choice that you're not worth fighting me for."

"But I am. I am worth fighting for."

She said it with as much assurance as she'd ever known.

Leto's nostrils flared on a long, deep inhale. The muscles on either side of his jaw bunched, with radiated movement up to his temples, to his tattoo. "Yes."

That moment fled, like clinging to smoke and expecting it to hold her in return. Nynn followed him out of the Cage. Her body and her mind felt equally abused. She was still buzzing with an indescribable tingle of violence. If she wanted anything from Leto of Garnis, it was to strip his armor and become combatants of another sort. She wanted to get rid of her edginess, rid of the confusion that kept her from thinking clearly.

She exited the Cage just in time to see Leto and the Old Man squaring off. Before, she'd seen only deference from Leto when talking with the head of the Aster family. "Keep him away from her," Leto said with unmistakable force. "Feel free to ask him why."

The skeletal man's smile never faltered. Never even changed shape. "You overstep."

"You brought this on us all."

Leto didn't even wait for the Old Man's dismissal; he simply turned and walked out of the arena. Now Nynn was not only confused but also bereft of her partner in this madness. Although she followed him, she was unable to refrain from looking back toward the Asters' patriarch. That smile remained. Her skin shivered up her arms and down her spin.

*Keep him away from her.*

Nothing about the fight compared to the way her brain fractured on the most random thoughts.

"Trouble in paradise," came a voice at her shoulder.

Nynn found the near-inseparable pair, Hark and Silence, suited up for their match. Only once had she fought Hark. He had a don't-give-a-damn demeanor that he backed up with canny, daredevil tricks. Nynn had been in the complex for only three or four days when she'd met Hark in the practice Cage. He hadn't even needed to borrow her gift in order to leave her busted and humiliated. His brown hair was shot through with blond streaks that seemed out of place in their underground world. As if he . . . belonged on a beach. A *beach*. The word sounded unfamiliar in her mind, but she knew it was right.

Silence whispered something in his ear and he laughed. He had a big laugh and a big smile and a *really* big *nighnor* in his right hand. The left he wrapped around Silence's trim waist, as if the woman might actually require protection of any kind. Ever.

"Tell me," Hark said. "Since you're in a unique position of knowledge."

"Unique?"

Hark's smile was infectious. She might've been sucked into his good humor had she been in a less cataclysmic mood. "You've spent more time with the grand Leto of Garnis than anyone. No one can remember a neophyte thriving so well under his tutelage."

That knowledge sank in slowly, like water eroding stone with only drip after drip.

Leto. Neophyte. Survive. *Thrive.*

"Mostly," he continued, "they're made ready to fight and do well to hold their own. You seem to have become his special project. That means you're unique. And that means, as his most doted student, I'm curious . . . Have you ever seen him so defiant? Toward the Old Man?"

Nynn swallowed back her reply. She'd registered the strangeness of it. On some level, she understood that it had to do with her. These two warriors, with their bizarre whispers—Hark's disarming smile, which was almost a weapon of its own, and Silence's cool, appraising stillness—they knew something she did not. She hated them for their mockery.

"Good hunting," she managed to say.

Another whisper between them. Another private smile. Their names were announced and they turned toward the Cage. Hark tipped two fingers to his brow, as if in salute. Nynn wanted her collar disarmed so she could fry them both.

Despite her disorientation and a labyrinth of hallways, she searched until she found the weapons room. Leto was standing with his back to the door, which bothered her more than she could say. He was not a man to turn his back on any potential threat. That warriors such as Hellix and those from the other cartels were still within the complex should've been enough to keep him on guard. Instead, he'd placed both hands on the wall, as if propping it up. His head was bowed. Had she not recognized the armor and his distinctive tattoo, she would've thought her initial assessment wrong.

Yet . . . he was Leto.

"Which blade should I have chosen?" she asked quietly. Everything sounded muted once beyond the din of the arena.

"The gilt-edged one."

"Why?"

He pushed away from the wall and retrieved the dagger in question. "This one is thin enough to be wielded as a whip—slicing rather than hacking."

"What lesson was I supposed to learn from picking the wrong one? Weren't the odds bad enough already?"

Leto swept the blade. The air parted in a swish of sound, as if molecules could be split as easily as skin. "Now you know you can win even when conditions aren't perfect."

"Oh, because you were perfectly happy with being chained together. I saw your frustration."

"That wasn't frustration." He tossed the weapon aside so that it slid beneath a metal bench. "That was humiliation."

"We won."

"Yes."

She swallowed. She inhaled. She prepared to ask the next question as if swords and shields would be drawn. "What did you say to the Old Man? You looked . . . defiant."

"I will not be chained again."

That didn't answer her question. It was a statement, as if he'd made a decision.

*Keep him away from her.*

What had he meant?

She dared reach up to touch his collar, although she risked her hand in doing so. Danger pulsed off him like the explosive potential of gasoline. He might combust at any moment, and she had no idea what would set him off. Were his sexual promises in the Cage truthful? At the moment, those promises were the best she could hope for.

That made her situation sound passive. She wanted him to honor those blunt, hard-edged promises. Her body was keyed up, desperate, starved in ways she'd never know.

For now, she only touched his collar. "You've been chained for a very long time. I would've thought your senses acute enough to know that. To feel the weight on your neck. To recognize the satisfaction of walking into a Cage and feeling these monstrous devices set us free." The metal was warmed by the heat that pulsed from his majestic body. Her fingertips prickled. She didn't touch skin, but she touched the one thing that had been with him nearly as long. "Leto of Garnis, what would you be without this?"

His eyes blanked. No emotion there. No connection. "I'd be a better Cage warrior."

✦ ✦ ✦

Leto had hoped that returning home would erase how unsettling the match had been—before, during, and after. The return should've been simple. Drink *golish*. Pick a woman from among the selection kept by the Asters for just that purpose. Release this grinding tension.

He could rely on none of those easy routines. First, he had Nynn's initiation ceremony to attend. Then . . . he had Nynn. He'd boasted that she would come to him, but he didn't trust his judgment regarding the woman. After all, he'd never spoken to the Old Man as he had after the match. Yet what he'd said was vital. Whatever Ulia had done to Nynn's mind would not last if Dr. Aster continued to test the boundaries of the telepathic block. Instinct alone had caused Nynn to draw her weapon against the man. Any further contact might snap her mind in two.

That prospect shouldn't bother Leto on a personal level. He had been tasked with helping Nynn survive for three matches. This was one down. Two more to go. The thought of Nynn's sanity fracturing in the process added weight to his burdens.

Their return to the dorms was heralded with raucous shouts and congratulations. Leto accepted the well-wishes of his fellow warriors, and from those who hadn't been chosen for the evening's contest. Silence and Hark had won their match, as had Hellix and Fam. Their gloating made Leto's teeth clench together.

Through the narrow corridor leading to the dorms, they filed into a common area where the *golish* was already flowing freely. Leto hadn't shed his armor. He wouldn't until he stripped naked that evening and cleaned himself in his quarters. Some of the men washed each other in the communal baths, a practice that held no interest for Leto.

Wearing his armor was a sound choice, rather than habit. He was uncomfortably aware of his body's reaction to the thought of Nynn, let alone seeing her enter the common room. The lights were softer here, more inviting—less like the industrial wing inhabited by the humans. This was a space for lounging in the few moments when warriors were free to relax.

She had cleaned and changed into a clean set of her silk-lined, leather training clothes. Her short blond hair gleamed, and tiny droplets of water clung to individual strands. He tried to remember the feel of her long tresses between his fingers—the beautiful hair he'd cut out of necessity—but his blasted senses failed him.

That she had washed and found a spare set of clothes meant someone had shown her to her newly appointed dorm. She would still be his responsibility, but not to the same degree. She would be a Cage warrior who determined her own regimen and sparred with whom she chose. He would no longer dictate every waking and sleeping hour.

Leto sat up from the bench and tunneled his fingers across his freshly buzzed scalp. He shouldn't care, shouldn't want, shouldn't be so Dragon-damned tormented.

This had to stop.

"Congratulations, Nynn of Tigony," he said.

The room quieted at the sound of his voice. He had enjoyed that influence for nearly two decades. Only now, when faced with the one person who should've ranked lowest of their group, did he feel his power slip. Nynn was looking at him, with eyes so pale that her irises were more like light than color. Her freckles added depth and beauty to golden skin, while the confidence she wore across her shoulders and up her spine said what no words needed to express.

She had won.

"I think we're all eager to get on with your initiation. Not since Hark's arrival have we welcomed one into our own."

Nynn's expression was placid, despite the fierce burn in her eyes. She was practically laughing at him. He could tell. The power he had taken for granted was being stolen, minute by minute, by a fierce woman who made him *feel*. He hadn't felt for years.

"Be careful what you wish for." Hark sat hip to hip with Silence. He wore a short-sleeved shirt—some holdover from the clothes he'd brought with him upon volunteering to fight. Silence absently stroked her thumb over a crescent-shaped scar on Hark's inner arm. Leto had never given much thought as to why the man served the Asters, but now he knew. The crescent was evidence of the Sath bonding tradition known as the Ritual of Thorns. Not to pay debts or to earn favors, Hark had come belowground to be with his wife.

"Why is that?" Nynn asked, jarring Leto's thoughts.

"Initiation is no pretty process," Hark said. "My screams may have been a tad less than manly. Maybe just a bit. I try to be as studly as the rest of these meatheads, but of course, there's no keeping up with so much testosterone. I have to taunt them with the fact I'm getting laid more than once a month."

Silence sighed softly, as if vexed by his chatter.

"I haven't wished for any of this." Nynn lifted her chin and stared the jester down. "But now it is my privilege. My right."

"This is never going to work," Hark muttered to Silence. He played with two shards of black rock as if they were three-dimensional puzzle pieces. "You know that, right? It's impossible." Only when she rolled her eyes and took the pieces did Hark return to Nynn. "Anyway, wanting it or not doesn't mean it won't hurt. 'Cuz that thing is a bloody *bitch*."

Lamot, another elder who'd retired from the Cages in the good grace of the Asters, arrived with his equipment. Nynn's confident expression wavered only once, as she glanced toward Leto. He met her where Lamot prepared the needle and ink.

"I have a tattoo." Leto could not remember the feel of her silken hair in his hands, but he would never forget her fingertips along his scalp. "Now you'll have one, too. The emblem of the Asters."

"Where?"

"Your choice."

She raised her brows to his shorn hair. "Didn't that hurt?"

Her eyes added to that unfinished sentence. *Didn't that hurt . . . considering your gift?*

"Hark didn't lie. It will hurt. Our physiology means it's a more aggressive process than with humans. More like scarification, infused with ink."

"And this is the reward I get for having flattened Weil?"

"Lucky shot, neophyte," came Weil's reply.

Nynn turned deadly cold eyes on her. "A win's a win."

The woman cleared her throat and returned to a conversation she may or may not have been having with Fam.

"Choose." Lamot motioned to his special chair, which was outfitted with various restraints and clasps. "Then sit."

She eyed the chair with obvious trepidation, but she didn't hesitate in her choice. "My shoulder blade. Left. Armor won't conceal it."

Lamot nodded. As Nynn sat, he set about fastening her into a position where her upper body was immobilized. Leto knelt before her. He took her hand. "You deserve this. Breathe into the pain. Take it into yourself. You've already done and survived worse."

*Keep this woman safe.*

Ulia, that twice-evil Indranan witch, had told him that. He wanted to set it aside as the strange babble of a mad meddler, but Leto could not. A strengthening part of him didn't *want* to set it aside.

One day, she would be released from her captivity. He harbored no further doubts that she could and would survive another eleven months and regain custody of her son. When that day came, she would be released from the mental block that kept her sanity intact and her gift contained. When she awoke, she would find her golden skin marred with yet another scar bestowed by the Asters—their serpent on her shoulder.

He moved to stand.

She grasped his wrist. "Don't. Stay."

"I will. Breathe with you, remember?"

Leto no longer cared who heard or what they made

of his relationship with his neophyte. *No, not neophyte.* She was his protégé now. His partner. That meant keeping her safe. That meant keeping her safe from a future where the Asters would scar her forever. He remained proud to wear the symbol of their house, but Nynn would take a blade to her own skin rather than live with their brand.

He gave her hand another squeeze before pulling free of her grip. As Lamot readied the soldering gun and well of ink, Leto whispered in the man's ear. "Not a serpent. Give her the mark of the Dragon."

# CHAPTER TWENTY-ONE

Leto held a bottle of *golish* to her lips, but Nynn refused another drink. She could endure the pain more than she could endure the embarrassment of vomiting in front of her new comrades. The strong drink would've knocked a human being unconscious after a few ounces, but for Nynn, for a Dragon King—they needed to drink it like water before feeling the numbing effects. The warm withdrawal from her body began at her toes and crept upward. Her shoulder blade would be among the last parts of her body to be anesthetized.

"I want to be awake," she said to Leto, who knelt before her. The harsh lines of his face had not eased since their exit from the Cage. Deeper in his eyes, however, she found something like concern. He looked on her as if nothing mattered more than ensuring that she would not only survive, but become stronger for it.

Again.

She was bent over a wide, flat attachment to the front of the chair, as if leaning over the top of a taller, rounded student desk like . . . "Jack . . . ?" Nynn mumbled.

The first burn of the cauterizing needle scattered thought. She bit her lower lip until she tasted blood, and she sucked air through her nose. She would *not* cry out. Only hours before, Nynn had been chained to Leto and they had both emerged victorious. There was no place for weakness in their world.

That didn't mean the pain was easy to absorb. She flinched against it. Her body wanted to be in charge. No wonder Lamot had strapped her to the strange chair. Those who held any reservations about receiving the mark of their fellow warriors would've fled with the first touch of the stinging needle.

The straps around her torso left her arms free. A comfort. She didn't want to let go of Leto's hands. He was an amazing man. His fine, impressive armor no longer gleamed, but the streaks of clay and blood added to his vitality. That armor wasn't for show; it was worn by a conqueror. The scar along his top lip was more proof. She remembered the scars on his back, which stretched beneath crisscrossed straps of leather. For a Dragon King to be scarred required a serious wound.

*She* had scars.

"Why do I have scars?"

Leto's eyes widened briefly, before his stoic expression returned. He gripped her hands more tightly and shook them, as if trying to restore feeling rather than deaden her to the pain. "Focus. This will only get worse."

"I don't want to be numb."

"That's exactly what you'll want. Soon."

The straps bit into her lower back and across one shoulder. After that initial shock, the other shoulder sizzled with slowly gathering agony. The scent of burning flesh made her crinkle her nose, as if it emanated from someone else.

"No. I don't want to be numb." She hissed and shuddered. "I've been numb before, when . . . Leto, why do I have scars?"

"All warriors have scars."

She held a strangled sound in her throat. "How did you bear this? You with your senses?"

"*Golish*. Drink."

"*No.*"

She looked for other distractions. The other warriors had resumed their relaxed celebrations, but few kept their attention away from her for long. Flickers of interest. Curiosity that couldn't be contained by conversation. What sort of initiation was this, where those she'd join treated her scarification as casual entertainment? Only Silence refused to be bashful. She tipped her head to one side and kept her eerily black eyes trained to where the needle dotted Nynn's shoulder blade like never-ending bursts of fire. What was it about the woman? Direct in her gaze, blank in her expression—in that calm setting, she seemed like a living mannequin.

Yet she had a partner. Hark was hers, and she was his.

Nynn shut her eyes against a stab of envy that bit with the ferocity of the tattoo needle.

"You want me to do well," she whispered. For him. For them alone. "In all things."

"Of course. Your success—"

"Come off it. All other reasons aside, you want me to do well. Why?"

He shook his head. "I don't know."

"You didn't have to."

The *golish* was traveling up her spine. Rather than

giving Nynn the comfort she should've welcomed, it made her heart race faster. She was leaving her body on a wave of panic that felt so familiar she could almost taste fear—some old fear, like iron and lime on her tongue, mingled with the blood from her lip.

"I didn't have to," Leto said quietly, although she couldn't be certain of that. Everything sounded soft and shadowed at the edges. Her vision was covered over with shades of coal and mud. "But I did for you."

"Don't want to go." Peering through dank colors the opposite of her beautiful gift, she saw how fiercely she gripped Leto's hands. Her knuckles were white. They wouldn't be cold, not with his warmth to surround her. "They take him. If I go, they'll take . . ."

She shuddered and hiccupped on a flash of pain that had nothing to do with the anguish of the soldering gun.

Leto shook free of her grasp and framed her face with his hands. "Do you see me? Nynn, look at me."

His voice was less powerful when she was so far away, but his rumbling authority remained. He had trained her. He had trusted her enough to fight beside him. She didn't understand what was happening—there in the complex, there in her mind—but she understood the sound of his voice. What's more, she responded to it.

"You want this," he said. "You want a mark to prove who you are and what you've accomplished. No one will ever take that from you."

She grinned, although it felt sloppy across her lips. "You'd try if you thought it'd make me listen."

Leto didn't grin. He didn't alter the forceful hold of his hands—thumbs at her temples, fingers spanning back into her hair and beneath her jaw. "Are you listening, Nynn?"

"Yes, sir."

He bowed his head at that. The smallest dip. Yet his arresting stare remained fixed. He wasn't letting her go, not even with his gaze. "Sleep now, knowing this will be the last time you'll be numb. I won't let it happen again. The pain is yours. The pleasure is yours. I promise you that."

She smiled again, feeling drunk, limp, gone. "You promise me pleasure?" The words didn't sound as if they came from her. So different. Liquid and subtle and inviting.

He lowered his mouth to her ear. *No one else can hear us,* she thought. Despite their combined efforts, she was losing him to the beckoning darkness. Only a few more words made it through the fog. "Yes, Nynn. I promise you pleasure."

Leto nearly slumped with relief when Nynn passed out.

"Never seen that before," Fam said conversationally. He lounged on one of the padded benches, with his own bottle of *golish* in his hand. Three empty bottles were lined up at his feet. "You sure she's one of us? Really?"

With an ache in his legs borne of unfamiliar tension, Leto stood and stared down at Fam. "She is."

He didn't wait to see the shorter man's reaction, instead turning to assess Lamot's progress. "Nearly finished," the old man said. "But—" He nodded toward Fam. "That one's not wrong. I've never seen anyone resist that strongly. Most are giggly on drink before the first touch of the needle. I even heard Silence speak."

The woman visibly flinched, which was the strongest reaction Leto had ever seen in her outside of combat. Hark raised his brows. He wore a wide, teasing smile. Silence's stiff body language suggested retribution of one kind or another later.

"Really?" Weil sat forward on her knees. "And what did she say?"

Hark's smile never wavered. "She said, 'Shut the fuck up, you Reaper shit.' Oh, no, that was me. Right now. To you."

"Out!" Leto's shout reverberated against the far wall. "All of you. Get out."

"Someone needs more private time with the new champion?" As if he needed more reason to lose temper, Leto turned to find Hellix propped in the doorway to the recreation room. "Seems your dorm would be more appropriate." He shrugged. "Or hers. I hear tell you would've lost without her today."

Hark had gathered up his gear and his last bottle of drink, with Silence following behind. Even Weil, still red in the face from Hark's insult, was sensible enough to ready her departure.

"A warrior who fights with a partner wins and loses with that partner," Leto said. "I want you to leave."

"I suppose that means you don't want to be reminded of the obvious. My whip lashes will mark her as surely as any tattoo."

Leto felt hewn of rock and deep, motionless rivers of ice. Good. Any other reaction would mean crippling Hellix where he stood. He satisfied himself with the image of grabbing Hark's *nighnor*, smashing it against Hellix's skull, and praying to the Dragon that the man woke up so he could do it again. "The subject of permanent marks is not one suited to you. How long did they have to hold the knife against your skin? I hope you were in more pain than you inflicted on Nynn."

"Unlikely. Your girl screamed loud enough that every man in the complex got hard."

Yes, Leto would do Hellix permanent damage. One day. But he would do so when Nynn could witness the act with the satisfaction she deserved. "You are twisted."

"Wait. What is this?" Fam barged past and knocked Lamot back from where he'd been hunched over Nynn's shoulder. "A dragon? That doesn't make her an Aster."

The other warriors returned. Even Silence frowned. She glanced between the tattoo and Leto's face. Weil cursed quietly under her breath and smoothed her frizzy red hair in that habitual way of hers. Hawk actually yawned, but the reaction didn't mask his initial flash of surprise.

Fam had taken his usual place at Hellix's side, which made him appear even weaker. A pantomime warrior. "You'll answer to the Old Man for this. He'll have Hellix whip the damn thing off her back. Can't say that doesn't have a certain appeal."

"The Old Man will be no concern of yours." That icy river still claimed Leto—for the better. "Are you finished, Lamot?"

The older Dragon King turned off his soldering gun and used a cloth to wipe away streaks of blood and ink. For motionless, speechless moments, everyone in the room stared at the tattoo. A perfect depiction of the Dragon. Not the fire-breathing monsters from Pendray myths, and not the snakelike creatures with great heads and lolling tongues, as the Garnis depicted. The Tigony, with their penchant for sidling up to the humans as the source of their long-standing power, had even gone so far as to portray the Dragon as a woman named Medusa.

Each clan had its own interpretation.

This, however . . . the tattoo on Nynn's shoulder was *the* Dragon. It contained elements from all of the Five Clans' mythology, blended into a cohesive creature.

"Now doesn't that make your hair stand on end." Hark shook his head. "How did he know?"

"Shut up, Thief," Weil said. "Or we'll ask how *you'd* know. Your kind keeps too many secrets."

"I'm not a Sath elder, although it would be interesting for a day or two. Imagine all the mysteries I could solve about our people." He leaned nearer to Weil, who was considerably shorter. "What secrets do the Pendray keep?"

She raised her red brows in challenge. "How to dispose of Dragon King bodies without anyone being the wiser."

"Go," Leto said. No shouts now. "Lamot, you, too. Thank you for your work."

The contentious, infuriating lot filed out. Some did so without fanfare. Leto closed his mind to Fam's parting question to Hellix. "Think he'll wait till she wakes up before he fucks her?"

Fists clenched, jaw rigid, Leto stood alone. Only his breathing and Nynn's very, very quiet respiration filled the heavy quiet. He hadn't meant to add to her panic. The *golish* should've been a good thing, as Lamot had said. Leto had appreciated its effects more than once. For Nynn, the numbness must've chipped away at the barriers Ulia had constructed. Memories of being drugged? The terrors of the labs had returned to her in bits and frightened gulps.

*Why do I have scars?*

*Jack . . .*

He'd hoped the drink would blunt her pain and keep those memories from intruding. That assumption had been wrong enough to make him wonder which version of Nynn would awaken. Or if a fractured mind would make her into something altogether new.

He shook his arms until his ligaments and bones and tissue worked in concert. He'd needed to lock down his instincts to keep from mauling Hellix. Carefully, he unfastened the straps that trapped Nynn to the supporting chair. She slumped against his chest.

Only then did he wish he'd taken the time to remove his armor and wash. He would've liked to feel her body resting against his. Very little between them had been gentle. No matter how much he desired her, he craved the gentleness he knew she was capable of.

He stroked sweat back from her temple. Eyes closed, her brow was smooth and untroubled. The split bite marks on her bottom lip were already healing. That symbol of her distress and pain accentuated her exotic beauty by plumping her lush mouth. She was too pale, unnaturally pale, and her freckles stood out as constellations across her nose.

He'd never seen constellations, only heard tales from his mother.

Leto of Garnis. Full of ridiculous, fanciful notions. His mind had no place in his body if his body was to survive. Pell would never be safe. He would never fight in another Grievance to help perpetuate their line.

He would never father children of his own.

*Why for my sister but not for me?*

With motions far rougher than he would've liked, he lifted Nynn from the chair. She was still propped against him, in a way that gave him a clear view of her tattoo. Leto had been tempted, as Hark had, to ask Lamot how he'd captured the *idea* of the Dragon so accurately. It belonged to all of the clans, in a way that made all other portrayals seem purposefully wrong.

As eerie as that was, it was a question for another time. Nynn was his concern now. He had come to care about her. Yes, he cared enough that he would not see her permanently marked by the men she despised—men she would remember one day.

A more selfish reason was that she would never forgive him for letting it happen.

He'd been reviled before. The air around him was filled with the stench of unresolved anger, jealousy, and rage, much of it pointed at him. Being champion had afforded him respect and fear, the latter of which would turn against him when the opportunity arose. He trusted none of them.

To be hated by Nynn, however, was unsettling.

He shook his head as he lifted her from the chair. Nothing was making sense. She'd hated him throughout weeks of training. She'd hated him when he treated her as lab filth, watched her dress, cut her hair. She'd hated him when he used Kilgore as punishment. Why would this be any different?

Because he'd become vulnerable.

He'd enjoyed Nynn's companionship as a neophyte, because she was a challenge. He'd enjoyed it even more when she stood by his side as his partner. No one else had ever held his hand in the dark, and no one else had needed him to hold.

She wouldn't get out of his way, or quit talking to him, or stop touching him. *Touching* him. How could he keep from opening himself to this woman? He'd have thought of a way by now, had it been possible. That meant one day, when she was free of the mental blocks and reunited with her son, she would hate him just as much as the Asters.

He liked having her there. As he held her over his shoulder and carried her toward his dorm, he liked knowing she would share his bed—quietly at first, as she healed and awoke from the *golish* stupor. Passionately later.

He had promised her pleasure. And he had promised to keep her safe.

In body, that had been an easy vow. But her mind? What would be left of her when she returned to herself? Nynn would leave him. And Audrey MacLaren would never forgive him.

# ✦ CHAPTER ✦ TWENTY-TWO

Nynn awoke by slow, slow, slow degrees. At first only her mind worked, behind the dark of her closed eyes. She never thought her sense of smell could be so powerful. Wherever she was, she was surrounded by masculinity—leather, metal, musk. That wasn't just any man. It was Leto. She could smell him in ways she'd never imagined, as if each of her cells had been designed for taking in his fragrance, appreciating its notes as she would scent the blood of a warrior soon to be bested.

Now that she knew he was near, she wanted her other senses back. Soon. Which would return to her first? Taste, apparently, which wasn't nearly as rewarding. Blood stained her tongue with the bitterness of copper. Overwhelming it was the sweet remains of the *golish* that had sent her into this nightmare tunnel where her body and mind had parted ways.

*Make that stop. No more.*

She wanted to hear him, see him, feel him.

"Nynn."

She nearly purred at the sound of her name. There was another sense. She could hear him. More than that, now she knew he was nearby. His voice was quiet thunder and distant winds. Elemental. Stronger than man, and even stronger than Dragon King. She wanted to hear her name again, even as she imagined the shape of his lips as he formed the word.

Warmth enveloped her. She was protected. She was safe in ways she hadn't felt in . . . Her memory didn't go back that far. Or couldn't. Some dark force blocked the way. She preferred sinking into the comfort of the moment, no matter how disorienting her awakening.

That warmth moved. His hands. He was touching her, skin to skin, maybe even body to body. That delicious heat was all around her, from her cheek to her toes. Was she lying with him? In his room? She shivered, and he pulled her closer.

"Nynn, come back."

On her first try, her voice was barely more than a rasp. She swallowed past that painful ache—the most immediate of so many aches clamoring for her attention—and tried again. "To you?"

"Yes." He stroked her forehead. "Come back to me."

Big, assured hands caressed up and down her arm. She melted into that rhythm. She must've been lying near him, perhaps on top of him, because every concession her body made elicited more from him. She shifted closer, and he gave her more. Deeper strokes of his fingers along her sore muscles. Longer pulses of his wide palms, until her hip and thigh came within his reach.

"Give me a reason," she said, the words breathy. "Dark is safer."

He kissed her temple. That such a ferocious, unyielding man could deliver a kiss so soft made her closed eyes prickle with tears. She couldn't remember the last time she'd been comforted, and she couldn't remember the last time she cried. *Abnormal,* some deep corner of her mind screamed. *Impossible.*

*Remember.*

"Dark is safer." She would keep saying it until it was true and she could hide there forever.

Another kiss. "But then I can't see your eyes."

Nynn groaned. Unfair. So beautifully unfair.

"Open your eyes for me." His breath brushed her temple as he spoke. Another form of touching. Another comfort. "I want to see your eyes and know that you want to be here."

"Where?"

"In my bed. In my arms." Those arms flexed subtly, as if she needed a reminder of his brawn. The beat of his heart sped as he talked. "I want to keep touching you. I want to do more than touch you. But I won't do it if the *golish* still poisons your thoughts and leaves you unable to say no."

"I won't say no."

"You need to look at me when you say that."

She was identifying more detail now. His chest was bare. He was on his back. She was lying on her side. Was he wearing any clothes? Was she? The thrill that she could be naked in his bed shot tingles of electricity through the rest of her numb places. She was Tigony. Gathering electricity was her gift. She imagined it to be the key to bringing her body back to life.

Slowly she opened her eyes, expecting a sharp shaft of light. Yet the room was nearly dark. No fluorescents in here. No bare bulbs. Details came into focus with the same sloth. A gleam caught her attention. The scant light that shone from a far corner caught on a pristine set of armor hanging on a wall. And three other sets of armor, actually, of different designs.

They hung . . . at the end of a narrow bed.

Aside from a sink, a footlocker, and a few hygiene products, the room was empty. Stark. The lack of decorations accented what was most important to Leto of Garnis. His armor. His life's work.

Then why was she in his bed? Nothing else mattered to him. In that violent place, there was no room for distractions.

Maybe that's why they lay together in the near darkness. It *was* a violent place. If two people could find a moment's respite, why deny herself? She wanted him. Her body—beaten and aching—craved his. As long as she was condemned to surviving, forced down in the underground darkness, she might as well enjoy what pleasure they could give one another.

*Condemned?*

*Forced?*

Shivering fear tingled up from her toes and lodged at the base of her skull. A headache exploded with the concussive force of releasing her gift. She groaned and pushed her forehead against Leto's chest.

"What is it?"

"Headache," she gasped. *"Fuck."*

He sat up, urging her to do so. The blackness was back as she squeezed her eyes shut against the pain. "Head between your knees. Bend low."

Deadly hands turned tender as he massaged up the

back of her neck. Nynn groaned again, this time because of the relief he provided. The headache burned like a brand in her skull, but he forced it back, back into a corner. Soon he was paying equal attention to the tense flesh between her neck and shoulders. Only when he kissed along the top of her spine did her body react with want rather than gratefulness.

She realized that she was wearing her undergarments—the tank top and lightweight cotton shorts. At that moment, she appreciated that small measure of privacy, even if Leto's legs circled around hers. He kept his distance; she couldn't feel the press of his groin against her lower back. She had no idea whether this caress affected him as a man, or if he was once again taking care of her like he was tending a prize animal.

"Come," he said brusquely. "I'll take you to your dorm. You need sleep. These few days have been trying for us both."

For the first time since regaining consciousness, she turned to face him. Leto had held her for who knew how long. Looked after her. Gave her shelter against a world that clawed at her calves, up her thighs, trying to drag her down.

His expression was the most open she'd ever seen of him. The stern set of his mouth was lax, as if he'd just exhaled. His scarred upper lip didn't seem so stern now, just softer and more vulnerable. She could almost picture the moment of his injury—and the desire to comfort him—as opposed to seeing the intimidating scar left behind. The tight brackets around his mouth had eased. He looked younger. Powerful, yes, but without the same burdens.

He wore briefs similar to hers, made from the same cotton that felt like rough homespun cloth. The chest he'd kept covered by armor was bare. She'd always known his body was marvelous, but to see the bare, shadowed proof was overwhelming. Where to look first? Strong pectorals were swirled with a dusting of dark hair. Wide shoulders were capped with striated muscle that led down to thick biceps and the powerful cords of his forearms. His seated posture folded defined abdominals more tightly together, like masculine origami hewn of flesh. Ligaments and ridges bunched between his ribs.

She wanted to trace her teeth down every hard line and sweeping curve. She wanted to test his strength, to taste it. Even there, with so much unsaid, she had unconsciously started to touch him. Just her fingertips within the cradle of his calloused palms.

His eyes were hooded and dark, propping up shields she wanted to tear down. Why was it so important to find out his character?

*I care for him. I want to know what sort of man I care for.*

Cupping his jaw in both hands, she brought his gaze up to meet hers. "I've only been in my dorm room to change clothes and wash. Why would I want to sleep there when you're here? For that matter, why would I want to sleep at all?"

"And your headache?"

"You made it better." She shrugged. "They seem to . . . I don't know. Come and go. Flashes, then gone in a few seconds."

He hesitated. His mouth tightened in some twist of

emotion she couldn't begin to interpret. "This will change things."

"You don't deal well with change."

An answering grunt.

"Leto?"

Another wordless noise in his throat. His expression might be more open, but she could do with a few more assurances.

"As champion, you have your choice tonight," she said, pushing her fingers up, up into his soft, cropped hair. "Who would you choose if it wasn't me? And don't lie. By now, you should know that I can tell the difference."

"No one else."

His voice was as rough as when they sparred, but layered with very different feelings. The eyes he finally trained on her were just as dark, just as intense. Goose bumps raised on her arms because of the desire he couldn't—or no longer wanted—to hide. Frank, sensual anticipation gathered in her stomach and pulsed up, down, *out* until her body ached to be kissed. Everywhere. She wanted that rough mouth in all the ways a man could satisfy a woman, and she wanted to worship him in return.

"And me? Do you want me to choose someone else?"

*"No."*

His primal growl intensified her need. She'd fought him for so long. She'd fought beside him. Now, if they were to fight, they would do so in pursuit of release.

"This is me looking right at you. This is me making a choice that has nothing to do with Dragon-damned *golish* or the heat of battle's aftermath." She leaned forward and brushed her mouth against his. Restless, greedy hands helped her balance as she held his taut shoulders. "This is me saying you won't sleep tonight, and you won't spend tonight with anyone else."

A smile livened his grim expression. "I said you'd come to me."

Leto had rarely, if ever, used an attempt at humor to disguise his real emotions. Would leading them down this path ease the strain against Nynn's mental defenses or snap them in two?

Would it matter in a few seconds if she kept touching him?

She pushed up on her knees and positioned herself between his open thighs. The bed was not wide. He'd always been uncomfortable in the thing. Now that closeness was an unexpected benefit. He wanted her closer still.

"Yes, Leto. I've come to you. You win. From one champion to another," she said against his cheek, "that's quite a thing for me to admit."

"You have quite an ego after only one round."

"You like that I do. I'm what you've made of me."

Again he stifled a surge of something like guilt. He had done his best to train her, but in the end, her success hadn't been his to shape. He wasn't some Indranan witch, able to rearrange her thoughts and make her into a whole new woman.

Yet how was he not responsible? Ulia deserved only part of the blame. He could've kept her alive as long as was required of them both. Instead, he'd wanted her to be a grand reflection of his prowess. The applause she'd received had eclipsed any he'd ever received, and even then, he'd been able to absorb the glory because she was his creation.

He had tried to transform her, as surely as had Dr. Aster.

Nynn of Tigony was more powerful now, more assured, but she was not free.

Why that mattered to him was impossible to tell. *He* wasn't free, and that had never bothered him.

*She has a son. Her husband was murdered.*

If she had remembered either of those things, she wouldn't be kneeling between his legs. Which made him the greediest Dragon-damned bastard when he took hold of her hips.

"That's more like it," she said against his temple. "Show me what you can do, Leto of Garnis. Show me."

She knelt at the perfect height to showcase her torso. The tank top concealed her breasts but hugged their firm, high shape. Her nipples had tightened. They strained against the cotton, lifting and lowering with each breath. She dug her nails into the caps of his shoulders. Wide, lush lips softened until they parted completely. She licked her upper lip. That pure sensual invitation sent a rush of blood to Leto's cock. He'd been hard around Nynn before—and he'd been hard when atop her, there in Kilgore's room. This was different, just as it was different from any other reward fuck after a fight.

This was intimate.

"You were right," he rasped. "I don't like change."

She edged forward, changing the position of their legs so that she straddled his hips. A shift, a dip, and she settled the soft apex of her thighs over the proof of how much he wanted her. That proof made him groan, while her eyes rolled closed. "I like *that* change. Always so much the warrior. Always so hard." She ground her pelvis against his. "But this is the kind of hard we need tonight."

Leto's control snapped. He couldn't hold it together for both of them. She wanted to be taken. He would take her.

What had been a slow awakening to temptation became rougher, faster. He stripped her tank top in a move so quick that she gasped. Perhaps reflex made her cross her arms over bare, beautiful breasts. He caught both wrists and pinned them at the base of her spine. Any other woman—Dragon damn, *any* other woman—would've bowed to his show of strength. Nynn couldn't escape his grip, but she still had weapons. She bared her teeth and thrust out her chest.

"Yours," she said.

Such a dare.

Leto tugged her wrists down and back, arching her spine. He fixed his mouth on her left breast and sucked. No warning. No soft kiss. Her gasp was a molten tide that spread through his body. She shook her shoulders from side to side—small attempts to break free of his binding hands. The movements only heightened his arousal. She wasn't going anywhere, and better still, she didn't want to.

Her flesh was firm and soft beneath his lips and under the flick of his tongue. He toyed with her beaded nipple. Soft strokes. Deep, pulsing licks. Each drew a different noise from her throat. He wanted to learn each one and how to re-create it. The trail he left between her breasts was warm and wet. She shivered when he scored his roughened cheek against another firm nipple.

Again she struggled against how he'd restrained her wrists. "I want to touch you."

Leto trailed hot, openmouthed kisses up her neck, to her jaw, behind her ear. "Where would you touch first?"

"Down your sides. I want to scratch you until you flinch."

"And when I flinch?"

"You'll fuck me." She surged forward to catch his mouth in a fierce kiss. Passion was a storm between them, with the crackle of her electricity and the ferocity of his senses. A collision. "Because I don't want soft anymore. Soft is for later."

He groaned against her throat. *Later*. That promise. There would be more time. More encounters such as these. She would learn his shivers and groans as surely as he'd taught her how to fight.

With one more hard sweep of his tongue between her lips, he let go of her arms.

She hadn't played coy. Nynn ripped her nails down his sides and along his flanks. He hissed. He bucked his hips. Her answering moan was exactly what he'd needed to hear. She was primal, strong—the partner he'd never known he wanted.

*Needed.*

"Feel that?" He growled against her lips, then clenched her ass. Pulled her hips down. Ground against her. Closer, with the rhythm that fueled their bodies. "Feel how hard I am for you?"

She shoved her hands between them. Hot, slender fingers slid inside the waistband of his shorts. "This?" She encircled him, gripped him. "This is for me?"

"Teasing bitch," he said with a smile that was half-pain, half-ecstasy. "Should I show you what's mine?"

"Yes."

Even in the haze of arousal, Leto knew he couldn't flip Nynn over and drive into her the way he wanted. Her back was too scarred and tender. She might seem oblivious to what had taken place during the last few hours, the last few days, but he couldn't forget her pain if he tried.

Instead, he used his strength—he loved being strong when it came to dominating this woman—to turn her onto her knees. He pulled down her shorts. With firm purpose, he fit his whole palm between her legs. She was wet. Wet for *him*. Every time he assumed he'd reached the height of his desire, he found another reason to blow past his limits.

Nynn arched her back like a cat, pressing more firmly against his hand. They both shared a hissed moan.

Leto tugged down his own shorts and positioned his prick at her slick entrance. She stilled. He didn't breathe as he bowed over her body. He circled his free arm low across her hips. She could struggle and thrash from the waist up, but her hips, her pussy—they were his to control.

At the sight of her fresh tattoo, he fought those misgivings. He made them disappear, just as he had the ability to make even the most vocal crowds disappear when he fought. Single-minded.

"You wanted me to show you." Against the hollow behind her ear, he growled his anticipation. "*This* is mine. And this is our reward."

# ✦ CHAPTER ✦ TWENTY-THREE

With one strong buck of his hips, Leto filled her. Nynn cried out, arched, surged back to take more. She couldn't remember a man before him—that's how deeply he stroked, how the pulsing cadence of his body overwhelmed thought. It was all she could do to brace her hands against the wall at the head of the bed. He held nothing back. She'd seen him fight and seen him hold his temper. Both required strength. Different kinds of strength.

Now he used that strength to drive into her. Every withdrawal made her want to weep. The loss of his hard length stole the air from her lungs. He didn't leave her for long. A half heartbeat later, he was back where he belonged, where she needed him—flush, hip to hip, buried to the hilt. She ached. Slick. Greedy. Each thrust pushed her higher and closer to an animalistic release. She wanted to be that mindless. She wanted Leto to make her scream.

Bowed over her, he pulsed hot flashes of sensation across her back. His chest hair scraped a gentle tease over her skin. His breath was harsh, fast, matching the rhythm of his thrusts.

He pressed his mouth against her temple. "Say my name."

"Leto."

"Say that you love this."

"Dragon dammit, Leto. I love this."

"Say that you want more."

"More," she gasped.

"I broke you once." His pace increased, bodies straining. "I'm going to break you again."

"Wrong, wrong, wrong." The chant felt right. Matched their desire. "My turn. Going to break you, sir."

He shifted to kneel upright. One strong hand grabbed her damping collar and pulled. She had no choice but to arch her spine. That position left her more vulnerable. What little control she'd had to toss her head was taken. For Leto, to Leto, she was actually eager to give over that control.

Even that wasn't enough for him. He released her collar with a harsh curse and clenched her hips with both hands.

She looked back over her shoulder to see his face twisted in a grimace of absolute rapture. He stared at a point on her lower back. The tense way his arms arrowed down to her pelvis bunched his pecs together. They gleamed with sweat. His mouth was open. Each drive of his thick, weighty shaft wrested an exhaled grunt from his wide chest.

"Look at me," she said between bouts of sensation that gathered and built. She was a living embodiment of her gift—glowing, ready to explode. *"Leto."*

Maybe she had learned some of his techniques, because her sharp command snapped his gaze toward hers. His pupils were dilated. He looked like a god bent on laying waste to cities. Their kind had done as much. That they could fuck with such intensity stole her mind.

He was beyond speech. She was nearly there. But she wasn't going to let him make good on his boast.

"Break me. Try. It won't happen. All you'll do is come before I'm satisfied." She moaned sharply when he reached around to circle two fingers over her clit. "You're too proud for that. You won't let yourself."

"I can."

"Then come first. You can—" Another gasp when he pressed his fingers deeper as he rubbed her clit. "You can think about it afterward. Shame, like losing. Or you can make me beg for you. I *want* to."

"Beg. For me."

She shook her head and dipped it down into his pillow. Smelled of him. The whole room smelled of him and of sex.

"Give me that," he rasped.

Fuck, she wasn't going to last much longer. His fingers were clever, strong, unyielding, even as his prick slammed home, stealing everything but need. But she needed *this*, too. To own him. "You want to hear me beg more than you want to come."

His frustration became a bodily force. "Yes. *Yes*. Do it, Nynn."

It wasn't a game now. Wasn't difficult. She gave herself over to the mass of sensations. Colors blended with sounds blended with the knowledge that he surrounded her. They couldn't stop now if they wanted to. "Please—ah, *bathatéi*. Leto, please. Make me— I want to—"

Her voice was broken when she screamed. That shrieking release throttled down to a low, low moan as pleasure scorched her nerve endings and whirled thought into feeling.

Just *feel*.

Leto's strokes became tighter, shorter, less controlled. His hands were vises digging into the meat of her hips. She looked back in time to see him point his chin toward the ceiling. That gorgeous expanse of masculine beauty strained. His release was a groan and a string of deep, truncated curses. He ground his pelvis against hers, wringing the last sparks of sensation from them both.

Still panting, he withdrew and sank heavily onto the mattress. With one agile movement—how was he still capable?—he swirled her body down and along his. They were glorious, shimmering with an afterglow that was nearly palpable.

Nynn smiled against his chest, licked his salty skin. "See? Now I've broken you."

He rumbled something inarticulate and pulled her flush, chest to chest. "We both knew you would."

"Did we? I doubt that. Stubborn man."

"In that regard," he said, kissing her crown, "I've met my match."

Leto awoke with a shiver. Some dream. Remnants stuck to his thoughts like having walked into a spiderweb. Two children. One slightly grown, in pain. Another just born. Small, red-faced, yelling at the world.

His skin was cold. Nynn still slept across his chest, but his feet, legs, and one arm were bathed in an unnatural chill. Her heat had only so much power to keep the worst at bay.

He wanted to hold her tighter, or pull a tangled blanket off the floor and wrap it around them as surely as they held one another. He did neither, unwilling to wake her.

Bright and beautiful, her gift was the most amazing thing he'd ever seen. Yet every day, she gave him more of herself.

*Break her.* What a lie. She'd taken everything thrown her way and absorbed it like he could absorb the force of a punch. He was staring at the shadows on the ceiling, wondering when he'd lost his way.

She was becoming even more of a slave to the Asters, just as she was prying his mind apart.

He touched his collar, suffering through another bone-deep shiver of dread.

*Leto of Garnis, what would you be without this?*

The skin along the edges of the collar was scarred by callouses. He wondered what he would look like without it wrapped around his neck. He couldn't think back far enough to remember, and even then, the face in the mirror would've been that of a young man. He'd been eager to follow the path forged by his father, even though that path had meant suffering, sacrifice, and ultimately death.

Leto would live and die in the Cages.

He shook his head, closed his eyes, but nothing eased the truth: He didn't believe that anymore. What's more, he didn't *want* to believe it.

For the first time in two decades, he remembered wails of agony—his mother's voice, shredded into hoarse strips of sound. The crowd had cheered as it always did when strong men fell. His father had been made to look defenseless, slaughtered like a sacrificial lamb. He'd been made to look weak when Leto had never known a stronger warrior. A stronger *man*. Not himself. Not anyone. For years, he'd endured match after match, guiding his wife through multiple pregnancies until they had what few Dragon Kings could claim: a new family.

Who else could've bid that family good-bye, kissing wife and children perhaps for the last time, every time he entered a Cage? Who else could've delivered the whip marks that still scored Leto's back, all in the knowledge it would make his son a more resilient fighter? When faced with the same prospect now—of whipping Nynn to make her tougher—his skin tried to peel away from his muscles. The idea was that revolting.

His father had been the epitome of honor.

What Leto felt, lying there with Nynn, was selfish and ugly by comparison. His pride had been humbled, which was not necessarily a bad thing. He'd been riding too high as the Asters' champion for too long. This infection of greed and petty wants was deeper.

He wanted out of the dark.

The single person who might be able to lead him free of such a place was in his arms—and she wasn't even a real person. She was a warped version of the woman who'd once been more determined than the passage of time.

Somewhere out there, held in a box or a cell by Dr. Aster, was a little boy named Jack MacLaren. Leto had helped erase the one person who would walk through hell to save that child.

Nynn stirred, which added another layer of unease

to the cold wrapped around his exposed limbs. Cold wrapped around his *heart*.

He'd known it was wrong from the beginning. Hadn't he?

No.

She'd been right. Brainwashed, she'd called him. He wished he could scrub it clean, start over, sink back into that numb, rote place where his misgivings didn't bite his insides. He should've been sated, having won a tough match and fucked a lush woman.

Instead, he was beginning to wonder what sort of man he would be if Nynn snapped. If she became Audrey again. If she burst into pieces as violent as the fireworks thrown off by her gift. Living in the dark was one thing. Knowing it surrounded him and defined him was another. He could endure that darkness, even contentedly, had Nynn been his partner for good. His mind touched on Silence and Hark. That sort of comfort. That sort of light and promise.

But what kind of man would he be if he kept Nynn from her child?

"You're really out of it," came a sleep-soft voice.

"Hm?"

"I've said your name twice."

Leto opened his eyes and found Nynn propped on her elbow, looking down at his face. She touched his brow. He inhaled deeply. Soaking in her lax, rested beauty was as much a pain as it was a balm. He shouldn't have cared. He should've let her training be harder, meaner, more selfish—to protect his family. Nothing more. He hadn't known that his capacity for selflessness extended beyond them.

"What's going on in that head of yours?"

Leto forced a small smile. "Have you changed so much that you think I have anything in this head of mine?"

"Changed?" A frown tipped her brows together. "For the better, I hope."

He gave in to that need to cover their cooled bodies by grabbing the tousled blanket off the ground. "Changed," he said softly.

"No, no." She shrugged out of the blanket and stood up from the bed. "I want to see my tattoo. I remember at least that much." Another pause. Another frown. "I keep . . ."

Leto sat up. "What?"

"I keep losing time."

"What *do* you remember?"

"Glimpses of you." She ducked her head, then pulled on her wrinkled cotton shorts.

Unable to resist that seductive call, he joined her standing in the middle of his small room, holding her from behind. Her dragon seemed to glow in the scant light. "Which glimpses?"

She turned her face and grinned against his inner arm. "How about glancing back at you as you came? That was a good one."

"Wicked," he whispered against her hair. "Tell me another."

"You held my face as Lamot seared my back. I want to see what he put there. I think I've earned it, don't you?"

There was no putting off the inevitable. He nodded.

Although the room had only one mirror, there above

the sink, he retrieved a breast plate from the wall. It was polished to a shine that was nearly as revealing as a mirror. Nynn held the breast plate and shifted. Recognition came in the form of a soft inhale.

"That's not a serpent."

"No."

She peered closer. "A . . . Leto, what does this mean? Did Lamot do this?"

"No," he said again, as grim as delivering news of a death. "I told him to."

Whirling on him, she thrust the breast plate into his hands. Stark, strong anger shone from her face. In the last twelve hours, he'd seen her determined, depleted, triumphant, panicked, and ravished. Now she looked ready to steal his skin and sew it into the leather of her armor.

"And why was that? It was easy to joke about being a champion alongside you, but now it's not so funny."

"What does that mean?"

She jabbed her forefingers against both of his temples. "This, you Dragon-damned bastard. You commit sacrilege on my skin and keep the Asters' symbol from me. Am I still such a neophyte that I don't deserve what I've earned? I fought for them the same as you did."

Leto wanted to smash his mace against everything he could see. Then he'd start again, catching what he missed the first time. He'd kept her from wearing the permanent mark of the family that had ruined her life, and she'd turned it into some sick competition. The irony was strong enough to punch through his resistance to change.

Change wasn't going to let him be. Walking into the

training cell where Audrey MacLaren was held prisoner had been the first step toward this moment. Nothing that significant could be recognized as it happened.

*Tell her the truth.*

*Keep her safe from the truth.*

Muscle and strength weren't enough for him to solve this puzzle. But they might be enough to keep her alive and honor the goal she'd forgotten. No matter what he did, he wouldn't hold Nynn again. She would become his enemy; her furious expression said as much. That knowledge wedged needles into his joints, until every movement—forward, backward, even standing perfectly still—was agony.

The safety of her mind and, eventually, the safety of her son depended on becoming her rival. She would despise what remained of her year of captivity, but stubborn woman, that bitterness would keep her strong.

"Yes," he said heavily. "I told him to withhold the family symbol."

A flare of her nostrils was her only reply. Hair a spiked tangle, breasts still bare, she looked more like a wild Pendray than a woman of royal Tigony lineage. "Then we do this the hard way, you *lonayíp* piece of shit. I'll fight beside you, *champion*, but don't expect any warning next time. You'll know I've used my gift when it throws you to the ground and you lie there like a steaming heap of shit."

She deserved her anger. He deserved his anger, too, although he didn't know where to aim it.

Crossing his arms, he retreated to the old ways. The old places. He'd lived in the complex long enough that he almost convinced himself he welcomed the homecoming—rather than hating the creature he was becoming.

"What does that mean, neophyte?" he asked, needing the distance of that old insult.

"It means that the next time we step into a Cage, you'll be fighting me, too."

# ✦ CHAPTER ✦ TWENTY-FOUR

If you're in agreement," said Hark, that grinning idiot, "today will be the day."

Leto stood in the weapons room. He'd been mentally preparing for his upcoming match where, for the third and hopefully last time, he would be paired with Nynn. For their second turn in the Cage, a month before, they'd been manacled at the wrists. Maybe this time, for added sport, the Asters would chain them at the neck.

Apparently pairing him with a woman who'd rather incinerate him than stand with him wasn't interesting enough.

The Asters knew. They knew he and Nynn had fallen out, even if they didn't know the reason. For giving Lamot the command to change Nynn's tattoo, Leto had endured twenty lashes by one of the family's hulking human thugs. Nearly, very nearly, he would've preferred being whipped by Hellix. To turn his back and take his punishment from a human had been a withering blow to Leto's pride. That incident, three days after earning that first dynamic victory with Nynn as his partner, only added to the cracks in long-held beliefs.

He was only as valuable as his last success.

In every other respect, he was a slave.

As Nynn progressed through the weeks, appearing more and more content with her lot, she became a living mirror of how he'd spent his life. That she served the people who'd ruined her family was even more devastating. She'd called him brainwashed. Now she was. Literally.

After standing to his full height, he looked down at Hark—and kept his fists firmly at his sides. The man's smile was fraying Leto's already tissue-thin temper. "In agreement with what?"

"That today's the day." He nodded toward where Silence leaned against the wall. A line of swords and shields reflected her placid expression, unnerving black eyes, and white blond hair. "Silence and I have taken what we need from this place. It was needle in a haystack for a while, but we're all set. It's been surprisingly satisfying to follow a hunch and have it work out. But now it's up to you."

"Speak plainly. Nynn and I fight next."

"Yeah, about that." Hark handled a pair of sickles as if he might select those weapons rather than his usual *nighnor*. "See, big guy . . . we are your opponents. I'm surprised you hadn't noticed. And I'm a little disappointed. Being completely ignored doesn't say much about our ability to intimidate."

Leto blinked. He was surprised, too. So caught up in the strife he expected to face with Nynn in the Cage, he hadn't moved through his tried-and-true routine. He hadn't been this clumsy since he was a green kid.

Then again, he'd never faced decisions that threatened to rip his life in half. He'd trained. He'd fought.

He'd won. Those had been the three tenets of his waking days and the dreams he relished at night.

*Had been.*

He was no longer that arrogant young man. Nynn had become worse than a stubborn neophyte. She was trained and she hated him. That hatred showed in every skewering stare and frenzied attack. Her mastery of her gift bordered on the sublime.

Sublime and devastating.

His right arm still throbbed where she'd landed the full force of an energy burst. Five days ago. Even the fresh lash marks on his back had only hurt for two. Something about her gift had the ability to wedge under the skin and leave traces of that Dragon-damned electricity behind. He itched with the pain of it.

"So," he said. "We fight. I hope this isn't your way of asking for mercy."

Silence hid her mouth behind her hand, but her eyes crinkled around a concealed smile. Hark laughed outright. "We'd never beg quarter and you'd never give it. A waste of breath."

"You know a great deal about that."

"Generally. But not this time." Bright blue eyes morphed from idiotic geniality to the sharp focus of a merciless killer. Intense. Unrelenting. Leto knew from experience that the man was capable, even brilliant on occasion. This was something else entirely. "Are you listening, Leto of Garnis? We know you can, even past these Dragon-damned collars. Listen to the silence."

Leto glanced at the woman who still leaned against the wall. She lowered her hand, tipped her head, and began to speak.

Only, her voice was more like a sigh. Leto fought past the damping powers of the collar. He'd worked diligently to make that possible, never thinking he would one day use his repressed gift to hear words among a woman's sighs.

What he heard he could not believe.

*Found both halves of the idol.*

*Deactivate the collars.*

*Living gold.*

*Waiting for this.*

*Go free.*

The plan Silence whispered in his ears—practically in his mind—made him want to wring her slender neck.

"And you've been hiding this the entire time?"

She lowered her eyes, apparently done with her end of the conversation.

Hark stood close. "Not all of us bought into the system. Some . . ." He looked back toward his lover. "Some of us had never planned to stay. There is an outside world and it's pretty damn fabulous. You, fearless leader, need to be introduced to it for the first time."

"Do you always make plans with madness at the root?"

"No, but there's patience. That should be her real name, you know."

Leto couldn't go through with what they suggested. He still had his sister to care for. This was the final match before earning his reward for Pell. Her well-being had been his aim for nearly four months, since first meeting his new neophyte.

*Let it go*, a deep, greedy voice said. *You can't afford to care.*

He could take care of Pell. He could . . .

"And what of Nynn?" he asked, having known the whole time that he couldn't leave her out of his decision.

Silence selected her preferred shield, the one with the serrated edges. Hark shrugged, then hefted the nearest *nighnor*. "Her brain is a mud puddle. Tell us a way to guarantee her restored mental health and we're all over that. Ready to skip right to the endgame."

Nynn was falling away from him. Things that fell eventually crashed and shattered. For nearly two months, he'd lived with the shadow of who she was. He'd sworn to keep her safe. In body, she was, whereas he was cursed with too many overlapping memories that swirled into gray clouds. At night, when he slept alone in his dorm, he simply remembered her kiss, her smile, and the feel of her body. That satisfaction was gone now. Knowing it had existed at all was an internal scar he would bear for the rest of his life, one spent in darkness and brightly lit Cages.

During the waking hours, however, he watched her. Had she given him any sign, he would've been able to select the right course. A softening of her expression? She might have forgiven him and he would work to get Nynn back. A frown of confusion as old memories filtered through? She might be close to breaking past the barriers in her mind.

He'd seen nothing except the balls of energy she hurled around the practice Cage. All he knew, all he felt, was her fury. It blotted out everything else.

"No." Leto grabbed a mace and a shield, strapping the latter in place. "I won't go through with it. If you try, I'll take you both down."

"You'd rather let her sleepwalk through the next ten years?" Hark was smiling again, but the expression was cruel, completely void of mirth. "Or until some Kawashima or Townsend bastard takes off her head at the next Grievance? She'd die and she wouldn't even know the reason. Her little boy . . ."

"How did you know that?" Leto growled.

"Silence and patience. I have my partner, Leto of Garnis. Yours seems to have gone missing. Tell me these last few weeks haven't been like fire under your skin."

"Shut up, you Thief bastard."

"And you're a remnant of the Lost." Hark stepped back, hands spread wide. One still held the *nighnor*. "How appropriate. So lost."

Silence looked between them, until her bizarre tickling voice became real sound. "I don't want to be numb. She said that to you."

She'd actually spoken, and the words cut Leto to his heart.

The two departed, with Hark calling over his shoulder, "Good hunting, my friend."

Leto stood, chest out and spine straight. He no longer wanted to be numb either. He'd been selfish for too long. After this match, with Pell safe, he would do what Nynn needed—even if that meant tearing into her thoughts with his bare hands.

He looked down at his hands. Scarred. Calloused. Too many years of abuse for his body to repair itself. If using force would make this better, he would've done it already.

Nynn smiled at Silence and Hark as they entered the Cage. It was a nasty smile. It felt nasty on her lips. Yet she would've traded her partner for either of those Sath Thieves. Leto of Garnis was still shackled to her—although not literally. No one entered the ring to bind them together. She didn't think she'd be able to stomach another such round. Chained as a pair, they took the applause as a pair. The champion of the Asters got to take equal credit when her gift blew the air out of their opponents' lungs.

She wanted to scratch the tattoo on her shoulder. Scratch. Peel. Rip it off. This was her third match. Leto fought for a promise for his sister. Nynn intended to appeal to the Old Man. A new tattoo. A serpent. One that proved she belonged among his best warriors.

First she needed to win.

Thousands of people bellowed their eagerness to get the evening's final match under way. Nynn bounced on the balls of her feet, back and forth, and loosened the ligaments of her shoulders. Leto had wanted her to use the whip-thin sword edged with gold. She'd stuck with her heavier, austere choice and her right arm had compensated. She was stronger now. Strong enough to take her place as the Asters' champion.

The bell sounded.

The collars winked out.

The fight was on.

Nynn had gained so much control of her gift, but it remained a slow process. Build the energy. Release it. She hovered back as Leto took on the paired Thieves. Her opportunity would come. If she had her say, her partner would stand dead center of the blast.

Leto was in fine form. Fast. *So* fast. By the time his eyes set on a target, his body was already there. The mace swirled in his wake like a contrail.

She shook her head. Pressed fingers to her temples. Sometimes words came to her that didn't make sense. She saw the image of a plane, with a defined trail of white lancing the blue sky in its wake.

She lived in the complex. She was losing . . . missing . . . something.

"Move!"

Nynn snapped back into her head with a crash. Leto's warning had come just in time. She raised her shield and deflected Hark's pouncing assault. He'd stolen Leto's agility and speed. She landed on her back, shield over her chest, with Hark balanced there—practically squatting. He looked over the rim with that infuriating smile.

"Are you sure you don't like being numb?"

Mouth open, Nynn couldn't speak, could barely think. She let her body take over. The collars reactivated, so it was strength against strength. She used momentum and a trick of balance to fling Hark away. Bounding to her feet, she found Leto dodging Silence's fierce shield.

The break was brief, as the collars deactivated again. Her gift, coming and going on a whim, was like drowning—catching a breath—drowning again. Whoever was in charge had shortened the bursts, perhaps to compensate for her ability. She couldn't get the rhythm of it. Every time she gathered enough concentration to hurl a ball of energy, she lost it again.

No.

It wasn't the collars this time.

The Sath had teamed up to take the power from her. Beyond a blue blaze of light and her own red fury, she saw Hark laughing. Silence was nearly . . . *sympathetic*.

Leto's shout was drowned in a sea of pure energy. The force slammed into her like taking a wrecking ball to the chest. The back of her head connected with one of the octagonal frames. She had a brief moment of déjà vu. Once, long ago, she'd let go—let it all go—and had wound up with her head smacked flat against the pole.

Then the image was gone, because she was screaming. Fire lanced across her body. She practically felt the metal of her armor dissolving into hot glue. Or, Dragon-damn, maybe that was her skin. Her nerves swam and collided. No relief. No air. No telling up from down from death. Her lungs felt crushed in on themselves. Even if she had a thousand bones, they would all be shattered. Pain beckoned her toward unconsciousness. She tried to keep her eyes open but failed.

With her body made vulnerable, and her brain left defenseless, a concussive force of another kind slammed through her skull.

Crowds? A Cage?

Leto was shouting at the Sath. "What the fuck was that?"

"A test," Hark replied. "We can't rely on a weak link."

At the man's mock salute, Leto took up his mace as if to resume the fight. The crowd thundered its approval.

*"Leto!"*

Her scream jerked his head. He ignored both Hark and that thumping call to violence by kneeling beside Nynn. He lifted her head and brought it to rest across his thighs. A manic bubble gurgled up from what was left of her consciousness. "Not a good pillow."

Why did she need him? Why had she bellowed his name? He was her tormentor and her captor. Only, the shelter of his arms made her shudder. His body forced her to feel pleasure and relief and utter confusion.

"Nynn, open your eyes. Now, lab filth. Open your eyes and look at me."

She flinched. *Lab filth.*

*Why do I have scars?*

Leto leaned close, but that didn't make understanding him any easier. "I lost," he said. "*We* lost. That applause is for the Thieves."

"What happens to us now?"

"You survived. That was the agreement. I think it will depend on which way the Old Man wagered." He unfastened what was left of her armor, which still smoked and hissed. "But now we'll know."

"Know what?"

"If he can be trusted."

Nynn tried to push him away, but he was too powerful. "You're talking blasphemy."

"He's not a god," Leto hissed. "He's a *lonayíp* human. *We're* the gods."

The world had gone gray until the lights looked like glowing thunderclouds. He wasn't making sense. Jealous still? No . . . They'd lost.

"You blame me."

"You idiot woman. Whether he lost money or won, the Old Man promised my sister would be cared for. All I needed to do was keep you alive for three matches."

He dragged her to standing, despite her protests. "I have."

She sneered.

"Fine," he said, jaw fixed. "*We* have. If he honors his word about Pell, then he might do so with regard to your son."

"My . . ."

Images flooded back. A man she loved . . . and blood. A little boy . . . and tiny, precise wounds. She saw her mother and a house demolished by a blaze of fire. She recalled Malnefoley—his years of friendship and support, and the decision that had made her an outcast.

More memories, this time of captivity. Humiliation and rage and promises she believed would free her son. Violence and endless hours of disciplined training. She'd been Leto's warrior to mold. They had been lovers, too—as close as man and woman could be.

The halves of two different lives smashed together and spiked from her forehead to the base of her spine. She remembered a soothing copper light and a voice speaking directly into her mind. A serpent's voice.

Ulia. Telepath. Gift.

All that she'd been, both Nynn and Audrey, had been blocked. Wiped clean.

The darkness could take her now. All she knew was bursting apart, as surely as her gift burst into fields of light. She didn't—couldn't—

"I have scars because of Dr. Aster," she said haltingly. "I met Caleb MacLaren in school. He was my husband and he's dead. Dragon damn, Leto." She smothered her cries by shoving her knuckles into her mouth. "I hated you, but I *don't* hate you. You're . . . You've helped me survive. Resist the Asters. For—for . . . my son."

"Yes." His expression was intent, eager. "Make that leap, Nynn. I'll catch you. Just tell me his—"

"Jack." She closed her eyes against another blinding wash of pain. White and black fused as if neither existed. Nothing did. Just the agony of nearly having lost something so precious. "How did I forget him? How could I?"

"This isn't the time."

*"Isn't the time?"*

"Trust me. By the Chasm and the Dragon, can you do that?"

"Tell me why. Leto, I don't have anything else. Give me something to *know*."

"Now is when we'll see if the Old Man can be trusted." Leto hauled her along his side, then kissed her temple. "About my sister, and about Jack."

# CHAPTER TWENTY-FIVE

Leto needed to get Nynn out of the Cage and back to the complex before too many pressures caused her mind to implode. Already, when he looked down into her heavy-lidded eyes, he saw nothing but defeat.

Sweat tinged with blood trailed down from her hair. A human would be dead by now. The concussive force. The blow to the back of her head. Her feet tripped along, but at least she was holding up the majority of her weight.

*Get her out of here.*

*Keep her safe.*

That wasn't going to happen.

Although victorious, Silence and Hark stood quietly by. They were good warriors—better than good—because they had perfected self-defense of a different kind. Blank disinterest from her. Grinning idiocy from him. Those expressions were exactly what everyone anticipated seeing, which had allowed them to appear good little soldiers for so long. Leto had never considered them allies, but at that moment, he grasped at the best he could find.

Their plan . . .

The Old Man entered the Cage, as did Dr. Aster and the Pet.

The crowd quieted.

The Old Man was given a microphone. His rasping, crushed voice was even more threatening when amplified. "Our champion, Leto of Garnis. Defeated!"

While thousands celebrated the novelty, an honorable, *loyal* part of Leto pinched into a stone that dropped through to his gut. Emerging undefeated had been the goal. Once. Too long ago to remember. Now, he held Nynn, who was mostly conscious. He had dragged her through three matches, dodging her wrath along the way. He had succeeded.

Yet having to let go of that former glory was like ripping out his ribs. He needed his ribs. He needed his pride. The latter had been pulverized.

The rumble of shouts quieted as the Old Man continued gloating. Maybe that answered whether he'd be wrathful or pleased with the outcome. Had he lost part of the Aster fortune, Leto might as well resign himself to an execution in the preliminary round of the next Grievance—Leto, who'd won the entire tournament at age sixteen.

Again, he felt a tingle of that old simplicity. Fight. Win.

Nynn groaned and coughed up a fleck of blood.

Nothing was simple now.

Amid the chaos, the Pet walked with ethereal poise across the scuffed clay floor. She wore her customary black leather, from her spiked collar down to slim-fitting boots. Intensely black hair swept in freakish disarray across her brow, around her ears, down her neck. None of it mattered. She was a riveting beauty—untouchable and cold, but with features pure and unsullied, as if she'd never conjured a single thought.

She hunched close to Nynn's body, touching, almost caressing the shattered armor.

"What in the Dragon . . . ?" Nynn whispered.

"No. *Because* of the Dragon."

"Who are you?"

The Pet focused her bright green eyes on Nynn. "The Chasm isn't fixed."

"You've said that before. I don't understand." Her body was going into shock as she shivered against Leto's side.

"Jack is waiting for you. Nothing will ever be perfect for our kind. But you will hold him again."

With a strangled gasp, Nynn faltered. Leto caught her in his arms. At least his strength was good for something, because his thoughts were a tangle of wire and chain. He strode past the Asters and out of the Cage. The doctor's laughter trailed after him like a dirty stench.

The stench of the labs.

Just out of sight of the madness in the Cage, Nynn sputtered back to life. She fought him, hard enough that they both collapsed onto the concrete floor of a walkway in the rear staging area.

"Say something," he growled.

Too much. He couldn't process this much at once. So he took it out on her.

"Talk to me, you useless woman!"

"Let me kill him." She rolled onto her hands and knees. The dragon on her bare shoulder blade gave off that ominous, beautiful glow in the corridor's dim light.

Her armor was a lost cause, but the steel in her body remained. "He's in the Cage. Right now. I'm going to kill him."

"With what? Are you going to spit on him, too?" He grabbed her chin with none of the gentleness the Pet had used. "You'd better learn to play dumb *fast*. I don't know what's happening in that head of yours, but it's all shaken loose. That's true, isn't it?"

"Yes. Everything. I don't—like a car crash in my brain."

Leto exhaled. "Brave girl."

"I don't understand any of this."

He'd have thought himself too tired and abused, with his pride burned to cinders, but he managed a sick smile. "Then we're partners again. I don't either."

"She said Jack is waiting for me."

"That doesn't mean a Dragon-damned thing. She's like the doctor's extra limb. Whatever she said was something he *wanted* her to say."

He pushed to his feet. He could save Pell and keep Nynn from getting herself killed. If either of them was harmed, he'd take his rage out on Silence and Hark. The plan they'd suggested was tantamount to anarchy. What they'd actually done was take the choice out of his hands.

*For the best.*

He'd never adjusted well to change. Everyone knew that. Now he needed to move as quickly in his mind as he could with his body. He was no longer the Asters' champion, and his future was not clear. All he knew was that Nynn remembered her son. That eased the tightness in his chest that he'd carried for months.

Leto pulled her face nearer until their foreheads touched. "We haven't much time," he said. "We'll have to take the bus back to the complex."

"There's snow outside. We're somewhere high altitude."

A shudder traveled across his body in a slow but leveling journey. "Is that what it is? That smell of cold?"

She touched his face. "Yes, Leto."

"You're back to thinking about getting free."

"Aren't you?"

"Hark and Silence have a plan."

"Incinerating me with my own gift," she said with a hard twist of her lips. "Great."

"I don't know that I trust them either. But right now, you need to do just as I told you. Play dumb. Be as brainwashed and compliant as I was."

"Was?"

He nodded while pulling her to her feet. "Was."

"I don't know whether to gloat or celebrate."

"Both. But *later*. If they think you're useless or dangerous, they might send you back to the labs."

"I'd see my son again." Her hands fisted within his.

"But without the means of setting him free. Think like them. The long game." He dipped his head, only briefly. "It's something I'm not used to doing."

Darkness passed through her eyes. He watched it as if her soul were being poisoned. Voice flat, body trembling, she said, "I was Audrey MacLaren."

*Not again, Nynn. Don't go.*

But he forced his stiff neck to nod.

"Before that, I crippled my mother so badly that she'd begged for death. How could I have forgotten that?"

"You . . . ?" He touched her cheek as understanding dawned. "The psychic block. Calm yourself, or you'll never sort through the answers."

"I was already a killer. Who knew? I was meant to be in the Cages all along."

"You weren't. Not you. Not down here." The vehemence of his reply startled them both. Logic be damned, he was being selfish—and it felt amazing. "Do this, Nynn. Do it or they'll *take you from me*."

Her expression softened. She leaned into where he still cupped her cheek. "We can't have that, now, can we?"

Then, as if by the trick of some magician, her gaze went hazy and heavy-lidded and dead. She was no magician now. More like a blunt instrument. She straightened her shoulders. Even in that ruined armor, or perhaps because of it, she looked every inch a soldier tamed by the Asters. Humbled, yes, but still proud, ready to rise again.

He recognized that posture. He recognized that stance and that vacant acceptance. He'd seen it in the mirror every day since his adolescence, when defeat was more common than victory.

"I've turned you into a fiend." His throat was tight enough to gag him.

"You've taught me how to survive. Let's keep it that way."

A curt nod.

They cleaned and stowed their weapons, soon joined by Hellix and Weil. Weeks had helped the woman recover from Nynn's attack during her first Cage match.

"Well, well," Hellix said. "The Thieves figured out how to turn your freak against you. The champion taken down." His sneer warped into a smile without mirth. A pitiless expression. "Maybe your punishment about her tattoo will be the first of many. I'd love to be the man who struck the lash on both of your backs."

At Leto's side, Nynn didn't even flinch. Because she didn't remember, or because she was that in control? She'd teased Leto, and she remembered Jack. He had to trust that her blankness was an act, just as he'd encouraged.

"How did your match fare, Hellix?"

"I'll rip out your tongue, lab filth."

She arched a golden blond brow. "I guess that answers my question."

With that snide reply, she put an end to Leto's doubts. Nynn was back. She was returned to him. Now to keep from letting everyone else know that.

After the rest of the Asters' warriors returned their weapons, they walked toward the airlock corridor. Silence and Hark assumed no boasting posture, each flicking glances at Nynn. Silence kept her expression as placid as always, but Hark radiated an air of accomplishment paired with eyes brimming with curiosity.

They'd done their part, it seemed, even without Leto's consent. He may well owe them an apology—and the serious consideration of their plan.

As if nothing had happened, the Dragon Kings offered their wrists and accepted their manacles. Leto was shocked by the urge to fight back. His imprisonment was real. The heavy metal cuffs biting into Nynn's slender wrists were real.

As was the one-two-three thump of the Old Man's shuffling rhythm.

His steps echoed down the corridor long before he came into view. Perhaps he took to the shadows on purpose. Even Leto could not discern the exact shape of his body as he approached. That should've been possible, even while wearing the collar.

Other steps followed: one set assured, one like a ballerina on tiptoe.

Cold swept across Leto's skin. Nynn had been able to mask her true feelings when faced with Hellix. But when faced with Dr. Aster? The man who'd abused her and who still held her son prisoner?

Leto could only trust that her mind was clear enough for strategy. Otherwise, he'd be forced to make a choice—one that shook him to his bones. He could play along just as well, hoping for the guarantee for Pell's care to be honored, or he could risk his sister's safety by jumping to Nynn's defense.

Nynn felt each and every one of her scars.

Not the ones Hellix had carved into her back, although she knew they were there. They would heal in time.

No, the scars she felt were burning reminders of hell. They scorched beneath her skin, where cauterizing blades had rendered even Dragon King cells unable to heal. She looked down at her left hand and remembered the anguish of when Dr. Aster had broken each middle knuckle. No one else would ever notice the difference, but she did. Her fingers didn't line up just right.

Scars.

More scars.

And he held her son captive, if Jack was still alive.

She banked a shudder and cut that thought off at the

knees. Jack was alive. She would've felt it carved into her marrow, had he been killed. She'd endured that grinding agony when Caleb was murdered.

Her task, as it had always been, was to keep her boy safe. That meant suppressing the nearly overwhelming urge to jump on Dr. Aster, wrap the manacle chains around his neck, and smile as he turned the color of a bruise. She would snap his neck.

A glance at Leto's profile revealed the same determination. He was trusting her, just as he had in the Cages. He was trusting her to remember all her training, and that his sister's future was on the line, too.

*I hate them. I hate them all for what they've done to us.*

*Us.* Because she and Leto were in this together.

She realized now that he had saved her from wearing their mark forever—the serpent that circled his skull. She owed him so many different apologies. She'd never get to tell him if she gave hint of her true feelings.

"Leto." The Old Man's voice was as raspy as dead leaves. "You did not emerge as champion."

"My apologies, sir."

"No apologies." His warped smile was a chilling reminder that while Nynn hated the doctor, he was born of equally maniacal stock. "Silence and Hark performed wonderfully, as did you both. The family made a fortune today."

The Sath pair were infuriating in their ability to match completely blank expressions. Even Hark, the smiling bastard, registered no emotion. Plans and tests and weak links. The Tigony were not the only tricksters among the Five Clans.

Nynn was still missing too many pieces to keep up.

The Old Man grinned and leaned heavily on his cane. "Your performance couldn't have been more entertaining. I'm very pleased."

"I'm glad of that, sir," Leto replied. He sounded humbled but no less arrogant—quite the feat.

"And you, Nynn of Tigony? How do you feel?"

"Gratified that I did my duty for the family." She couldn't quite make herself say *sir*, when calling Leto by that title of respect had become a teasing joke between them.

"Good, good." The Old Man ushered his son into the conversation. "You kept your partner whole for three matches. Such a remarkable job of training such a stubborn mind."

Nynn remembered a time in the recent past—Dragon be, so many memories returning—when Leto would've taken genuine pleasure in such praise. She didn't dare assess his expression to see if that was still the case.

*Trust. Oh, Dragon damn. Just . . . trust.*

"You not only survived, Nynn, but thrived in your natural element. I knew you would become remarkable. Your part in tonight's drama was equally important." He spread his hands. "Although you didn't technically win the fight, I offer your choice of rewards."

She felt rather than saw Dr. Aster become more attentive. He'd studied her for more than a year. He knew her weaknesses better than she knew her own. But those had been the weaknesses of a distant, grieving woman named Audrey. The sadistic doctor had no idea who she was now.

*Long game,* Leto had said.

Shutting away the request that Jack be freed was almost simple, but not without pain. She knew what she needed to do—stay hidden—and she would not deviate from that goal. Although she would never sacrifice him for a moment of selfish comfort, she was able to ask for that comfort when there was no choice to make.

"I didn't technically win the fight," she said, purposefully echoing his words. "But I would ask for the reward offered a winning warrior. I want a partner tonight. I ask to share Leto's bed."

Again, Leto stiffened. She was as attuned to him as she was to her own breath. Anyone with his senses would've been able to read them both like fresh newsprint. The men she faced were beasts in anonymous gray suits, but they were still human.

The Pet, however . . .

Hands clasped around the doctor's upper arm, she made a noise that sounded more feline than human. Contentment? Appreciation? Nynn didn't think it was because she'd chosen Leto over another warrior. Instead, the strange woman looked up with an expression of having shared a secret victory.

Pale, ethereal, possibly insane, the Pet *was* a Dragon King. If Nynn had ever doubted, she knew it as fact now. But what clan was she? What power did she possess?

"Request granted," the Old Man said. "I'm glad to see that the Cages have brought out the more carnal side to a Tigony. No one would've expected that, but I enjoy seeing arrogance brought low."

He glanced toward Leto. He might as well have hunted for signs of life in granite.

"Now, Leto, the time has come to honor the promise

we made. Pell will no longer be a burden to Yeta and her young family. You will never need to worry about her future. My son will assume responsibility for her care. She will live out the rest of her days within the safety of his personal residence."

"His personal residence, sir?"

"Yes, my champion." A cagey, disgusting glint matched in the eyes of both father and son. "My son never likes to be far from his work. He lives in the labs. And so will Pell."

# CHAPTER TWENTY-SIX

Leto needed Nynn's kindness. Wanted it. Knew his sanity depended on it.

Yet they sat side by side on the bed in his room, not touching. He hadn't moved since their return, when they'd cleaned and changed clothes. He couldn't move now. His heart had been carved out with a machete. It no longer beat. It no longer had reason to.

"You held your niece," she whispered. "You told me so."

His throat ached. He wanted to claw at it until the collar fell away or his head popped off. Death for a Dragon King. He deserved it after trusting such twisted men. He'd believed their promises, dispatched dozens at their command, and brought damned and innocents alike into the fold—training them, yes, but feeding them the same brainwashed lies.

Only Nynn had ever gotten it right. He was the fool.

His fists looked so powerful resting on his thighs, but he didn't feel powerful. "Do you trust any of your memories right now?"

She stroked his bare shoulder, soft but not tentative. Her hair smelled of snow. She'd answered that mystery for him: a name for that scent of sharp, crisp air. "You're right. I don't trust much of anything, except that I'm here with you."

"And that makes it better?"

Nynn's flinch meant he'd gone too far. As her trainer, he would've gloried in drawing forth an unchecked show of fear. It would've been proof of his intimidation.

He dropped his head into his hands and scraped the back of his skull. She crawled behind him on the bed. After stripping her shirt, she draped across his back and held him around the chest.

"You couldn't have known." Her breath stirred him more gently than the precious weight of her lithe torso, but no less intensely. "Whatever they've done, they did it *to* you. They did it to me as well. We've had so little to hope for. What person, human or Dragon King, would've refused the chances that have been dangled in front of us?"

"They've let us stay here together. Another prize, I suppose." She tightened her hands around two fistfuls of his flesh. He closed his eyes and leaned his head back. "The things I want aren't mine to keep. That's what it is to be a slave."

Nynn licked the top of his spine. She'd never be able to lick all the way up, reaching his hairline, because the collar barred the way. A barrier he'd worn—suffered under—since his earliest memories. He'd wanted glory and respect. Now he wanted to kiss Nynn's bare neck and he wanted to see the snow, even if the glare blinded him for days.

And his family. His fear outweighed his hopes now. What had been fighting for their future was now a matter of staying strong just to save them.

"You don't feel like a slave." She tensed her fingers again. Dug into skin and muscle. Pressed her breasts more firmly against his back. "You don't think like a slave. Not anymore."

Nynn's ministrations tempted him to dive into her embrace, join with her body, lose his thoughts in a burst of release. He couldn't. Not yet.

"I held her," he said quietly. "She was so small that she fit in my two palms. I thought I would drop her until Yeta showed me the right way to hold her. Black hair. Beautiful golden skin. Her face was peaceful when she slept, then tight like a wrinkled ball when she woke and cried. I watched my sister rock her. I watched Dalnis duck away, overcome by even more emotion than I felt." He shuddered an exhale. "I'd been so proud, Nynn. I'd fought for a decade so that they could hold a child."

"And her name?"

"Shoshan. Shoshan of Garnis." He rocked up to stand. Nynn still knelt on the bed, bare from the waist up. The solace she offered was so compelling. "Was she even real? And if she was . . . If I fought so that Dr. Aster could help Yeta conceive . . . Then why were you able to give birth to Jack? A natural-born Dragon King. What have I been fighting for?"

She stood with innate grace. Kind but insistent hands—hands lined with callouses that matched his own—pulled his gaze down from the ceiling. It was either stare at the ceiling or at the perfect swell of her breasts. He was a hungry, greedy man. Had he freed his angered beast, he would've turned her over the bed and fucked her. Again. Like they'd done before.

He was not the beast the Asters expected. He was a

man who wanted this woman, her sighs and compassionate touches and respect. All of her. A good thing, because Nynn wouldn't let him look away. When he found that familiar mix of stubbornness, smarts, and a glimmer of humor in her eyes, Leto didn't want to.

"You've been fighting for your own version of survival. You've been fighting because you thought you were doing what was right for your family."

"Now Pell will live under Dr. Aster's so-called care." The bile that rose into his mouth held the taste of poison. "She could've been safe with Yeta. I thought . . . Dragon damn, I thought I could give her something better."

"You can still. We can for both of our families."

"More hopes."

She brought him down to meet her. A kiss of compromise. Slight, sweet, and vivid enough to shine light into the dark places he'd kept hidden. "Hopes *we* control. Nothing they dangle in front of us, but the ones we make for ourselves."

"How is that better?"

"They can't enslave our thoughts."

He pulled her into his arms and held on. They had little else but the shared comfort of two bodies and two minds shying away from pain.

"Thank you." Her soft words brushed moist heat along the thin skin of his collarbone.

Confused, Leto pulled back enough to see her expression. "For what?"

"I wear a dragon on my back instead of a serpent. That was because of you. I was smug and satisfied when the Asters whipped you for that. I thought you got what you deserved. Thought you'd been jealous of . . . Fuck. That you'd made the choice out of some warped pettiness. Instead, you did it to save me."

Leto was surprised to find himself smiling. Slight. Chagrined. But it was still a smile. "You said you had a serpent inside you. You didn't need another one." He frowned. "You also said, 'Burn it down.' Do you remember that?"

She began to tremble. Her voice was a chatter of teeth and sloppy consonants. "Can we . . . ?"

"And what you said about your mother?"

"I don't want to. Leto, please. It's fire in my mind. Too much."

"For now. Too much." With his arms closed around her, he kissed the top of her head. "I want you again. I think I've wanted you from the start."

A shaky sob rattled from her chest into his. "After seeing me naked, how could you not?"

"Would it upset you to hear that I've used that technique with every neophyte?"

"Did every neophyte turn you on?"

"No. They whined or begged or cried, so that I wanted to make it worse for them. Keep my pity at bay. You pushed back. Naked. Defenseless. You made me feel like I was the one being tested."

"Your secret's safe with me," she said with a trace of laughter. "Because I didn't see anything close to that."

Another kiss. Arms tighter. "But here. Tonight. Nynn, not like last time."

He didn't have the words to ask for more. Didn't know how to match emotion with language.

She pulled him down for another kiss. Her naked

chest brushed his as she balanced on tiptoes. Such a beautiful miracle of touch. "Have we fought enough, Leto? Tell me we have—at least each other. Tell me that my warrior wants caring, because that's what I want to give."

"Your warrior?"

"You've kept me whole and safe and *mean*, even when it was directed at you and when I made stupid decisions. I blamed you when I couldn't tell one pain from another." She nipped kisses along toward his shoulder, talking as she went. "You were the nearest extension of the Asters. I could take it out on you when I couldn't harm them. But you never faltered. The long game. Save our families. You were strong enough for both of us, when I couldn't be."

"And what has that strength accomplished?"

"I'm here. You're here. Will the skills you've taught me vanish? No. Which means when the time comes to . . ." She swallowed tightly. "When the time comes to burn it down, I'll be your partner in that, too. So yes. *My* warrior."

"But not tonight."

"No, not tonight." She caused goose bumps to flutter down his arm with the lightest caress. "Leto, show me how tender you can be."

Nynn didn't know if she had asked too much until he cupped her shoulders. The wide, implacable wall of his body urged her backward. She was at eye level with the undeniable strength of his chest, which was shaped by muscle and shaded by the sharp, soft angle of light from the single lamp in the corner. Memories layered on memories, with the present caught in a dark, swirling cloud. She had once seen the world as would an artist. Audrey MacLaren. Art teacher. Widow. So much of herself had been taken, as a child, as a lab experiment, and then as a Cage warrior.

Rather than go mad from the anger and pain, she sought the man who would take her mind away, at least for the night. Leto was breathtaking. He had been from the start, no matter how she'd resisted him. Now, as she lay perpendicular on the bed, she could admire him fully. Heavy muscles clung to strong bones. His skin shone dark copper, and his black hair all but absorbed the light. She breathed out. The resentment was gone. All that remained was the privilege of admiring a man built for violence—and who dared to offer gentleness.

His gaze held no violence. She found surprising hopefulness among currents of desire that were practically caresses. Along her cheek. Through the valley between her breasts. Down to her belly where anticipation grew. She was fire and bronze, all things hot and resilient. That power was within her, but his open appreciation made her giddy and weightless.

Soon his weight would hold her down. She wanted that. The security and protection. The seductive mindlessness.

"You stare." His two words, as raspy as sandpaper. She shivered. His gaze shifted to where her nipples beaded.

"So do you."

"Too much to look at."

She extended a hand. "It's like the sun on the snow. You think it's too much, but you can't look away."

Leto paused in the act of removing his plain shorts.

He was already hard.

Nynn continued to stare. She knew she should find his eyes and return to the idea of gentleness that she had initiated, but he was too impressive. They'd been too quick the last time, although tactile memories of biting, kissing, fucking reminded her there was nothing to regret. Just a different sort of need.

Now she could admire his prowess in full. So aroused, his cock lifted high. It appeared as lengthy as her body remembered, as thick and weighty.

Although she'd been holding out her arm in invitation, she levered off the bed and took hold of his hips. She couldn't resist tasting him. Tongue first, just a circle around the clean, broad head.

Leto hissed. His hands curled beneath her jaw and lifted her chin. He loomed over her, as if standing as majestically as a mountain was his gift from the Dragon. "I will not be gentle if we begin like that."

"Women have done this to you, then?"

"I've practically forced this on women."

"Big difference, Leto. Stand still. Enjoy. And know that I'm enjoying it, too."

She liked that his hands tightened around her face, a reminder of the strength he held in check. Every lick and swirl and long, languorous suck drew different reactions from him. Sometimes hisses—those were especially good, telling her she'd taken him by surprise. Sometimes grunts and truncated thrusts, when she'd back off. She didn't want to veer too near to the sharp vigor they'd shared before. Mostly his reactions were told through those hands framing her face. Twitch. Tense. Fingers twisting into her hair.

He was too big to take as deeply as she wanted. She used the clasp of her fingers to make up the difference remaining between her lips and his body. The rhythm she chose was slow and so, so deliberate, even though her body began to hum a potent charge. Since she'd learned to use her gift, she equated arousal with the explosive force. Gathering energy . . . then the release.

This gathering was achingly patient. The release would be complete.

After dragging her tongue along the length of his shaft, she moved to take his throbbing head back into her mouth. Those hands lining her jaw reminded her that, when he wanted to be, Leto was in charge.

*"Enough."* He sounded just as bestial as ever. His eyes, heavy-lidded and fathomless, marked the only difference. He looked stunned. And eager.

Nynn expected his resolve to crumble. She had pushed him too far. Her warrior would shove her back across the bed and take what his body demanded. She wouldn't mind; he would be satisfying her needs as well. But she'd hoped they were more than that.

He proved they *could be* when he dropped to his knees.

"Off with these," he said, tugging her shorts. She had no say—a compromise of sorts between being taken and being coddled. "My turn."

Nynn opened her knees even as he pushed them wide. "You've done this to women, then?"

She'd meant it as a teasing echo, but the skin across his cheekbones tightened as he grimaced. "Not often enough for you to appreciate any great skill."

"I like an honest man."

Lying back on one elbow, she guided his face down until the first rush of contact made her gasp. His lips were hot, but his tongue was even hotter. He lacked finesse. He did not lack patience or intensity. Nynn arched and tipped her pelvis forward. He hooked an arm under her ass to position her as he wanted. His other hand grasped her breast, softly kneading, looping his fingers over her nipple in a pattern that matched the pulse of his tongue.

Breathing heavily, Nynn offered no resistance when he pushed her breastbone in a signal for her to lie back. He eased two fingers into her sheath. He must've appreciated her whispered curse because he grinned against her inner thigh. A rumbled curse of his own trembled up her legs and pooled where his fingers pulsed.

Without thought, she began to speak in the old language. Not Tigony or Garnis. Not Sath or Pendray or Indranan. There was a language even older than the Five Clans, and she knew its words.

Leto paused. Looked up her body. Those nearly black eyes held as many questions as promises of lust and satisfaction.

"I'd forgotten," he said softly, in that same lost language.

"Me, too."

She caressed his cheek, which was roughened by sharp stubble. The ancient spell wove between them, until speaking English or even her clan's tongue would've seemed like sacrilege in the bubble of time and space they'd claimed for themselves.

"Then this is how we're supposed to make love," he said. "Even down to the words given to us by the Dragon."

"Making love."

A frown etched between his brows. After a few more luxurious strokes, so deep where she yearned for more, he eased his fingers free. His features still revealed the riddles of his thoughts, but he lifted up and over her body. They were still sideways across the mattress. His feet must've been planted firmly on the floor. Nynn could only flick her attention between his taut expression and the hand he'd clamped around the base of his prick.

"That's what we're doing, Nynn. Making love."

She smiled, almost relieved that his confusion came from something so simple. Although none of this felt simple. "Yes, we are."

She pulled him down as she lifted up, that same dance of compromise, as they balanced each other. Dovetailed one another. His mouth tasted of her body, which was both shocking and amazingly intimate. Soon that taste was licked and kissed away until she found only Leto. His heat and the sharp sweetness of his tongue swished over hers. Rough breaths puffed between them in a quiet, tender duel.

Nynn was restless. The place he'd filled with such care, with only two of his blunt fingers, needed more. She needed the heavy erection jutting out from the body he held rigid.

She touched one of his unsteady biceps. "This from my warrior? Shaking?"

"You take everything from me." He positioned himself at her slick opening and pulsed inside. No quick thrust. Not even a tease—just the gentleness she'd asked for. Hard, thick, almost asking permission. "Just as you give everything to me."

"Give me everything now."

He shook his head. "We're making love. Those *are* the right words for what we're doing. Because I am not a beast."

"No. You're not."

"And I'm not just your warrior."

Tears burned beneath her lids. She couldn't breathe except in pained little gulps. She lifted her hand and touched the collar she'd always hated. Now she had so many more reasons to despise the things.

She'd asked him once, and she asked him again. "What would you be without this?"

His answer . . .

*Oh, Dragon be. Please.*

With eyes as dark as midnight, as expressive as dance, he pushed his full, throbbing length into her waiting body. Nynn opened her mouth but made no sound. Only shuddered at the rightness of their joining.

He leaned down, cradling the back of her head. She clung to him, wrapped her legs around him, moved with him.

Against her temple he whispered, "I'd be a better man."

# ✦ CHAPTER ✦ TWENTY-SEVEN

Leto wanted to close his eyes and bask in softness. This was what softness felt like—not just Nynn's body, which welcomed his with trust, warmth, and an intimacy so fierce that it stung each nerve. This was the softness of letting down his guard. He gave in to her keeping. So often he'd believed he was the one to keep her safe, but that protection traveled in two directions.

He needed this moment as much as he needed victory.

No, that's wasn't true. He needed this more than victory, because he'd lost in the Cage. Although his pride had been damaged, he had not dried into dust. Unmanned. Ashamed. No, he still breathed. He breathed the scent of the woman who was teaching him different ways of seeing the world. The world he knew was small, tight, dark.

If he shut his eyes, glorying in unfamiliar sensations, he'd be back in the darkness. He stayed with Nynn, with her clear blue eyes that shimmered silver in the pale light. He stayed with the way her moist lips parted. Every deliberate slide into her slick, tight pussy drew forth a gasp or a sigh or a little cry. He moved slowly, giving himself a brief moment to wonder which sound would come next. He liked changing the angle of his thrusts just enough to catch her by surprise.

She clutched his flanks with edgy fingers, urging him with restless pulses. Her nails were blunt, but that didn't mean her sharp journey from his hip to the top of his spine was any less potent. He shivered under the weight of his vulnerability and released his confusion with a trio of sharp thrusts. Nynn's heavy breathing ratcheted down to a moan. *Oh yes.* More sounds to find. More softness edged with the passion and strength they both possessed.

While crossing his arm beneath her back, he turned her to lie fully along the bed. He'd thought of taking her again, in the interminable days after they'd fought. He'd imagined that she would ride him, so as not to aggravate her tattoo and the wounds on her back. Two months on, she was healed. Reality meant he could lever his body over hers and claim her. One day she would straddle his torso and set the pace, but not this night.

He braced his weight on his elbows. Despite the hazy desire in her eyes, she was completely fixed on him, as if he was the answer to every question she'd ever asked.

Him. Leto of Garnis. She believed he could be better than he was. *More* than believed; she expected it.

While drawing out the agonizing pleasure of their joining, he almost shared her belief. Warriors fought and bled and fucked. They didn't make love in a way that put a partner's satisfaction above their own. Leto felt that way now. No matter how urgently he wanted to thrust—hard, deep, unrelenting—he held back. That resistance tapped into long years of training. He was strong enough to be patient. He basked in the moments of soft splendor, waiting for the moment when Nynn would need him to be anything but.

He bowed over her body while she explored his. Hands and fingers and even her heels found rough crevices and made them smooth. She calmed him in ways he'd never thought possible. So very aroused yet somehow *lethargic*. He dropped his forehead to hers.

"I've never had this." The admission made his rhythm falter, along with his heartbeat. He hadn't meant to say anything so personal, even as they shared such a personal act.

She cupped the side of his face in the way that made him shudder with a sense of belonging. "Beautiful, isn't it?"

Leto pushed away his body's needs and lifted from hers. "*Bathatéi.*"

"What?" On her elbows, Nynn's confusion was written across her brow.

"You have felt this . . . this . . . Dragon damn, Nynn, it's beautiful. And they took that from you. Your husband . . ."

He'd never felt more humiliated by his inability to make a point.

Nynn's face had paled, so distinctive in her pain or fear. The golden tone of her skin drained away and left behind the pattern of freckles he had memorized.

She didn't shy away or stop touching him. He'd expected both. When faced with a reminder of that loss, how could she not? Just the opposite happened. She touched him with more assurance and more vigor.

Leto swallowed to quell the monster in his blood. "Because you remember it all now, don't you?"

"Yes."

Guilt overwhelmed him. She was in possession of memories they hadn't discussed. That meant she had her husband back—the life they'd shared, the life that had been ripped away from her.

Nynn stroked where his inner thigh met his groin. He flinched. She caressed him again, until the flinches eased into calm. "Breathe," she whispered.

Now he closed his eyes. She changed position on the bed so that she knelt at his side. Leto was enveloped by softness once again, this time nestled between her breasts. He breathed just to soak up her scent.

"Caleb was taken from me." Her halting words feathered across the buzzed hair and the crown of his head. "And yes, I ache with the knowledge of what we could've shared. We'll never have that."

"I was as brainwashed as you first said. I was part of the system that made your family suffer."

"You were a boy raised to be a man with no choice as to how that happened. Do you yearn to kill and maim, Leto? I don't believe you do. You've never hinted at enjoying the blood for blood's sake. It's all been for your sisters."

"And for glory," he said wearily. "You've felt it. We both know how intense it can be."

"Just like we both know the unfairness of it all. And who *really* caused it. I'll dig their graves with bare hands if I have to, because the Asters will not escape the punishment they deserve."

"You'll have help digging those graves, if they deserve such a courtesy." The cadence of her touches was so soothing. Leto crisscrossed his arms behind her back and held tight. "I can't replace your husband."

"Of course you can't." She lifted his head and held his gaze. "That doesn't mean I want to be alone forever."

"I never thought I'd be anything but alone."

"What about your family?"

"I've fought for their safety, but I can't speak to them. Sometimes they exist more as goals than people. There are moments I regret that I wasn't born one of the Dragon-damned Heartless. At least Indranan warriors can communicate with those outside."

"No." She kissed him so tenderly that it might have been a daydream, but her hand was still at the juncture of his thigh and groin. Nynn was no daydream. "You are Leto of Garnis," she said against his mouth. "You are a Dragon King. And if you let me, I could love you."

He bracketed her head in his hands. "Could?"

Her expression took on a teasing glint—a glimmer of silver to lead them out of the black. "You have to admit, we haven't been on the same side very often."

"It felt right when we were."

"Yes. It did. And it does now." She arched into his touch when he threaded hard, possessive fingers into her hair. "I asked for you, remember? I want to be here with you. To be on the same side and know it's forever."

"We can't promise forever. Not down here."

"Then we get out of here."

He shook his head. "Not possible."

"I wouldn't do it with the stupid, impatient trust I gave Kilgore. Instead, you're my warrior, and I light up like Dragon-damned fireworks." She grinned, slid her warm palms to his shoulders, and gave him a good shake. "Then you could love me, too."

*Could?*

There was no "could" about it.

He loved her. Nynn of Tigony was a firework, so bright and beautiful in a place that had never known either. He needed that light, craved it. More meaningfully, he was grateful that she'd shared it with him. He'd taken to heart that he would keep her safe because *his* heart was at risk. To lose her now would mean losing a part of himself he hadn't known existed, liberated of everyone else's wishes but his. And hers.

"When we're free," he said with his lips against her bare shoulder. "That's my promise."

"Now you get to promise that you won't stop again."

She stretched back against the mattress, with her knees negligently parted. The pink wetness of her sex made him want to taste. He dipped low and licked. Nynn's hands flew to the back of his head. Another new sound. *Greed.* A combination of *yes* and a groan and a curse word older than the Five Clans. She was salt and sweet, hot and pulsing against his tongue. Each questing swirl revived his arousal. The past was the past—painful, and not without a demand to be avenged.

At that moment, however, Leto was finally able to set his mind aside and let his body loose. Reflex. Instinct. Selfish need. Every satisfying lick made Nynn writhe. Her hands stroked faster along the back of his head. Dragon be, she could drive him mad with her enthusiasm. They had matched from the beginning, not in goals, but in resolve and pure stubbornness. He put that stubbornness to its most sensual use, flicking faster, sucking deeper. His prick swelled in response. He was so ready.

This was a claiming, and it was mutual.

"Leto! Please, here with me. Not by myself."

The breath punched out of him. Without thought, he was over her, kissing her, inside her. The slow softness they'd given each other was still there, in the way they caressed and in the encouraging sounds of pleasure. Little gifts. But Leto could not be gentle, pushing, pulsing with that word repeating in his mind. *Claim.*

"I'm here," he said on a gasp. With his head tucked next to hers on the pillow, he drove with gathering speed. Each stroke was stronger. Her tight legs and quick hips met him each time. "We do this together."

Previous orgasms had all been explosions, full and potent and as hard as he'd fucked. This time, with Nynn stretched beneath him and her breath breaking to pieces, he felt his climax building and building. It could've been seconds. It could've been years.

"Nynn, tell me. Tell me you're close."

She had no words, only the fierce arch of her spine and a mangled cry. The clench of her sheath around his cock broke through the gradual build of his pleasure—broke through, then dragged him into an abyss that seized his muscles and locked his bones. His last thrust was as deep as she could take, and she took all of him. Every thick, aching inch. He growled his satisfaction into the pillow, where Nynn had already turned her head, kissing his temple. She licked away the sheen of sweat.

When his breathing quieted, he rolled off and around so that she tucked along his side. "Again," he said into the near-dark. "I want that again."

"Tell your prick." Her voice was sleepy, but he heard a smile.

He kissed her hair, grinning in return. He was *grinning*. "Dragon Kings have remarkable powers of recovery."

"Yes, they do." She yawned and snuggled more deeply into his embrace. "Imagine what it could be if you could use all of your gift. All of those amazing senses."

The thought was almost too much to handle. He'd overload. But that made him hate the collar even more. He had touched, tasted, inhaled Nynn's distinct beauty. All of it *blunted*. He was half-tempted to drag them to the training Cage and make love to her without the barrier that stood between him and his true power.

But no, that would be a poor substitute. Nynn had been right. They would be free.

"After the match . . ."

Leto's scratchy, rumbling voice broke their long, long silence. Nynn may have dozed, but for minutes at a time. It was as if her body only wanted brief moments of sleep so that she wouldn't stray from him for long.

"Hm?"

He cleared his throat. "After the match, you said that you'd killed your mother."

Old pains seized her heart. She wanted to curl into a ball and curl and curl until she couldn't be burned by flame. It had been banked for years, but if she let it, her mind could become that long-ago house on fire.

"I'm sorry," he said. "I didn't know when else to ask about it. Tomorrow, there's no telling, Nynn."

"I know." She inhaled his salty, masculine scent. She breathed him again, knowing *she* was the perfume that didn't smell quite like Leto. "I'm half Pendray," she said, not knowing where else to begin the tale.

Leto made some noise in his throat. "Makes sense now. Freckles like them. Ears a little pointed at the top. And your gift, a blend of rage and electricity."

"That's what I've assumed, too. Well, since finding out the truth of it." She shifted against his side, glad for his protection. "My mother was Leoki of Tigony. She never revealed my father's identity, afraid our clan would punish him. When she refused, she was banished. I was left in Mal's care."

"Mal?"

"Malnefoley."

Leto chuckled softly. "I suppose only you can refer to the Giva by such an informal name."

"Maybe, yes. My mother was his aunt, but she was only five years older. He protected me, and I defended him from those who called him the Usurper. I wasn't trained in the martial styles for no reason. But I was still an outcast because of my bloodline. I lived a step apart." She shrugged, adjusting those painful childhood slights. "Eventually my mother returned. Mal made sure she was accepted at the fortress."

"The privilege of the Giva?"

"More like the power of a man coming into his own." She sighed. Dragon be, this weight on her chest. She never wanted to feel it again. "But my mother was . . . unstable. Whatever she'd endured out in the world had not been kind. Mal was losing the ability to protect her. Things were tenuous enough when . . ."

Nynn blinked back tears. They were welling inside her, with no other outlet. Telling the rest of the story would make crying inevitable. Leto was still looking at her, his grave features etched with concern and a sympathy she never would've thought possible from the great champion of the Asters. Not at first, anyway. Now she knew that he felt a great deal. She took refuge in the comfort he offered wordlessly.

"You've seen what my gift can do. I didn't know how to control it. The house. Our house, there in the Tigony complex. I was sitting next to my mother on her bed. She had a fever, raving, half lost to the world. Then I was fire. The first explosion of my gift."

"You remember it now?"

"Not . . . entirely. I remember people's reactions to it. Grief. Accusations. Hatred. But the actual moment the house exploded and she burned?" She shook her head as tears dripped toward the pillow. "Thank the Dragon I don't remember. When Mal's personal doctor said she would never recover, she begged to be killed. Mal took the responsibility himself when he wielded a Dragon-forged sword to take her life."

Leto petted the tears away, then kissed the corner of her lips. "So when they let some Indranan witch dredge your brain, they hid more than just your gift."

Nynn managed to nod, although her neck was stiff and cramping. "They took most memories of my mother. I became Tigony in name only. Blending in with the humans became a better option. I emigrated to the States. Studied art. Fell in love with Caleb. Became a teacher."

A sob shook her shoulders, then overcame what remained of her control.

Leto pulled her into the hollow of his curved shoulders. He held her, even rocked her gently. The words he said in their ancient, Dragon-given tongue were a comfort, even if her tears drowned out some of the words. She'd lost so many versions of her life, then regained them in pieces only to have them taken again. All of those gifts and thefts had led her to the moment when a Cage warrior held her as if he could take her grief into his own warm skin—the Cage warrior who'd taught her how to forge a life of her own.

The sound of metal scraping into a lock shocked Nynn back to herself. Leto had jumped clear of the bed and grabbed his shorts before she blinked. He threw clothes at her and grabbed a shield and curved sword off his wall. Perhaps he'd been awarded them as prizes after some victory or another, but he held them now like a man ready to defend his home.

Maybe he was, because the lock began to turn.

# ✦ CHAPTER ✦ TWENTY-EIGHT

If anything proved how weak he was in the scheme of the Asters' cartel, Leto knew it the moment his privacy was invaded by three armed guards. The shield and sword he hefted were no better than toys when the intruders leveled cattle prods and rifles loaded with napalm bullets. Without his gift, Leto was a medieval knight against an army from the future.

"Nynn of Tigony," said one of the helmeted men. "You're coming with us."

"Where—?"

The man leveled his prod at her as she yanked her tank top into place. "No talking."

Another of the guards gestured to the armaments Leto had snatched off the wall. "Put those down."

All this time, Leto had believed he was worth more. Now he was staring at faceless human opponents who aimed rifles at his bare chest. Faceless humans had come to take Nynn away.

Without his collar, his decision would've been simple. Take them out. Three guards laid out on the ground. With it, however, he needed to gauge the outcome. He couldn't be sure that he'd incapacitate the guards before one of them hurt the woman he loved.

*The woman I love.*

Dragon damn, that realization had felt so right when holding her close. It had become a weakness. He would never recover from the pain of losing her.

*That won't happen.*

Leto dropped and did a somersault. He thrust his shield between Nynn and the guard holding the prod. Electricity sparked off bronze and jolted up his arm. He swung the sword low and took the guard out at the knees. The crunch of breaking bones was muffled by plastic-bonded armor. Behind his helmet, the guard's scream was muffled, too.

Angered beyond words, Leto used the language of violence he'd spoken since he was a child. He thrust the shield into Nynn's hands and snatched up the fallen prod. Swirling it like Weil did with her lance, he jammed it into the second guard's stomach. A buzzing, gurgling sound was followed by the stench of singed plastic.

Two napalm bullets fired. That premonition feeling he experienced on occasion in the Cages showed him where to escape the trajectory of the bullets. He used sword and prod in a one-two attack against the final guard. Another bullet fired into the ceiling. Its lasting, unnatural green glowed until chunks of concrete rained down.

Leto turned to search for the other two bullets. One sizzled in the middle of the pillow he and Nynn had shared. The other burned in a pool of green dead center of the shield.

He ripped the shield away before the bullet ate

through the bronze. Nynn leapt at him with a fierce shriek. Leto's reflexes and his Dragon-damned collar saved him from taking a knife to his throat. He used momentum to roll with her until he lay stretched over her body.

"You *really* wanted to keep that shield."

She smacked him across the face. "I didn't know it was you!"

"And this?" He yanked the knife from her hand.

"Guard's boot," she said, nodding toward the first man fallen. "Leto, what the fuck is this about?"

He pulled her to her feet. Efficiently, she grabbed her training gear and strapped it on. Silk-lined leather wasn't the same as armor, but it would serve. The set of armor he retrieved from the wall had been his prize after the last Grievance. Yeta had miscarried three months later, so he'd never worn it in combat. *Tainted.* Now it was nothing more than a tool. The gilt trim and onyx inlay may as well have been plain steel.

An alarm sounded.

Nynn flinched mid-motion as she gripped two weapons—the guard's knife and Leto's ceremonial sword. She met his eyes, then tossed him the sword. "Too heavy for me," she said with a tight grin.

"You're learning, neophyte."

"You really want your ass singed."

"Not particularly." He picked up the napalm rifle and checked the ammunition. Seven left.

"You're a Cage warrior and you're amazing—but that looks completely wrong in your hands."

"It's because I'm a Cage warrior and I'm amazing," he said tightly. "This *lonayíp* toy is for cowards."

"Then you're holding it why?"

"Because we'll be facing off against other cowards." He nodded toward the first guard. "Can you handle the prod, too?"

She'd already stripped an ankle scabbard and tightened it around her thigh. Knife stowed, she took up the prod and accepted the smallest shield from his wall of trophies. At least the Asters had been trusting enough in his subservience to allow him that. He'd walked around without manacles and with weapons on his wall because they'd believed him so neatly broken.

"How many charges does this thing have?" Nynn adjusted her grip on the prod so that her thumb rested on the trigger.

"I've only ever seen it used once at a time. No one gets up afterward."

The alarm continued to cleave the air. It was all Leto could do to find a balance between using his senses and protecting them from damage. A Dragon King could lose a limb and never grow it back. He didn't want to test whether losing his hearing could be permanent.

Yet he could always rely on his speed—nearly as powerful as within the Cages. He pinned Hark to the wall with a rifle before even registering the man's presence.

"What in the Dragon's name is going on?" Hark choked out.

"I'd ask the same of you. Wasn't this part of your plan?"

Hark coughed. "What plan would possibly involve you killing three guards and setting off alarms?"

"You and Silence wanted a diversion so you could deactivate the collars. This looks a lot like a diversion."

"If this was our doing, I'd be holding her hand and we'd be getting the fuck out of here."

"Where is she?" asked Nynn.

"Our room, probably grabbing our packs. Do you have cold weather clothing?" At Leto's blink of confusion, Hark rolled his eyes. "We didn't plan this, but we can use it. Are you coming or not?"

"Really?" Nynn was frowning. "You and Silence planned an escape?"

Silence snuck behind her and grasped Nynn's head with her hooked forearm. The woman pressed the tip of a petite dagger at the soft juncture between Nynn's jaw and ear.

"For six months," Silence whispered. "Let him go, Leto."

Despite his renewed surprise at the woman's voice, Leto assessed her posture. He knew her affection for Hark and read the determination in her black eyes. Leto backed away. Hark doubled over to rest his hands on his thighs, coughing the pressure out of his abdomen.

Leto tightened the last strap of his armor. "We'll need another name for you now."

Silence only shrugged and released Nynn.

"I told you, it should be Patience," Hark said. "You're lucky she likes you both. Normally she would've cut rather than turn all civil." Then he spoke directly to her in what must've been some Sath code—or maybe one they'd devised together.

She nodded.

Hark grinned as if they'd agreed to a friendly sparring match. "Now, unless you're excessively fond of the things, it's time to take off these Dragon-damned collars."

After taking down additional guards, Nynn and the others reached the training Cage arena. Hark carried two large duffels while Silence and Leto collected what weapons they could. In a telling gesture, Leto winced and rubbed one ear with the back of his hand. The alarm must be killing him, even with the collar still active and in place.

The pair was likely insane—some sort of Sath madness—only adding gasoline to a fiery situation. Nynn wanted to be the one wielding the lighter fluid and matches. That meant she needed to take a chance on Silence and Hark. If they could get free of the dampening field, if they could escape the complex, if they could find her son . . .

And if Pell was being held in the labs, they would find her, too.

During the night, during the last few months, she and Leto had fused. That was the only way she could explain why the safety of his sister now ranked with saving Jack.

With a ring of stolen keys, Hark locked the arena door behind them. "The others need to stay out of here when we make with the big bang. If this works, they can fight their way free."

From her duffel, Silence produced a small black dragon idol. The tiny hairs on the backs of Nynn's hands stood. Why should a little figurine produce such a visceral reaction?

"Hark was playing with that during my initiation," Nynn said. "It was in two pieces."

Silence nodded, turned her around, and placed the idol at the back of the collar. With a snap and a strange, rusty groan, the steel dropped away. Nynn jumped at the chance to touch her own skin, which was raw in the center and calloused at the edges.

Then came a flood. Unchecked, her gift surged to life under her skin, even more powerfully than in the Cages. It seemed that even in providing a measure of freedom to fight as Dragon Kings, the Asters had discovered a way to keep them small.

"Leto," she said, catching his gaze. "You're going to love this."

He submitted to Silence as she fit the tail of the dragon idol into the hated lock. "Where did you get that? You've been hiding it?"

Hark stood beside his woman. "Half of it was here. Silence found it. Isn't that cool? Like any old rock—although, granted, we had an inside track on where to look. Don't ask. You wouldn't believe us if we told you. The other half came with me from Hong Kong. It's not just a city of hot prostitutes and really, *really* high buildings."

While Silence spirited the idol into the folds of her armor, Hark sobered in that unnerving way of his, turning his jester switch from on to off. "So yes, we've hidden it. And we waited."

"Dragon-damned Sath with your patience."

"See? *Patience*. You're catching on. We have thousands of years of experience keeping our mouths shut. Something of a clan specialty." He grinned. "Although I didn't get the official rule book."

The collar unsnapped and dropped with a metallic

thud. Leto gasped, then groaned. He wrapped his hands around the column of his throat. A manic beauty filled his chocolate eyes. Nynn had seen that expression when he'd pressed her body into the mattress and strove toward satisfaction, finally overtaken by the strength of his release.

He looked to the ceiling and roared an unnamable pain. *"Twenty years!"*

While Silence and Hark unlocked one another, Nynn found her lover and caught his face between her hands. He was inhaling short, heavy breaths, his face distorted by anguish.

"I did everything they demanded and more," he rasped. "They kept this from me."

Nynn nodded. "They did. Now it's time to dig those graves."

They stared at one another. A bright golden glow gathered between their faces. It had happened before, but never like this. They generated their own energy. Nynn reached to touch it. Nothing. It was entirely pure. She could see individual molecules as they shivered with unspent potential.

"That's it. Living gold." Hark sounded awed. "That's what we were waiting for."

When Nynn blinked away her amazement, she found the couple staring at her and Leto.

"What is it?" Nynn thought her head should hurt. How could something so potent be without consequences? Yet she felt stronger than ever, and closer to Leto—joined in new, inexplicable ways.

Hark slugged Leto on the shoulder, which would've been a very bad idea under other circumstances. "Come back to us, my friend." He eyed the ceiling where the unseen alarms continued to blare. "It's gotta be hell, but we need you."

Silence led Nynn by the hand until they stood at a far corner. Her eyes were dark marbles, like the unblinking gaze of a raven. "Weakest right there."

It was like hearing a cat start talking.

"Weakest?"

The clamor of metal caught her attention. Leto was racing in seemingly haphazard directions, so fast that her eyes couldn't follow. Was he testing his powers, or being overwhelmed by them?

"Leto! We need you!"

He snapped to her side. A huge, unbelievable grin took ten years off his face. The care and grim thoughts were momentarily lifted. His throat was a column of scars and overlapping callouses. He would never be rid of that mark, nor his tattoo. Perhaps having his powers in full—not returned, but for the first time—would be compensation.

"Okay, folks, we have one shot," Hark said. "And even this is . . . well, let's say I'd like to get out of this alive, but I'm not holding my breath."

What he explained was ridiculous. Ludicrous. None of it was possible, and yet Nynn felt deep inside that this was a strange destiny. That four Dragon Kings with such compatible skills could come together, *work* together. She could almost feel the tattoo on her shoulder buzzing with excited approval.

"Too bad we don't have an Indranan with us," she said. "I'm half Pendray. The Dragon would be pleased by the cooperation of all Five Clans."

*Don't be so sure.*

Nynn and the other two stared at Leto. He'd spoken right into their minds.

He appeared almost embarrassed. "I've always felt it." His words were halting. "I could almost see what an opponent was going to do before it happened. The only Dragon Kings who can fight like that are the Indranan."

"The Five Clans it is, then. That'll be nice and all kumbaya." Hark flicked a glance at the door. "We'll sort family trees later."

"Yes." Nynn took Leto's hand. "Let's do this. Burn it down."

# CHAPTER TWENTY-NINE

Leto was in pain. He was buzzing. He was furious. He was *himself*.

Only when he felt the roughness beneath his fingertips did he realize he was touching his neck. He didn't even know its contours. Hidden from him for two decades. Although he would bear those scars until he died, he would never wear a *lonayíp* collar again.

Another surety was harder to accept.

*I'm one of the Heartless.*

Had his mother been Indranan, or had Dr. Aster done . . . *something* to ensure Leto's conception and birth? Pell had been incapacitated by her gift. Was she a crossbreed, too? Nynn was, and she was powerful—so powerful. And her son was half human. Perhaps that explained some of the Dragon Kings' trials. Split and segregated, bigoted and aloof, they'd retreated into tight-knit clans and doomed themselves to extinction.

"We're not going die." Even his voice sounded different. Some combination of his liberated senses and his voice box free of a permanent metal grip.

There was no more time to delay. He turned to face

Nynn. Their gazes caught. They held hands. At the far end of the disorienting golden tunnel of light, he found her icy blue eyes. She looked scared, elated, anxious.

"Never let me go," she said.

"Neither of us is in the habit of letting go of the ones we love."

She blessed him with a radiant smile that added more gold to their intimate bonfire. "Be ready to keep up, sir."

His heart pinched. "Make me proud, neophyte."

He could only watch as Nynn pulled the golden energy into her body. He couldn't imagine what Nynn could do with this much pure energy at her disposal. The Pendray in her must be the difference. She wasn't a pure, polite, straight-thinking Tigony. She possessed a wild touch of berserker.

His job was to keep the berserker calm and speed her to safety just before the full concussive blast neared its peak. For Hark and Silence, they had the task of channeling Nynn's gift. Two wrathful blasts were better than one. For Leto's peace of mind, he hoped the split would save Nynn from flat-out exploding. She'd lost control before.

Leto recalled the tattoo on her shoulder, now more a premonition than anything he'd done to save her from the Asters. It was as if Lamot had uncovered the color and shape that had already been there. Nynn, who carried a piece of the Dragon.

Did that mean she could succumb to her own inner violence, falling into the Chasm as the Dragon had done?

The golden energy disappeared. She threw her head

back. Her whole body shook, as if his hands were live wires she'd caught while standing in a puddle of water. Lightning burst and sparked outward from where they touched. With his wild senses careening around the arena, collecting information he could barely process, Leto heard voices, guards, keys.

Hark and Silence positioned themselves before the section of arena wall they claimed was weakest. Leto found a strange sympathy for them. If no other Dragon Kings existed, the Sath would be as powerless as humans. No gifts to steal. What would it be like to only borrow the unfamiliar? They would never know in advance what intensity they prepared to take into their bodies.

*A test,* Hark had said. *Can't rely on a weak link.*

There in the Cage, they'd already tasted a sample of Nynn's power. Leto's long games looked like snap decisions compared to these two.

A tremor in Nynn's mind, a cry, a truncated scream. Between them had grown a bubble of fireworks and sputtering light. It doubled in size until its perimeter sizzled Leto's skin. His sense of touch was radically sensitive. He jerked back, slipped, lost her hands.

"Nynn!"

The bubble was as tall as she was.

Just at his peripheral vision, he saw Hark and Silence touch. Just hands. A quick squeeze. Silence had a lovely smile. He looked away, unwilling to intrude on what may have been two lovers' wishes for luck. Or their goodbyes.

The bubble burst in a furious blast of fire and stinging electrical currents. Leto was faster. No wonder they'd wanted to restrict what the Dragon had bestowed. He grabbed Nynn around the waist and pulled her to the far side of the Cage. She was limp in his arms.

The blast was a tidal wave pouring over them in an arc of molten light. The Cage, which had been the bedrock of his existence, shriveled and burned like paper in fire. Briefly, the Sath pair was silhouetted against the onslaught. He cringed closer to Nynn and groaned as his eyes were stabbed by indescribable brightness. Pain ricocheted between his sockets and the back of his skull.

Leto gave her a shake. Maybe too hard. He couldn't tell how loud he shouted or how fast he moved. "Don't you leave me."

"Going . . . nowhere."

The last of what had been forged steel landed in bits and chunks, all brittle and black like charred wood. Leto realized that much of the training arena looked the same way. Their insane plan had worked. What looked like singed wood was enclosed where layers of metal girders and roofing had been. Maybe it still was metal, just altered beyond recognition.

Light filtered through crags and cracks in the rock, and streamed in great gushes through a gaping hole where Silence and Hark had stood. The hole was almost as big as the octagonal base of the obliterated practice Cage.

"You meant it," he said, pulling her into his arms. "Burn it down."

"Hell yeah."

"You're a wreck."

"You should see your face."

"You want a pretty boy instead? Can't help you there." He kissed her forehead. "Time to leave. You promised to show me the snow."

"What if I killed them, too? Silence and Hark?"

"Then they died on their terms. Free."

Nynn stumbled over the rubble and into the bright glare of late midday on an artic field. She'd assumed it would be morning, but the artificial markers of time in the complex didn't match the turn of the earth. She'd also imagined mountains. This was just flat. Flatness without end. Features mashed together into a stark wash of ice on white on blue.

That wasn't to say it was devoid of life. Hark and Silence stood staring at the white wasteland. They looked like refugees from a coal mine.

"Where's your pack?" Nynn called.

Hark looked over his shoulder with a teasing grin. "Someone's Dragon-damned gift has a nasty kick. Our packs are ash. On the upside, we thought we'd need supplies for a long foot trek. I'm glad we can be proven wrong *and* still survive the shame."

In the distance, maybe two miles away, stood another complex. It was aboveground and ringed with helicopter pads and smaller buildings that looked like private, individual villas. Nynn knew without question that the actual game Cage was inside.

Perhaps she and the other warriors had traveled that short distance on some convoluted, disorienting path, because those two miles could've been traversed in mere minutes. Their bus rides had taken a good half hour. She didn't trust much about her perspective from that time, but she read it as another Aster trick to keep their slaves subjugated.

One long, squat building among the others was lit for business.

*That bastard has my son.*

Leto climbed out behind her and staggered. He shielded his eyes. Nynn wrapped her hands around his upper arm, hoping to steady him. She'd never expected to get this far. The tortures of the previous year—no, the tortures that extended back into her childhood—had nurtured a fatalistic streak she only recognized now that the cold sun touched her face.

Training, fighting, hating . . . they'd taken on a numbing cadence. Saving Jack had become a mantra, not an actual *thing*. No wonder Leto had been able to continue without question for so long. He would've kept fighting forever, to make sure his sisters were safe and that his clan name continued.

But if he *had* continued, he never would've seen the sun or the snow.

Eyes shut, he tilted his face up and panned across the horizon until he faced the sun where it arced toward evening. The thick muscle of his neck was shaded by the angle of his uplifted chin. Callouses and raw skin were reminders of his captivity, and of how intensely his freed gift must be amplifying that moment. He swallowed, opened his mouth, and slowly, slowly, opened his eyes.

The shudder that worked down his body fed into Nynn through her hands, and maybe through her pores. Intimate and elemental.

*Beautiful pain.*

Those two words, spoken with his roughened voice, tickled between her temples. Beautiful pain. Yes, that was it exactly. She looked at the sun, stared at it, dared the elements to take what remained of her. Nothing could. She wasn't numb anymore. She was in pain, the beautiful pain of being awake, finally awake.

"A little help here, firecracker," Hark said. "We need to clean up our mess. I'd rather not share this lovely snow-covered holiday with a passel of guards."

Nynn blinked away from the sun and looked toward Hark. His face was partially obscured by black dots strewn across her vision. Funny that she could look upon the bright colors of her own gift, and through the golden tunnel of light she and Leto could create with their gazes, but the sun was still the sun—more powerful than all of them. Even Dragon Kings needed humbling.

Nynn gave Leto's arm another squeeze before joining Silence and Hark around what now looked like a pit. They'd been living in a pit. Dozens of the Asters' guards were trying to climb to the surface.

The Sath must've been gaining control of their uninhibited gifts, too, because Nynn felt as if they were only borrowing her light. They shared it. They weren't Thieves but comrades in arms. Nynn concentrated on building her power, layering, gathering the energy of the sun and the electricity in the cold arctic air into a lethal ball.

An inner confidence told her when it was enough. She was able to disperse the bright ferocity rather than launch it like a megaton bomb. Silence and Hark shaped it yet again. Together the three remade the gaping hole. Rock fell and twisted, melting into fresh lava before cooling in the frigid air. She staggered back and dropped ass-first into the snow. What remained of the blasted exit was a giant scar on the ground. Steam poured skyward.

"One door opens," Hark said, "and another closes. Ta-dah."

A big hand reached down. Leto helped her creak to her feet. Without speaking a word, she and the others began a fast trudge to the distant outpost.

A few hundred yards of snow had numbed her feet before she frowned. "Why are you two coming with us? Do the Asters hold relatives of yours?"

"Nothing so selfless. We can't walk out of here."

Leto's armor clanged because of his fast pace but he wasn't even winded. Likely he could travel there and back a dozen times before Nynn and the others ran a quarter of the distance.

Nynn stopped. "Wait. Leto. I'm slowing you down. All of you."

"What are you talking about?"

"Just like how they channeled my gift. They can borrow yours. The three of you can make it to those buildings—fast, together."

Leto charged into her space in that restrained, angered way of his. "Leave you here?"

"Yes. You could carry me, but that would be three people digging into your strength. The alarms have already warned the guards at the labs. We don't have time to let them fortify. And we need you as strong as possible to take on those who have."

"You are my partner."

"But right now," she said, "I'm your liability. These

two have been lying in wait for months. They helped us get free. You'll have them at your back, and they'll have you at theirs." She touched his face, ran her thumb over the scar along his upper lip. Out in the daylight, that streak of silvery pink was easier to see. "I'll catch up. Go, please. Find Jack and Pell."

Sometimes the words that shivered out of his mind, into hers, were as distinct as if he'd spoken. Sometimes they were just feelings. Did all Indranan work that way, or was it because he was crossbred? She only felt his desperation. She felt it and echoed it. They would do what they needed to. Their goals would not waver. Even if that meant parting. Her heart was as hot as the rock she'd turned into molten slag.

After a curt nod, he turned away and took a breath. The strength of it lifted his scarred armor. He was a mountain preparing to run—the most impressive thing she'd ever seen. Nynn had only blinked when Leto and the strange couple churned snow in their wake.

She stood there. Blank. Frozen. Colorless and bereft. When tightening her fists, she could still feel the old breaks where her knuckles had been crushed. Escape was not the same as safety for their loved ones. And as much as she loved Leto of Garnis, having lost sight of him amid a cloud of powder white, she didn't need him for exacting revenge.

# ✦ CHAPTER ✦
# THIRTY

Leto was part of the world rather than trapped beneath it. Tiny shards of ice as small as grit scored his face and his gloriously bare throat. Inhaling the air stung his nostrils with pure cold, and he could've sworn he could still smell Nynn—her sweet, feminine scent on the wind. Every time he'd stepped into a Cage, he'd thought his gift was in full force. Not even close.

*This* was what it was to be a Dragon King.

Even with Silence and Hark gathering some of his power for their own, he processed details at a pace that should've made his mind spin. He put each in correct places: environment, velocity, potential threats, and the effect his run was having on his body.

That was an unknown. After all, he didn't know his limits now.

But he realized that his limits didn't matter. He would do what he'd always done. He would fight until he emerged victorious. These stakes were the highest of his life.

As the outpost gained shape and size, he signaled to his unlikely companions. They responded as they would have in the Cages. Instantly. Efficiently. They split away from Leto to flank the building to his left and right. As long as their goals overlapped with rescuing Pell and Jack, they would be welcome allies.

The lab was more like a fortress. He circled but could find no way in. He was on the verge of returning for Nynn—her gift would've made fast work of this hellish place—when his senses sizzled. He sniffed the air. The hair at the base of his skull prickled. Without diverting power to his conscious mind, he ran based on instinct, following the path Silence had taken. Around a sharp corner. Down a long stretch of marble and ice and iron.

The low building they'd assumed to be the laboratory was menacing. It was an eerie blight on the white landscape, even more pronounced than the hole Nynn and the Sath had punched out from the ground. This place radiated with screams. Leto couldn't tell if he heard the screams with his ears or his brain. His newly freed Indranan powers almost overwhelmed the senses he'd trusted for a lifetime.

The arena that housed the battle Cage was huge. It looked even more impressive in its stone housing than from his usual vantage in the center of the action. He veered away from it, intent on finding the source of his sizzling awareness. The sensation was hot and sputtering, pressing out from his forehead and temples. Something was coming. Violence.

The moment he realized Silence's footprints had gone missing was the moment he glimpsed the source of that sizzling crackle. A small device on top of a generator at the rear of the squat building was blinking *red, red, red*. For all his training, he had no idea what it was.

He wanted to strip his armor and beat it against the marble wall. Useless. Being out in the world was as new as a being born.

Yet he wouldn't let himself retreat into maudlin. Whether scent or sound, something gave Silence away. He wasn't surprised to find her crouched on one of the slim eaves, two stories up. Any warrior who didn't admire her elegant balance was a fool. She was looking down at the explosive device that had skittered cold up Leto's spine—a cold very different from the newfound snow and ice.

"What is it?"

Silence shook her head, cracked the knuckle of her right thumb, and mouthed, "Boom."

Tallis of Pendray leaned lower over the handlebars of his snowmobile. Dark goggles protected his eyes. He left no skin exposed to the elements. Riding three vehicles deep on either side of him were the Honorable Giva and five members of the nameless underground. Tallis wasn't a member of that secret network. He didn't want to be. His missions were personal. Perhaps that's why he pursued them so doggedly.

For more than a year, he'd suffered guilt so strong and potent that sleep was nearly impossible. The strength to hold back his rage—the berserker rage he'd suppressed when living among the humans—was beginning to ebb.

He'd killed and he'd done worse. And he regretted none of it.

Except for what he'd let happen to Nynn.

She'd been just another step toward the Sun's

prophecy of uniting the Five Clans—steps he'd taken since murdering a Pendray priest. Only after leading the Asters' guards to Nynn's home had Tallis realized her identity, and that some means were too sickening to stomach, no matter the noble ends.

He needed his conscience washed clean of her pain. And he needed revenge against the Sun, the living goddess whose dreamtime deceptions had guided his life for too long.

The snow was beginning to blend into dreamtime. Predictions and prophecies were streaked by each new spray of crystals. He shook free of those dreams' seductive hold, only to find himself back in the light of a waning sun and surrounded by his own kind. Despite his appearance at the Council, rumors insisted he was dead or some crazed myth. That was for the best.

He tightened his mouth. His resolve was unshakable; his course was set as if by the Dragon. He still had work to do on this earth.

Tallis could barely see the massive complex on the horizon. They had no Garnis among their number, but that was no surprise. Leto and his siblings were the only ones of the Lost that Tallis had known, even in his far-ranging travels. They could've used the amplified senses and speed of a Garnis warrior. The elements conspired with the gathering dusk to obscure even the defined outline of the huge arena's walls, let alone potential threats.

The Giva sped to the front of the triangular formation and motioned toward another distant spot. Not the outpost.

Smoke.

They had no need to signal one another to converge

there first. The seven snowmobiles turned in a wide arc to cover the last few miles of the loud, chilly trek. Through what must've constituted years of work, the rebels had located this desolate Canadian stronghold. A thousand miles of tundra seemed appropriate when tasked with hiding the secret of conception.

Dark clouds rising into the snow blue sky reminded him of the day, months earlier, when Nynn had inadvertently revealed the outpost's exact location. Nynn had destroyed part of Dr. Aster's lab. That had been the proof the rebels had needed to convince Tallis, and the proof he'd taken to the Giva.

Throttling down his vehicle, Tallis pulled alongside Malnefoley. The man's hatred for Tallis had been banked only long enough to rescue Nynn. But they were both caught up in bigger events than the Giva realized.

A female rebel lifted the visor of her helmet. "What is that?"

They looked at a smoking, blackened swath of earth. Falling snow melted even before it touched the surface that radiated waves of heat.

"GPS says that we're above part of the complex," said another.

He was Pendray, although he claimed no association with any of the Five Clans. It was the nature of their loose network that those who wished to remain unaffiliated were allowed that right.

"I recognize this." The Giva's words were strong, although blunted by the wind. He wiped his mouth with the tail of a scarf pulled from his parka. "This is my cousin's work. I haven't seen it in . . . Dragon be, I haven't seen it since the day Leoki died."

"Should we look for an entrance?" Another rebel. Another nameless face. "We know the Cage warriors live and train in a secret facility. They won't be at the outpost."

"But Nynn will be," said the Giva. "Or else she was killed in creating this. Either way, the lab is my first priority."

"What about the Dragon Kings down there?" The Pendray man nodded to the cooling slag. Only hours before, it must've been covered by the same endless snow. "They could be trapped, collared, and at the mercy of human guards."

"I'm not the Giva in this place." Even wrapped in gear to protect against the cold, Malnefoley's exposed features were striking. He was as classically handsome as the gods portrayed in Greek art. Symmetry and strong grace. Optimism and light to Tallis's darkness. "If you want to find an entrance and save what warriors you can, the choice is yours. I'm going to find my cousin and learn what the Asters know."

With that, he affixed his goggles and sped toward the outpost. Three of the rebels stayed behind, while the rest followed Malnefoley's snowmobile. It would remain a mystery whether they did so by rational choice or because, even there, Malnefoley was still the Giva.

Tallis revved the machine's engine and tore through the snow in pursuit.

They closed in on the outpost, which was more like a coliseum of the Tigony's ancient reign. Made sense. The men and women who fought in the Cages were latter-day gladiators—just as powerful and just as powerless. Playthings of the richest people on the planet.

Playthings of the cartels.

Tallis was a man of sideways steps and measured moves. Riding headlong into any situation was just wrong, and yet he needed to do it. His all-weather suit felt infested with lice and the slithering tails of rats. He wanted to be gone, but he battled his destructive temper and stayed the course.

He would atone for the hell he'd brought down on Nynn. And he would have his revenge against the Sun, who'd convinced him that twenty years of murder was in the service of a higher calling.

Maybe then he might be able to forgive himself.

*And there she is.*

Nynn of Tigony was trudging through the blinding white, seemingly alone on the endless, icy tundra. Dragon save him, his niece was returning to the laboratory where he'd handed her over to Dr. Aster.

Nynn was no more than a quarter mile from the complex when she felt an ominous drone. She slowed. That same droning hummed beneath her feet. Her vision was whitewashed, her lungs burned, and sweat glued the protective layer of silk to her skin. Only that threatening vibration made her stop completely.

Two pairs of snowmobiles roared past her, then circled back in wide symmetrical arcs. She had no weapon other than her gift, although the thought of using it made her breath hitch in short, shallow gasps. Not out of fear. Out of pure fatigue. She could gather and amplify energy, but that process seemed to leave her weaker each time. If the figures on the snowmobiles had weapons, if they were loyal to the Asters, she would need to take her chances.

One skidded to a stop ten feet in front of her. She tensed. Every maneuver Leto had taught her was coiled in her limbs. They could shoot her, or they could fight. She would win if they chose the latter.

The figure lifted his goggles and threw back the hood of his parka. Bright blond hair shone bronze and copper and gold in the fading sunshine. He always had seemed like some creature made of precious, untouchable treasures, with the blue waters of the Aegean reflected in his eyes.

"Mal!"

She catapulted forward so fast she thought she'd knock him from the seat of his snowmobile. But he'd always been strong. Despite disagreements, they caught each other in a flurry of hugs and quick words of explanation.

"Now Leto has gone ahead. We have to go."

"Who's Leto?" he asked, frowning.

"He's . . ." She climbed behind him on the snowmobile and grabbed around her cousin's waist. "He's more than I can explain right now. Mal, just ride."

Three other people fell in line behind their Giva. They made short work of the distance remaining to the arena outpost. Hard to believe she'd fought with such gusto and pride within those high, forbidding walls. Caught in Ulia's mind trap, she'd wanted to win so that the Asters would be pleased. The bumping speed of the snowmobile over ice only added to her distress.

She concentrated until two thoughts remained. *Save Jack. Keep Leto.*

Those would be her two most important goals for the rest of her life.

The patter of what sounded like rain arced around them. Sprays of ice shot up from where bullets struck, some ordinary, some glowing with napalm. One of the snowmobile drivers was hit dead center in the chest. Whether man or woman, Nynn would never know. The body swelled green from the inside out where it hit the ground, and would continue to burn until someone used a Dragon-forged sword to end that misery. The vehicle tumbled to a sputtering stop, useless.

Mal grabbed her hands and pulled her tight against his back. They leaned forward so far that Nynn grasped the throttle. She could barely see, could only trust and try to keep them riding straight. Mal balanced, then lifted his arms. The sky shrieked with a crack of lightning. Another. Then another. He gathered them like the stems of flowers, then hurtled them like javelins.

Marble with brick underlay shattered out into the snow. Smoke obscured the damage he'd done. Nynn shuddered against his back as more streaks of lightning cut the deepening afternoon blue.

The machine guns went silent.

Mal took control of the snowmobile, then throttled it to a stop.

The sudden silence was like pain in Nynn's ears. She was probably speaking too loudly when she asked, "How did you know where to strike?"

Removing his goggles again, Mal nodded toward another driver—a woman who'd removed her helmet. "Indranan. She showed me their minds."

"And you *let* her?"

The woman scowled, but Mal lifted his hands. His face had hardened in that way she knew so well. The expression said argument was no option. "You'd rather I guessed? Or turned the building to rubble?"

Her spine stiffened, but she managed to propel her frozen body from the seat. "I remember now, cousin. Everything."

At least that got to him. He inhaled sharply before his narrow lips softened with obvious regret. The Honorable Giva, unnerved. "I'm glad," he replied quietly. "Not for your suffering, but because you've been freed."

"I *fought* to be free." The others followed as she picked her way through what Mal had destroyed.

Inside, she was hit by a sudden headache as her brain adjusted to the change from cold to pleasant warmth. One intake of breath was followed by a flood of bile at the base of her tongue. Her stomach pitched.

*The lab.*

She'd been right. Oh, by the Dragon. She was back in hell.

That meant she was only steps away from Jack.

"Prisoners or enemies." Mal's voice was authoritative but calm as he spoke to the Indranan woman. "Can you find any?"

She shook her head, then shuddered so hard that Nynn could see it ripple across the thick parka. "There's another Indranan here. More powerful. The best I can do is keep her distracted."

Unless the Asters kept another tame Indranan in the complex, Nynn knew it would be Ulia. So many scores to settle, but her thoughts remained focused.

*Save Jack. Keep Leto.*

A flurry of guards stormed along the two corridors

that intersected at the building's destroyed corner. Another Dragon King in a parka—dark hair tipped with silver, eerily familiar features—shed his winter clothing. Power bunched up the line of his back. "Giva, you take half. Time for those tempers of ours."

Stunned, Nynn watched the man flare into a full berserker rage. No weapons. No armor. Just the ferocity of a Pendray warrior who held nothing back. He tore through the guards along the left corridor, while Mal strode down the right. Sparks of lightning shot from his fingertips and pulsed from the walls. She followed the berserker—a living tornado—because he was mowing through the guards at a quicker clip than her deliberate cousin.

The stranger jerked her to the side, just as another stream of napalm bullets shot down the hall. He moved nearly as fast as Leto, but without the elegance, as if his Pendray gift made him too angry for physics to restrain. Half of her could relate.

Pinned to the wall, she watched as the stranger kicked two more guards within inches of death. She slipped free and picked up a discarded napalm rifle. Dragon, she didn't know how to shoot the thing. She'd be better equipped with her fists or a dagger. Funny how what had been important training in the Cages was trumped by how to aim and shoot.

"Go," the man shouted.

She saw a clearing between the bodies and hurried through corridors, past rooms that began to ring with familiarity. She knew this place by its smell. She'd been prodded down these hallways—and sometimes wheeled by gurney. The surgery theater on the right. The prep room on the left. Farther down, the containment cells where she'd been strapped to tables.

She began to scream Jack's name, although the logical woman at the back of her mind knew fury and desperation were liabilities. Didn't matter. Just saying his name with the knowledge that he might hear was too much to contain.

A shadow in her periphery.

She whirled.

Hark used a flat hunk of sheet metal to knock the barrel of the rifle away, just as Nynn fired. Green glowed in the austere marble just behind his head. His eyes flared wide. A quick exhale and a small smile. "That was close." He nodded toward another long hallway. "Any clue? Down there?"

"Yes," Nynn said. "That's the one."

Armed, she and Hark hurried on. Every corner was both familiar and disorienting. Pain ricocheted through her body, as if the rooms she passed could reach out and reenact the torture. A year lost. A husband lost. But, Dragon-willing, not her son.

The lights snapped off. She and Hark bumped to a stop. What had been disorienting was terrifying now.

"Firecracker," Hark whispered. "Do your thing."

Nynn sparked to life. She glowed with electric energy. Just a lantern given to her by the Dragon, lighting her way.

She focused. Took two steps. And saw the Pet at the end of the hall.

# ✦ CHAPTER ✦ THIRTY-ONE

Everything Leto prized was inside a building set to detonate.

He searched outside, with Silence close behind, until he found a service entrance half-buried by the snow. Here, at least, his body was all he needed. Perhaps another man's fingers would have gone numb, but Leto's sense of touch didn't wane. He cranked the service door open with a grunt and a shove.

That smell. *Lab filth.* He nearly coughed on the potent reminder of how Nynn had first come into his care.

Within a supply room, he found repair equipment. Pipes. Hammers. The tools of humans, perfect in the hands of Dragon Kings. He grabbed one of each, and slung three more hammers in the belt of his armor. Smiling, Silence snatched a pair as well. Leto adjusted his grip, but hand-to-hand violence was nothing compared to the blast waiting to take out the entire building.

"Quickly."

He tore down the hallway leading from the service entrance. The three guards he met were fallen men within seconds. Silence dispatched any who lingered on the bright side of consciousness when he moved on. She was a living shadow. Only her white-blond hair gave her away in the half-lit gloom.

They stepped into what must've been a main corridor. Dazzling. Sterile. The stink of fear had nearly been rubbed clean by bleach.

"Can you hear voices?"

Silence tilted her head, her black eyes going distant. Leto felt the touch of her gift as she soaked up some of his powers—his senses and the strange new currents of telepathy. She blinked free of her slight trance, then pointed.

Leto nodded. "My thoughts, too."

They found a hallway that seemed as anonymous as the rest, but it was lined with doors no higher than Leto's waist. Each was labeled by metal plates. He used the claws of the hammer to pry open one of the doors. When it wrenched free, he stumbled back—not because of momentum, but because of the stench. An inhale from Silence was as compelling as a cry of indignation.

Inside one room huddled a thin woman, maybe thirty years old. In the next was a robust man in his fifties, who was completely devoid of clothing and hair. A third revealed another woman, scarred in patterns that nearly matched those Nynn bore.

All were Dragon Kings. No lustrous skin tone. No superiority. They were not warriors and would never fight in a Cage, but these abused wretches were his people.

He pried open doors as Silence led prisoners into the light. Most collapsed against the corridor wall, blinking furiously. He remembered rumors that Dr. Aster kept his test subjects physically fit. None of the freed prisoners was too weak to move, although some wore bandages and splints. Instead, they seemed stunned. Some curled into themselves, as if the open corridor was scarier than sleeping in metal boxes. Their lethargy made him appreciate Nynn's fierce attempts at self-defense. She'd come at him with a chunk of concrete. These people stared with blank confusion.

His heart beat faster as he neared the last of the doors. The head of one hammer tore away. He flung it aside and retrieved another from his belt. Pry. Screeching metal. Pry again. The burn in his muscles was nothing compared to the fear in his heart—that he would find Jack or Pell, or that he wouldn't.

"Dragon be!" came a shocked voice.

Leto turned to find a tall blond man in cold weather gear at the far end of the tunnel. Between them stood Silence, with two dozen of Aster's test subjects on the floor. Leto lifted his pipe and half crouched, ready to defend these people. "Who are you?"

"Malnefoley of Tigony."

"The Honorable Giva," Leto said slowly.

He could see the resemblance now. Nynn and the Giva shared the same coloring and the same perfection of features. Only, this man didn't have Nynn's freckles or the slight point to her ears. He was pure Tigony, and he wore the lineage well.

"You must be Leto."

"I am."

The Giva gestured to another pair of Dragon Kings, a man and woman, as they flanked him. "We'll keep these people safe. Go. Finish your work."

Leto had started on the next door before the Giva

finished speaking. He should tell them about the detonator. To what end? Two dozen dazed faces were ready to panic at the smallest threat. Even if five healthy Dragon Kings managed to get every prisoner outside and away from the building, they would be stranded on the tundra. And there was no guarantee that the bomb was limited to the outpost, lab, or arena. The whole underground complex could be wired.

The best he could do was give these people a taste of freedom, for however long they had left.

He pried open yet another door.

*Pell.*

At first he didn't recognize her. He couldn't count the years since last seeing her face. She was on her back, with her head pointed toward the opening. Beneath her was a rolling pallet. They simply . . . *wheeled* her in and out of what may as well have been a coffin.

Leto had fought for this travesty.

Some part of him had held out hope that it wasn't that stark, that brutally true. But seeing Pell's etherally still face stole the last of his hope. The Asters were murderers and liars.

He forced steadiness into his hands as he rolled her pallet into the corridor. He caressed her brow, half surprised to find she'd matured into a lovely young woman. The tightness in his chest wouldn't ease. Her skin was warm, but she didn't respond to his touch. She was beautiful and would never awaken. All he'd ever wanted was her comfort, but now—knowing what had been done to him and to Nynn during their adolescence—he wanted her well.

If the building didn't burn around them first.

He kissed her forehead. Silence's face was etched with sympathy. She touched two fingers to where Leto had kissed, then nodded. Leto shuddered at what he took to be a wordless vow.

On he went. Three more doors. Three more people to set free. The first after Pell's revealed a young boy.

Leto froze.

"Jack?"

The boy's head jerked up. His eyes were Nynn's eyes. The same brilliance and intelligence, but tempered with so much fear.

"Come with me, Jack. Your mother is waiting for you."

The fear, apparently, was only part of what he was capable of feeling. Wariness, then aggression took its place. He looked more like Nynn with every breath. "What's her name?"

"Audrey MacLaren."

"Her *other* name."

"She told you that, did she? Stories in the dark?" The boy nodded, which made Leto smile. He'd never smiled with more vicious pride. "Your mother is Nynn of Tigony, and she's been burning buildings to the ground to find you."

Hark walked cautiously toward the Pet. Nynn could barely keep her gift from obliterating the corridor. Her light blazed until the marble glowed white and sparkled with snaps of power.

The Pet leaned against the far wall with her hands at the small of her back. She looked tidy and small, like a teenage girl who'd accidentally wound up with an ancient woman's maturity behind her strange, piercing eyes.

"Hark, who is she?" Nynn asked.

"A soothsayer." Although he seemed at ease, Nynn noticed the loose bend in his knees. With any breath, he could spring forward and wield that hunk of sheet metal offensively. "She sought out Silence. 'Wait for the living gold'—and believe me, 'living gold' is the perfect description for when you two stare at one another. Then we'd know it was time to go."

"But why?"

"Something about the Chasm." He frowned. "But also something about keeping the children safe."

Nynn flinched. "What children?"

"All of them," the Pet said. "In the labs. I saw which would survive whole of mind and body, and which would not. Then . . . decisions were made."

Hark scowled. "Dr. Aster doesn't hold the secret to conception?"

"No, but he never stopped looking—to the misfortune of those housed here. *I* bought him time."

"Do you have any idea what you've done?" Nynn whipped across the hallway and caught the Pet around the throat—a throat unblemished by any collar. Sparks and flickers of white-hot light shot out from where their skin meshed. "You helped perpetuate this horror."

Although she gasped for air, the Pet's green gaze was unapologetic. "Your Leto knows about slavery. He's not the only one."

"Where is Aster?"

"Helicopter."

"He left you?"

"I *stayed*. I'll be hunted now. Unless . . ." With a grimace of a smile, she showed off brilliant white teeth in tiny, even rows. "Will you kill me, Nynn of Tigony? I've seen it both ways."

Doubt stilled Nynn's wrath. Could she kill a woman who had done nothing more concrete than stand at Aster's side? She'd believed Leto a useless, brainwashed thug. There was no telling what the Pet had done to survive. She could be as guilty as the sadistic doctor, or as innocent as a child born to the dark life of the Cages.

The decision wasn't Nynn's to make, not with Mal there. She exhaled, relaxed her grip, and let the woman go. The Pet didn't flinch or dart away. She only tipped her head, retaining her deliberate means of moving—a woman as fluid as water.

The dark-haired Pendray stranger who'd cleared the way through the guards caught up with them. "If you want to strangle the little freak, let's take her with us."

"Tallis," the Pet said evenly. "How interesting to see you here. Nynn deserves an introduction before you run again."

Nynn caught his eye. He flinched. And looked away. That eerie feeling of familiarity covered her skin like a fast-growing mold. "Tell me."

The stranger swallowed and met her gaze for the first time. Head proud. Chin lifted. "Nynn, your father was named Vallen of Pendray. He was my older brother. And I owe you a debt beyond words."

"Yeah, we don't have time for that," Hark said. "I'm Sath, remember? Borrow a little here and there? This green-eyed girl is a soothsayer, which means right now I'm seeing a big ball of flames and very crispy Dragon

Kings. Couldn't tell you why, but she doesn't think this building has much of a future." His attention flicked to a chuck of wall just behind the Pet. "And I don't think it's because of the Giva."

Nynn grabbed the Pet and swirled to one side, where Hark protected them both with the bent shield. Concentrated blasts of lightning scraped through the whitewashed inner walls. Mal ripped through marble and cinder block like shredding a paper towel. The blasted, blackened hole was large enough for her cousin to step through.

Leto followed . . . holding Jack.

Nynn leapt to her feet with a cry that was nearly a scream. She snatched her boy from Leto and crushed him to her chest. She smoothed his hair back from his dirty face and kissed him. Again and again. With a sense of disbelief making her shiver, she buried her nose in his hair and inhaled past the lab's sterile stench. Jack. *Her Jack.*

"Baby, oh, by the Dragon." She breathed his name, like a mantra against the madness of having nearly lost him. She would never know his suffering. But then, he would never know hers. Perhaps they could protect each other that way.

"You told me never to swear by the Dragon." His voice sounded different. How could she have forgotten its timbre? No, this was different. Darker and artificially mature.

"There are exceptions."

Wariness clouded eyes so much like her own, which shone with a golden tint. "You'll explain all of it to me."

"Yes, baby," she said with a shiver. She pulled him

close again and met Leto's gaze over her son's shoulders. "Thank you."

She recognized distress in Leto's dark eyes. They were narrowed so tightly that his lashes nearly touched.

"What is it?"

"This building." He glanced at Jack, then closed his eyes. *Set to explode.*

Nynn flinched as if burned. Not just the tickle of his voice in her brain, but the terrorizing words he delivered. "We could leave. Snowmobiles. The Sath borrowing your gift."

Silence and the Indranan woman from the snowmobile stepped through the hole. Together they supported an unconscious woman. Her head lolled at an angle that suggested she hadn't had control of her muscles for a long time. No resistance at all.

"Meet Pell," Leto said quietly, helping them lower his sister to the ground. "And there are dozens more, Nynn. All of Aster's test subjects. We can't make it out—not all of us. Even with my gift, I don't think I could move that quickly. If Silence is right about the detonator, we have roughly twenty minutes."

"Is that why the guards have gone?" She shook her head. "And the alarms. When did they stop? Everyone who could flee has already left."

"Including the other telepath," said the Indranan woman.

"Ulia?"

"Gone with Aster." The Pet still sat on the hunk of sheet metal Hark had used to protect her from Mal's blast.

Leto stepped to within inches of Nynn. "We could

leave," he whispered. His damp breath feathered over her lips. She couldn't be sure if he spoke out loud or into her mind. The sensation that had been unnerving with Ulia was comforting from Leto. "You and me. Jack and Pell. I could get the four of us out. The Sath could take care of themselves."

"And the others? And those who've suffered?"

He nearly shrugged—so slight. "I've never fought for anything but my family." With a glance toward the fair-haired boy Nynn still clutched, he added, "That means both of you now."

Nynn's heart jumped at the chance. Her family. A new family. Safe and away from this place of nightmares.

"I haven't seen this one either," the Pet said without inflection.

As if caught stealing, Nynn blushed. Her skin flared hot, then frigid cold. She met the gaze of each person in that blasted corridor. Mal and the dark-haired stranger. The Dragon Kings who'd come to their aid. Even the Pet and the Sath couple. That didn't take into account the men and women—the children—who'd suffered at Aster's hands.

She wasn't a soothsayer, but Nynn saw her future.

She nuzzled her son's hair and drew in a breath, then kissed him. "Take him. Keep him safe, as I know you would've kept me safe for the rest of my days."

Mal stepped forward in the wake of Leto's confused silence. "Nynn, what is this?"

"You know what I can do. I take the energy from the air and make it mine. I own it. This detonation will be no different."

She said it with the confidence of a woman who

knew her place in the world. She'd always envied that confidence when watching Leto in his element. Now it was hers—not the serpent she'd imagined when filled with Ulia's twisted intentions. No, this was a destiny she'd never imagined. She would save her new family and these precious few Dragon Kings.

"I won't let you do it." Leto's rough, battered features bunched around an expression of fury.

She touched his cheek. "You know there's no other way."

"I'll stay, too," Mal said. "I can help absorb the energy."

"The Honorable Giva? No way." She quickly kissed his cheek. "Our people need you. I understand that now."

Mal's head bowed. She'd never seen him humbled, but maybe her awkward forgiveness held that power. If for no other reason, she was glad to have said it.

Hark was the first to move. He and Silence lifted Pell between them. "Twenty minutes isn't much time, people."

"Out." Mal's voice held all the authority of his station, plus that added punch of charisma and assurance he'd possessed even as a child. "All of us. We need to escape the blast radius and take as many of the prisoners with us as we can."

The group mobilized. Nynn slipped through the hole in the cinder block wall. She wanted to take Leto's hand, but he held his crude weapons at the ready. His profile was grim as they ran side by side. She cradled Jack's head instead. She remembered his weight, the cadence of his breathing, his shivers of fear—and she held on tighter. The time she had to hold him close was coming to an end.

She sobbed against the side of his head.

She'd been mistaken all along. She held her boy—the child she had conceived in love with her dear, murdered Caleb—and she was still fighting for him. That didn't mean she would be the one to raise him. The realization shot spikes through her chest and pierced her heart.

Leto growled at her side. "I know what you're thinking, Nynn, and you're wrong. He'll never be alone. And neither will we."

# ✦ CHAPTER ✦ THIRTY-TWO

"I have to do this," Nynn said, her throat pinching shut. "You know there's no other way. If the worst happens—"

Leto's expression was black with fury. "*No.*"

"—then Jack will still be safe. Dozens of lives in exchange for one Dragon King? Our people are so scarce. This is taking advantage of the odds. Other warriors like Weil may still be alive down underground, too. And what if I can save this place from the worst of the destruction? No matter how he acquired the information, or what he did with it, we need to learn what Dr. Aster knew. Tell me I'm wrong. Deny me any of this."

Leto stopped with a sudden jerk, took her by the shoulders. "You made me see you and hear you and feel you because you were so Dragon-damned stubborn. Now you want to leave me."

"I don't want to!"

"I've seen the snow and the sun now, but without you, I'll live in the dark forever."

She inhaled sharply.

His every hardened feature was pleading—pain-filled eyes, a compressed mouth, nostrils flaring in that way she knew, when he was trying to hold on to his temper. "I need you, Nynn."

Never, not ever, had she expected to hear such a thing from him. Her stoic teacher and her tender lover. But those words spoke of a desire for forever. She would've honored him in a heartbeat had she trusted any promise she could make in return.

They were close enough to a hallway that she remembered. Small doors. Small chambers to trap the most powerful beings on the planet and keep them meek. She heard pitiful sounds and whispered, fearful words, which meant Leto heard them, too.

She released the back of Jack's head and twined her fingers with Leto's. "They need us and they need you," she said, huddled into Leto's waiting embrace. "*I* need you . . ." Her voice clogged with tears in her throat. "I need you to be with me on this. I can't do it any other way. I can't leave you and leave Jack without knowing you were proud of me. I'll go down fighting, Leto. Nothing you've ever taught me will have been wasted."

That got to him. She could see it take hold behind the eyes she'd taken so long to read. He swallowed tightly, and she was oddly gratified to be able to see his Adam's apple bob. Such a small gift: his bare throat.

She touched it with fingertips still shaking, although her resolve didn't waver. A strange calm had overtaken her, even as her heart shattered. So much of life she would never know.

One for the many.

"They still wear collars, Leto. They deserve to survive and know what it is to have their gifts returned and to feel that beautiful pain for the first time."

Leto leaned close and brushed his lips against hers. "This, my brave girl. *This* is beautiful pain."

*My brave girl.*

His words became her new mantra. She could save Jack but she could not keep Leto—only his quiet, stoic benediction. With one more kiss, when she gathered his taste on her tongue, he stood upright. He still wore the ceremonial onyx-tipped armor that made him larger than life. A god. The warrior who would raise her son.

As Leto turned to lead the others in their tasks, she trailed her fingers across the back of her son's hand. Then his softness was no longer hers to touch. Jack began to call for her, reaching back from over Leto's shoulder. Against her son's frightened, suddenly incoherent sobs—sobs that nearly shook her to cowardice—she watched them go.

*I'll come back for you.*

She wanted to protest the words Leto whispered in her mind, but he and Jack slipped completely out of view.

Leto scooped up two thin, unresisting patients and slung them over his shoulders. He raced into the vast cold, cursing the disappearing sun and the snow he'd quietly longed to see. None of it mattered now. Just the people he ran to safety. He could move fast enough. He could get them all out. He could save Nynn, too.

Then they'd be together—a real family he could hold and watch grow and love.

He banked his thoughts and kept them tucked in the dark, where he had once been held captive. He delivered the two he carried to the makeshift meeting area the Giva had established two miles away from the arena, where Jack waited with the shivering, shocked patients. The snowmobiles ran circuits, too, and the Sath stole little chunks of Leto's speed to do what they could. By last count, they had under three minutes and fifteen people to save. Leto cursed the Dragon for tipping the odds so heavily against Nynn.

His neophyte. His lover. The woman he'd hoped would be his for the rest of his life as a free man.

Two more test subjects reached the checkpoint. Although the number they'd pulled to safety was growing, huddled together in the snow, blinking even in the twilight, the remaining number was a weight on his chest.

"Silence, Hark—no more. Stay with Jack and Pell. Let me do this at full speed."

"I'm going with you," said the man named Tallis. Even Leto had heard of the Heretic, although his knowledge went no further than a sense of foreboding and distrust. "I'll do what I can to dismantle the detonator. Two gone in exchange for these people. Not so bad."

Leto protected himself from any more of the man's grim fatalism by racing back to the outpost. The arena shed long, dark shadows over what remained of the lights inside the lab.

He returned to the corridor of death. Eight remained. Outside, he heard the thrum of two snowmobiles. Then came the glimmer of Tallis's energy and the sharp crackle of the Giva—distant, but near enough to honor his promise to help Nynn.

Two more prisoners freed. Leto was fueled by fear and desperation and Dragon-damned grit. Time could fuck off. That human expression fit best. He wouldn't give up on Nynn, and while he still breathed, he would not bow to an enemy.

Even if that enemy was time itself.

When the charges set off, Nynn had a blink of warning. She was overwhelmed with heat and pain. The charges kept coming. A chain reaction.

Her body tensed and her mind shut down. Pure instinct, as old as the Dragon. Millennia of power tempered by millennia of sacrifice. She saw it all as clearly as the scorching storm that boiled down the corridor. The force smacked her chest with the power of buses at full speed. She inhaled and sucked it into herself, into pores and cells and the follicles of her hair. She breathed lava and the concussion of endless waves of fire. Her lungs blistered. Perhaps the ends of her fingers and toes had turned to ash; she couldn't feel them.

That fire was hers. She owned it. She was a daughter of the Dragon. The wall of searing heat gathered in front of her as a ball of living flame. The roof of the labs blew open, into the sky she couldn't see. All was red. All was orange and yellow and evil. Her control of the energy was so close to nothing. She could only keep it, focus it, shoot it upward.

Fighting. Still fighting.

*My brave girl.*

Leto's words were a chant even when her skin felt like it was peeling off. Soon her muscles and her bones would dissolve. She knew the moment when she'd lost the fight. Her body went cold. The fire took her and she felt no more pain. Shivers, uncontrollable shivers, swallowed her without mercy as she called out Leto's name.

Her life was at an end.

No, the pain was . . . gone.

"*Nynn!* Dragon damn you. Open your eyes."

So slow. So terrified of it not being true. Because she thought she heard Leto.

Her eyelids fluttered. She was that out of body, as if her lids worked of their own accord. Finally they parted to reveal Leto's scarred, uncompromising face.

"You're not going anywhere," he growled. "I promised I'd come back for you. You heard me. Don't make me a liar, Nynn. Talk to me. *Do it.*"

Her throat felt papery and charred. Yet she could still swallow. She could still talk. "So bossy."

Leto enveloped her in a fierce hug. His heart galloped beneath her ear at the speed she knew he could travel. She'd worked so hard, but even she knew she was oddly still. His rasping exhale was a brush of warmth against her cheek. Good warmth. The kind that meant safety, not destruction.

"Where is your armor?" she asked.

"Shed it. Faster that way."

"How many lost?"

"I don't know."

"Leto, no! I could've held on a little longer."

"*Lonayíp* woman, I grabbed you up through a wall of pure fire. You were being consumed by it, like the Dragon swallowed into the Chasm. Nynn, I couldn't hear your thoughts or your heartbeat. Nothing left of you but a tiny pulse of life." He bowed his forehead to hers. Only then did she realize they lay together in the snow. That was the cold she felt. "I wasn't leaving you to die." His blunt, wide palms framed her cheeks—his warmth battling the bristling cold. "Do you hear me?"

She gulped cold air into her singed lungs and burrowed her body into his warmth. "I hear you."

"I can't imagine my life without you. I had my arms around you and was running free. Saving you was saving myself. You've given me a taste of a life I never knew I could have. For me, for you, for Jack—I wasn't going to give that up. I've sacrificed too much to lose you now."

"But the last prisoners?"

Leto exhaled heavily. "I've always lived with the choices I've made."

He smoothed sweat-sticky hair back from her temples, which exposed her heated flesh to the elements. She liked the shock of cold as she returned to herself.

"But that doesn't mean the death of more innocents today," Leto continued. "That Pendray man did what he could with the detonator. Hark said only half of the charges went off. He and Silence found the remaining patients several hundred meters back from the outpost. The Pendray was nowhere to be seen. He's gone. Even the rebel Indranan woman can't feel a trace of him."

She shook her head, which still roared with the sounds of whirling flames, like an enraged predator. "Where's Jack?"

"With your cousin. The Giva helped you, as he said he would. He took part of the energy, too."

"He's a damn fool."

"He's related to you."

She hurt all over, but Leto's rough caresses began to heal her from the inside out. "You were my tormentor once. Maybe all of that harsh treatment led us here. I wouldn't have survived without you, Leto. I wouldn't have known my strength."

Nynn couldn't hold it in any longer. The energy she'd funneled through her body had left her depleted. Completely depleted. Sensation returned—a mixed blessing as the memories of flames remained. The very real threat of an arctic night remained. She shook until her teeth clicked together. Yet a sense of joy began to warm her from the inside out. She'd defeated her own fears and, with the help of members of all Five Clans, she'd helped save almost three dozen Dragon Kings from Dr. Aster.

Tears froze on her cheeks, but Leto kissed them away.

"Here," came a familiar voice. "I believe this young man belongs to you."

Looking up from the protection of Leto's solid chest, Nynn found Malnefoley kneeling in the snow. Jack jumped from his arms and folded into Nynn's. Leto closed his embrace around them both. Her grateful, awed sobs came in earnest then. Jack. Leto. She was holding them both. That Aster and the Indranan witch had escaped was a fight for another day. She was too busy thanking the Dragon for each breath she shared with her family.

"I've communicated with the outside world, if you can believe it," Mal said. "Who needs the Indranan when we have satellite phones?" He looked exhausted. Quietly sure of his place, but exhausted. "Rescue helicopters will be here in an hour. Then we'll search what's left of the underground complex for survivors."

"And the Pet?"

"She's under my protection now. Or my custody. Whichever winds up being more appropriate." He smiled tightly and turned to leave them in privacy.

"Mal? Who was that man? He said he was my father's younger brother."

The Honorable Giva stopped, his back still turned. "Tallis of Pendray. The Heretic. And yes, your uncle. One day I'll tell you the sins he confessed to me." He looked over his shoulder with a glare as powerful as his lightning strikes. "But not tonight. Enjoy your family, cousin."

He returned to the people who needed him—who would need him more than ever now that the power of one of the cartels had been upended.

Although confused, Nynn took Mal's advice. She was safe. Really, truly safe. Leto kissed the top of her head, and she could've sworn he whispered prayers of thanks in their old, old language.

Four snowmobiles pulled up alongside them. Two faceless Dragon Kings merely nodded before gunning their machines into the dark. Hark, however, grinned with his usual misplaced levity.

"We're throwing in with the rebels for now," he said. "We have an idol to return to our clan, and a few collared brethren to free along the way. That sounds far too noble for me, but I'll survive. I have it on tenuous authority we'll see each other again—sometime between now and our return from the Sath leadership. Won't *that* be a pleasant reunion? At least it'll be warm in Egypt."

He tipped his chin toward his partner in a gesture to get going.

Silence smiled down at Nynn and the two men in her life—one barely formed, one scarred and just as new to the world. "Take care, friends."

Then they were as much a part of the night as the stillness and stars. Leto helped Nynn stand, so that he could lead her back toward the huddled bundle of shivering bodies. Leto knelt next to Pell and touched her cheeks. "Jack, come sit with my sister, will you? Her name is Pell. And you're both cold."

"It's all right," Nynn said to Jack with a growing measure of calm. "I'm right here. And I'm never going anywhere without you again."

Jack threw his arms around her neck and kissed her there—there, where she wore no collar and could feel his small, sure gesture. "Love you, Mama."

She swallowed back tears as her son scampered from her arms and laid down beside Pell's motionless body. He huddled under a makeshift blanket that may have been from the young woman's gurney. Nynn considered her survival and her reunion with Jack—let alone her love for Leto—to be miracles. There had been no future for Pell before, and she would've died in the labs. Maybe now . . .

Leto settled behind Nynn, with his legs crisscrossed around hers. He'd held her that way on several occasions. She adored the safety and possessive weight of his limbs wrapped around hers. She leaned back against his chest, reveling in the man who'd become hers through a hell she would spend years trying to understand. At least she would have Leto to hold her throughout it all.

Over her shoulder, looking up at him, she whispered,

"I love you, Leto. I'm glad you came for me. I could've given all I had, but that wasn't my right. It would mean sacrificing you and Jack, too—your happiness."

He leaned close and kissed her. Tenderly at first, but then with the growing heat of having survived. Together. His arms were her refuge. His heart was her home. His soul was the treasure she'd never knew she sought. She could never put right what had been lost, but she could look ahead to years filled with boundless potential.

Leto's tongue stroked over hers. Passion and power. Sweetness and sweat. They were everything and more.

"I love you," he said with that rough, deep rumble. "Be mine. Be mine . . ."

As the distant sound of helicopter rotors filled her with another surge of hope, Nynn smiled against his mouth. "Always, my warrior. No matter what the future holds."

Continue reading for an exclusive excerpt from

# Blood Warrior

The Dragon Kings
Book Two

by

Lindsey Piper

Coming August 2013 from Pocket Books

Tallis shed his heavy leather jacket and levered over Kavya, the legendary goddess known as the Sun, where she sprawled on the ground, sheltered by the canvas tent. He wore sturdy military-style cargo pants, while she wore only a silken sari. She would be able to feel his desire taking physical form.

"Should I kiss you again?" He touched her only from the waist down, where he used the weight of his lower body as more threat than seduction. Arms straight, he braced his hands on either side of her head. "I'd learn secrets about the Sun you're too arrogant to admit possessing."

"More of the so-called justice you seek? I've done nothing to you!"

"You know my weaknesses better than I do. Every fantasy—even those I can't arrange into thought."

"What are you talking about?"

"You've used that knowledge against me for years," he said, voice deepening with anger. "If I resisted, you invaded dream after dream like some Dragon-damned monster. You'd raid another corner of my mind to find more secrets." He was still aroused. Kissing her had been calculated, but he'd been swept into the vortex where fantasy swirled with reality. "Is it any surprise that I desire you in person?"

"You have the only mind I've never been able to read. How could I have done anything to your dreams?"

A clamor of voices came from beyond the tent's dingy white canvas. For a moment Tallis thought she'd managed to telepathically call for help, but she wore no expression of triumph. Then came more voices, more chaos.

He edged away and grabbed the deadly Norse seaxes he'd kept out of her reach.

His sense of hearing gave away her attack from behind as Kavya swung a cooking pot. The determination and, frankly, the vehemence in her glittering brown eyes was pure surprise. Ropes around her ankles meant she had one chance before losing her balance, but she made the most of it. The bulk of the pot hit his shoulder. One seax with its etched blade and honed edge skidded along the bare rock floor.

She rolled onto her back and grabbed the hilt with both bound hands. A quick slice parted the ropes at her ankles. She spun so that she knelt again, bloodying her knees. Shins braced against the ground gave her more stability. The split skirt of her sari bared the sleek skin of her thigh.

Although his shoulder ached, Tallis could only grin. "I'd hoped there was more to you than words and specters."

"Why would you think that of someone you kidnapped and profess to hate?"

Her eyes were bright and widely spaced, wedded to the high, rounded apples of her cheeks. She had a tiny nose and a chin that, for all her defiance, was softly shaped. Tallis shivered. This was her, *really her*, not the witch who'd infected his dreams for two decades. The real Sun, this woman Kavya, was the perfect compromise between truth and fantasy, virgin and whore—a bound innocent holding his blade.

Although she remained still, she vibrated with near-visible energy. Tallis could practically smell the heady cologne of her fear and focus. Her telepathic seductions were vile, but the surprising resilience of her fighting spirit made him smile more deeply.

"I like to think," he said, "that when I break you, I'll have broken someone who deserved the worst I can dish out. Seems you're in the mood to make me a happy man."

"Happy? I want you dead." A look a horror crossed her face. She inhaled sharply, which lifted the supple curve of breasts draped in silk.

Tallis chuckled. "You didn't mean to say that, did you?"

Exaggerating the ache in his shoulder, crouching before her, he shifted his weight onto the balls of his feet. Rather than leap, he leaned and swept his right leg. The toe of his boot caught her behind her upper thigh with a hard kick. He yanked. Between the blow and the pull, she fell hard onto her side.

She coughed, struggling for air. He pushed forward with two crouched strides and snatched the stolen blade from her bound hands.

"The Sun can fight. Gratifying, but it won't change anything." The gathering ferment outside the tent caught his attention again. "Stay. Unless you want to remain unaware of what's happening among your flock."

Her mouth was . . . gorgeous. There was no other word. Bee-stung lips twisted into a sneer. "Do it."

"That's the only command of yours I'll obey."

Intending to piss her off, he took one more taste of the lips he'd never believed could be real. Seeing her in the flesh, tasting and smelling and touching her—those intimacies made her night visits more ephemeral. They were mere shadows compared to the sweet bitterness of the kiss he took without permission.

She bit him. Tallis reared back. He swiped a hand against his mouth and came away with blood.

"That wasn't very nice, goddess." But he was still grinning.

Both seaxes firmly grasped, Tallis peered outside again. Dusk approached to take the place of full sunlight. Amiable pods of Indranan had been gathered around their fire pits. Now they hurried around wearing frightened expressions.

*Strange.*

Tallis's own clan, the Pendray, were generally insane and suffered from historic self-esteem issues, but at least they displayed what they felt without pretense. They were boisterous and unapologetic. The Indranan, however, were made of mystery. To see the camp transformed into a frenzied, buzzing collection of scared souls was shocking—so many emotions laid surprisingly bare.

"Let me go," came the persuasive voice at his back. "Whatever grudge you hold against me, you know I can calm them."

"No. Their panic will remain unaddressed by their savior. Seeing you discredited and ruined has always been my goal, no matter how much I like kissing you."

The fervor outside the tent died down, but only because hurrying worshipers had frozen solid. Their attention was focused on the altar.

Tallis narrowed his eyes. A man stood where Kavya had delivered her morning benediction. He was tall, with a commanding presence. His hair was brown, his features sharp, his clothing black on black. Among those gathered in the valley, his layers of leather and protective plates of silver armor stood out like a burn on a child's skin.

No matter Tallis's grudge against the Sun and her cult, this stranger was pure violence.

"You were expecting someone else," the man intoned, his words hypnotic. They echoed back across the valley in a one-two punch of spellbinding power. "You were expecting a savior. I'm here to say there is no such thing. And there's no such thing as reconciliation between the Northern and Southern factions of Clan Indranan. There never will be."

Tallis grabbed Kavya by her hair and dragged her to the tent's opening. Her face went chalk white. The paleness looked sick and unnatural on a Dragon King, and especially eerie when it leeched the soft charisma of her beauty.

"Who is that?" Tallis was more disturbed than he would have liked, but the unexpected was always a threat.

"That." She swallowed. "That is Pashkah of the Northern Indranan. My brother."

If skin could turn to ice, Kavya's became as cold as the glaciers along the Himalaya's Rohtang Pass.

She hadn't seen Pashkah since she was twelve years

old, but she would never mistake his stance, his face. Even as a boy, his expression had been freakishly blank. Devils and ghouls were nothing compared to his uncanny blankness. Had she been able to understand him, with telepathy or her senses, she might have been able to save their sister, Baile.

But in those final moments, Baile hadn't wanted to be saved. Before Pashkah had taken her head, she'd wanted his just as much.

Every Indranan was born as a twin or, in Kavya's case, as a triplet. Siblings grew up knowing that the Dragon had divvied up their true potential in the womb. *Learn to share*. So few did. By committing fratricide, an Indranan could unite the pieces of shattered potential. The ability to read another's mind was the most intoxicating, terrifying gift among the Five Clans. To keep from wanting more was the ultimate responsibility.

The Heartless.

Kavya had never protested her clan's derogatory nickname. She'd simply fought to rise above its hideous legacy.

Now, having reduced their family to a series of grim victories, Pashkah stood within a few hundred meters of success. He would take Kavya's gift and add it to the power he'd stolen from Baile. He would become thrice-cursed with his true potential sewn together in violence—while the never-ending shrieks of two dead sisters destroyed his sanity.

Tallis shook her by the hair. "What is this, part of your big announcement? Bring in muscle to make sure everyone complies?"

"This is my brother having found me after decades of searching. This is . . . this is the brink of chaos."

She jerked free. At least now she knew the identity of her captor.

Tallis of Pendray. The Heretic.

She still wasn't able to read his mind, but his honed Norse seaxes held residual memories so strong that she'd caught flashes of his true self. His life on the run.

A man of myth. But still a man.

"You don't need to be a telepath to sense the panic." She tipped her chin toward where Pashkah owned the altar—the altar she'd hoped would be host to an evening of peaceful triumph. "Those are lambs being herded toward a butcher's knife. Nothing I've done, no matter your delusions, will match the crimes Pashkah is capable of committing."

"He's your brother. I wouldn't expect anything less than deceit and mind-warping delusions."

Kavya's heart was expanding with each beat, until it shoved against her trachea. Everything she'd worked for was at Pashkah's mercy, while the notorious Heretic kept her from helping her people. "Do you hate me so much that you deny the obvious? Look at the men at his back. Each one of them is twice-cursed."

"You can tell? You're reading their minds?"

"I don't need to. They're Pashkah's Black Guard. Whole communities have been rolled over by their arrival."

"He kills Dragon Kings? The Five Clans would've heard about that."

Kavya shook her head, her eyes filling. "Not killing. Trying to *breed*. The Black Guard were responsible for the Juvine forty years ago, when women were stolen from the South and held captive here in the mountains. Retaliation after retaliation followed, reviving the same hatreds that split our clan three thousand years ago. By trapping me, you've given him unchecked permission. The Black Guard will continue its spree."

Tallis had fascinating skin—smooth except for those places where emotions pushed to the surface. So animated for a Dragon King, he frowned with his whole face until it took on the gravity of a pending typhoon. Finally he seemed to be taking her fear seriously.

"Unbind me," she said, pressing her advantage.

"So you can flee? What do you think I am?"

"An idiotic, brainless Pendray *thing*. Always thinking with your cocks and your work-worn hands, if you think at all. All I want is to face my brother without ropes around my wrists." She forced strength into her voice just as she'd forced calm into her body. "You wanted me discredited among my followers, not martyred. Remember?"

"That I can agree with."

"First obeying me, now agreeing with me. You'll be undone by dawn."

"Suddenly you expect to live that long," he said with an edge of a smile.

"You have no idea the consequences if I don't. Forget martyrdom. I'll be the dead soul that gives Pashkah what he's always wanted: the powers of a thrice-cursed Indranan."

Tallis shook his head. "Ancient myth."

"No, *fact*. Just like how the Heretic seems to have graced me with his presence."

That caught him off guard, but only for a moment. "So you admit it. You know who I am."

"That doesn't mean your accusations hold merit."

He silenced her by dragging a seax nearer to her

flesh. Although she shuddered, she appreciated the knife more than his kiss. She could endure pain. Life had taught her those lessons and the means of coping with what no one should have to endure. The surprise of pleasure, however, was still frothing in her veins. Every hair stood on end. Her skin pulled toward his touch and his Dragon-damned kisses.

The conflicting emotions were too much to process. As telepaths, the Indranan learned how to put emotions in boxes. Her own went in one box, separated and classified and memorized—the better to make sure they were really hers. Impressions and ideas from other people had boxes of their own, like quarantined contagions.

The tip of the seax was as fine as the point of a needle. Engraved scrollwork along the blade caught the last of the dying sunshine. Tallis slid the tip between her wrists and sliced the ropes with one swift cut. No wasted motion. Perfect mastery of his weapon.

"Members of the Sun Cult," came the voice that sent hot dread up her spine and ghostly chills back down. "Your leader is no longer here. Because I am her brother, Pashkah, you can imagine the consequences if I take her life—or if I already have. Perhaps she's merely fled, leaving you to my mercies."

The Black Guard marched to the edge of the altar.

Pashkah didn't smile, but contentment shimmered around him in a swirl of charcoal fog. "I have no mercy."

Additional members of the Guard dragged a pair of men into sight and thrust them to their knees, flanking Pashkah.

Kavya gasped. "No, no, no . . ."

A hand wrapped around her mouth. She struggled

until Tallis's words found their way into her short-circuiting brain.

"Quiet," he hissed softly. His arms were strong around her, which was welcome rather than abhorrent. She was ready to shudder apart, disintegrated by fear and outrage. "Who are those men?"

"Indranan representatives. My allies from the Northern and Southern factions. Oh, Dragon save them."

Pashkah was a man of his sick, malevolent word. He stood over the representatives and spread his hands with a flourish. "These are the presents the Sun was going to offer at dusk. Omanand of the North. Raghupati of the South. She would've stood behind them and smiled that calm, happy smile as they shook hands. Ended the civil war. Healed the breach. Wouldn't that have been lovely?"

"Is that true?" Tallis asked against Kavya's cheek.

"Yes," she whispered. "A foundation for lasting peace. But it doesn't matter now. Nothing will matter now."

One of the Guardsmen handed Pashkah a sword.

Tallis drew in a sharp breath. "That's Dragon-forged."

Her lucidity was slipping away along with her hopes. She was physically ill, so painfully, violently ill. "Yes. The only weapon that can kill a Dragon King."

Pashkah lifted the blade. With one blow, he beheaded Omanand. With another, he separated Raghupati's head from a body that flopped onto the altar. Terror echoed through the valley like the shrieks of demons.

Kavya saw only blood.